Kathleen Schoonover

Kathleen Schoonover

The Pony Tale

4/20/02

For Jerry ~

Kathy

♡

THE STANISLAUS WORKSHOP

Thank You

To my husband Sam
To my son Michael
To my editor, Rita Carlos
To my consultant, Suzanne Hagan
To my friend and artist, Nick Santoleri
To all my friends

♥

FIRST STANISLAUS WORKSHOP EDITION, JULY 2000

Published in the United States of America by The Stanislaus Workshop, a division of Renoir's Nephew, Ocean City, New Jersey.

ISBN 0-9702136-0-3
Web address: www.theponytale.com

Printed in the United States of America by Quinn-Woodbine Inc.
10 9 8 7 6 5 4 3 2 1

In Loving Memory of my Father

James Stanislaus Cooper

One

Einstein said that there are only two kinds of people in the world: those who believe that everything is a miracle, and those who believe that nothing is.

He also said that all matter is ninety-nine percent empty space.

When I was forty-two years old, I realized that my journey through the universe in this spinning web of nothing had to be a miracle. There was no other way to explain life as I knew it, even if it was an illusion.

My enlightenment occurred one starry night in Stockholm, as my family and I stood arguing in the gutter adjacent to City Hall. That we were in Stockholm was a miracle in itself, but the real miracle was the magic about to unfold in my life. That night in the City of Water, I resolved my life-long existential crisis. After being locked inside of my head for thirty years, my illusory prison finally crumbled and I was free to live.

I had sentenced myself in 1969. It was late July, and I was floating on the Atlantic Ocean in a multi-colored vinyl life preserver.

It began as a sunny beach day in Atlantic City. We were there on vacation, Philadelphians seeking respite from the heat and clamor of the city.

The mood that particular summer was a weird blend of solemnity and surrealism—after all, an American flag was flying on the moon. That we could put the flag there ourselves caused mixed feelings in people. If we could go to the moon, what else were we capable of?

We were reminded every day of another human capability: the ugliness of war, beamed to our living rooms via satellite.

In my twelve year-old brain, power plus destruction equaled mass destruction, and the threat of my own mortality sent my consciousness into a tailspin. Worrying that my life might be over momentarily, I began to entertain a serious mid-life crisis at the age when puberty should have been twisting my thoughts.

As I was bobbing up and down on the Atlantic that day, perhaps a little high on vinyl out-gassing, a dramatic change was occurring in the sky overhead. I failed to notice because I was staring toward shore, watching the silent movie of the family that was moving toward the right.

Actually it was my family and I was moving toward the left. According to Einstein, it didn't really matter who was moving. The point was, there was an ocean between us, and I had to swim like mad to keep from drifting away.

As I drifted, I noticed my sister Margaret on the beach. She lay on a pink towel, ponytail draped gracefully across her chest, one knee up and bent. She looked uncomfortable, but she looked good on her towel. Margaret was obsessed with looking good, and as a result she was often oblivious to current events and her surroundings.

Margaret's ponytail was a mail-order version that cost her two weeks' allowance and had to be secured with a dozen or so bobby pins. She called it "sultry brunette", which was custom-matched to her own hair by a team of experts.

Apparently the experts were having a bad day when they filled Margaret's order. Her ponytail made her hair seem upside-down, lighter at the roots and darker at the ends. The short piece of hair sticking out where she had removed her color swatch gave her the appearance of an Indian girl with a feather behind her ear. In her mind she looked exotic, and Margaret lived her Pocahontas fantasy in full glory while the rest of us watched in quiet bewilderment.

Margaret was "at that age", as my mother explained. Actually, she was at that age for as long as I could remember. I learned through the family underground that it began at two and a half, when I was born and when Margaret developed a precocious interest in cosmetics.

My father blamed my Aunt Vicky for Margaret's obsession, since she had given Margaret a pint-sized vanity and bench for Christmas in 1957. My father was always unjustly accusing someone, so we never took him seriously.

Another family member, who wishes to remain anonymous, felt that Margaret's obsession was a mechanism constructed to deal with sibling rivalry. If Margaret looked really good, then maybe the new baby (me) wouldn't get all the attention. It worked well for her—who could ignore a three year-old who bore a striking resemblance to Cleopatra?

Poor Margaret. She didn't want to go swimming with me that day, even though she loved the water. She was too self-conscious.

"Hey Margaret, wanna catch some waves with me?"

"No, Tony. Not now. My stomach's a little puffy today. I'm going to lie here and keep it flat."

"Your stomach doesn't look puffy."

"Oh yes it does! I'm not going to parade around the beach looking like this."

"Who cares if your stomach is puffy? Stomachs are supposed to look puffy—look at mine." I inhaled and blew up my stomach like a blowfish.

"Oh my God, do I really look that bad?" Margaret asked desperately.

"Oh no. Your stomach is nowhere near as puffy as mine—you're flat as a pancake compared to me. You don't look at all puffy," I tried to say convincingly.

"If I wasn't so puffy you wouldn't be working so hard to convince me that I'm not puffy," Margaret sulked.

The repeated abuse of the word puffy made our conversation sound alien. Was puffy even a real word?

"I'll tell you what, Margaret. I'll let you use my life preserver; put this around your waist and nobody will even see your stomach." I thought I had the perfect solution.

"Are you kidding? Those wide stripes will only accentuate my problem. I may as well put up a sign right here in the sand advertising that I'm fat."

Margaret shifted her position and adjusted her ponytail. I knew it was time to give up. There was no convincing Margaret that her puffiness fell within the acceptable range of normal bloat.

So Margaret posed on her towel like a mannequin, coming to consciousness only when the lifeguards would ask her to move to accommodate the incoming tide. Then maybe she would go for a swim, since the water was right there.

Margaret lived within the confines of her obsession quite successfully, with a little help. Margaret had come to depend on me to "fill her in" on everything she missed while preoccupied with her appearance. In exchange for my acting as her personal reality consultant, Margaret took care of my cuticles.

Although Margaret was instrumental in keeping my hangnails in check, at times I felt the arrangement was unfair to me. I had a hard enough time keeping my own affairs in order, let alone managing Margaret's. But someone had to take care of her; she seemed too frail to be left to her own recognizance. Although I had willingly accepted the position, I often felt that I was selling my soul for the price of a cheap manicure.

I went through life paying attention to details, so I could give accurate re-enactments to Margaret when she needed a reality check.

I looked down at my life preserver. Was it losing air? I turned it so I could see the air nozzle. The plug was still firmly in place; it probably had a slow leak. I decided to paddle closer to shore in case my life support was failing. As I did, I caught a glimpse of my younger brother Jerry, who was ten years old at the time.

Jerry was belly-down on his towel, staring into the sand. Every so often Jerry would grab a handful and let it sift through his fingers, looking at the sand as though seeing it for the first time.

Infinitely curious about the microscopic world, Jerry could spend hours inside his head building a universe of atomic *Legos.* Jerry lived well in that minuscule world, but had a bit of difficulty living to scale.

I had asked Jerry to go swimming with me, but he didn't want to go either.

"C'mon, Jerr. Let's go in the water!"

"Nah, Tone. I just want to lie here."

"C'mon. The water's warm."

"Nah—too many critters in the water."

"What? Jellyfish?"

"Nah—invisible critters. They coat your skin and live in your creases."

"Jerry, don't be ridiculous!"

"I'm not. I read about them in *Microcosmos.* They look like armored dinosaurs."

"Dinosaurs that we can't even see?"

"Yeah, with rows of teeth."

It was senseless to argue with Jerry; he always had a comeback supported by documented research. You were always left with the feeling you were sorry you asked, as he tortured you with details about which you'd much rather be in the dark. So I left Jerry on his towel to ponder his world that no one else could see.

As I saw Jerry from a distance, I realized how "removed" he actually was. I imagined a conversation that the couple to his left might be having.

"Mildred, do you see that boy on the striped towel? What do you suppose is wrong with him?"

"Oh, I don't know, Martin. Poor thing probably didn't get enough oxygen at some point. He looks normal enough, but he can't be right—all he can do is lie there and stare into the sand. Poor thing, he'll probably never have a normal life."

"Well, Mildred, maybe it's hereditary; I think that man singing is his father. He doesn't look like he's wrapped too tight."

My gaze shifted to my father and I could tell he had begun to hear the music. I didn't need to be within earshot to know he was singing; a swing of the hip or the kick of a foot was all I needed to see.

My father seemed to have an internal switch that controlled two modes of operation: he was singing or he was pissed off. When there was no song you could be absolutely sure that war was imminent.

When Dad was in his singing mode, we weren't a very good audience—not that we wanted the alternative. But it got a little old, and we tuned Dad out like the hum of the refrigerator. Our oblivion spared us public embarrassment. When people stared at us we checked to see if we had ketchup on our faces or toilet paper sticking to our shoes, forgetting it was Dad who was making us motley.

At that moment, being out of earshot and viewing only his antics, I realized how bizarre Dad's habit really was. And it wasn't any accident that our beach chairs and towels were arranged in a half-circle under the sun; it was surely Dad's amphitheater, with him plopped at center stage. We were on the set of South Pacific, and I wasn't surprised that we were at the wrong ocean.

At times Dad's singing was downright dangerous. On the way to the beach that day we almost had an accident. Dad swore that a man in a blue van cut us off and forced him to ride the pavement on two wheels. I never saw the blue van in question.

Jerry and Margaret didn't even notice that our ride had become lopsided. Jerry wore an expression that meant he was doing mental calculations, and Margaret was meditating on the centerfold of a girl's magazine. Some guy with shaggy hair was speaking to her, and only to her.

I yelled, "Dad, what are you doing on the pavement? Watch out! You're going to hit that old lady walking the poodle!"

"I see them! That god-damned blue van pulled out of nowhere and cut me off. The friggin SOB, I'll show him," Dad snarled, with nostrils dilated.

"What blue van? I didn't see any blue van," I said. What I had seen was my father momentarily close his eyes while belting out a rather dramatic chorus of whatever Tom Jones song he was singing (they all sounded the same to me).

"Are you calling me a liar?" Dad snapped.

I felt like saying "How could you see a blue van when your eyes were closed?" But I kept my mouth shut. There was an old lady and a poodle at stake.

Dad's yelling brought Jerry and Margaret into conscious awareness.

"What happened?" Jerry and Margaret asked simultaneously.

"Oh, you should have seen the huge blue truck that almost wiped us out—Dad had to go up on the pavement to save us!" I said.

Dad looked at me. "You're damn right. That J.O. wasn't paying a god-damned bit of attention to the road! He could have killed us."

Those were my thoughts exactly.

So I held on tightly for the rest of the ride, one more block. I didn't understand why we had to drive; the beach was only four blocks from our beach house. But Dad was lugging his stage set, so we needed the car. I hated the car during the summer: the metal dashboard became a radiator, and I was the lucky one to sit up front since Mom hadn't come with us.

There was no longer the question of whether my life preserver was losing air: tiny bubbles were tickling my waist.

I suddenly realized Dad was becoming smaller and smaller. The undertow was pulling me out to sea, and its force jolted me to consciousness. There were only a few people left in the water, and it was getting dark. I decided to start paddling to shore before it started raining.

As I paddled, I noticed the figure of my mother on the boardwalk. She looked up at the sky and then down at her purse three times before fumbling through her belongings. Something pink emerged. It was a cheap plastic rain bonnet stashed for unexpected downpours, and she scrambled about her head to attach it.

From a distance, the pink bag over her beehive hairdo made Mom look as if she was balancing a bag of cotton candy on her head.

Mom didn't like the beach, so I thought it was strange that we went to the shore for vacation every year. She claimed to be allergic to sand fleas, but I knew the real reason for her absence: the Atlantic City Boardwalk was brimming with fine gift shops, and my mother was building a "collection".

Mom had a weird fetish for ceramic tableware that resembled the food it was meant to serve: a big cabbage for coleslaw, a potato that could burst with mashed potatoes, a butter dish that looked like a stick of butter with one pat missing. She had acquired a rather impressive collection of the inedibles, and when not in use, Mom proudly displayed them in the corner hutch of the dining room.

When I was very young I had recurring nightmares about those dishes; they somehow came to life and my mother served a dinner of giant hollow crudités. "There will be no dessert if you don't finish your plates!" Mom yelled, dusting the lattice-top of the pie server.

So Dad took us to the beach while Mom scoured the souvenir shops. We didn't care because it meant we'd escape the exfoliating ritual of being smeared with sand-laced Coppertone. Dad didn't care if we got sunburned.

As I watched my mother in her pink armor, hairdo unthreatened by the pending storm, I remembered her biblical explanations of the weather. She said that clouds were angels' pillows, and rain was angels' bath water draining from their tubs.

I'd argue that there was no dirt in heaven, so angels wouldn't have to bathe.

"Some things you just have to take on faith," She would say.

It was evident that some angel had pulled the plug on our day at the beach. It was about to rain and I would probably be struck by lightning for making fun of my family.

It began to rain just as my feet hit land. Dad was scurrying to break down our camp, and was half-way into *Singing in the Rain*, with a chorus of raindrops beating on canvas umbrella tops. Margaret wore a distraught look and a towel around her head turban-style. Jerry was carefully pouring sand out of his sneakers to eliminate any monsters that might hitch a ride home on his big toe.

"C'mon, kids," Mom was yelling.

While Dad went to get the car we took shelter under the awning of the Peanut Shoppe, enjoying the smell of freshly roasted nuts while we waited. In a bizarre twist of fate, a cotton candy display was located in the window just behind my mother. If I blinked my eyes her face became lost in a sea of pink and she became one with the display.

The absurdity of the whole thing amused me and I began laughing.

Mom looked at me. "What's so funny, Tony?"

I tried to keep a straight face. Fifteen other people had also taken cover under the awning, and they were staring at me. "Oh, nothing," I said. "I don't know—I forget."

"Well, it couldn't have been too funny if you've forgotten already," Mom said, moving her head back into position with the cotton candy display. What were the chances of that happening? Mom had a cotton candy head, and cotton candy appeared behind her.

God was playing with my head, testing me to see if I could keep a straight face during the comedy of errors he'd construed. I couldn't. About to break down, I tried to think of something sufficiently sad enough to destroy my humor. It was pointless. With fifteen strangers as my audience, I roared with laughter and fell to my knees.

When I was able to regain my composure, I looked at the soggy crowd. They were staring and whispering, obviously making laymen diagnoses of my condition.

Mom looked at me, puzzled. "Tony, what is it that is so hilarious? Jerry, help your brother up."

I was unable to answer Mom, paralyzed by the realization that I had just made a complete fool of myself in front of a gawking crowd.

Margaret looked mad. "I know why he's laughing. He's laughing at my hair!"

I looked at Margaret. I couldn't even see her hair; it was wrapped in a towel.

"I knew I shouldn't have gone into the water," Margaret said, retreating into silent sadness.

Why was Margaret so upset? Because her hair had gotten wet?

While still on my knees, I begged God to stop daunting me. Jerry approached me from behind and helped me to my feet.

"Are you O.K.?" Jerry asked.

"Yeah, I'm O.K.," I lied. I had a splinter in my knee from the boardwalk.

It seemed as if we waited an eternity for Dad to bring the car. While Jerry admired a plastic Mr. Peanut that could hold coins in his belly, I listened to the muffled whispers of the crowd:

"You know, Mildred, that hysterical boy *is* related to the singing man."

"Yes, Martin, I know. Strange group—I wonder how they all manage together. Must be like the blind leading the blind. What a bunch of poor souls."

But Mildred and Martin didn't understand. I had been laughing at something really funny. They just couldn't see the cotton candy in the window. I was really the sane one of the group.

It was pointless to convince myself that my "spell" was normal. I had made a fool of myself, and tried to disappear behind Martin's beach chair. As I reassured myself that I would never see those people again, the smell of freshly roasted nuts singed its mark on my olfactory memory.

While driving back to our rented beach house we discovered that Margaret's ponytail had been swept out to sea by the unusually strong undertow, which explained her new look and disposition. Pocahontas had been scalped, and she bore an expression of such shame that we felt sorry for her and agreed to chip in and finance a new ponytail.

Eventually Margaret was able to regain her pride and enjoy the rest of the vacation, although swaddled in a blue bandanna that appeared to be tied a little too tightly.

When we returned to the house the rain had stopped and we were instructed to use the outside shower. Margaret, being at that age, was permitted to use the indoor facilities.

As I showered in the slippery wooden stall, my thoughts returned to the bizarre imagery of that afternoon: Jerry lying hopelessly in the sand, Dad swinging his hips in song, Mom the cotton candy head, and Margaret, the victim of Mother Nature's fury. Where did I fit in? Was God just having fun with me? Would I awaken one day to realize it was all just a dream?

I was suddenly jolted to reality by my butt hitting the concrete shower floor. It wasn't a dream—I slipped in the filthy old shower and pulled a muscle in my groin. God had spared the lightning rod in exchange for something much slower and drawn-out.

I stood and turned off the water. If I moved a certain way, an excruciating pain shot through my groin. I awkwardly dried myself, not doing a very good job, since I couldn't bend to the right.

I dressed my clammy body and stepped out of the shower. A warm breeze evaporated some of my sogginess, and I felt a little better. I headed toward the back steps.

I walked into the kitchen just as Mom was unveiling her latest acquisition.

"Isn't it lovely? It's numbered," Mom said to Dad. The numbered article was a cookie plate that looked like a giant waffle. "I'll have to make a big batch of pizzelles as soon as we get home so we can get some use out of it."

Dad wasn't paying attention. He was staring out the kitchen door, lost in thought.

Sensing that Mom needed someone to share in her excitement, I walked closer and began to admire her new *objet d'art.*

"This is super, Mom."

"Oh honey, you're sweet, but I'm no supermom."

"Huh?"

"Only twenty thousand were made," she continued, "so one day it will be worth something."

It was hard for me to imagine that there were 19,999 women out there as smitten with ceramics as Mom. But I faked an interest to not rain on her parade. Her collection was important to her, and my interest in it, although insincere, was endearing. The camaraderie that evolved as a result of our mutual appreciation of inanimate fruits and vegetables became the emotional glue that bound us.

My father turned from the window. "What time are Harry and Vicky getting here?"

"Around 4:30, if they don't run into traffic," Mom said, carefully placing the ceramic waffle on display in front of the window over the kitchen sink. "Here, now. This will be safe until we go home." Mom then added, "I hope it doesn't rain tonight, so we can put the kids on the amusements."

"You know, Leona," Dad said, "I was thinking that tonight might be a good night to take the kids to the Wax Museum. We'd be indoors and wouldn't have to worry about the weather."

Jerry walked into the kitchen when he heard the Wax Museum mentioned. He was spooked by people being immortalized in wax, and didn't want to go; I didn't want to go either. But the idea was endlessly fascinating to Dad, and every summer we had to go to the Wax Museum at least once. We always went kicking and screaming as though being taken to the doctor for our annual shots.

Maybe we'd be lucky and would be *put on* the amusements, as Mom had suggested. I laughed as I visualized Dad carrying Jerry and dropping him into a spinning teacup like a lump of sugar with flailing limbs.

"Well, we'll see what happens," Mom said. She was only listening with one ear, because she had a tomato pie ready to come out of the oven and was nervously looking for the pot holders in her rented kitchen. She found them and removed the pie, which had cooked unevenly and was burnt around the edges.

"Oh fiddlesticks. This hasn't cooked properly."

Dad rushed to the rescue. "Not to fear, my dear. I'll fix it." He proceeded to trim the burnt crusts from our sorry-looking snack, and put the middle of it back into the oven. "Give it five minutes, and it will be perfect," Dad said triumphantly.

Five minutes later, Mom retrieved the pie; we heard her voice echo from the oven walls: "Oh no—not again!"

At that instant, Margaret walked into the kitchen. "What's Mom doing with her head in the oven?"

Mom removed her head and the tomato pie from the oven to reveal an embarrassing situation for my father: he had not *fixed it* at all. Nothing was different about the tomato pie except that it was smaller. Jerry began to laugh.

Dad ignored him. "If at first you don't succeed, try, try again." Dad proceeded to trim the pie for the second time, and burst into song: "When the moon hits your eye like a big pizza pie, that's amore!"

Dad returned the pizza to the oven, confident that he would triumph. "This time, only leave it in for three minutes!"

They were a long three minutes for my father. He paced, wearing oven mitts like a pair of boxing gloves, anxiously waiting for the sound of the buzzer. It finally sounded, and we ran to the oven to share in Dad's glory.

Dad opened the oven door and looked in. "Turn off the god-damn oven!" He had been defeated by a particularly stubborn tomato pie. It was burnt around the edges and smaller yet.

Jerry spoke at the wrong time. "Dad, I think the problem is that the pan is too big for this tiny oven. Ovens work by convection, and the heat can't circulate…"

Dad interrupted Jerry. "So when did you win the god-damned *noble* prize? This pizza isn't cooking properly because the oven has a lousy god-damned thermostat!" Dad stubbornly trimmed the burnt crusts for the third time; only a six inch square of salvageable tomato pie remained.

Jerry, trying to stir hope, quantified Dad's blunder. "Don't worry, Dad," he said. "There's thirty-six square inches of pizza, giving us each 7.2 square inches, more than enough to hold us over!"

Dad glared at Jerry. "Never mind! You can eat my 7.2 inches! I'll eat the crust—there's nothing wrong with it." Dad stubbornly ate the crusts without scraping the black surfaces.

Not knowing when to back off, Jerry added, "Well, at least it's only us. If Aunt Vicky and Uncle Harry and Tommy were here, then there really wouldn't be enough."

We then heard their car pulling into the driveway.

Dad looked at Jerry. "Well, I guess there isn't enough now."

Because our portions were so small, we were able to finish our snack before they even reached the back steps.

"Hello, everyone!" Aunt Vicky yelled, entering the back door.

Dad ran to help her with the grocery bags she was lugging.

"What's cooking, good-looking?" she said to Dad.

Dad, still sulking over the tomato pie incident, gave Aunt Vicky a dirty look.

"What's the matter? I'm not here two minutes and you're giving me dirty looks," Aunt Vicky responded.

"Oh, everything's fine," Mom said, hugging Aunt Vicky. "Anthony's just a little upset over the tomato pie."

"What tomato pie? Is there any left? I'm starving."

"Will you forget about the god-damned tomato pie, Leona? It's over!"

Aunt Vicky read Mom's non-verbal cue; she changed the subject and greeted Margaret. "Margaret, doll! How are you?" She squeezed Margaret and then stood back to give her a once-over. "You look great. I love what you've done with the bandanna, how you've extended the color."

Aunt Vicky was referring to the eye shadow and mascara that was carefully matched to the shade of blue in Margaret's skullcap. Aunt Vicky always complimented Margaret's appearance as part of her greeting; that pleased Margaret to no end. In addition to being a third-grade teacher, Aunt Vicky was a very established *Avon* Lady. Aunt Vicky's stamp of approval was an affirmation of Margaret's glamour.

I looked at my father: he was rolling his eyes. He still blamed Aunt Vicky for Margaret's obsession; in fact, he had cursed Aunt Vicky earlier that day.

"Margaret, hurry the hell up. I need to get in there."

"I'll be out in a minute. Jeez!"

"A minute's up!"

"Dad, I'll be right out!"

Mom went to referee. "Anthony, what's the problem?"

"I'll tell you what the problem is, it's your god-damned sister. She planted the seed that has taken root in the bathroom. When I have kidney failure, I'm sending her the hospital bills!"

Dad and Aunt Vicky locked horns a lot, and Mom did a lot of changing the subject in a futile attempt to keep peace.

"Where's the little guy?" Mom asked.

"He fell asleep, so Harry's waiting with him," Aunt Vicky replied. "It won't be long."

Uncle Harry was O.K. in my book, although the rest of the family seemed to have a problem with him. I thought it was a simple lack of communication. Uncle Harry had a speech impediment that could most accurately be described as a problem with contractions. He never knew where to put the N, and he usually put it in the wrong place, along with a few superfluous N's. As a result, his speech was often garbled, sometimes contracting when he should have been expanding, and vice-versa.

Dad and I went outside to greet Uncle Harry.

When Uncle Harry saw us approaching, he quickly stubbed out his cigarette. Uncle Harry must have been ashamed of his smoking habit; whenever we'd catch him smoking, he quickly tried to get rid of the evidence.

"Harry, you made great time! We didn't expect to see you until at least 4:30."

"Well, luckily we didninit hit much traffic. Isninit great to get lucky once in a while?"

"It certainly is," Dad responded. "How's business been?"

"Oh, you know, same old shit. A day doesninit go by that we are ninit knee deep in it."

He was a plumber.

"Well you have that in every profession, old man," Dad said. "I see the little guy is fast asleep."

"Yeah, five minutes in a car is all it takes. He canninit keep his eyes open."

The little guy was my cousin Tommy: four years old, thirty-five pounds, muscles of steel. He could also swing with the best of orangutans. Tommy was actually pretty cute when he was sleeping, but when awake his cuteness was overshadowed by the fact that we were always blamed for his actions.

One Christmas Tommy dropped a candy cane behind the bookcase in our living room, so he did the logical thing: he moved the bookcase to retrieve it. Unfortunately, he scraped the varnish off the hardwood floor in the process. Not surprisingly, once he'd had the candy cane in possession, he didn't bother to move the bookcase back.

Having heard the commotion from the kitchen, Dad ran into the living room to find big scuff marks in the floor.

"Now why in hell would you move that bookcase from the wall? Can't we ever get together for the holidays without some kind of god-damned trouble?"

"We didn't do it!" Jerry said desperately. "It was Tommy. He dropped a candy cane behind it."

"So Tommy dropped a candy cane behind it, and I suppose he moved it all by himself so he could get it," Dad said, punctuating his syllables with sarcasm.

"I did not, Uncle Anthony."

"Of course you didn't. I don't know which one of you boys did it, but you're both in trouble. Lying on god-damned Christmas—you should be ashamed of yourselves!"

Jerry and I looked at Tommy. He just sat there looking petite, shrugging his shoulders.

So over the years we developed a love/hate relationship with Tommy. We hated having to pick up his slack, but we respected his brute power.

"He shouldinit sleep much longer," Uncle Harry said. "Why don't we take the bags in while we're waiting?"

Uncle Harry opened the trunk and began unloading their bags.

"Give me that suitcase, Harry," Dad said.

"No, I'll get that one, it's heavy. Here, you take Vicky's vanity bag. It's only half the size."

"It may be only half the size but I'm sure it's twice the god-damned weight—give me the friggin suitcase!"

"Whatsit the problem, Anthony? I just didninit want you to hurt yourself is all."

"I've been struggling for ten years with that vanity bag and I'm not carrying it into the house, period!"

"I just donut understand your attitude sometimes, Anthony. You shouldinit be so uptight; gonna give yourself a heart attack."

"I'm going in!" Dad said abruptly, ending the conversation.

The little guy finally awoke and we were instructed to play in the backyard until dinner. The backyard was a square concrete area enclosed by a chain link fence.

"What do you want to do?" Jerry asked.

"I dunno, what is there to do?" I responded.

"We could count the little diamonds in the fence and see how many there are."

"Nah, that's boring."

"I wanna go in!" Tommy wailed, heading for the back steps.

Tommy must have gotten into someone's way in the kitchen; within a minute Dad was yelling out the back door: "Didn't I tell you boys to play outside until dinner was ready?"

"But Dad, there's nothing to do out here," I yelled.

"Well, use your god-damned imagination! Can't you behave for ten minutes?"

Tommy descended the steps with a puss on his face. Jerry began to spurt ideas again; they were too abstract.

"Let's play hide and seek," Tommy said.

"We can't. There's no place to hide," Jerry said.

"I can hide in the shower."

"Then we'd know where to find you."

"You can pretend you don't know where I am."

"That's dumb," Jerry said.

"I don't care. I'm hiding in the shower! Don't care what you say!" Tommy yelled, stomping toward the shower stall.

"You're nuts, Tommy! It's all slimy in there!" I yelled.

We could tell by the sound effects that Tommy was using the spigots and towel rack to climb around the shower walls.

"He's crazy. It's slippery in there," I said to Jerry.

"You're darn right. There's enough bugs in there to kill you."

"I didn't see any bugs in there."

"Of course not. They're too small to see with the naked eye. What do you think all that slime is? It's millions of small animals suspended in water—protozoan *Jello*." Jerry spoke as if everyone but me was versed in microbiology. "Yeah," Jerry added, "I made sure not to touch the walls; I even wore my flip-flops in there."

I thought back to my own shower experience: clumsily falling on my butt, my back sliding down the shower wall on the way down, hugging the shower wall while regaining my composure after the fall. God would punish me with a full-body case of athlete's foot. I would become a leper for making fun of my family. I should have taken the lightning.

"Apparently the people who own this place have never heard of bleach. Poor Tommy's going to be a mess when he comes out of there," Jerry said sympathetically.

Sure enough, Tommy emerged from the shower coated with a nice layer of specimen. Jerry ran to help him.

"You need to take a bath, Tommy. You're all slimy," Jerry said.

"I yam not!" Tommy yelled.

"Yes you are. Feel your arm."

Tommy rubbed his arm and ran into the house screaming. Before we could blink, Dad was scurrying down the back steps.

"What in hell did you boys rub all over your cousin? If you keep this up, there will be no Wax Museum tonight, period!"

Perhaps the situation would have a good outcome, I thought.

"Get in the house, now!" Dad yelled.

We ran inside to find Mom loading meatballs into a pot of gravy. "Now, boys. Why did you rub gunk all over the little guy? You boys are older and should be setting a good example. Now Aunt Vicky has to give him another bath."

"Oh, Mom, he was filthy anyway," Jerry said. "And we didn't do it! He was acting like a monkey in the shower stall. That's where the slime came from."

"Now, Jerry. Don't talk about your cousin that way, it's not nice," Mom said, turning to me. "We have a half-hour before we have to start cooking the macaroni. Why don't you boys play a game of *Candy Land* with Tommy when he gets out of the tub? That would make amends."

I was tired of being the little guy's fall guy. But I agreed to play the baby game anyhow, because my mother had that tone in her voice: would you rather comply or deal with your father's wrath?

"I want to be green!" Tommy yelled.

After the episode in the shower, he was well on his way.

We were sitting at the kitchen table trying to get to the gingerbread house while the adults had drinks in the living room.

"I'm hungry," Tommy complained.

"Well, we'll be eating soon. Just play the game," Jerry said.

I rolled the dice and got doubles. I moved my red gingerbread man to a favorable location on the board, and Jerry yelled, "NO!"

"What do you mean, no?"

"You moved thirteen spaces. Rolling doubles will always yield an even number. Hence two dice," Jerry babbled.

"I did not move thirteen!" I protested.

"Where were you?"

"I was in gumdrop village."

"No you weren't. You got your foot stuck in taffy and lost a turn."

"I did not. That was the turn before," I said defensively.

Our argument was interrupted by a loud crash. Tommy was dangling from the hanging plant in front of the kitchen sink, and Mom's new pizzelle dish was on the floor, shattered neatly into little squares. Tommy jumped down just before the adults reached the kitchen door.

"Oh heavens, my plate!" Mom yelled, looking at the pile of rubble, her beloved plate reduced to its lowest possible terms.

"What the hell have you done now?" Dad yelled. "There will be no Wax Museum tonight, period. Don't worry, Leona, we'll get you a new one tomorrow, and take it out of their allowance."

"Dad, Tommy did it," I yelled. "He was hanging from that plant and he dropped Mom's plate."

Before I could utter another word, Dad went off. "So now Tommy is *Tarzan* swinging from vines. Please, *do not* insult my intelligence!"

While I acted in our defense, Jerry analyzed the physical debris: "Look how the plate broke neatly into squares; that could only mean that the force was distributed evenly through the plane of the cookie—I mean the plate. This is very unusual. I think the pizzelle design could have some interesting engineering applications."

"So when did you win the god-damned *noble* prize?" Dad blurted. Whenever Jerry baffled Dad with figures or technical jargon, Dad retorted with his *noble* prize put-down. We had no idea what he was talking about until later that day.

"Well, it's just an interesting phenomenon," Jerry sulked.

A word like phenomenon was ill-fated at that point in Jerry's plight. In his heart and mind, Dad knew that Jerry was brighter than he was; it infuriated him when Jerry, though unwittingly, rubbed his nose in it.

"Oh, Anthony, enough about the broken pizzelle," Mom said. "Let's get the macaroni cooking so we can eat."

We went in different directions to sulk until the macaroni finished cooking. Jerry offered to clean up the mess, and swept the little squares into a baggie so he could study them in more detail later.

I went outside. After being in the house with my family, counting the diamonds in the fence seemed a charming distraction. I sat down and started counting, near the gate.

I reached a count of eighty-seven diamonds when my eyes crossed and I lost my reference point. I began again, counting only to thirty-six before my vision became kaleidoscopic. Dizziness forced my eyes shut; I'd lost my place, again.

Visual impairment became a real nuisance; I decided to run my finger along each link, counting blindly to avoid the pitfalls of sight. I moved boldly from my reference point.

My new method worked like a charm; only two more rows to go, and I hadn't been lost once. I was so preoccupied with counting in four digits, I hadn't noticed Jerry approaching me.

"Jerry! You scared me!" I yelled, forgetting my diamond count.

"I'm sorry, Tony. I didn't mean to scare you. What the heck were you doing?"

"I can't believe you made me lose my place—I'm not starting over again!"

"Tony, calm down. Listen to me. Everyone is watching you from the kitchen window."

I looked toward the window. Sure enough, the four adults had taken cover behind the leaves of the hanging plant. I wondered how long they'd been watching me.

"Tony," Jerry said, "what the heck were you doing, anyhow?"

"What do you mean, what was I doing? I was counting the diamonds in the fence."

"Are you nuts?"

"What do you mean, am I nuts? You're the one that came up with the idea."

"I didn't mean to count each individual diamond. No wonder we couldn't figure out what you were doing. It never occurred to me that you would use the long method. We thought you were losing it—you looked possessed," Jerry laughed.

"What?" I asked in disbelief.

"Well, who in their right mind would count each one?"

"What are you talking about?"

"Oh Tony, come here. Let me show you something," Jerry said, whipping a ruler out of his back pocket.

"Wait a minute," I said. "You didn't say we had a ruler."

"You didn't bring yours?"

"No, I didn't bring my math book or my ruler to the shore with me; we're on vacation, remember?" I said sarcastically.

"You don't need your math book," Jerry said. "It's just number per square foot times number of square feet. An even shorter way to do it would be to…"

I stood looking at Jerry in disbelief for a very long time; my eyes, still recovering from the counting trauma, began to play tricks on me.

Jerry was then wearing a long white vest covered with pockets, each bulging with a different measuring apparatus. The triple balance beam strapped to his back made him look like a turtle.

I blinked and the tool vest was gone.

"Tony, what are you looking at?"

"Nothing," I said, readjusting my focus. "So why didn't you tell them I was just counting the fence?"

"Tony, I swear to God, I didn't know what you were doing."

I believed him. Because Jerry could compute without a pencil and paper, he thought everyone else could as well. I let him off the hook.

"Anyhow, Tone, I came out to tell you that Granny's almost here; she left Ocean City a half-hour ago."

"How do you know that?"

"She called the people next door, and asked them to come over and tell us."

"How did she get their number?"

"I don't know, what does that matter?"

It didn't matter. All that mattered was my forthcoming salvation. When Granny arrived, I wouldn't feel so nuts.

"Hey Tone, wasn't it neat how the pizzelle shattered?"

"Yeah, Jerry, real neat. I won't need any more entertainment for at least a week."

"Real funny, Tone. You know, you'd have a lot more fun if you'd enjoy the simpler things in life."

Simpler? How could using calculus to clean up a mess be simpler than just doing it and getting it done? I didn't argue; it would send Jerry onto a tangent and he'd never shut up. I needed some quiet time to sort through the mess in my head.

The one thing I'd inherited from my mother was my opportunistic appreciation of changing the subject. I suggested to Jerry that I may have seen a jet ascending through the sky. He was fascinated by trajectories.

"Where?" Jerry yelled excitedly, running to get an unobstructed view.

He would be out of my hair for at least a few minutes; I sat on the back steps to wait for Granny.

We called her "magic" Granny to differentiate her from "far-away" Granny, who lived in Italy. We'd never met far-away Granny, but she used to send us weird-looking birthday cards.

Granny was the only one in the family with whom I felt at ease; she had a way of making me feel so normal.

Granny lived in a mansion. Well, maybe not a real mansion, but it was a mansion compared to our house.

When you walked into Granny's house, the rest of the world ceased to exist; it was a place of such enchantment, there was room in your soul for nothing else. Everything in Granny's house was non-ordinary. There was a story behind everything, and those stories told such a tale of magic that at times they were unbelievable. Those stories captivated our attentions and our imaginations.

Granny's furniture was perched among a small forest of trees, each specimen carefully calibrated to its light conditions. Some were mature trees, growing sideways across the ceiling.

Granny and Poppy collected plants the way some people collected figurines. Each marked a special occasion: their first anniversary jade plant, an ivy bought on vacation in Miami, the thirtieth birthday euphorbia. They had even purchased two green children on their honeymoon, the oldest and tallest of their clan.

The tree collection was well-integrated into their family structure; as children, Mom and Aunt Vicky were often jealous of the attention the plants received. "Why do I have to go to bed, you let the plants stay up all night!" or "I think you love the umbrella tree more than you love me!" they would cry. Granny laughed in hindsight as she recounted the story.

To shed more light on their plants, Granny and Poppy strategically placed mirrors throughout the house. While sitting at the dining room table, one had visual access to every room on the first floor. My father wasn't privy to that, and on more than one occasion made a complete fool of himself.

The mirror arrangement emerged from Poppy's fascination with optics. He had been a mathematician, and knew every visual trick in the book. In the window behind each tree hung several crystal prisms that scattered rainbows across the room. The mirrors synergized this effect; on several charmed afternoons we had witnessed a light show so spectacular we were catapulted into bliss. When we had to go home, we sulked. Why weren't there rainbows in our house?

Another unusual thing about Granny's house was the pictures. Where there were no mirrors, pictures were hung, and those also told a story. There were portraits of people, landscapes, and especially, paintings of flowers. Those paintings were collected as Granny and Poppy traveled the world, attending math symposiums abroad.

Granny's art collection was only one of many collections. She also collected rocks. They weren't ordinary rocks; Granny's rocks were bursting with colored jewels. The most interesting and beautiful rock was covered in a shimmering white powder; its interior was layered with crystals resembling pointed blue ice cubes. There was something magical about that rock. It even had a magical name; Granny said that it was called *Celestine* because it fell from the heavens. We believed the Celestine geode was somehow responsible for the cloud of magic hovering over Granny's house.

Their offices were on the second floor, the most interesting rooms in the house. My grandfather's office was like a museum; there were pictures of famous scientists, and Poppy himself was in the pictures. He had become quite friendly with these comrades, meeting them in Europe, or getting to know them on the ship en route. In science class, I had no trouble envisioning the faces of Einstein or Enrico Fermi—I had seen their pictures hundreds of times.

I was also on a first-name basis with Mark Twain. On a pedestal next to Poppy's desk stood a bust of Twain, below which read an inscription: "To get the full value of a joy you must have somebody to divide it with." If I sat at the desk and stared at the bust for a length of time, strange things would happen. Twain would wink at me or stick out his tongue. On one occasion, I'd even thought Twain had something caught in his throat; I whacked his stone back twice before halting my daftness.

There was a blackboard in Poppy's office that we were allowed to use. Granny said that Poppy had erased that chalkboard over a million times; strangely, it showed little evidence of wear. Granny claimed that Poppy held the chalk effortlessly, moving it across the slate with minimal friction: "The chalk was an extension of his mind; it glided through time and space manifesting ideas."

Granny's office was adjacent to Poppy's. Along one wall stood a huge mahogany desk that housed multiple cubby-holes and drawers. Granny hadn't called it a desk; she called it an escritoire, which we couldn't pronounce as kids. The desk was over two hundred years old; Granny had fallen in love with it in an antique shop in Paris, and Poppy had it shipped back as a surprise.

Next to Granny's desk was a stack of leather hatboxes, which resembled a large brown wedding cake. Jerry and I would sit on the first tier, hypnotized by our environment. Sometimes Granny would disassemble the cake and read aloud one of the letters, which constituted the filling. At the ages of eight and ten we stopped sitting on the cake because it would no longer support our weight, but the reading of the letters continued.

On one wall of Granny's office was a border painted in bright silver; it was the musical notation for the first few bars of her favorite Bach Concerto. Granny loved Bach the way some people loved chocolate or cigars. Sometimes she would play the record for us; we listened *and* watched the silver notes being sounded.

My love of Granny's house was overshadowed by the unrequited love I felt for my grandfather. How could I love someone whom I'd never met? Why did Poppy have to die when my mother was just a girl? It wasn't fair that I would never meet him. But at least I got to know him, through my Grandmother.

Granny did a superior job of keeping Poppy's spirit alive. His office at home remained unchanged for thirty years, living on as a shrine to Poppy's memory. It was physically disturbed only once a week to be dusted, not by the cleaning woman who did the rest of the house, but by Granny herself. That ritual kept Poppy close to her heart; the office was dust-free.

Granny had done such a wonderful job of keeping Poppy's spirit alive, that we three kids never really thought of him as being dead. We fantasized that he was away on an extended symposium, and someday, he *would* come back.

I suddenly realized how long I'd been sitting on the back steps. I was so lost in thought, it was as if I really had been sitting on the wedding cake in Granny's office. It was my first out-of-body experience. Fate projected me to ordinary reality—I was whacked across the back so hard with the screen door that it sent me hurling into the thorn bush next to the steps.

My father had barreled out the back door after an argument with Granny. Apparently she had not been there two minutes when Dad perceived a facial expression as an air of condescension on my grandmother's part. Picking the last thorn from the center of my chest, I wondered why no one told me that Granny had arrived. I'd been waiting all that time, and was the last to know .

"Where the hell did you come from?" Dad snarled.

"What?" I asked.

"What the hell are you doing in that bush? You're going to poke a hole in your shirt. Get out of there!"

Thanks to Dad, I had been tortured by an acupuncturist gone mad, and he was worried about poking a hole in my shirt. What about my puncture wounds?

"Dad, you knocked me into the bush with the door when you came running out like a banshee!" I yelled.

"I think if you were on the steps, I would have seen you, and maybe you deserve a little smack for the way you just talked to me," Dad snickered.

So, Dad could smack me in advance for something I might do, after being provoked by him! His game was beginning to make perfect sense.

I blew into the house on veritable storm of condescension. I knew I'd pay later; I didn't care. At that moment, revenge and escape had been more pressing. Granny was waiting for me.

Jerry was in the kitchen drinking a glass of lemonade.

"Why didn't you come outside and tell me that Granny was here?" I asked.

"I didn't know where you were. I looked out the back door and couldn't find you."

"Jerry, I was sitting on the back steps the whole time."

"You were not, Tony. Not when I looked," Jerry said matter-of-factly.

"Jerry, I never left the back steps."

"O.K., Tone. Whatever you say. I must have overlooked you."

"What? How could you have overlooked me when I was right in front of you?"

"I'm not sure, Tone. But I guess I did, if you say I did."

"I didn't say you did—you said you did!"

Once again, Jerry and I were at a stalemate, confused by our language. It would take us a minute to figure out exactly what had been said; Jerry was always the first to utter, "Yeah, right."

A similar farce usually sprang from my conversations with Margaret. Our impasses, however, were based not on complete sentences but on single words, such as the word *puffy* on the beach that day. It was strange.

It was even stranger that neither Dad nor Jerry had seen me on the steps; at the time, I had even wondered where I was myself. Was it possible that I had disappeared for an instant or two?

I suddenly heard a strange ripping sound and realized the fabric of my reality was being torn to shreds: I had just entertained the possibility of my disappearance. I had to be nuts, driven to insanity by a bad chromosome that was a birthday present from my father. How could life be so absurd?

I then heard angels plucking Bach on their celestial harps, in musical accompaniment to my flight from neurosis to the sanctity of my Grandmother's world.

"Tony, my love!" Granny said, squeezing me hard, but not too hard. Everything Granny did was perfect, never underdone nor overdone. "How's my sweetheart?"

"I'm better now that you're here," I squealed.

Granny looked radiant in her flowing white outfit. She always wore white in the summer because it reflected the most heat. It was one of the ways in which Granny stayed cool, while the rest of us sweated like hogs. My father hated that Granny was able to remain cool; I found it fascinating.

Granny also smelled good, like flowers after a rain. Granny believed you could enter heaven through your sense of smell; small brown bottles of flower oils filled most of the shelves at the back of her desk. Occasionally she would open the bottles, and we would be transported to a lavender field in Provence or a southern plantation dripping with magnolia flowers in full bloom. Sometimes Granny would put a small dab of oil on a cotton ball so we could take our imaginary gardens home. It was comforting to stop and smell the roses while knee-deep in the culture shock of returning to big Anthony's territory. At times those cotton balls became our only wads of sanity.

Finally Granny had arrived. She would keep everyone in line and help reweave my reality.

Mom had followed Granny into the kitchen. "Tony, would you go outside and tell your father we're having him for dinner with some honey?"

Did she say we were having my father for dinner? A wave of nausea moved through me. "What did you say, Mom?"

"Oh, Tony, go out the back door, find your father, and tell him it's time for dinner, honey," she repeated slowly.

Oh. But the thought of having my father for dinner had already done its damage. I wiped the sweat from my brow and tried to think of something pleasant. Approaching the back door, nausea consumed me. Arriving there, I instead focused on exploiting my father's blatant vulnerability: he was sitting in the same spot where I'd been perched before my accident. I imagined giving my father a little retaliatory hurl, but couldn't muster the guts to pull it off. I timidly opened the back door just enough to let my voice out. "Dad, it's time to eat."

"Watch the god-damned door, don't be winging it into my back!" Dad spewed.

Having partly accomplished my mission, I fled the scene.

"Tony," Margaret said, "help me set the table." I did as I was told while everyone took their place at the crowded table.

We sat down to a dinner served in very ordinary dishes, which was unusual. We passed our plates to the adults so they could *fix* them for us. I'd always thought that expression was odd; to me it conjured images of the adults working with porcelain shards and a noxious adhesive.

Mom was putting macaroni on my plate when I had to say something. "Mom, no meatballs for me." I still hadn't released the thought of having my father for dinner.

"What? No meatballs?"

"No, no meatballs for me," I repeated.

"Why not?" My father demanded. "Usually you're like a god-damned cannibal."

That was it. I could never eat meatballs again.

"Suit yourself, honey," Mom said.

"You know," Granny said, "it's not a bad idea to have a purely vegetarian meal once in a while. Meat can be terribly hard to digest."

My father had to have the last word. "Well, just don't be complaining later that you want some flesh!"

Everyone rolled their eyes in a gesture of mass disgust. The collective feeling of lost appetite almost required the removal of a few place settings from the table, but Mom came to the rescue and changed the subject.

"I hear it's supposed to be hot tomorrow, 104 degrees inland and 96 at the shore," she said.

"Well," said Aunt Vicky, "I guess we'll be spending a lot of time jumping waves and eating popsicles!"

"Yeah!" Tommy squealed.

"Anthony, Did you say something about a wax museum? Ivent never been to one before. What, are the pictures made of wax?" Uncle Harry asked.

"No, no Harry. They're figures of famous people carved and molded in three dimensions; it's a very fine art."

"Isninit interesting. Iyamin dying to see it. Did they do Gina Lolabrigida?"

"Oh Harry!" Aunt Vicky yelled, "What are you going to do—get off on a wax figure in a low-cut dress?"

"Vicky," Mom said, "have you heard that furniture store on Frankford Avenue is going out of business? It may be your chance to get a coffee table at half-price."

"Really?" Aunt Vicky asked, eyebrows arched like horseshoes.

Mom had gotten Uncle Harry off the hook.

I looked at Jerry and we communicated telepathically.

"Yeah, they're a real bunch," Jerry thought.

"Can you believe they get excited over a bunch of human candles?" I thought back.

We looked at Granny; she winked at us, as if applauding our powers of perception.

"Speaking of carving, Anthony, how's the soap sculpting going?" Aunt Vicky asked.

Oh no. That was a sore subject, since I had taken a bath with Dad's *Statue of Liberty*. Dad's art was washed down the drain, leaving no evidence that it had indeed been his best work. And I was responsible for dissolving his masterpiece. My question was, why did he leave it in the bathroom if we weren't supposed to use it? How could soap be just for *show*?

Soap was my father's medium and our bathroom was his gallery. His little figures weren't carved of *Dial* or *Palmolive*; Dad made his own soap with *Crisco* and a caustic chemical called lye. I couldn't comprehend why lye didn't burn one's skin. Jerry tried to explain its chemical transmutation, but it was pointless since my understanding of hydrocarbons was so unsophisticated. As usual, I was sorry I'd asked; actually I hadn't asked. I knew better. Jerry had volunteered the information.

"My carving is going just fine, thank-you," Dad said, glaring at me.

He was lying. His sculptures looked flat and could never stand alone; they always required a leaning post, like the side of the toothbrush holder or two Dixie cups arranged *just so.*

"Well anyhow," Dad continued, "we were going to the Wax Museum until the boys made me punish them. But I suppose if they've learned their lesson, we can still go."

Dad turned to Jerry and me. We looked at one another, each silently begging the other to speak first. What could we do? If we said yes, we'd have to go to the Wax Museum. If we said no, we'd be punished for being defiant.

"Well, boys, has a cat got your tongue? Have you learned your lesson or do you require further punishment?"

"Oh, we've learned!" Jerry and I yelled in unison.

"Well then, let's get ready to go!" Dad said, so excited over the coming attraction that he charged from the kitchen like a bull.

As we walked the boardwalk toward the Wax Museum, I followed Granny like her shadow.

"Granny, you were awfully quiet during dinner. Is anything the matter?" I asked.

"Oh no, love, everything's just fine. What could I have possibly added to *that* conversation? As you mature, you'll learn there are times to talk and times to be silent and observe," Granny said, squeezing my hand.

That made sense. If you didn't say anything, you couldn't get into trouble. Why hadn't I thought of that myself? I resolved from that moment forward to say less and observe more. Granny was never off the mark.

We were only a block from the Wax Museum when Aunt Vicky stopped walking, so we all stopped. She was looking at Margaret.

"Honey, what's that on your chest?" Aunt Vicky asked.

"What, Aunt Vicky?" Margaret responded.

"You have a big white streak across your chest, right here." Aunt Vicky pointed to the area above Margaret's tank top.

"That's the shadow of her ponytail," Jerry said. "I knew that would happen. The sun was blocked there but gave her a tan everywhere else."

"What ponytail?" Aunt Vicky asked.

"My ponytail that was swept out to sea. It happened today when I went in the water; it was so embarrassing!" Margaret said, bursting into tears.

"Margaret, honey, don't cry. Why not grow a ponytail of your own so it won't come off?" Aunt Vicky asked consolingly.

"I'm not always in the mood for a ponytail. It's nice to be able to go either way," Margaret whined.

"Well then, you can order another one when you get home. You look perfectly lovely without it. Now dry those pretty eyes; your mascara will run," Aunt Vicky ordered.

Poor Margaret, forced to wear her shame like a scarlet letter. She managed to compose herself as we approached the Wax Museum, in time for the next fiasco.

"I'm treating tonight!" Dad boasted. He wanted to be the one whom everyone thanked for that enchanting evening.

Dad removed his wad and curtly dangled his stash in plain view.

Granny laughed.

"And what are you laughing at?" Dad asked sarcastically.

"Nothing, Anthony. Can't a person just quietly chuckle to herself once in a while?" Granny asked.

"Yeah, once in a while. But it seems as if you're always snickering. You think I don't know you're laughing at my money?"

"Laughing at your money, Anthony? Don't be ridiculous. What could possibly be funny about your money?"

Nevertheless, an argument about funny money ensued. I wasn't sure if Granny had been laughing at Dad's money, but I had been. Dad had the curious habit of carrying only one-dollar bills, so his bankroll would look and feel more impressive than it really was. Dad didn't realize that everyone was on to his game.

Big Anthony was determined to have an altercation with Granny. "Didn't you ever hear that expression about putting all of your eggs in one basket? I lose a dollar and it's only a dollar. I carry nothing but twenties, and I've lost twenty dollars; you do the math," Dad said, with a false sense of triumph.

"Well," said Granny, "I guess you've never heard the expression by Mark Twain: put all your eggs in one basket and watch that basket." And then she added, "When a gust of wind blows away your bankroll, you'll have a much better chance of catching one bill rather than twenty."

Granny won, but Dad had to have the last word. "I'll never be out of luck because some sucker can't change a twenty-dollar bill," Dad retorted.

"And one day, Anthony, you'll realize that foolish games can get you into trouble."

I knew Granny's words meant something, but I wasn't sure what. How could Dad's one dollar bills ever get him into trouble?

Dad turned and walked towards the ticket booth. "I'm generous enough to foot the bill and all I get is shit," Dad mumbled under his breath. "That will be five adults and four children, please."

The cashier looked at Dad. "Excuse me, sir. Children must be twelve and under."

"My son is only twelve—going into the seventh grade is all," Dad said, pretending I was the party in question.

"No, sir," said the cashier, "I was referring to the young woman in the blue bandanna. Surely she's at least seventeen."

"Oh yes, forgive me. I forgot that we just recently celebrated her thirteenth birthday. Make that six adults, please." Dad's cheeks were as red as the carafe of wine he had downed with dinner.

Margaret spoke. "Dad! I'm fourteen years old! You'd try to pass me off as a little kid just to save a buck?"

"Margaret, not now, dear," Mom said, as she quickly ushered Margaret through the front doors to avert a scene.

Once inside, Margaret continued to pout her azalea-colored lips. "I can't believe you did that to me, Dad. Why are you always treating me like a child?"

"Don't argue with me. If you didn't wear so much god-damned makeup maybe you'd look your age!"

Mom hated Dad's cursing, especially in public. "Now, now. Let's enjoy our visit here and stop arguing. That policeman over there is looking at us. Let's move along."

Jerry and I remained together while the rest of our motley bunch went to ooh and aah over the lifeless wax movie stars. We found a bench near the exit so we'd be ready and waiting when the others had finished gawking.

"Tony, it sure is hot in here, isn't it?" Jerry whined.

"Yeah," I replied. "It doesn't feel as if the air-conditioning is working. I can't wait to get out of here."

"Me too," Jerry said pathetically.

We had a long wait. Jerry gave me a scientific treatise on every subject imaginable, including the effect of temperature on bacterial growth. Finally I could bear the heat and Jerry's babbling no longer.

"I'm going to find the others. I can't take it any more," I said to Jerry.

"Me too, Tony."

We searched but couldn't find the others. Finally, I turned a corner and caught a glimpse of my father. "I see Dad, he's over there," I said, relieved.

"Where?" Jerry asked.

"Over there, next to John Wayne."

"Dad!" We yelled simultaneously. Dad didn't hear us; he was intently studying John Wayne. We approached and Jerry yelled, "Dad, we've been looking all over for you!"

"Kids, come here. Have you ever seen a pair of ears that looked so real?" Dad asked.

We looked at John Wayne's ears. "They do look real," Jerry said.

Dad was enthralled. "Now I've seen some real ear wax, but never wax ears that looked so real," he said in amazement.

Jerry and I looked at him as if he was crazy.

"Where is everyone?" I asked my father. He was still admiring the Duke's ears.

"Well, there was some trouble and Uncle Harry and Aunt Vicky and Tommy were asked to leave. They're waiting outside," Dad said matter-of-factly. "I don't know where your mother and grandmother are."

"Trouble? What kind of trouble?" I asked.

"Tommy broke the wax policeman's arm," Dad said.

Jerry was intrigued. "Was it fractured or did the whole thing come off?

"I'm afraid he broke the whole thing off," Dad said.

I was confused. "Dad, are you talking about the policeman who was staring at us when we first arrived? I thought he was real."

"No, he was wax."

"But he looked so real."

"Now you've got it; it's what a wax museum is all about—taking you by surprise."

Jerry was getting nervous. "Where's Mom and Granny?"

"I don't know. Maybe they went outside to wait with the others. I'll be out shortly. I have a few more models to inspect," Dad said, brushing us off.

"C'mon, Jerry, let's get out of here."

The air outside was a few degrees cooler but extremely muggy. Uncle Harry was scolding Tommy, telling him it wasn't nice to twist people's arms, even if they were made of wax.

"Mom! We were sitting by the exit; how come we didn't see you leave?" I asked.

Mom looked flustered. "It was so warm in there, I turned around and left. I can't remember a summer so hot. As soon as your father comes out, we'll go for ice cream."

"Where's Granny?" I asked.

"Oh, she's meeting us back at the house. She ran into people she knew and they went for coffee."

"She ran into people who she knew *here*?"

"Well, she said that she knew them."

How disappointing. I had spent over an hour listening to Jerry's lectures inside that stinking Wax Museum and everyone else was waiting outside. And, Granny was gone!

The heat was becoming intolerable, and so was my paranoia. Jerry had informed me that it took only hours for a few bacteria to have several million children, and I kept thinking about that slimy shower. Surely those children had become grandparents on my skin—children grew so quickly! Not only were they multiplying on my skin, but by that time they had undoubtedly invaded my bloodstream. Surely my fall into the thorn bush had created hundreds of portals of entry for the greedy slime balls.

I was desperate for a bath, but could hear my father: "You took a shower before dinner! You don't need a bath. There are seven other people that need to use that bathroom. You're not going to inconvenience everyone so you can sleep fresh as a daisy!"

"But Dad, that outdoor shower is filthy. I can't go to bed with this kind of bacterial count," I pleaded.

Suddenly, it dawned on me that I was arguing with my father and he was still inside the Wax Museum. He left me no choice; I'd have to figure a way to get filthy by the time we got back to the house. Then I'd have to take a bath; how many times had Dad told us that we couldn't get into bed with a filthy ring around our necks? He'd have to give in.

Ice cream. That was it. When we went for ice cream, I'd drop mine down my shirt and get sticky. Then I'd have to take a bath. I'd show him.

Finally Dad emerged from the wax museum. "Leona, did you see John Wayne's ears?"

"Yes I did, Anthony. Now let's move along; I promised the kids some ice cream to cool off."

Mom couldn't have seen John Wayne's ears, but she did the smart thing and changed the subject.

We flew into the ice cream parlor like a bunch of hungry pigeons, and viewed the myriad of flavors through the cold glass windows. While the others looked for a palate pleaser, I searched for the dirtiest, messiest flavor available.

Finally it was my turn.

"What kind do you want, Tony?" Dad asked, looking at me suspiciously.

"I'll have a double dip of Mississippi Mudpie on a sugar cone, please!"

Dad chimed in, "On a cone? Are you sure? It might be easier to eat that out of a cup; you don't want it to fall over," he warned.

What? Was he on to me?

"Oh, I don't care," Dad said. "Get a cone if you want. Just be careful!"

Oh no—he was forewarning me! He would really fume when I dropped the whole thing down my shirt. The "shits" and the "goddammits" would fly like missiles. I didn't care about the repercussions. I just wanted a bath.

"I'll take a cone, please," I said.

The waitress handed me a top-heavy cone of the darkest, dirtiest chocolate ice cream I had ever seen. God was on my side! "Thank you very much!"

I overheard Mom and Aunt Vicky conversing in the background.

"Boy, little Tony is certainly a polite child, all the pleases and thank you's," Aunt Vicky remarked.

"Yes, Tony's a delight," Mom said, turning to wink at me.

While my Mother and my Aunt discussed my admirable qualities, I was busy plotting my ice cream's demise. I couldn't let the ice cream just plop off the cone. It might roll right off my shirt and I wouldn't get dirty *enough* to justify a bath. It had to be more calculated: I would have to pull my shirt out at the neck and dump the whole thing in. But how?

The answer came to me. I'd wait until Uncle Harry spoke. Because of his problem with contractions, everyone had to stare and really concentrate to decipher his words. With Uncle Harry on stage, no one would be watching me, and alas, no witnesses to my crime.

Ice cream began running down my arm, and finally Uncle Harry had something to say. "Isninit remarkable how they can make a ball of wax look so human?"

That was it. On his next contraction, my move was going down.

"Doesninit…"

I grabbed the ball of frozen mud and shoved it down my shirt. "Oh no, my ice cream!" I yelled.

Everyone turned and looked at me.

"Where is your ice cream, Tony?" Mom asked.

"I dropped it down my shirt, by accident!" I cried.

"Well, of course it was an accident. No one would purposely put an ice cream cone down his shirt; that would be insane. Come here and let me help you," Mom said, motioning me toward her.

"I told you to get a god-damned cup," Dad yelled. "How could you drop a whole ice cream cone down your shirt? You had to have a cone! You never listen!"

"Oh, Anthony, don't be so hard on him. He can take a bath when we get back," Mom said sympathetically.

"He can't be tying up the bathroom all night! Seven other people need to use that bathroom; he can shower outside!"

I wasn't going to use that slimebox again. "Oh Dad, not in the dark, please!" I begged.

"Since when are you afraid of the god-damned dark?"

Mom saved me. "Tony, of course you can take a bath inside. Just don't dilly-dally."

We couldn't get back to the house quickly enough. To my relief, Mom had packed an antibacterial soap; I unwrapped a fresh yellow bar as the tub filled. What a day, and my groin was still killing me.

As I lay back in the tub I thought about Jerry. Why did he have to be so graphic? He knew I hated bugs, especially ones you couldn't even see. I scrubbed and rinsed myself three times to make certain I'd killed every last scoundrel. I then decided to lie back in the hot water so the heat could soothe my poor groin muscle. Just as I became completely relaxed, it sounded as if someone was going to bust down the door.

"Tony, god-damn it! You've been in there long enough. You don't have to inconvenience the other seven people in this house so you can sleep fresh as a daisy!" Dad yelled.

My bacterial population had been annihilated; my groin would have to wait. "O.K.!" I yelled.

I got into my pajamas and went downstairs. Granny was sitting in the living room, reading a book.

"Granny, you're back!"

"Yes, sweetie. You were in the tub when I arrived. Sorry I missed you on the boardwalk. I ran into some friends from Philadelphia and we went for a cup of coffee."

"You must know a lot of people. Wherever we go you always run into somebody you know."

"Well, I've had a lot of years to meet people."

"Did you hear what happened at the wax museum? Tommy and Aunt Vicky and Uncle Harry were kicked out."

"What? Are you pulling my leg?"

"No, Tommy broke the wax policeman's arm and they were forced to leave."

"Well, I guess Tommy didn't realize the power of his own strength."

"Granny, how can a little kid be so strong? I think he's stronger than me, and I'm twelve years old."

"Everyone has strengths and weaknesses. Tommy's strength happens to be physical. You're blessed with a different kind of strength; you have mental strength."

"I do?" I asked in disbelief.

"Of course you do," Granny said.

"Then how come I don't feel mentally strong? Sometimes I wonder if I'm nuts because nothing seems to make sense to me."

"You poor, sweet child, sometimes it's hard to make sense of life. But don't ever think you're the one who's nuts."

"It's my dad; he's the one who's nuts, right?"

"No, honey, your father isn't nuts either. He always thinks people are out to get him, that's his problem. But we have to have compassion for all people, even the obnoxious ones. Underneath our personalities, we're all the same."

"We are?"

"Yes we are, honey," Granny said. "You have to learn the virtue of patience. You have to be like a tree, and stand tall and firm, even during a storm."

"But what if a storm knocks me down?"

"Well then, you have to get up and take root again. As you get older you'll learn how to hold on tightly so you aren't uprooted."

"Granny, do you like my dad?" .

"Of course I like him. I may not always like the things he does, but don't forget what I said: in our hearts, we're all the same."

Maybe Dad wasn't so bad, after all. I had to keep reminding myself to be patient. Granny was right.

"Honey," Granny said, "why is your knee all red?"

"Oh, I got a splinter when I fell on the boardwalk today."

"You fell? How did you fall?"

I thought about the incident in front of the Peanut Shoppe. It was a long story, and I was too hot and tired to re-enact it. "Oh, I was just being clumsy."

"Well, let me help you remove it," Granny said. "I have a needle in my sewing kit."

Normally the word *needle* would have sent me into shock, but my experience in the bush that day had desensitized me.

Granny returned with her sewing kit and the small gold lighter that she used to light candles.

"You're going to burn it out?"

"No, I'm going to use the flame to sterilize the needle."

"So the needle's going to be hot when it goes in?" I asked. "Is it going to hurt?"

"Not one bit," she said. "I'm going to let the needle cool before I start. Just sit back and relax."

I leaned back on the sofa and got comfortable. I knew I could trust Granny not to hurt me.

"Tony, remember that day we went to Pennypack Park in the spring? Weren't the waterfalls magnificent?"

"Oh yeah," I said. Granny had taken me there during Easter vacation. It was beautiful, like Granny's house, but without a roof. The only sounds were falling water and the songs of birds; everywhere you looked, there was a green sense of calm. We never wanted to leave, but of course we had to.

"O.K., Granny, you can start digging it out now."

"Oh, it's out already," Granny said.

"But I didn't feel a thing."

"That's because your mind was somewhere else," Granny said. "Your mind wasn't free to feel the pain because it was somewhere else."

Granny was right. My mind was in Pennypack, even though my body was in Atlantic City. Just like that afternoon, when my mind was in Granny's office and my body was sitting on the back steps. So why was I able to feel Dad whacking me with the back door but not a sewing needle piercing my kneecap?

"Can we go to Pennypack again when we get home? Just the two of us?" I asked Granny.

"What about Jerry and Margaret?" Granny asked.

"Margaret won't want to go; she has a hard time walking in the dirt in high heels. She won't care," I said.

"What about Jerry?" Granny asked. "His feelings might be hurt if we don't include him."

"Oh," I said. I didn't want to hurt Jerry's feelings, but he was distracting. I enjoyed walking through the woods and simply observing; Jerry always had to give a lecture. When Granny and I went alone, we didn't say a word until we got in the car to go home. It was much more relaxing.

I had an idea. "What if you took Jerry to the *Franklin Institute*? Then it wouldn't be unfair if we went somewhere without him."

"Good idea," Granny laughed. "When we get home next week we'll make plans."

"Thanks, Gran. We'll have fun,"

"We always do. Now why don't we go and look for the others? I think they're on the front porch."

"O.K.," I said, following Granny.

Dad and Uncle Harry were sitting on the front porch drinking beer, talking about the wax museum.

"So do they have wax bones, too?" Uncle Harry asked Dad.

"For crying out loud, Harry. What the hell do you think?"

"Ivent never thought about it before, but I guess they need some kind of support."

"They're as solid as a god-damned rock, Harry. What the hell's the matter with you?"

Granny interrupted their conversation. "Are you two still obsessing on the wax museum?"

"What do you mean, obsessing? Just because you have no appreciation of fine art, you accuse us of obsessing?" Dad sneered.

"She does too," I said. "Granny has her own art collection!" How could my father have said something so ludicrous?

"Who asked you?" Dad snarled.

Before I could say anything, Granny spoke. "I didn't mean it in a negative way, Anthony. I find your appreciation of wax sculpture quite fascinating."

"Right," Dad said. "You think I don't know what you're implying? It just so happens that you didn't see my *Statue of Liberty*, because your grandson here used it to wash his armpits last week!"

"I didn't know what it was!" I yelled.

"You didn't notice the god-damned torch?"

"Oh, Anthony, you don't have to take it out on poor Tony. Maybe you should consider displaying your sculptures somewhere else to avoid confusion—perhaps get a curio cabinet."

"Now that aininit a bad idea, Anthony," Uncle Harry said. "Then there wouldinint be any accidents in the bathroom."

"Who the hell asked you?" Dad said. "Everyone in the god-damned house knows if the soap is tan not to use it!"

I thought about Dad's statement. What about *Fels-Naptha*? Was that off-limits too? It was tan. I knew what he'd meant but needed a little private one-upmanship. Who the hell was he, talking to my Grandmother that way?

Granny ignored Dad and addressed Uncle Harry. "Where did the others go?" She asked.

"Oh," Uncle Harry said. "They went to the store to get Tommy some candy. Poor kid, he isninit happy unless he's pumping in the sugar. Went through a whole box of Mallow Cups last night when we wereninint looking. Can you imagine? He even got a five-dollar prize card in the last one, and almost went through the roof! Haveninint ever seen a kid get so excited over a toasted marshmallow cup. But I guess Idedid get excited too if I won five bucks. Not sure though, because I'vent never didninit won anything in my life, so I donut know how Idedid react." Uncle Harry rambled.

"O.K. Harry. We get the picture," Dad said. "The kid likes candy and you have no luck. You can spare us the details."

"Well," Granny said, "maybe we'll go and meet them. What do you say, Tony? Do you want to get dressed and go with me?"

I thought about it; I was comfortable in my pajamas, but I would never say no to Granny. Besides, if I didn't go, I'd be tortured by my father.

Before I could respond, Granny said "Never mind, honey, here they come."

The others were just turning the corner. Tommy was carrying a big bag.

From a distance I could see two bandannas shielding Margaret's pride—she'd added one to drape the eclipse-marking on her chest.

As they approached, I realized how exhausted I was. What a day, and it was so hot.

"You look tired, honey," Granny said.

"I am, Granny. I'm going to bed soon. Besides, it's too hot to do anything."

"Let me tell you a little secret," Granny said, ushering me off the porch and toward the driveway.

"What secret?" I asked excitedly.

"Remember how you couldn't feel my removing the splinter because your mind was somewhere else?"

"Yeah?"

"You can use the same trick to cool off when it's really hot."

"You can?"

"Yes, what you have to do is imagine that you're somewhere cold, perhaps swimming in a pool of ice water or building a snowman in the backyard in the middle of February."

"Really?"

"Yes, Tony. It's called mind over matter. You use your mind to change your perception of things. Your mind can't be hot and cold at the same time. When it's really hot, convince yourself there's snow falling around you, and actually see the snowflakes, frosty and cold. Before you know it, you're in a winter wonderland and it isn't so hot anymore. Try it and see."

"Is that what you do, Granny?"

"All the time." Granny was going to say something else, but was interrupted by Jerry.

"Hi Gran! What are you guys doing?" Jerry asked.

"Oh, we're just talking," Granny said. "What did you buy at the store?"

"Look, I got these little candies shaped like shoes—you want one?" Jerry asked, presenting a half-melted chocolate resembling a wing-tip without its tip. It was so hot that Jerry's little shoes had melted into a brown mess in his hand.

"Oh shoot—they're melting! How could I have been so stupid? I should have considered the melting point of cocoa butter when I chose my candy. I knew I should have picked the Swedish Slippers," Jerry whined.

"Swedish slippers?" I asked.

"Yeah, you know. Those chewy red things. They had some that looked like bedroom slippers," Jerry said.

I wondered why anyone would want to eat anything remotely resembling an old bedroom slipper or a wing-tip that had stepped in something. Why was candy even molded into weird shapes? Couldn't chocolate just be a bar, or Swedish taffy just be a piece? I wondered if Swedish slippers were even made in Sweden.

"Granny," I asked, "are Swedish slippers actually made in Sweden?"

"Well, probably not. The recipe just originated there."

"Where exactly is Sweden, Gran? I forget," Jerry asked.

I could tell by Jerry's rapid eye movement that he was spinning an imaginary globe.

"It's in northern Europe between Norway and Finland."

Jerry had located Sweden on the map in his head—his eyeballs stopped rolling.

"Have you ever been to Sweden?" I asked Granny.

"Yes, but it's been a long time. Poppy and I went to Stockholm when his friend won the Nobel Prize," Granny said.

"The noble prize that Dad's always screaming about?" I asked.

"It's not the *noble* prize. It's the *Nobel* Prize, named after Alfred Nobel, its benefactor. Your father just mispronounces it."

"What is the Nobel Prize, anyway?" Jerry asked.

"The Nobel Prize is an award given to scientists who make important discoveries."

"Like the Academy Awards?" I asked.

"Yes, exactly. Only the winners are scientists instead of actors."

"So what is Stockholm like, Granny?" Jerry asked.

"Oh," Granny replied, "Stockholm is amazing. They call it the City of Water. Everywhere you look, there is water."

"Was it fun to go there?" Jerry asked.

"Oh yes, especially during the week of the prize ceremony. A subtle yet powerful energy filled the air; the town was brimming with the finest thinkers on the planet. It was as though the water surrounding the city had absorbed the intellectual pulse that was beating in the mind of humanity. It was a wonderful experience."

"I'd like to go to Stockholm one day," Jerry said.

"Well anything is possible, Jerry," Granny said. "Anything that you dream about can come true, if you believe it hard enough."

"Yeah, one day I'm going to Stockholm," Jerry said, looking skyward.

Mom and Aunt Vicky came looking for us. "So there you are," Mom said. "Tony, you're ready for bed?"

"Yeah, Mom. I'm really tired. I'm going to sleep early tonight," I said. "Besides, it's too hot to do anything."

As we approached the front porch my eyes met Granny's. "Remember what I told you," her eyes said.

As sweat dripped from my brow, I tried to imagine that I was back in Philadelphia, in the midst of a snowstorm.

Two feet of snow had fallen since daybreak, and I was working furiously to clear the driveway so my father could pull in when he got home from work. I wanted to play at the park before dinner, so I tried to move quickly. Pain impeded my progress; I had lost one of my gloves, and my left hand was frost-bitten. A chill traveled straight to my bones. By the time I had finished, I was numb. As I wondered how much play time was left, a horn beeped. It was Dad, signaling me to get out of his way: "Do you want me to run you the hell over?" There would be no playing in the park. The sound of Dad's car pulling into the driveway was Mom's cue to put dinner on the table.

My mind returned to the heat of Atlantic City.

"Tony, do you want something to drink before you go to bed?" Mom asked.

"Yeah, Mom, would you make me some hot chocolate to warm me up?" I asked, hugged myself in an effort to keep warm.

"Only you would want something hot to drink when it's almost a hundred degrees. What the hell's the matter with you, are you sick or something?" Dad snarled.

"Tony, we don't have the ingredients here for hot chocolate. Are you feeling all right?" Mom asked.

"Yeah, I'm just tired," I said. "I'm going up now."

I couldn't believe how well Granny's trick had worked. Although I had just made a fool of myself, I didn't care. All I wanted was to go to bed and be alone, to mull over the strange events that had unfolded that day.

I pecked Mom and Aunt Vicky goodnight; I hugged Granny and thanked her for coming.

I went into the house and headed for the stairs. Jerry yelled through the screen door at me: "Don't worry, Tony, I'll be right up."

"Dear God," I prayed, "can I please just have a few minutes of peace and quiet? I promise I won't ask for anything else, ever again."

I crawled into bed and pulled the cool sheets over my weary body. I thought about what Granny had said earlier: underneath our personalities, we're all the same. So why did we seem to be so different? I was sure, however, that Granny knew what she was talking about; she knew everything. Still, I had a hard time imagining that my father and I were the least bit alike. Perhaps it would happen gradually over time; maybe one day I would awaken to discover that I *was* my father. Perhaps I would even come to be known as *big* Anthony—God forbid!

I closed my eyes and tried to think of something pleasant. Just then, Jerry walked in the bedroom. "Hi Tony. Are you asleep?"

"Almost, Jerry. I'm really tired." I hoped Jerry would get the hint: I couldn't endure his incessant babbling. My mind couldn't process the quantities of information that spewed from Jerry's lips. Especially that night, after the day I'd had. Maybe I'd be spared; Jerry had undressed quietly and slipped into bed. He was probably tired too.

Just when I thought I was off the hook, Jerry spoke. "Tony?"

"What?"

"Do you think colors look the same in outer space as they do on earth?"

"No, they're probably brighter."

"Oh really? Why do you say that?" Jerry sat up in bed and I knew I was in for a whopper. "Do you think it has something to do with the atmosphere?"

"Yeah, the atmosphere." I had no idea. I had said something, anything, to shut him up.

"But how?" Jerry asked.

"I don't know, Jerry. Can I just go to sleep? I'm exhausted!" I pleaded.

"Well you can't just state a hypothesis without some kind of support."

"The only support I want right now is the pillow under my head."

"You don't have to be mean," Jerry said, appearing hurt.

I didn't want to hurt Jerry's feelings. "I'm not trying to be mean," I said. "I just want to go to sleep."

Jerry was silent for a few moments and I began drifting off to sleep.

"Tony?"

"Wha-at?" I yelled.

"I know you put your ice cream down your shirt on purpose."

"I did not."

"Yes you did."

"I did not, it was top-heavy!"

"Exactly," Jerry said. "Being top-heavy, your ice cream's center of gravity was high. Under ordinary physical conditions, it would have rolled quickly off your shirt and onto the floor. You must have introduced energy into the system, namely by giving it a shove in the right direction. You dumped it down your shirt!"

"You don't know what you're talking about, Jerry."

"Yes I do."

"No you don't."

"Yes I do. But don't worry, I'm not going to tell. I know you just wanted to take a bath. I saw the way you were sweating during our talk about the shower slime," Jerry said sympathetically.

"Well, you made it sound so gross."

"I did not. I presented a scientific fact: bacterial growth is temperature-dependent."

"Yeah, and it was hot as hell in that damned Wax Museum."

"You don't have to curse, Tony. You sound like Dad."

He was right.

"Well," I said, "how would you feel if you thought that bugs were crawling all over you?"

"I'm tired," Jerry said. "Let's go to sleep."

"Oh, so now I'm wide awake, and you want to go to sleep," I said.

"Jerry!"

"Jerry!"

He was asleep. So my mad scientist-brother had it figured out. But I didn't have to worry; Jerry would *never* tell. Although he sometimes drove me crazy, there existed a heartfelt bond of loyalty between us, similar to that shared by prison cell-mates.

I closed my eyes and tried to go to sleep. As I did, the weird imagery that I had witnessed that day skated across my mind in a jumble of shapes and colors.

The last image I remembered was that of my father driving to the beach. My life preserver had become the steering wheel of the car, and someone had purposely let the air out of it. A hissing sound shifted to a current of profanities as the steering wheel became a limp heap of vinyl in Dad's hands. Unable to negotiate his turn, Dad drove onto the boardwalk and smashed into the window of the Peanut Shoppe. Broken glass and nuts went flying, as tufts of cotton candy escaped to freedom and became pink clouds overhead.

The next morning I awoke in a pool of sweat. It was the summer's worst heat wave; I couldn't wait to go downstairs for a cold drink.

Dad was already dressed, reading the newspaper at the kitchen table. He looked as if he was ready to jump out of his skin.

"Dad, what is it?"

He didn't answer me.

"Dad, what happened? What are you reading?" I began to wonder if there had been an accident on the moon.

Finally Dad spoke. "Well, I guess it was a good thing we went to the Wax Museum last night. It was our last chance."

"Why?"

Dad held up the newspaper so that I could read the headline: "RECORD TEMPERATURES AND FAULTY AIR CONDITIONING BLAMED IN WAX MUSEUM MELTDOWN."

"Oh my God! Did they completely melt?"

"No, but they're sagging pretty darn badly."

Jerry walked into the kitchen. "What's all the commotion?"

"The wax museum people melted!" I yelled.

"What?" Jerry asked, perplexed.

Dad read us a passage: "Museum losses are estimated at 1.2 million dollars. Figures lost an average of 3.2 inches in height and suffered a marked sagging of facial features. Several of the taller wax models have become hunch-backed, and most have lost their hair."

"Sounds just like the aging process," Jerry interjected.

Dad continued reading:

> The museum is forced to close its doors and will not re-open this season. Investigators are looking into the possibility of foul play in the incident. Meanwhile, a security leak across the police line allowed an unknown photographer to shoot pictures inside the museum. He

> made his getaway on horseback before police could apprehend the film. The National Gossip has reportedly paid over one million dollars for a photo of Raquel Welch as she would appear at the age of ninety-four.

"Foul play? That's ridiculous," I said.

"No it isn't," Jerry said. "It could have been arson at a reduced temperature. Maybe the owners wanted out, and saw a window of opportunity during the heat wave. All of a sudden the compressors just gave out? I don't buy it. What I can't figure, though, is the part about the horse."

"Well, all I know," Dad said, "is that I'm glad we didn't squander our last opportunity. To think we almost didn't go because of the way you two boys misbehaved."

"We did not. It was Tommy. After the way he broke the policeman's arm, you still don't believe us?" Jerry pleaded.

"Just go and eat a donut!" Dad ordered, returning his attention to the newspaper.

While eating our donuts, Jerry noted an interesting point. "Hey Tone. Funny thing is, those wax models should have been pretty soft and pliable because of the heat. Seems like that cop's arm should have pulled off like a piece of taffy instead of making a clean break."

"I think you've been playing too much *Candy Land*," I replied.

"Well, think about it," Jerry said. "Wax has the property of malleability. Tommy should have been able to stretch that arm at least fourteen feet before it tore at a point equidistant between the wrist and the shoulder."

"I don't know the physics, but it must have been pretty bad if they were thrown out. We'll have to ask Tommy."

We never questioned Tommy about the wax policeman that day. We forgot about it, in the anticipation of going to *Steel Pier*.

It seemed as if we would never leave the house that morning.

Mom had to go and buy a replacement pizzelle, and it took Aunt Vicky over an hour to mix four shades of liquid makeup to match Margaret's tan and conceal her ponytail negative.

Dad and Uncle Harry sat forever at that kitchen table arguing about the Wax Museum meltdown. Poor Uncle Harry, arguing with Dad meant using a lot of contractions containing N's.

Granny left early that morning to clean up Tommy's mess at the Wax Museum. It happened that Tommy had gotten off on a technicality: the policeman would have melted anyhow.

I waited on the front porch to remove myself from the comedy of errors that was transpiring inside of that rented beach house. Perhaps when we returned to Philadelphia my life wouldn't seem so strange. But there was always the chance my life would grow even more pathetic.

I closed my eyes and prayed for the strength to maintain my sanity. "Please, dear God, make my life more normal when I return to Philadelphia. You're really just playing with my head, right? I just haven't gotten the joke, right?"

I promised God that I would never ask for another thing if we could just go back to Philadelphia and start living like a normal family.

Two

"Tony! Da Plane! Da Plane!" My wife Maria was impersonating that little guy on TV again. Actually he'd been on TV years ago. He was gone but not forgotten, forever immortalized by word association.

I thought, which two words would I want to stand by me? Before I could think of something clever, Maria interrupted my train of thought.

"Tony! Da Plane! Da Plane!" She repeated, in a slightly more excited intonation.

"Yeah, I see it," I replied half-heartedly, wanting to return to the conversation I'd been having with myself.

We were driving on the New Jersey Turnpike and a 737 was getting ready for takeoff on the runway parallel to us. The holiday traffic was thick, on the highway and the runways of Newark Airport.

We were going to Philadelphia for Christmas. We had spent Thanksgiving with Maria's family in New York, so we were bound and obligated to spend Christmas with mine. I wasn't looking forward to the trip. My father was in one of his moods, and our last encounter hadn't been pleasant.

I looked to my right and noticed that the 737 had begun taxiing down the runway in preparation for its ascent. For several seconds we drove south in unison, until the plane began gaining distance and we were looking at its tail-end. For a few stupid minutes, I accelerated in an effort to keep up with the soaring jet. The 737 inevitably won, and finally it was airborne. Sensing defeat, I decelerated down to my previous cruise-control speed of sixty-eight miles per hour.

For several minutes I stared at the south-bound jet, watching it become smaller and smaller in my field of view, until it appeared to almost disappear.

What could have been easily mistaken for a speck of dirt on my windshield was really tons of steel, lots of human flesh and several pounds of smokehouse almonds being slung toward Miami. How could any of our perceptions be trusted? Maria was right: things weren't always what they seemed to be. Perhaps we weren't on our way to Philadelphia; maybe we were on a rollercoaster, and would be getting off soon to try our luck at winning a giant stuffed Panda Bear.

"Tony!" Maria's tone jolted me. We were indeed on the Turnpike and I had just been spared a collision.

"Tony, you almost sideswiped that truck!" Maria yelled. "What were you doing?"

"I'm sorry. I was lost in thought and didn't even see him," I apologized.

"That's obvious. Will you please pay attention so we can arrive in one piece?" Maria pleaded.

"O.K., I'm sorry," I said, looking into the rear-view mirror at the tractor-trailer behind me. The driver was holding up a sign, obviously for my benefit. I tried to read his message: urna, followed by a hole in the paper. What did urna mean? I then realized there were dashes between the letters, and the letters weren't reversed the way they should have been. The driver had taken the time to write in mirror image.

"U-R-N-A-Hole," I said, finally getting the driver's drift.

"Who's an a-hole?" Maria yelled.

"That truck driver is calling me an a-hole. Can you believe it? What kind of jerk would take the time to write nasty messages in mirror image?"

"The kind of jerk who has been sideswiped more than once," Maria said sarcastically.

"Oh come on, you're going to defend him?"

"You're the one who wasn't paying attention, and it was a harmless way of venting anger. Besides, you could have ran yourself off the road trying to reverse his letters," Maria said wryly.

"I get the point. No one was hurt, so can we drop it?"

"It's been dropped," Maria said cynically. "I really don't know what is with you today; you need to relax."

"I have to suffer the abuse of my father for two days, and you don't know what's with me? You're a shrink—figure it out."

"I really don't appreciate the way you condescend my profession. The abuse is all in your head. Your father may be a little hard-headed and stubborn, but his antics hardly constitute abuse. Besides, things are not always what they seem to be. Why don't you lighten up?" Maria was irritated.

I hadn't meant to undermine Maria's life-work. I knew she was a legitimate therapist—how could I forget? That Maria was a psychiatrist was the source of private torment for me: was I a heathen, having married this poor, sweet woman not out of true love, but for what I had to gain—a lifetime of free therapy? Was my love for Maria just a sham constructed by my ego to keep my psychosis simmering within a socially acceptable range?

Why was I even asking myself those questions? Of course I loved my wife. I had fallen in love with her before I knew she was a shrink. No, wait a minute, I did know she was doing her rotation in psychiatry when we met. But I wasn't her patient before we married, not technically. Had I been just a sick opportunist? I wasn't sure.

But Maria hadn't helped me. She always answered a question with a question, or she accused me of over-analyzing. Most annoying was her habit of rationalizing the things that seemed absurd to me. Maria's idea of help was a good swift kick into the labyrinth of inner turmoil. What kind of help was that?

I wasn't using her. If I was in the marriage for mental health reasons only, surely I'd have bailed out when I didn't get what I thought I had coming.

I suddenly realized how hurt Maria would be if she knew I had questioned my love for her. I could just imagine the look on her face as she slapped me and proclaimed that I'd never loved her. Well, it wasn't the truth, and she'd never find out. Not unless she breached my privacy and read my journals, which described in lucid detail how low I had really sunk.

But I did love her. Maria was right. I was over-analyzing.

"C'mon Tony, let's go," Maria said.

"What?" I mumbled. I looked around and realized that I had pulled into the rest area and parked the car with absolutely no recollection of having done so.

"I thought you said you needed something to eat."

"I did?"

"You don't remember saying that you wanted a bite to eat? It was only two minutes ago. Tony, are you feeling all right?"

Before I said anything, I had to think. Maria didn't need to know the danger she'd just escaped, having been driven by a lunatic who forgot he was even driving.

"Now I remember," I lied, to spare her feelings. I remembered how vulnerable I'd felt when my father would close his eyes while driving.

"Tony, I'm driving the rest of the way. I think you need to take a nap—and don't argue!"

As we approached the food court, I noticed the trucker with whom I'd had the incident, parked in one of the gas bays. Was he really refueling or was his hand-lettered sign just a precursor to the shoot-out that was about to occur? I decided I was being paranoid and walked quickly into the building.

"Honey, will you get a pack of crackers for me? I'll be back in a minute. I want to use the ladies' room." Maria disappeared down a tunnel of pink tiles.

I stepped toward the fast food counter, looking for a reasonable facsimile of food.

"May I help you, Sir?" A severe-looking woman with the thickest, most unruly eyebrows I'd ever seen was glaring at me from behind the counter.

"Yes, you," she said. "What do you want?"

"Are your hot dogs all-beef?" I asked.

"Chili or plain?"

"Don't you use the same hot dogs for both?"

"One chili, one plain," she yelled. Apparently she misunderstood and thought I ordered both.

"I'm sorry, mam, I wasn't ordering both, I was…"

"Cancel that one chili, one plain!" She yelled with gusto. "Your order, sir?"

"Oh, forget the hot dog. Just give me a soft pretzel, but one without salt," I said grudgingly.

"One pretzel, no salt," the woman yelled, even though she was the one approaching the pretzel display to retrieve it. She inserted her hand and removed a pretzel with a heavy coating of salt.

"Mam, I said no salt!" I yelled.

"I heard you sir—no salt!" She then proceeded to roll and massage the pretzel between the palms of her hands, the salt falling like snow into a pile around her feet.

I was quickly losing patience. "I'm not going to eat that pretzel after it's been handled that way."

"You said no salt. This is no salt. One dollar and twenty-five cents, please!" She demanded.

"Pardon me, but I'm not paying for a pretzel that's been man-handled!"

"I am a woman," she roared. "I do not appreciate your referring to me as a man."

"I said man-handled! It's a figure of speech!"

"You are very rude, sir. I will not wait on you. Step aside please or I will call security." She meant business. "Next!"

I couldn't believe what had transpired. That one-eyebrowed counter lady had refused to serve me.

Maria walked out of the ladies' room. "Did you get my crackers?"

"I didn't get anything; that woman behind the counter refused to serve me and threatened to call security," I said, in sheer and utter disbelief.

"Tony, what did you say to her?"

"I'll tell you what I should have said: I should have told her to pull her hair net down over her eyebrows because they're in violation of sanitary code!" I felt better after a little verbal retaliation.

Maria interrupted my gloating. "I really can't believe your attitude today. This problem with your father is turning you into a maniac. Why don't you wait in the car? I'll get something out of the machines. I'll be out in a minute." Maria walked away, rolling her eyes.

I walked to the car, wondering if that had really just happened in there or if I had imagined it. Maybe Maria was right: I was letting the thing with my father get to me. I needed to relax.

I looked toward the gas bays and saw the driver of the tractor-trailer getting into his cab. Great, I thought, he'll probably be tailing us all the way to Philadelphia. I got into the car, as a passenger.

Maria returned. "Do you want crackers or pretzels? I got both."

"I just want to pull out of here before that psycho truck driver does; I don't trust him."

"Oh, Tony, will you stop it? It's Christmas Eve. Please don't ruin this holiday for me!" Maria pleaded.

Of course I didn't want to ruin the holiday for Maria. Poor, sweet Maria, married to a jerk like me. She worked with nut cases all day and had to have me for a husband. What was I thinking, making her work such long hours? I was going to relax and give poor Maria a break. Perhaps I had blown the whole thing with my father out of proportion. As Maria and the 737 had reminded me, things were not always what they seemed to be.

"Mind if I turn on the radio?" I asked Maria.

"Not at all. Maybe some Christmas music will get you in the spirit," she said. "Why don't you take a nap?"

"No, I'm fine. I'm feeling better. You're right, I'm getting upset over nothing. Besides, I'm looking forward to seeing Jerry. I haven't seen him since August. I can't believe it's been so long; I wonder what he's been up to?"

"Well, I hear he's bringing a date to dinner tomorrow."

"Who told you that?"

"Your mother told me. She called last week. I forgot to tell you."

"What else did she say?"

"Oh, nothing much. She couldn't really talk because she was getting ready for class. Oh, she did say your father received a big promotion at work."

"Why didn't you tell me?" I asked in disbelief.

"I'm sorry, I've had a busy week," she said nonchalantly.

I was stunned that Maria could have forgotten to tell me such an important piece of information. If Dad had been promoted, the heat would be off me.

"I can't believe you forgot to tell me."

"I'm sorry, Tony," Maria said. "And besides, once you get something in your head, there is little to be said. Can we drop it? I'm trying to drive."

"It's been dropped," I said sarcastically.

We sat for several minutes in silence, listening to the radio and eating our packaged snacks.

Finally, Maria spoke. "You never finished telling me the story about *Steel Pier*," she said.

"Where did I leave off?" I asked, hoping Maria could provide a clue.

"You were sitting on the porch while your father and Uncle Harry argued about the Wax Museum meltdown."

The floodgates of my memory collapsed. I proceeded to rehash the incident that had been eternally twisted, embellished, and even re-created as a drama for television in my father's head.

"Well," I said, "the day unfolded as usual, with Dad yelling at Margaret to hurry the hell up. We finally got to Steel Pier around noon, and split into groups. We were to meet at the diving horse at three o'clock." I took a deep breath and continued. "So we met at three o'clock and had a soda before entering the attraction. Everyone but Margaret."

"Why didn't Margaret get a soda?"

"She wasn't thirsty."

"Oh."

"So anyhow, we finished our drinks, and began walking toward the diving horse attraction when Margaret changed her mind and decided she wanted a drink after all. Dad said it was too late, that she had her chance, and they began arguing. The irony was, there was no time to get a soda, but there was plenty of time to argue. When we got to the attraction, the bleachers were full and we had to sit at the very top, which really infuriated Dad," I said.

"So we took our seats in the nosebleed section, and Mom opened a box of salt water taffy for us to eat. As I passed the box to Margaret, I could tell something was wrong; she looked as if she was about to faint. I asked her if she was all right, and she asked me to switch seats so she could talk to Mom. The first horse hadn't jumped yet; apparently they were having trouble convincing the horses that the rig was entirely safe."

"Very funny," Maria said. "So what was wrong with Margaret?"

"She had bad menstrual cramps and needed to take a *Midol.* You should have been there—it was a classic!" I snickered.

Suddenly I was there, transported back in time thirty years. I arrived at Steel Pier with a forty year-old brain and enough emotional baggage to fill a container.

"Oh Anthony, get her a lemonade so she can take a *Midol*; she's in terrible pain," Mom whispered.

"I think we've already had this argument. Why the hell couldn't you get a drink when everyone else did, Margaret-Ann? You could have taken your little pill down there and been done with it!"

"But I didn't have cramps until we climbed to the top of these bleachers," Margaret whined.

"Well, we would have found seats at the bottom had we arrived on time, but I seem to remember a little trouble on our way in," Dad snarled.

"The perspective is much better up here anyhow," Jerry interjected.

Dad glared at Jerry.

"Oh, forget it," Margaret sulked. "I'll just swallow them—I don't even need a drink."

Margaret swallowed one of the white tablets; it went down the wrong way, and she began choking.

"Margaret, are you all right?" I asked.

She couldn't answer me because she was choking; obviously she wasn't O.K.. I began hitting her on the back to dislodge the *Midol*. It was stuck, so I hit her harder. The *Midol* spewed forth and accelerated in a projectile arc that ended on top of a man's baseball cap three levels down. He never knew what hit him. It was a red baseball cap, and it looked as if a bird had gotten him.

"Anthony, now will you get her a drink? She can't swallow a pill without any liquid in this heat," Mom said.

Dad arose without saying a word and stomped down the steps of the bleachers.

"Here they come!" Jerry yelled excitedly.

He was referring to the first horse and diver who were finally crossing the platform. When they arrived to the bottom of the ramp, the horse backed away. With a lot of prodding, and little choice, the horse ran up the ramp and stood for a millisecond with knees knocking before taking the plunge and falling into the tank below. The crowd roared.

I thought, this is entertainment? What was so amusing about scaring a horse half to death and watching it free-fall forty feet before it hit a tank of water? And how had they persuaded two hundred people to sit on bleachers on the hottest day of the year and actually pay money to watch that atrocity?

The horse, obviously shaken, struggled to exit the pool from a ramp on the far side of the platform. Just as the horse climbed from the water, I caught a glimpse of my father entering the attraction. He was walking slowly, carefully balancing the lemonade he was carrying.

Unfortunately, the platform, which Dad had to walk across, was wet from tank spill-over. Dad was paying more attention to balancing the lemonade than to his footing; he slipped across the platform and went down on his butt. As he did, cold lemonade and ice landed at the feet of the horse that had already been pushed too far. Dad regained his footing but was only able to progress a foot or two. The horse, who had become quite unruly, thrashed his wet tail about in such a manner that it slapped Dad in the face and knocked him down.

Dad jumped up, obviously wondering if anyone had noticed. All two hundred spectators had witnessed Dad's slapping and were roaring with laughter. Dad glared toward the top of the bleachers, fumed, and stomped away from the attraction.

"C'mon, kids. I think we'd better go," Mom said.

"Oh, do we have to?" Jerry said. "We've only seen one horse dive."

Margaret turned to me. "What just happened?"

"Dad was slapped in the face by a live ponytail."

"You're kidding?"

"You didn't see it?"

"No."

"How did you miss it?"

"I was thinking about something else," Margaret said.

Of course she was. It was a good thing one of us had been paying attention.

"Tell me about it later when I do your nails," Margaret said.

"C'mon, kids—and pretend you didn't see what just happened to your father!" Mom said.

Mom said that for our own good. If Dad thought we missed his skid across the platform, he'd think others had missed it too. Eventually he'd be able to convince himself that no one had witnessed his slapping, that the laughter was a response to something else entirely.

Dad, with one red cheek, was waiting for us outside of the attraction. As we approached, Mom said, "Anthony, you didn't miss a thing! What do you say we head back a little early and watch some TV in front of the fan?"

Dad began walking, and we followed in silence. No one said a word about what had happened. In fact, not much was said for the rest of the day. We pretended not to see Dad being slapped in the face by the ponytail so he could pretend it hadn't really happened.

The charade didn't last. Jerry, of all people, slipped and mentioned the ponytail incident at lunch the next day. So began my father's saga, one more card of woe to add to the deck stacked against him.

I turned to Maria. "Can you believe something so bizarre could actually happen?"

"Are you sure you're remembering it correctly, the way it really happened?"

"Are you accusing me of embellishing the story?"

"No, I'm just trying to make a point. You're looking at the incident through forty years of experience, which colors your perspective. Furthermore, if I asked the rest of your family what happened that day, I'm sure I'd get five very different stories, so who knows what really happened? All we can ever know is five different perspectives of reality. Which one is more real? We'll never have an answer to that question."

"You're telling me that none of us will ever know what really happened?" I asked sarcastically.

"Basically, yes. So why not relax and enjoy the ride?"

Was she being literal or metaphoric? Why did Maria always answer a question with another more disturbing question? Was she that much help to her patients? Maybe I was getting exactly what I'd paid for—nothing. Surely Maria could donate all those left-over five minutes that had been paid for by someone else; I was her husband! What did I have to do, start nonchalantly leaving my insurance card on her dresser?

"C'mon, Tony, don't space out. You scare me sometimes."

So my behavior scared someone who had seen the whole wretched gamut of human behavior. That made me feel great.

"I'm not spacing out," I said. "I think you're right. I do need some shut-eye." I hoped Maria would pick up my cue to stop talking.

Maria took my cue, and I closed my eyes. Perhaps Maria was right: maybe I did spend too much time trying to figure out things. Sometimes I felt as if my life whizzed by without my consent, as though I wasn't really living. That was it. From then on, I was going to start living and stop analyzing. I was making a breakthrough.

Smelling sulfur, I realized we were getting close to the city. I tried to get myself together so I could make a good presentation to my parents.

"So Jerry's bringing a date to dinner tomorrow?" I asked Maria.

"Yes. That's what your mother said."

"I wonder how Jerry met her?"

"She's his auto mechanic," Maria replied matter-of-factly.

"Really?" I asked, pondering what type of pick-up line Jerry had used down at the garage.

"I guess she fixes his car, but I'm not really sure. Do you have two dollars for the bridge?"

"Isn't the bridge free on Christmas Eve?"

"The bridge is never free."

We paid the toll and drove into Philadelphia. We were heading South on I-95 when Maria looked at me. "So you're telling me that after the ponytail incident at Steel Pier your father stopped his little singing thing?"

"Yes," I replied. "We didn't even notice at first, since we had tuned him out. But after a while the silence was deadening, and we took notice. On one hand we felt relieved of a great annoyance, but on the other hand we knew what the consequences would be."

"What do you mean by consequences?"

"Well," I said, "Dad seemed to have only two modes of operation: he was either singing or he was pissed off. We knew we were in for a rough ride."

"Tony, life is never black or white. I think you ignore the gray areas," Maria said. "I think you're working too hard. Real life is not a silicon chip."

I had been working a lot of hours, but Maria was wrong. She just didn't understand the advantages of looking at life as either/or. How else could we have written the Declaration of Independence on the head of a pin, for God's sake? Maria forgot that jerks like me had made her life easier through technology. She had no idea what my job at SuperSoft was about. She was trying to get back at me for the crack I made about her job.

"Turn right on the next street," I told Maria.

"Tony, I've been here a hundred times."

Right. Maria turned the corner and pulled into my parents' driveway behind my father's car, which looked as if it could use some attention from Jerry's new girlfriend.

My father obviously heard our car pull into the driveway: he was coming out the front door to greet us. I quickly got out of the car and opened the trunk, hiding for a brief moment behind the safety of sheet steel. I then heard Dad singing.

"Ma-ree-ya! I've just met a girl named Ma-ree-ya," he sang, slightly off key.

What? I had just finished telling Maria that Dad had given up his little singing thing, and the first words he uttered were burst forth in song. He always had to make a liar of me.

Dad was finishing his serenade to Maria when I closed the trunk and walked up the driveway with our suitcases. "Hello, Dad."

"Hello, Son," Dad said, slapping me gingerly on the side of the arm.

What was that? He hadn't called me son since 1993, when SuperSoft released the software that eliminated his job as a mechanical draftsman. And that good-natured slap on the arm? I began to wonder if I was in one of Jerry's parallel universes.

"And Merry Christmas to both of you," Dad added, leading us to the front door.

I entered the house and scanned its four walls. It had changed little since I moved out twenty years ago—same furniture, same decor. How could a house not change? It even smelled the same: Mom was obviously baking one of her award-winning apple pies. I couldn't wait until dessert.

I walked into the kitchen to find Mom.

"Tony, it's so good to see you!" Mom squealed, as she squeezed me hard and whispered, "I'm so glad you decided to come, despite the differences between you and your father."

"What are you talking about, Mom?" I asked, knowing quite well that she was referring to the one-sided feud that Dad had concocted.

"Oh you know, the darn computer thing. About time you both buried it."

"What do you mean, both bury it? Dad's the only one with the chip on his shoulder, no pun intended."

Mom squeezed my hand. "Oh, Tony, it's Christmas time. Let's make everything the way it used to be, everyone merry, drinking hot chocolate."

The absurdity of her plea struck me funny, and I laughed. "Sure, Mom."

Mom could bribe anyone with her hot chocolate, a recipe handed down by her great-grandmother. She used only the finest Swiss cocoa, and a barrage of secret ingredients that imparted a flavor similar to that of chocolate almond bark.

While Mom made the hot chocolate, I stared out the back door at the little plot of grass that had once seemed a continent. I wondered how so many things had gotten lost in that little patch of dirt.

Dad had taken Maria upstairs to put the suitcases in our room, and I wondered what was keeping them. I turned from the door, and discovered why everyone was so merry when they drank Mom's hot chocolate. To the pot of milk on the stove, Mom was adding a hefty squirt of Amaretto di Saronna. She stirred her brew a few times, then brought the wooden spoon to her lips. Mom sipped, shook her head, and added another generous dousing of Amaretto.

"Mom, what are you doing?"

"What do you mean, what am I doing? I'm making hot chocolate."

"With booze?" I asked, "I never knew you spiked our hot chocolate."

"Of course you didn't. Until now, it was a secret recipe."

"Have you always made it that way?"

"For the last forty years. But mum's the word. Go join your father and Maria so I can finish my work here," she said nonchalantly.

Mom was so good at her work that she'd been fooling everyone for years, expertly camouflaging the taste of alcohol with chocolate and spices.

"Mom, are you telling me that you served us when we were minors?" I laughed.

"Oh, it's not as though you kids ever got drunk or anything. Besides, a little shot never hurt anyone in the dead of winter," Mom said innocently.

We were children, unwittingly putting a few shots under our belts after a hard day of shoveling snow. It then occurred to me why Jerry and I were so popular in those days, and it probably explained why Michael Lioni had walked into a telephone pole and broken his nose.

I again laughed, but that time to myself.

Mom turned to me. "How about when I'm finished here we take our hot chocolate into the den and drink it in front of the fire?"

Mom wore a particular facial expression when asking a question—eyebrows scrunched together, cheeks up. For the first time, I realized that her eyebrows looked like horizontal question marks when she did that. They curved towards her nose, went straight out to her temples, and were finally punctuated by the freckles that were situated like mirror images on either side of her face.

"Sure, we could go and sit in front of the fire."

It wasn't a real fire. It was a faux fireplace, ablaze with several low-wattage orange light bulbs. I had no idea what the poker was for.

"Go and tell your father and Maria that it's almost time," Mom said.

I walked into the den and noticed a stack of boxes sitting next to the tree in matching wrap. The collective gifts looked like a giant

Rubik's Cube. I immediately guessed at their contents, and laughed aloud. We were getting new globes for Christmas.

Dad and Maria entered the den. "What's so funny?" Dad asked.

"Oh nothing," I lied.

Mom walked in and saved me. "I hope everyone's cold," she said matter-of-factly, carefully placing the tray of hot chocolate and cookies onto the coffee table.

"Cold?" I asked, puzzled.

"Yes. I made hot chocolate to warm everyone up." Mom spoke as though we weren't entitled to hot chocolate if we were already warm.

"Leona, these cookies look scrumptious," Dad said.

The hot chocolate was being served appropriately in mugs that looked like giant *Hershey's Kisses.* The point on the top was removable to accommodate your lips and nose.

"Great mugs, Mom," Maria said, with genuine amusement.

"Aren't they lovely?" Mom asked. "Margaret gave them to me for Mother's Day this year. The lids keep the hot chocolate nice and warm in-between sips."

"Speaking of Margaret, is she coming for dinner tonight?" I asked.

"Yes, she's coming," Mom said, "but she may be late. You know how crazy the shop can be at this time of year."

Mom was referring to the beauty salon where Margaret worked. Her life-long obsession with style paid off big; Margaret had quite a loyal following.

"How about Granny?" I asked. "When is she coming?"

"Oh, she'll be here tomorrow. Vicky and Harry are bringing her. She's entertaining at home tonight," Dad said, rolling his eyes.

I couldn't believe Granny was still throwing dinner parties at eighty-four, catered or not.

Mom passed my hot chocolate and two coasters. I brought the mug to my nose, scrutinizing the aroma for the slightest essence of alcohol; I could detect none. I took a sip and tasted the subtle flavors of almond and cinnamon, but could discern no booze.

Dad noticed my sipping the hot chocolate and rose from his chair. He lifted his mug and said, "I believe the occasion calls for a toast. To Leona, who has just finished her first semester back at school!"

We removed our lids and pushed our mugs together. Mom had just completed an adult evening course, Survey of American Literature.

"How did you find the course, Mom?" Maria asked.

"I saw it advertised in the *Inquirer*, honey."

"No, I meant did you find it interesting?" Maria spoke a few decibels louder.

"Oh, yes, immensely. It's amazing, the stories people can come up with."

We looked at Mom, waiting for her to say something else, but that was it. After a few seconds of silence, she changed the subject. "Well, your father is really the one who deserves the congratulations. He just got a big promotion at work!"

"Oh, Leona!" Dad said. "It's really no big deal. Well, I guess it is—an extra six thousand dollars a year!"

"Dad, that's great. What kind of promotion was it?"

"You are looking at Director of Quality Control of the *whole* operation. The globes are inspected inside and out; nothing slips by that isn't one hundred percent!" Dad beamed.

Dad had been working in shipping at the globe plant for about three years. How he had been promoted to Director of Quality Control was beyond me. Perhaps I hadn't given my father enough credit. That he was promoted at a time when companies were eliminating their older employees had to mean something.

"Yeah," Mom said, "he beat forty men twenty years younger."

I hadn't known that it was possible to *beat people younger*.

"I'd say we're on top of the world right now," Dad quipped. "But enough about me. Anything that you two need to tell us?"

Maria and I looked at each other, puzzled. "No," I said. "What are you talking about?"

"I was just wondering if we could expect to hear the pitter-patter of tiny feet anytime soon. Any grandchildren on the horizon?"

"Oh," I said. "No, not yet."

"If you two make me wait any longer, it may be too late," Dad said. "I'm not getting any younger."

"Don't worry, Dad. When the time comes, you'll be the first to know."

Dad looked at me. "I don't know what the hell you're waiting for. You're not getting any younger, either."

Mom rushed to my rescue. "Anthony, if you're so eager to have some little ones to play with, I could take a part-time baby-sitting job. It would be nice to have a young one to read to and play with."

"I don't want a child to play with, I want someone to carry on the family name. I don't have time for fun and games. I do have a job, and a rather important one."

Dad turned to me again. "You're not having any trouble down there, are you? Pants a little too tight? Maybe you need to start wearing boxer shorts."

"I am not having trouble down there. Maria and I will have a child when we think the time is right! I really don't think it is any of your …"

Before I could finish, Mom changed the subject. "Anthony, the fire looks dull. Do you think one of the bulbs blew out? It's usually a tad brighter."

Dad checked the fire. "No, all the bulbs are burning. It must be the way the sun is hitting this wall."

"Anthony, you haven't tried the pecan sandies. Here, take one," Mom said, handing Dad a large cookie.

"My, my. They are good. And you've added extra pecans."

Dad loved pecans. And I loved Mom for changing the subject not once, but twice, to divert Dad's attention from our reproductive failure.

Mom turned to me. "Honey, you look exhausted. Why don't you go upstairs and lie down for a little while before dinner?"

I was feeling weary. I'd had problems at work the day before, and the anxiety of the trip home stirred angst. Mom's elixir had taken the edge off, but I did need a little shut-eye. "Yeah, Mom, I think you're right. Maybe I will go upstairs and take a nap. What time is dinner?"

"Oh, early. Your father is going carolling with the group tonight so we'll be eating around five."

I glanced at my watch. It was already 4:10 and we had just devoured a pot of hot chocolate and half a tray of Christmas cookies. What was Mom thinking? I hoped the entree was light so I'd have room for apple pie. Mom made it from scratch with granny smith apples and a delectable crumb topping. It was the best apple pie in the world.

Dad rose from the table. "I didn't realize it was so late. Time for me to shower and get into my singing clothes."

I went upstairs and propped a few pillows at the head of the bed. I lay back and re-hashed the crazy events that had transpired that day: the irate counter lady, the psycho truck driver, our spiked hot chocolate. Was it me or was my life sprinkled with a little too much absurdity? Maybe it was me. Maria was an expert, and the only problem she could see was in my interpretation of things. If things were not what they seemed to be, what the hell were they? I couldn't figure it out.

I had promised myself earlier to stop questioning life and start living. What was wrong with me? Maybe there was no hope for my ever having a normal life.

My thoughts were interrupted by the sound of the bedroom door opening. I turned, expecting to see Maria, but it was Mom.

"Mom," I said. "What's up?"

"You had two mugs of hot chocolate and a baker's dozen of cookies!" She yelled.

"Yeah? So?"

"How many times have I told you not to spoil your appetite before dinner? I slave over a hot stove all day, and for what? For you to come to the table not hungry?" Mom yelled. Her demeanor was uncharacteristically wicked.

"But Mom, you served it to us!"

"That didn't mean you had to eat it! You'll spoil your appetite, I told you!"

I had never seen Mom that way. She then removed the sparkling candy cane pin from her chest.

"What are you doing, Mom?"

"I'm eating this big fat candy cane," she said, taking a bite of the rhinestones and metal. "There! Now no one will have an appetite."

"Mom," I begged, "don't eat it, you'll kill yourself! Are you crazy? You'll die! Mom, don't eat it, please!"

"Tony, eat what? Tony, wake up. You're having a bad dream. Honey, are you all right?" Maria asked.

I focused on Maria's face.

"Tony, are you O.K.?"

"Yeah," I said, "I'm O.K." For once, my nightmare had been just a dream.

"Bad dream?"

"Yes. I dreamt that Mom barged in here and threatened to kill herself by eating her Christmas jewelry."

"Well, Tony, it was just a dream. Time to get up; dinner's in ten minutes."

"O.K.. Just give me a minute to get my head on straight."

"I'm going down to help your mother with dinner; don't fall asleep again," Maria said, leaving the room.

I arose and brushed my hair, and decided to splash some cold water on my face. After I did, I felt better. I then remembered the apple pie, and felt even better.

"Tony! Dinner's on the table!" Mom yelled.

"I'm coming!"

Downstairs, everyone was seated at the table. "Margaret isn't here yet?" I asked.

"Oh, she'll be here shortly," Mom said. "One of her best customers lost a nail while stuffing a turkey, so Margaret ran over to fix her up. She won't be long."

Mom had the table dressed in the best of her non-edibles: salad bowls that looked like giant up-turned lettuce leaves, a flat pink pig that served ham, and a bread dish that was a foot and a half long and sprinkled with ceramic sesame seeds.

"Have a nice rest, son?" Dad asked in a rather friendly tone.

"Yes I did," I lied, looking at Mom's chest.

"Mom, where's the candy cane pin that you were wearing earlier?" There was then a reindeer perched on her chest.

"Oh," Mom said, "the darn thing broke right in half. When I went to take it off, it crumbled to pieces. Had seen its day, I guess. It was so nice of you to notice. I told Margaret that people do notice when you wear nice holiday pins, but she's so worried about everything matching. I told her that seasonal jewelry doesn't necessarily have to match your outfit, but some things we just don't seem to ..."

Dad interrupted. "O.K. Leona, we get the point. Your reindeer looks fine. Would you pass the carrots?"

Mom passed the carrot full of carrots to Dad.

"Why that's an interesting dish, Mom," Maria said.

"Oh, that carrot dish. I bought it when Anthony and I were first married. I never got too much use out of it, though. Anthony always hated carrots, until last year."

"I never hated carrots, Leona. You never made them; how could I hate something that I never had?"

"I distinctly remember your hating carrots; you always left them on your plate."

"Just because I left them on my plate once doesn't mean I hated them."

"Anthony, don't you recall eating carrots at that restaurant downtown last year, remarking that you never knew carrots could taste so good, that you'd always hated them?" Mom punctuated her sentence with her facial expression.

"You're asking me to remember something I said a year ago when I can't even remember the last time I've eaten downtown?"

Maria and I finished eating and discussed our plans for New Year's Eve while the carrot confrontation ensued.

"Are you calling me a liar, Leona?"

"Oh Anthony, calm down. I am not calling you a liar. Kids, would you like more ham?" Mom asked, pushing the pig toward us.

"Oh, no thanks," Maria answered.

"None for me," I said. I was saving room for apple pie.

"Well, I don't know what kind of false memory you're conjuring, but I have never hated carrots!"

"Well, Anthony, I remember what you said, but I really don't care to argue about it anymore."

"Let it go down on the god-damned record that I have never hated carrots. And furthermore, I don't want to hear the word mentioned again. I know what I god-damned like!" Dad snarled.

That Dad's blood pressure had risen because of a vegetable was interesting. Even more interesting was that Mom had let a half-dozen opportunities to change the subject slip by the wayside. Could it be she was tired of that game?

Dad finished his carrots in silence, eating every last one.

"We'll put a plate in the oven for Margaret to keep warm," Mom said. "I can't imagine what's keeping her. How long could it take to glue on one nail?"

"Maybe they're having trouble finding it; how big of a turkey was it?" I joked.

"Oh Tony, you silly thing. I'm sure Margaret will give her a new nail. They're not going to re-use a nail that's been mixed up in the stuffing all day," Mom said.

Mom and Maria cleared off the table while discussing the pros and cons of acrylic nails. "Well, I just don't have time to go and have my nails done every week," Maria said.

"Oh, I know what you mean, honey. Since I've gone back to school I haven't had time for a lot of things."

Mom was carrying what looked like a carrot cake to the table. Carrot Cake? I thought we were having apple pie. I supposed Mom was saving that for Christmas Day.

"And we're having god-damned carrot cake for dessert?" Dad yelled, as though Mom could have known about the carrot argument in advance and had made a carrot cake to get the last word in without actually saying anything. Or perhaps the whole argument was instigated by Mom, confident because she had cunning ammunition? Dad sat there looking like a muzzled bulldog.

I didn't dare mention the apple pie. It was better to let Dad's fervor dissipate. I overlooked my disappointment and took a bite of carrot cake; it was good, but it wasn't Mom's apple pie.

Once Dad got a little cream cheese frosting into his system, his mood quickly changed. "Well, I think this is going to be the year that Ivan pops the question to Margaret."

Maria spoke. "Oh, Dad, I think Ivan and Margaret are just friends."

"Oh no," Dad said, "They're more than just friends. Friends don't sleep over one another's houses all the time."

"How do you know they're sleeping over?" I asked.

"Every god-damned time I call Margaret in the morning he answers the phone."

"What time?"

"7 A.M."

"Why are you calling Margaret at 7 A.M.?"

"For various reasons. Why the hell does that matter?"

It didn't. So Ivan always answered the phone; that was strange. Were they living together?

Maria and I looked at each other, perplexed. We had assumed that Ivan was gay, and that he and Margaret were just friends. We'd never come right out and asked Margaret, though. Maybe Ivan wasn't gay? Maybe we had both made an erroneous assumption.

"O.K., Dad," I said, "even if they are more than friends, what makes you think Ivan's going to pop the question?"

"I'll tell you why. I went to Frankford Avenue the other day to pick up my watch, and out of the jewelry store walked Ivan, with a grin from ear to ear."

"So why does that mean he's popping the question?"

"You didn't let me finish," Dad said. "So I went right up to Ivan and said, 'now you look like a man in love.' Ivan squeezed the small bag he was carrying and told me how perceptive I was. I asked him if it was for Margaret, and he said yes, with a very starry-eyed look, I might add."

Perhaps Maria and I had been wrong about Ivan. I guess he and Margaret are lovers, I thought. Maria had been wrong too? She was supposed to be so good at evaluating people.

The kitchen door opened; Margaret had arrived. "Hello everyone. Sorry I'm late. Mrs. Pancoast needed a repair; she's having a big party tonight." Margaret walked around the table and kissed everyone.

"Tony, you're looking good. How's life in the big city?"

"Oh, life is big."

Maria looked closely at Margaret. "I like your new color," she said, referring to Margaret's light brown mane.

"Oh, thanks. It's called sandalwood. It's new on the market."

Whenever I saw Margaret, her hair was a different color; she had worn at least four hundred shades since 1975. But I had to admit, sandalwood was her color.

"C'mon, honey. Let's fix you a plate while everything is still warm," Mom said to Margaret.

"So I guess you've been busy with the holidays and everything," Maria said.

"Yes. Between work and packing I haven't had a spare minute."

"Packing? Are you going on a trip?" I asked.

"I wish. No, I'm moving next week. I'm taking an apartment closer to work. The traffic in the morning is killing me."

What a shame, I thought. Margaret's apartment was gorgeous. You'd never know it, judging the outside of the building, which looked rather plain and tethered. But inside, Margaret's apartment was brimming with fine architectural details and cornice moldings; the woodwork looked hand-carved. An apartment like Margaret's would go for about six grand a month in New York.

"Oh, that's a shame," I said. "Your place is gorgeous."

"Well, the new apartment will be gorgeous once I get everything into place."

Dad interrupted our conversation. "I'm sorry, but I have to leave now."

"I just got here," Margaret said.

"Well, I'm meeting the guys at six."

"What guys?"

"The carollers."

"Who are the carollers?"

"The Christmas carollers: you know, Deck the halls with boughs of holly, fa-la-la-la-la-la-la-la-la…" Dad sang.

"Oh, you've taken up singing again?"

"What do you mean, again? I've always sung. Can't a man do something good for the community without getting the third degree from his family?" Dad rose from the table. "Now if you'll excuse me, I'm going to brush my teeth and go."

Dad went to brush his teeth and then yelled goodbye from the living room.

"So, Margaret, what part of town are you moving to?" I asked.

"Oh, I forget exactly where it is; I have it written down at home."

She was moving next week and couldn't remember where. Poor Margaret. How had she survived all those years without me?

"Ivan knows exactly where it is, and he's driving the truck. I'll cross that bridge when I come to it; I've got too much else to do right now."

So, I thought. Ivan was driving the truck; they *were* moving in together. Maria was right: things weren't always what they seemed to be. Why couldn't I get that through my head? Even God had given me a sign, when that jumbo jet turned into a speck of dirt.

It suddenly occurred to me that I was probably in a lot of spiritual trouble. I prayed to God for signs, he gave them to me, and I ignored them. I wondered if I'd get hell or just an eternal purgatory of self-doubt and confusion. I'd take hell if given a choice—it would be a refreshing change.

"Tony!" Maria shouted.

I realized I had spaced out again. "What, Maria? I've been listening," I lied. "I like the pink one."

"Oh," Maria said. I thought I detected a tone of disappointment in her *oh*. Maria really liked to catch me off guard; she seemed pretty disappointed that pink had been the right answer. Luckily my subconscious was on overdrive and I had absorbed enough of the underlying conversation to make a knowledgeable comment. And Maria was disappointed to see that I was really paying attention, even though I wasn't. What kind of game was she playing?

"Will you guys be going to midnight mass with us tonight?" Mom asked.

"Oh, we'll never make it that late," I said. "We've been up since five this morning."

"Oh, O.K.," Mom said. "We'll try not to make any noise. What about you, Margaret?"

"No, Mom. I'm going to an open house later. I don't want to drink and drive."

"Well, we could pick you up," Mom said.

Right. I imagined Dad driving forty minutes out of his way to pick up Margaret, half-sloshed, to take her to church. Mom must have thought the same thing: "Maybe you could just say a prayer at midnight."

Margaret looked at the clock. "Oh my God—I've gotta get going. I have to stop home and get ready for the party."

She looked ready to me. I wondered what she had to do. How could I forget? She'd have to do her hair "different", shower, assemble an ensemble, pick out her jewelry, touch up her nails, put on her face and her perfume, evaluate the end product, make revisions, change her shoes, and decide what coat to wear. And then find a pin that balanced the entire presentation. If I had to go through that routine I'd either shoot myself or become an agoraphobic. What kind of life did Margaret lead?

Margaret hugged me. "We'll talk more tomorrow," she whispered.

"Bye, Margaret," I said, wondering if she was really going to tie the knot.

"Well, it's just the three of us now," Mom said. "What would you kids like to do?"

"Oh, we don't have to do anything," Maria said.

"Do you want to watch *It's a Wonderful Life*? Mom asked. "That's always fun."

Maria looked at me. "Sure, I guess," I said.

Something stopped me from leaving the kitchen: it was the apple pie. Even though it was no longer baking, its aroma was irresistible. "Mom," I said, "I know the apple pie is for tomorrow, but could I just take a look at it?"

I knew if Mom realized how desperately I wanted a piece of her apple pie, she'd cut a piece for me. I could hear her: "Oh, let me cut you a piece. We have to make sure it's O.K. anyhow. It's no bother." Instead, Mom was looking at me strangely.

"What apple pie?" Mom asked.

"The one you were baking earlier, when we arrived."

"I don't know what you're talking about, Tony. I didn't bake a pie today."

"But the whole house smells like apple pie."

"Oh!" Mom laughed. "It's my new simmering potpourri; doesn't it smell delicious? It's the apple tart fragrance."

"You didn't make an apple pie?" I asked disappointedly.

"Not this year. The granny smith apples were awful, so I skipped it."

I had been fantasizing for hours about consuming an apple pie that didn't even exist. I wondered what Maria was privately thinking about me.

"There's no apple pie?" I repeated.

"I'm sorry to disappoint you, honey. I can see you were really looking forward to some apple pie. You know, I think, let me check the cupboard."

Did I dare hope?

Mom walked across the kitchen with determination and began spinning the *Lazy Susan* in the corner cupboard. Nothing. She spun it again, a little faster, her head spinning as she surveyed the contents of the three shelves. I felt as if we were playing roulette, complete with sound effects. It wasn't until the shelves slowed down that Mom yelled, "yes, there's one left!"

I began salivating.

"Here, honey, I put these in your father's lunchbox, but he won't mind," Mom said, handing me a Little Donna's fried snack pie. Across the label, a disclaimer was printed: "Contains no fruit."

"I'm so glad I had one left for you," Mom said. "Want a glass of milk?"

"No milk," I said. "I think I'll save this for the movie."

Maria looked at me holding the Little Donna. "You're going to eat those Little Donnas? I thought you were sensitive to BHT?"

"BH What?" Mom asked.

"BHT," Maria said, "It's a preservative that Tony thinks he's allergic to."

"You have allergies, Tony? You never did when you were little. When did this all start? It's not asthma, is it?"

"No, Mom, it's not asthma. I'm just sensitive to preservatives. They've been known to cause nausea in laboratory rats," I joked.

"Oh, that's just a bunch of junk food hype," Mom said. "Your father has been eating two boxes of those every week for the last four years and he's still very much alive."

I calculated Dad's consumption. Twelve to a box, times two, times fifty-two, times four. Dad had eaten two thousand four hundred and ninety-six Little Donnas—and his colon was still intact? What was Mom trying to do, kill him?

I then pondered the other side of the coin: what if preservatives weren't really bad for you? What if they preserved you and allowed you to live longer? What if preservatives were really the fountain of youth? Of course the AMA wouldn't go for it, all those preserved people, living forever. But maybe there was a hidden side-effect. Maybe you'd live forever, but turn to stone. Perhaps Dad would become a piece of garden statuary in his great-great-grandchildren's back yard, *if* we were gracious enough to spawn some descendants for him.

"Tony!" Maria yelled.

"What?!"

"Your mother wants you to go into the living room and start the movie."

"O.K., you don't have to yell."

"Well, she asked you twice and you didn't answer her."

"It was three times, Maria," Mom added.

"I'm sorry. I was preoccupied."

"You were spacing out again," Maria scolded.

Why did Maria always have to say that? Couldn't a person have some quiet time to himself without it being labeled negatively?

"The movie is in the bookcase next to your father's chair," Mom said, putting the rest of the leftovers in the refrigerator. While she had her back turned, I hid Little Donna behind the toaster.

We got comfortable in front of the television and I pushed *play*. If only real life was so simple, I thought.

When I felt that Maria was sufficiently engrossed in the movie, I sat back to review the absurd events of the day. Why was my life so insane? I prayed, "Dear God, please give me some type of sign that it's all just a joke. It's not supposed to make sense, right? Just one more sign—I promise I'll listen this time. Just give me some type of sign."

I opened my eyes and thought I noticed some scribbling on the wall over the television. It was written too small to see from my chair, but I didn't want to get up and stand in front of the TV during the movie.

I looked at Maria. "Maria!" I whispered.

Maria turned to me. "What?"

"What is that scribbling over the TV?"

"I don't know," Maria said. "From here, it looks like a marquee."

"A car?"

"No, a marquee as in a sign. You know, a sign that over-hangs the roof of a theater."

"That scribbling on the wall looks like a marquee to you?"

"Oh come on, Tony. I don't have time for an inkblot test right now; I'm trying to watch the movie," Maria said, annoyed.

"Maria, you've seen this movie a hundred times," I said. "Does it really look like a sign to you?"

"Yes, Tony. I told you it looks like a sign. Now can I finish watching the movie?"

"I want to look at it more closely."

"Oh Tony, you're impossible!" Maria turned to Mom. "Excuse me, Mom. Do you mind if we put the movie on pause for a moment while Tony reads the handwriting on the wall?"

"By all means," Mom said. "It's about time he reads the handwriting on the wall."

"What do you mean by that, Mom?"

"Just read it!" Mom said.

I looked at Maria. "Come on, Tony, read the handwriting on the wall," she said.

"Read it!" Mom yelled.

I couldn't. I was afraid to look, but Maria forced me; she took me by the hand and led me to the wall behind the television. "Do it, Tony. Read the handwriting on the wall—it's your last chance!"

What was Maria talking about, my last chance? My last chance for what? I looked at the wall. The message seemed startlingly familiar; I had seen that acronym before. I read aloud, "U-R-N-A-Hole!" What the hell was that? I had asked God for a sign and he threw back an obscenity? I looked at Maria.

"Why are you looking at me?"

"I don't get it."

"So? You never get it; that's the whole point."

"What's the whole point?"

"You're always trying to figure things out, and you never will, because…" She pointed to the handwriting on the wall.

"Because I am an A-hole?" I asked pathetically.

"That's right. Now I believe you owe me forty-seven thousand dollars," Maria said. "I'll have my office bill you."

"What for?" I cried.

"For three-hundred and seventy-six man-hours of psychotherapy, and that's not counting all the freebies you got when the meter wasn't running."

"You had a meter running?" I cried.

"Oh, come on, you married me because you needed a personal shrink and thought you wouldn't have to pay? Get with the program," Maria said heartlessly.

"You'd charge your own husband? I can't believe you'd charge your own husband!"

Maria was shaking me, yelling, "Tony, wake up. Tony, you're just having a bad dream. Wake up, honey." I looked at Maria. It was morning.

"Merry Christmas, Tony," Maria said.

"Oh my God, it's morning?" I asked. "I have no recollection of going to bed last night."

"Oh, you were out of it. You fell asleep about five minutes into the movie—out like a light. Don't you remember my helping you up the stairs?"

"No. And I had the most awful dream."

"I could tell. You kept yelling 'charge me'. What was that all about?"

"Oh, I can't remember," I lied.

"You know, Tony, I really think you should take some time off after the holidays. Maybe we could go to DC for a few days, to the National Gallery."

"That sounds great," I said. "When we get home, I'll check my schedule."

My thoughts were interrupted by a funny smell.

"Maria, do you smell something burning?"

"No. What do you smell?"

"It smells like burning plastic."

"No, I don't smell anything," Maria said. "Are you getting up now?"

"Yes. Just give me a few minutes."

Maria went downstairs and I went to shower and shave. I finished quickly, paranoid that an electrical fire had started somewhere in the house. I didn't want to be wet and naked when I had to jump out the window to safety. By the time I finished in the bathroom the smell had dissipated, so I assumed it had been my imagination. I got dressed and went downstairs.

Maria was reading the paper in the living room. She looked at me and smiled. "You were right, something was burning."

"What?"

"Take a look in the kitchen."

I walked into the kitchen.

"Good morning, Tony," Mom said. "Do you feel rested now? You were so exhausted last night that Maria practically had to carry you to bed."

"I feel great, Mom. Merry Christmas."

"Oh, Merry Christmas to you, too," Mom said.

I couldn't see what my father was doing; he was hunched over the counter with a metal spatula.

"Dad, what are you doing?"

Dad turned to face me. "What I am doing is scraping the words Little Donna off the toaster with a spatula. Some jerk slipped a fruit pie behind the toaster and the wrapper melted to it when I made my bagel this morning," he said, arrogantly.

I'd fallen asleep and never returned the pies to the cupboard. I wondered if Mom had told Dad that I was the jerk responsible? I looked at Mom. She winked. She had played dumb on my behalf.

Dad had already released the word little and proceeded to scrape Donna off the side of the toaster. "What a waste of a perfectly good pack of fruit pies," he mumbled, scraping the last bit of plastic from the toaster.

Maria walked into the kitchen. "Can I help you with breakfast, Mom?"

"Oh, thanks, honey. Everything's just about ready. Why don't you pour some juice for everyone?"

"Did you have a good time carolling last night?" I asked my father.

"Oh, yeah," Dad said. "It's becoming a lost art; we're like an endangered species."

More like a dangerous species, I thought to myself.

"What did you say?"

"I didn't say anything." What—was Dad psychic? I hadn't said that aloud, or had I? The boundary between reality and my imagination had blurred.

We sat down to breakfast and discussed Dad's new promotion.

"You know, kids," Mom said, "they picked your father over the younger men just out of college."

Maria looked at Dad. "To what do you attribute your success at the globe plant, Dad?".

"Well, I'm not sure," Dad said, "but I think it has a lot to do with attitude. Some of those younger guys just don't realize how important the job is. After all, we're representing the whole world. If we can't make a perfect globe, what does that say about how we handle the real world?"

No one had an answer to that profundity.

I wasn't sure what Dad's job actually entailed. What would one do in quality control at a globe manufacturing plant—make sure a continent wasn't forgotten? I was going to ask Dad, but I couldn't get a word in edgewise. He was talking about the fury at the plant when the Berlin Wall toppled.

"My only regret," Dad said, "was that I wasn't at the plant when the Wall came down. The men were working around the clock to meet demand. And when the USSR split, all hell broke loose. It was a very exciting time, both historically and in the globe business. The men still talk as if it happened yesterday. I missed that, but my day will come. They say California will eventually break free from the coast; that will have a big impact on business."

We looked at one another. It was Christmas—did we have to entertain a major global cataclysm?

Mom must have felt the same way; she changed the subject. "Well, we'd better get ready, Anthony. We have to be at the Taylors' at eleven." She then addressed Maria: "Honey, you wouldn't mind checking the turkey once or twice while we're gone, would you? We'll be back around two."

"Sure, Mom," Maria said.

Maria knew absolutely nothing about cooking a turkey; she had never cooked a turkey in her life.

"What exactly do I have to check for?" Maria asked.

"Oh," Mom said, sensing the lack of experience in Maria's response. "I'll baste it before I leave. You can just check to make sure—oh, never mind. I guess there's really nothing to check. I was worried about a grease fire, but what are the chances of that happening?"

Maria and I looked at one another. A grease fire? Neither one of us felt qualified to handle a grease fire. Mom was leaving us in charge? What was she thinking?

"What time is the rest of the family arriving?" I asked.

"Around two," Mom replied.

"Yeah, if your grandmother's cult will give her the afternoon off," Dad said.

"What?" I asked.

"Yeah," Dad replied, "she's becoming a god-damned religious fanatic."

"Oh, she is not, Anthony. She's just friends with them; she's not one of them," Mom said. "She's catholic."

"What cult?" I asked.

"Oh, some religion, not a cult. Your father's exaggerating."

A momentary image of my eighty-four year old grandmother handing out daisies at the airport flashed across my mind.

"I am not exaggerating!" Dad yelled. "It's one thing after another with her. The woman is losing it, I'm telling you. We really should be thinking about assisted living!"

Were we talking about the same grandmother? Granny was the only one in our family who had her head on straight. She was much too self-driven to join a cult. The only reason Dad had suggested assisted living was that he wanted to be the first to loot Granny's house after her incarceration.

My mother rolled her eyes.

Rather than incite my father, I asked no further questions. I would talk to Granny later.

"C'mon, Anthony," Mom said. "We'd better get going. We don't want to keep the Taylors' waiting."

"O.K., Leona," Dad grumbled.

As they left for the Taylors', Dad grabbed one of the large gift cubes from beside the tree.

"What do you want to do?" I asked Maria.

"I think we'd better sit in the kitchen and watch the turkey. If there's a grease fire I want to nip it in the bud."

Why did Mom have to mention a grease fire? I had finally dismissed my electrical fire paranoia, and she had to plant another seed of fear. Making matters worse, several weeks earlier Maria had started a small kitchen fire with a pot of green beans almondine. They were the boil-in-the-bag type, and it was a real mess. Since then, Maria entertained her own paranoia.

"Refresh my memory, Tony," Maria said. "What do I have to do, throw baking soda on it?"

"On what?"

"On a grease fire!"

"Yeah, I think so."

"We should see if they have any, just in case."

"O.K.," I said. While Maria checked the pantry, I checked the kitchen cupboards. "Here's a box!" I yelled.

"Oh, good!" Maria yelled from the pantry.

As I retrieved the baking soda from the back of the cupboard, I caught the edge of the box on the door handle and ripped it. "Maria," I yelled, "get me a plate. I tore a hole in the box."

"I'll get a plastic bag; I saw some in the pantry."

Maria returned with the Baggie and we tried to slide the box of baking soda down into it. The box was just a hair too big, and we didn't want to rip the seam of the bag.

"Here," Maria said, "you hold the Baggie open and I'll pour the baking soda into it."

I did as I was told, and Maria dumped the white powder into the Baggie. When we'd finished, I threw the empty box into the trash.

We had another hour and forty-five minutes to kill in the kitchen. Maria and I talked for a while about going to the National Gallery, and then she said, "Tony, you watch the turkey for a few minutes. I want to go upstairs and freshen up."

"O.K.," I said. "You're coming right back, aren't you?"

"Yes, I'll be right back."

She didn't come right back. After twenty minutes I decided to abandon the turkey and see what was keeping Maria. I grabbed the baking soda and went upstairs.

Maria was sprawled across the bed reading. "I can't believe it!" I yelled.

"What?"

"You left me alone with the turkey so you could come upstairs and read?"

"Tony, you left the turkey unattended?"

"Yeah, so did you."

"Oh, I'm sorry, Tony," Maria said. "I was interested in this magazine that was in the bathroom."

"What is it?"

"It's called *The Writer.* It looks interesting."

"I've never heard of that magazine before."

"I guess your Mother has to read it for school. Will you go and watch the turkey while I finish reading this one article?" Maria asked pleadingly.

"Oh, all right," I said grudgingly.

I went downstairs and realized it was ridiculous to be held prisoner in the kitchen by my own fear and a dead turkey. I washed our coffee cups and went into the living room to watch TV.

I surfed through the channels but nothing interested me. I began watching a documentary on the Asian Tree Frog, but my attention wavered. I looked at the living room walls, and remembered the crazy dream I'd had the night before. I had been home less than twenty-four hours and had two nightmares under my belt.

I looked around and wondered why there wasn't any art in the house. I scanned the four walls of the living room. A small curio shelf displaying Mom's porcelain pony collection adorned the south wall. A large mirror, showing definite signs of de-silvering, covered the north wall. Photographs of Jerry, Margaret and myself as young children hung on the east wall. A crucifix stood alone, next to the front door.

My eyes returned to the porcelain pony collection. It seemed odd that Mom should have such a collection; after all, it was a horse that had taken her father's life. Back in the thirties, horse-drawn carriages delivered products to the Philadelphia neighborhoods. My poor Grandfather had been at the wrong place at the wrong time: as he crossed South Street he was struck and trampled by a horse. An autopsy revealed he had suffered a fatal blow to the head, and his life and career as a mathematician were cut tragically short.

I then looked at our portraits: the three of us were each perched on a pony. What could that mean? I was about to go upstairs and ask Maria if it was some kind of psychological mechanism, but I didn't get a chance. The front door swung open, and in filed the procession: Mom and Dad, followed by Aunt Vicky, Uncle Harry and Granny. When Maria heard the commotion, she came downstairs.

"Granny!" I yelled.

"Tony! You're looking good," Granny said, hugging me.

I gave Granny a once-over, looking for evidence of cult-brainwashing.

"Hi, Aunt Vicky," I said. "How are you?"

"Oh, I'm great," she said. As Aunt Vicky approached, I realized that two coats of reddish-purple lipstick were about to be transferred to my cheek. Uncle Harry tried to save me, but was unsuccessful. The transfer was *complete.*

"Uncle Harry!" I said, shaking Uncle Harry's beat-up hand.

Uncle Harry's hands were beat-up from opening boxes at the Giant Mart on Rising Sun Avenue. While the rest of the family assumed Uncle Harry had a big position in shipping, I knew for a fact that he was just a stock-boy. Poor Uncle Harry, he'd spent thirty years falling down the ladder of success. He'd lost his job as a plumber in the late seventies, and from there, it was a downward spiral.

"Well, how's life treating you in the big city?" Uncle Harry asked. "I can't believe it's Christmas again; isn't time going quickly these days?"

Something was strange. Uncle Harry was contracting fluently, almost eloquently. Maybe I had imagined it. I decided to stir a conversation with him to confirm my observation, but before I could, Uncle Harry beat me to the punch.

"What's that on your cheek there?" Uncle Harry asked. "Looks like you've got a nasty bruise."

I felt my cheek. "Oh, that's Aunt Vicky's lipstick."

"It figures. You'd think she could be a little more careful about smearing her lipstick around," Uncle Harry said. "Vicky, look what you've done to poor Tony's cheek!"

"Oh, I'm sorry," Aunt Vicky said, rubbing my cheek.

"Vicky, what are you doing?" Uncle Harry asked. "You're just spreading it around; now it looks as if he's been slapped."

"Honey, you'd better run along and wash your face. I'm sorry, dear. I must have forgotten to blot my lipstick. And it's supposed to be kiss-proof! That's what they say on the commercial, anyhow. You never know if they're telling you the truth. You wonder about commercials sometimes…"

Uncle Harry interrupted Aunt Vicky. "Will you please be quiet and let the poor boy go and wash his face?"

I'd heard enough evidence. Uncle Harry had speech therapy. There was none of the spittering and sputtering he was famous for. It was a miracle. I went upstairs to wash my face; as I passed Granny, she smiled, shaking her head.

I looked into the mirror. Uncle Harry was right: I did look like I'd been slapped. Something funny was going on; I had detected an air of defiance on Uncle Harry's part. But Uncle Harry was never defiant. He always followed Aunt Vicky like a lost dog. And the bitterness—where was that coming from? I surmised they were having trouble in their marriage.

I washed my face. Since I wasn't paying attention, water rolled down my arms and my shirt sleeves got wet, one more annoyance to endure that day. I dried my shirtsleeves as best as I could and went downstairs.

The women had gone into the kitchen to prepare dinner. Dad and Uncle Harry were sitting in the living room, discussing globe packaging.

"So what kind of materials do you use to package them?" Uncle Harry asked smoothly.

"Oh, the usual," Dad said. "A cardboard brace and Styrofoam peanuts."

"That's what I figured."

"Why do you ask?"

"Well, I've been thinking a lot about those peanuts lately. Seems to me that eventually we're going to be up to our knees in them."

"What the hell are you talking about, Harry? We throw them away; we don't let them pile-up around us."

"True, Anthony. But eventually, where are they all going to go?"

"You're nuts, Harry!"

Dad and Uncle Harry continued arguing over the Styrofoam peanuts, and I sat back on the sofa. Uncle Harry was right, I thought. Millions of packages cushioned by peanuts were shipped every day, and one day we could be buried in them. Why did Dad always have to refute everything that Uncle Harry said?

The front door opened: it was Jerry and his date. I almost didn't recognize Jerry; he had changed somehow. It was probably the mustache.

Dad jumped and ran to the front door. "Can I help you?"

"Help me? Dad, it's me, Jerry."

"Jerry?"

"Yeah, Dad," Jerry said, looking at me quizzically.

"I almost didn't recognize you," Dad said. "When did you grow a mustache?"

"Oh, I don't remember," Jerry said. "Dad, this is my friend Roberta. Roberta, this is my father, Anthony."

Dad and Roberta shook hands. Dad then held Roberta's hand and said, "Boy, you are certainly able to keep your nails nice and clean." Dad had assumed her nails would be filthy from working at the garage.

"Thank you," Roberta said, looking a little perplexed.

Uncle Harry and I went to greet Jerry and Roberta.

"Hi, Jerry," I said. As we embraced, I felt something on his back. It felt like a ponytail.

"Tony, why are you playing with my ponytail?"

"Sorry, Jerr. I just didn't expect to feel one. How are you? I haven't seen you since August. I've missed you. Been busy?"

"Oh, Tony, we're on the verge of something big. I'll tell you about it later. I want you to meet Roberta."

Roberta and I shook hands. Her nails *were* clean. I was about to ask Roberta how she became interested in mechanics but Dad interrupted me. He was looking strangely at Jerry.

"What the hell is that growing down your back?"

Jerry felt his back. "What are you talking about, Dad?"

"I'm talking about your hair."

"Oh," Jerry said. "I haven't had time for a haircut in months—it's easier to pull it back, out of the way."

"You mean to tell me that you've been too busy to get a god-damned haircut? Men don't wear ponytails! Do you want to look like a fruit?"

"Oh Dad, relax," Jerry said. "Let's make a deal: you won't worry about my hair, and I won't worry about yours. Where is everyone?"

"They're in the kitchen," I said.

We walked single-file into the kitchen. After the hellos and introductions, we were instructed to get out of the kitchen so the women could finish dinner. We returned to the living room, and Uncle Harry sat next to me on the sofa.

"So everything's going O.K. for you in the big apple?" Uncle Harry asked.

"Everything's just great," I said. I looked at Uncle Harry with discerning eyes; he seemed as if he really needed somebody to talk to.

"How are you, Uncle Harry? Is everything O.K. with you and Aunt Vicky?"

"Oh. You've noticed the animosity between us. I guess I haven't done a very good job of hiding my bitterness."

"What's wrong?" I asked sympathetically.

"Well, your Aunt has really disappointed me. All these years I thought she really cared, that she would help me if I needed help. I guess she didn't have the time, too wrapped up with *Avon* and grading papers. Mostly *Avon.* No time left to help her own husband. She has really let me down."

"What happened?"

"Well," Uncle Harry said, "you've probably never noticed, but until a few months ago, I had a little stuttering problem. The damned thing always undermined my confidence; I felt that I could never measure up. It made me very self-conscious, not to mention the effect it had on my career. The managerial positions always went to the smooth-talkers."

"What does this have to do with Aunt Vicky?"

"Well, she never did a thing to help me—she let me babble on like a damned fool!" Uncle Harry leaned closer to me. "A couple months ago, Vicky invited me to her classroom for show and tell. The kids were learning about the economy, and I was to explain how goods were shipped and sold for profit. Well anyhow, I thought she said 1:00, but she swears she said 2:00. I got there at 1:00, and the kids had to finish their math and English before my lecture."

"Then what happened?" I asked, wondering where the story was going.

"So I figured I'd take a seat in the back and wait; there was no sense in leaving and coming back. I slid into one of the empty seats in the back, which was hard since the desks were built for kids three and a half feet tall. Needless to say, I was a little uncomfortable, but it was better than standing for an hour."

"Oh."

Uncle Harry checked to make sure no one was listening. Dad, Jerry and Roberta were talking about cars.

"So," Uncle Harry continued, "Vicky told the kids to get out their English books, that they were going to learn about contractions. So she wrote some contractions on the blackboard, and I said to myself, hey wait a minute—I always thought there was more than one N! Why hadn't I known that? And then it hit me: there was a tin ceiling in the classroom, just like the one in my old third-grade classroom. I'd always been *fascinated* by the patterns in tin ceilings; I liked to count the squares and pretend each was a portal to another world."

I was confused. "Uncle Harry, I'm not sure what the tin ceiling has to do with your anger toward Aunt Vicky."

"Suddenly it dawned on me that back in third grade, I was busy staring at the ceiling and wasn't paying attention to the lesson on contractions. I thought I had a speech impediment, but I'd been daydreaming and never learned the rules."

I remembered having thought years ago that Uncle Harry's problem was contractual. I should have said something, but I was just a kid—what did I know? Here I had known a lot. But everyone ignored Uncle Harry's problem and pretended it didn't exist. How could I, as a twelve year-old, tear through that web of compassionate deception?

"Well," I said, "I still don't understand what this has to do with Aunt Vicky."

Uncle Harry must have thought I was taking Aunt Vicky's side; he became defensive. "Well, she's a third grade teacher! She could have straightened out my little problem in a matter of ten minutes. But she was always too busy going out on her *Avon* calls!"

"Well, maybe she didn't realize what the problem was; I'm sure she'd have helped you if she had known."

"Well, I think she did know, and it was her way of being in control," Uncle Harry said. "Will you excuse me? I'm going outside for a smoke." Uncle Harry went to get his coat.

So, I thought, show and tell could be grounds for divorce. It was a crazy world.

I looked at Dad, Jerry, and Roberta. They were still talking about cars.

"So, Roberta," Dad said. "What do you think of the new *Towne Car*?"

"I'm not familiar with it, Mr. Vitello," Roberta said.

"Oh." Dad moved a little closer to Roberta. "You don't mind if I ask you a professional question off-hours, do you?"

"Of course not, Mr. Vitello."

"Well," Dad said, "when I press the accelerator, my car sounds like it's choking, you know, a pitter-putter kind of noise. Do you think my distributor cap might be shot?"

Roberta looked perplexed. "I'm sorry I can't help you, Mr. Vitello. I don't know a thing about cars. You're asking the wrong person."

"You're an auto mechanic and you don't know a thing about cars?"

"I'm not an auto mechanic. I'm a physicist. I teach quantum mechanics at Princeton. Oh, now I understand. I was wondering about the car talk," Roberta laughed.

"What the hell is quantum mechanics?"

"Well, it's hard to explain in layman terms. We mainly study collapsing wave functions, but there are many different ways of looking at it."

Dad interrupted: "Oh, not another one who spends all day watching suds dissolve!"

Jerry spoke. "Roberta, you'll have to forgive my father. He doesn't mean to be so insulting. He just misunderstood."

Roberta was a good sport. "Oh, it's O.K., Mr. Vitello. A lot of people make that mistake. We do watch suds dissolve as a way of understanding chaos in closed systems, but there's a lot more to it than that."

"O.K., you can spare me the details. Leona is the one who said you were a mechanic."

Jerry looked at me, rolling his eyes. "Tony," he said, "Dad tells me that Margaret and Ivan are engaged?"

"I didn't say that," Dad blurted. "What I said was that Ivan was going to pop the question. We don't know if Margaret is going to say yes or not. You two should pay more attention to what is actually being said." Dad rose from his chair and headed toward the kitchen. "Now if you'll excuse me, I'm going to see what is holding dinner."

I looked at Jerry and Roberta. We shrugged our shoulders in unison.

"I was wondering why your father remarked on my nails," Roberta said.

My father wasn't in the kitchen more than twenty seconds when we heard the muffled sounds of a confrontation emanating from behind the kitchen door. A minute later the door swung open and Granny emerged, shaking her head.

"Boy," Granny said. "Your father is in rare form today. Pardon me for venting in front of you, Roberta. I'm sure you don't need to hear our petty squabbles."

"Nonsense, Granny. You don't have to apologize on my account."

There was an odd sense of intimacy between Roberta and Granny; Roberta had even addressed her as Granny. I surmised it wasn't their first meeting.

"Gran, how was your party last night?" I asked.

"Oh, it was wonderful, dear. I'm sorry you and Maria couldn't stop by, but I know you had a long day," she said. "Everything was lovely; there was a wonderful mix of people."

"Can I ask you something, Gran? I'm sure it's one of Dad's misconstructions, but he seems to think you're involved in a cult."

"Yes, you're right, dear. It is one of his misconstructions. He's upset over a donation that I made to the Jehovah's Witnesses. I'm sure he's afraid I'll give all my money away and leave nothing for him."

"Are you converting?"

"Oh, of course not, honey. We're just friends. We respect one another's religious differences. They needed some money for repairs, and it was just a matter of a friend helping friends. It had nothing to do with religion."

"How did you meet?"

"They were going door to door to recruit new members, but I told them I wasn't interested in changing religions at my age. One of the women happened to notice my African Violets, and we hit it off . They seemed nice enough, so I invited them in for coffee. I told them right up front that it was purely a social invitation; I had no intention of discussing religion. One thing led to another and they stayed for dinner. We've become good friends."

"Oh," I said. "Dad made it sound like…"

"Like I was losing it and was being taken for everything I've got?" Granny finished.

"Yeah."

Jerry looked at me. "Tony, when are you going to learn? You have to take *everything* Dad says with a grain of salt."

"Yeah, you're right, Jerry."

Granny put her arm around me and whispered, "Tony, why don't you and Maria take me home later? It will give us a chance to catch up."

"O.K., Granny. It would be a pleasure."

The front door opened; Margaret made her entrance.

"Granny!" Margaret hugged our grandmother.

Jerry introduced Margaret to Roberta.

"Nice to meet you, Roberta. I understand you're a mechanic." Margaret said.

"No," Jerry said. "Roberta isn't a mechanic. Dad got his story screwed-up again. Roberta is a colleague of mine at Princeton."

"Oh," Margaret said. "I thought it was a little strange, your dating a mechanic. But Dad loved the idea—thought he'd get his car fixed for free."

"Well, he was wrong again," Jerry said.

"Where's Ivan?" I asked Margaret.

"He's spending the day with his new boyfriend. I think he's in love," Margaret said nonchalantly.

"What?" I asked.

"Why do you look so shocked?" Margaret asked.

"Hold on to your hat, Margaret. Dad's been telling everyone that you and Ivan are getting engaged," I laughed.

"What? Everyone knows that Ivan is gay. What the hell is Dad talking about?"

Jerry, Roberta, and Granny looked on with interest.

"Well," I said, "Dad claims he ran into Ivan at a jewelry store on Frankford Avenue. According to Dad, Ivan had just bought you a ring."

"Oh, that's preposterous," Margaret said. "Once again, Dad is assuming. Ivan's new boyfriend owns the jewelry store; he bought me earrings for Christmas. Can you believe how he exaggerates?"

"Well," Granny said, "so far we have Jerry dating an auto mechanic and Margaret marrying a gay man. I wonder what else Anthony will come up with before the day's end?'

"Yes," I said. "I wonder what kind of crazy story he'll invent about me?"

Maria called us for dinner. "Hello, Margaret," she said. "Where's Ivan?"

"He's not here. I'll explain later," Margaret said, walking toward the kitchen.

There were place cards arranged at the table to eliminate any seating problems. From the corner of my eye I caught Uncle Harry switching his place card so he wouldn't have to sit next to my father. I laughed silently to myself until I realized that he had switched his place card with mine. I would be the one sitting at my father's left, which wasn't his good side.

We sat in our assigned seats, and Margaret removed Ivan's place card from the table.

"Where's Ivan?" Dad asked Margaret.

"He's spending the day with friends," Margaret said.

"What do you mean, he's spending the day with friends? What kind of man abandons the woman he loves on Christmas Day?"

"Dad," Margaret said, "where did you get the crazy idea that Ivan and I were lovers? We're just friends. It would be nuts to try and convert him."

"We're not talking religion here," Dad said. "We're talking about doing what's right. What do you mean, you're just friends? Don't you think he's good enough for you? You'd better wise up—at your age you can't afford to be too choosy."

"What do you mean, at my age? Forty-four is not exactly ancient. And besides, it has nothing to do with Ivan being good enough for me."

"Well then, what the hell is it? He doesn't think you're good enough for him? He's not exactly the cream of the crop. What the hell's wrong with him?"

"Anthony, for God's sake, Ivan's a wonderful person," Mom said.

"I've always liked him," Aunt Vicky said.

"Ivan's a doll," Granny added.

"Well, how the hell long is he going to string you along? Don't you have any self-respect?" Dad asked Margaret.

"It has nothing to do with self-respect," Margaret said. "Ivan and I are friends, nothing more. He has no interest in dating women, and my interest in him is strictly platonic."

"What the hell are you saying?" Dad demanded.

"What do I have to do," Margaret said, "spell it out for you? Ivan is gay; I thought you knew that."

"Are you saying that Ivan is a god-damned fruit?" Dad snarled.

"No, I'm saying he's gay, end of story. I really don't think his lifestyle choice is any of your business, and I don't care to discuss it."

"I just want to know one thing," Dad said. "Are you telling me that you're a lesbian?"

"No, I am not. Your problem is that you make too many assumptions, and as a result, you never get a story straight. Now can I please eat? I'm starving."

"Yes," Mom said. "Let's eat and stop this nonsense. It's Christmas."

I glanced to my right. Dad was staring at his watch in disbelief. I knew exactly what he was thinking. He had finally put two and two together, and realized Ivan was dating the jeweler on Frankford Avenue. His beloved watch had been handled by a homosexual, and the thought was too much for him to bear; he was devastated. The rest of us began eating, determined to enjoy the meal despite Dad's antics.

Maria passed the big brown potato and I took a generous helping. I was about to eat a forkful when I noticed a fly had landed on my spoon. That's odd, I thought, a fly in the middle of winter? I went to hit the fly with my napkin; instead, the force of my swat sent my spoon catapulting across the table, right smack into the gravy boat. Gravy splashed onto the cuff of my father's shirt.

"What the hell are you doing? You got gravy all over my shirt!"

"I'm sorry," I said, "there was a fly on my spoon."

"There are no god-damned flies in the middle of the winter; what the hell's the matter with you?" Dad asked, blotting the gravy with his napkin.

"Yes there was!" I then noticed the fly had landed on my father's spoon. "There it is, it's on your spoon now."

My father looked at his spoon. His nostrils flared and he looked at me. "It is the reflection of the god-damn ceiling fan spinning, it's not a fly! Are you on drugs or something?"

"Oh, Anthony," Mom said, "it was an honest mistake."

Maria looked at me.

"What are you looking at?" I asked. "You're always saying that things aren't what they seem to be."

"I didn't say anything," Maria said.

Everyone at the table looked at me. "I'm sorry about the disturbance," I said.

"Oh, think nothing of it, Tony," Mom said. "Those things happen to me all the time. I once thought that Mr. Thomas had hung himself, and it turned out to be his chest waders drying from the porch rafters. He's a fly-fisherman."

Everyone laughed.

"Yes," Aunt Vicky said. "One day last summer I thought we had a terrible ant problem, but Harry had missed the trash can when he went to throw away the coffee grinds. I sprayed the whole mess with Raid before I realized Harry was just a slob."

"I did not, Vicky, you're the one that threw the coffee grinds away. Don't you remember? You were in a hurry because *Avon* was calling. Don't blame me."

"All right, we get the point," Dad said. "Would you pass me the god-damned coleslaw?'

Mom removed the little bunny lid from the coleslaw bowl and passed it to Dad.

"Mrs. Vitello," Roberta said, "you certainly have a remarkable collection of serving dishes."

"Why thank-you, Roberta," Mom replied. "I've been collecting them for years. Sorry about the cranberry sauce. Anthony broke the cranberry dish last year and I haven't been able to find another one like it. I guess it was one of a kind."

"I didn't break the cranberry dish, Leona. What the hell are you talking about?"

"Oh, that's right, Anthony. You broke the corn server. Now I remember: one of the cranberries broke off and we were afraid of bacteria getting into the crack. Remember, Jerry? You're the one who discovered that problem."

"Yes, I remember, Mom. And I hate to give you more bad news, but it looks like a piece of celery has chipped off the stuffing bowl. There on the corner, do you see where I mean?" Jerry asked.

"Oh, you're right," Mom said. "That will have to go, too."

I wondered if we were going to spend all of Christmas dinner talking about the dishes. Had we nothing to say to one another other than to remark on the absurdity of the tableware? I superseded Mom in changing the subject.

"Aunt Vicky," I asked, "where's Tommy today?"

"He's in Kansas City. They're doing the Nutcracker. We'll be celebrating Christmas with him on New Year's."

"Really?" Roberta asked Aunt Vicky. "He's a dancer?"

"Yes," Aunt Vicky replied, "with the Pittsburgh Ballet Company. They're going to be on Broadway this spring."

"Really?" I asked.

"How long has he been in ballet?" Roberta asked.

"Oh, since college. We thought it was a little odd at first, you know, a boy in tights. But we understand that many male dancers are straight. You know, they like women. In fact, Tommy is quite a lady's man," Aunt Vicky said proudly.

"Oh, that's nice," Roberta said.

Whenever Aunt Vicky talked about Tommy's profession, she had to wriggle in the fact that he wasn't gay. Why was that an issue? If Tommy had been a tax attorney would Aunt Vicky have made the same assertion? On second thought, that wasn't a good example.

"Oh, Vicky, come on," Granny said. "Roberta wasn't asking you about Tommy's sexual preference. One has nothing to do with the other."

"I know, Mom," Aunt Vicky said. "I just didn't want her to get the wrong idea."

Granny looked at Aunt Vicky and shook her head. There was an awful lot of eye-rolling and head-shaking in our family. Had we not been related, would we have tolerated one another?

"Did everyone have enough to eat?" Mom asked. "Maybe we should go into the den and open the gifts. We can have dessert later."

"That's a good idea," Granny said. "I'll help you clean up before we leave."

We filed into the den. When we were seated, Dad began passing the boxes.

"You go first, Roberta, since you're the guest," Dad said.

"Why thank-you, Mr. Vitello," Roberta said, removing the wrapping. "Oh—it's a globe! Thank you very much. I don't have one. It will look great on a shelf in my office."

"O.K., Maria, you're next," Dad ordered.

Maria opened the gift and uttered the very same response as Roberta.

"Why don't you take it out of the box? I think you'll find our colorists have done a wonderful job this year. Water quality is up, so they've adjusted the shade of blue of the ocean," Dad said.

Maria removed the globe from the box and Styrofoam peanuts fell everywhere.

"Oh, those darn peanuts," Maria said. "They're such a nuisance."

"See," Uncle Harry said to Dad, "what did I tell you? They're a real problem."

"Shut-up, Harry. At least the globe is protected," Dad said. "Kids, isn't the water a magnificent color?"

"Yes it is, Dad," Maria said, spinning the globe on its axis. As she did, I noticed something peculiar.

"Wait a minute," I said, stopping the globe. "Dad, they misspelled Russia!" Across the northern part of Asia was the word *Rusha.* Dad had given us factory seconds for Christmas.

"Oh, I know," Dad said. "Some dummy in typesetting made a mistake. Other than that, they're perfect. It's a good thing I caught it on the first day of production. Only nine slipped by before I caught the mistake."

"How could something like that happen?" I asked. "Everyone knows how to spell Russia."

"It's really no big deal," Dad said. "You can use a little touch-up paint to correct the misspelling."

"I just don't see how someone could actually misspell Russia," I laughed.

"You don't have to make such a big deal out of it. Like you've never misspelled a word in your whole life, *Mr. Smartypants*? If you don't want the globe, don't take it. Just leave it here and I'll give it to someone who isn't such a god-damned perfectionist," Dad grunted.

"I didn't say that I didn't want it; I just think it's strange that someone could misspell one of the major superpowers."

"I've heard enough of your condescension—it's the last time I give you anything!"

"Dad, Tony wasn't trying to be condescending," Maria said. "He was just surprised. Weren't you, Tony?"

I was afraid to say anything, so I nodded and said nothing.

"O.K., Margaret," Dad said, "here's yours. And yes, yours has a mistake on it too, so don't even bother opening it; just take my word for it. Jee-Zus Christ!"

Margaret took her box and placed it on the floor next to her chair. "I didn't intend to say a word," she said wryly.

"I'd like just one god-damned Christmas without trouble," Dad grunted again.

"I think that's enough out of you, Anthony. You don't have to take the Lord's name in vain, especially on Christmas Day. I don't know about anyone else, but I'm sick to death of your cursing," Mom said.

It was about time Mom had put big Anthony in his place. Another opportunity to change the subject slipped by; Mom interjected a veritable confrontation instead.

Dad couldn't allow Mom to have the last word. "Well, if this god-damned family was a little more appreciative, maybe I wouldn't get so friggin worked up!"

"That's it," Mom said. "Roberta, you'll have to excuse my husband's ignorance."

Dad looked at Roberta. "Please forgive me, Roberta. I'm sorry if our little disagreement has made you uncomfortable. It just seems as if we can never get together without some kind of trouble."

Roberta didn't know what to say, or she was afraid to say anything. She nodded and shrugged her shoulders.

"Leona," Granny said, "why don't we clean up the kitchen now? The kids can take the rest of their gifts home and open them."

"That's a good idea, Mom. I don't like the tone in here."

Apparently no one had liked the tone in there, because everyone piled into the kitchen, over-eager to help in the clean-up. Dad stayed in the den, staring into the faux-fireplace as though contemplating ending it all.

I pulled Maria aside in the kitchen. "Can you believe him?"

"Well, you know how he is," Maria said. "Why do you always have to push his buttons?"

"You're going to turn this around and pin it on me?"

"I'm not pinning anything on you. You just never know when to quit."

"I don't? He's the one that had to go off like a raving lunatic."

"O.K., Tony. I don't want to argue about it. Mom, do you want me to wrap up the bread?" Maria asked, blowing me off.

"Yes, honey," Mom said, "wrap it up and put it in the freezer."

Jerry approached me. "Relax, Tony. You've got to admit, it was pretty funny. *Rusha*? I wish I'd been a fly on the wall when Dad caught that one."

"Yeah, you're right, Jerr. So anyhow, what did you mean earlier when you said you were on to something big?"

"Well," Jerry said, "I can't tell you too much until we publish our results, but I think we're on the verge of a big breakthrough. We've discovered that a whole set of forces works in tandem to mold an object's physical form. By manipulating some of those forces, we've been able to cause changes in an object's shape. The most exciting thing isn't what we're learning about structural development; it's what we're learning about the forces themselves. Bit by bit we're beginning to understand the unified field."

"Wait a minute," I said, "slow down, you've lost me. What are you talking about?"

"Well," Jerry continued, "we know that DNA contains instructions on what to make, and that self-assembly folds it together into a primary shape. But what's responsible for an organism's final shape and form? Why does a nose always turn out looking like a nose? Until now we've assumed that the guidelines for form were contained wholly within the DNA. But we've discovered that secondary instructions for form may lie within the unified field. Additionally, we've stumbled upon the fact that what we used to think of as gravity is really a multitude of forces working together."

"This is too deep for me."

"It's really quite basic," Jerry said. "By manipulating the forces that shape an organism, we can alter its form. The concept has been studied as it relates to gravity and space travel for years."

"So we're going to use gravity to do nose-jobs in the near future?" I joked.

"Oh, c'mon, Tone. The nose was just an example. Our goal isn't to manipulate anything. However, one can't study the force per se; you can only observe its effects."

"Was it a flash of insight? An eureka?"

"Actually, Granny gave us the idea, inadvertently," Jerry replied.

"Granny?"

"Yeah. You know how crazy she is about her plants; she asked me to build a rotating base for a jade plant so the leaves would get even light exposure."

"And?"

"The motor on it went awry, and it began rotating too quickly. The rotational motion caused a centripetal force that somehow acted in tandem with gravity, altering the force-field in which the plant was imbedded. As a result, the new growth had leaves of a very uncharacteristic shape," Jerry said, in one breath.

"A mutant?"

"Kind of," Jerry said. "So we thought, if centripetal forces affected form, then other kinds of forces would also affect form. The engineering department built various devices for us to test the idea; we discovered that forces act as a mold. It's unbelievable in its simplicity."

"Simple for you," I said, "but it's Greek to me."

"Well, just look at Granny's jade plant, and see for yourself," Jerry said.

"I will. How big are you talking? Are you talking grant-money big, or revolution in physics big?"

"I'm talking revolution, Nobel Prize big," Jerry said. "But we still have to develop the mathematical models."

The Nobel Prize. Wouldn't Dad have a fit if Jerry actually won the Nobel Prize? "When did you win the god-damned *noble* prize?" were Dad's famous last words. I prayed that my brother would win the Nobel Prize, not only for the achievement, but also for what it would mean to my father. All those years of the Nobel Prize put-downs would blow up in his face. Was life really so just?

"But Tony," Jerry said, "you have to keep a lid on it. Until we finish the math and publish our results, it would be too easy for another lab to steal our idea."

"Mum's the word," I said. "Can I tell Maria?"

"Tell Maria what?" Maria asked, approaching us.

I looked at Jerry. "O.K.," he said, "but do it later, and make sure no one overhears."

"Sounds like top-secret spy stuff to me," Maria said. "Tony, will you go upstairs and get our bags? Granny's ready to go."

"No dessert?" I asked.

Maria held up our take-out bag.

"Oh."

"Don't forget, Tone. Take a look at Granny's jade plant," Jerry said.

"I will. Just tell me one thing, Jerr. This mutant, it won't try to eat me or anything, will it?"

"Well, not literally, but it will spray you with digestive enzymes if it feels threatened."

"Really?" What kind of monster had Jerry created? I laughed as I visualized Jerry's mutant plant turning on its creator and stalking him on the streets of Stockholm. I looked at Jerry. He was laughing too. Had I been thinking out loud again?

"Why are you laughing?" I asked Jerry.

"No, not really. I was only kidding about the digestive enzymes. You set yourself up for that one," Jerry laughed.

"I guess I did, but how do I know what you're capable of? They're doing all kinds of weird stuff in labs. I read last week that scientists had genetically-engineered headless rats. Do they honestly think we need that public service? A rat without a head is still a rat."

"Tony, they're not trying to build a better rat. They're trying to understand the genetic mechanisms that control brain development."

"Yeah," I said, "it looks as if they've hit the rat on the head."

"Very funny," Dad said. "You could have at least waited until you'd left my house to insult me."

Jerry and I were so engrossed in our conversation that we hadn't seen Dad enter the kitchen.

"What?" I said. "We weren't talking about you. We were talking about headless laboratory rats."

"Is that right? Headless? What are you implying, no brains?"

"Well, yeah, I guess. No head would seem to indicate no brain."

"I've had just about enough of your insults. I don't know what the hell your problem is, but you can take your attitude somewhere else. I will not be insulted in my own home, on god-damned Christmas!"

"I don't know what you're getting so upset about," I defended. "We weren't talking about you; you just assumed that we were."

"Dad, Tony's right. You were assuming," Jerry said.

"The only thing I assume is that I will be treated with respect by guests in my home."

We were no longer family. We had been re-categorized as guests, and ungrateful guests at that. How had that evolved? Because I found it funny that some dummy had misspelled Russia?

"Here you go, honey," Mom said. I looked at Mom. She was holding my coat. "Here you go, honey, and don't forget to ring the phone twice so we know you got home safely."

My own mother was rushing me out the door on Christmas, and I didn't even care. What had my life become?

"C'mon, Tony," Margaret said. "I'll help you with your bags."

I was stunned. I went outside to warm up the car, slamming the door behind me.

I returned to retrieve our bags, and Margaret followed me upstairs. We entered the bedroom and Margaret looked at me. I knew exactly what she was going to say, because I'd seen that expression a thousand times.

"Tony, what just happened down there?"

"I have no idea."

"You turn your head for one minute in this family and a whole saga transpires. I'll never understand this family," Margaret said sadly.

"Well," I said, "from what I gather, Dad got mad because I laughed at the globe misspelling, and then he assumed I was calling him a rat."

"Yeah, Tone. Tell me something I don't know already. I was there. What I want to know is why."

"Why did he assume I was calling him a rat?"

"Oh, Tony," Margaret said, frustrated. "I know why he thought you were calling him a rat. You know something? I've never told you this, but you have an annoying way of skirting around issues. I ask you for an opinion, and all you ever give me is a blow-by-blow description of what I already know. Like you won't commit yourself by taking a stance."

"What do you mean?"

"Well, all our lives you've done the same thing. I look for a little support from you and all you do is re-enact the insane details."

"I thought you were looking for details," I argued.

"Why would I want an instant repeat of insanity rearing its ugly head? Once is enough."

"You're not going to believe it, Margaret, but I always thought you were daydreaming and needed me to fill you in."

"Oh, I was daydreaming all right. Dreaming of what it would be like to be a member of a normal family."

Really, I thought. Why had I assumed she was oblivious to what was going on?

"Well, if it makes you feel any better," I said, "I think they're all nuts."

"Thank you, Tony, for finally taking a stance. All these years I've been thinking it was me. What a load off my chest."

"Why didn't you just come right out and ask me if they were nuts or if it was you?"

"For the same reason that you didn't," Margaret said. "I thought it was me."

"So I thought it was me and the whole time you thought it was you?"

"Yes," Margaret said. "To tell you the truth, Tone, I always felt like you were using me, that you only needed me when it was time for a manicure."

"That's ridiculous, Margaret. I never even wanted a manicure. I thought it was your way of cornering me so that I could fill you in on what was going on."

"Why would you think I needed you to fill me in? I was there, remember?"

Why had I thought that? How could I think that Margaret was so shallow?

"Yeah, I remember," was all I could say.

"Well, I'm just glad to finally know it wasn't me, and now you know it wasn't you."

I was glad Margaret had clarified that. As to what we had actually just discussed, I wasn't sure. In fact, my whole holiday season had been one blur of confusion. I couldn't wait to go home.

"Not to cut you off, Margaret, but I'm kind of hot standing here in my coat. I'll give you a call over the weekend and we can talk some more, O.K.?"

"Sounds good. Here, let me take one of your bags."

We went downstairs; Granny and Maria were waiting by the front door. "Do you have everything?" Maria asked.

"Yes," I replied. "Jerry, give me a call. Maybe you and Roberta would like to catch a show in the city some weekend."

"Sounds good, Tone. I'll call you."

"It was nice to finally meet you," Roberta said. "Have a safe trip home."

"Bye, Mom," I said. "Thanks for everything. Tell Dad I said goodbye."

"Oh Tony, go and say goodbye to your father," Maria scolded.

I wasn't going to be the one to look like a jerk, so I did as I was told. Dad was sitting in the den, pretending to browse through one of his mail-order catalogs.

"I'll see you, Dad."

"O.K."

That was it, just O.K. I had done my part. If he wanted to continue the charade, he could do it without me.

I went into the kitchen and said goodbye to Aunt Vicky and Uncle Harry, then returned to the living room. "Ready to go?"

"Yes, we're ready," Granny said.

We said goodbye again and were on our way.

As I drove the Schuylkill Expressway, I had a flash of insight. Dad had jumped down my throat because he assumed that I was making fun of him. I had assumed that Margaret was so far-gone that she needed a reality consultant. Dad had assumed that Roberta was going to help him get to the bottom of his car trouble. I assumed that Mom had baked an apple pie. I blamed my father of assuming, when I was guilty of the same crime. I was just like him—I had turned into my father! I was about to crack.

I looked into the rear-view mirror at Granny. Maybe she could save me from breaking right in half. "Granny?"

"Yes, dear?"

"I'm confused about something."

"I know you are."

"How do you know?"

"Well, who wouldn't be, after that drama?" Granny chuckled. "I don't think there was a person there today who wasn't confused."

Maria suddenly seemed interested in my father's neurosis.

"What happened back there? Margaret couldn't figure it out either," I said.

"Well, I think your father's paranoia has reached critical mass. It made a mess of the holiday for everyone."

"I thought he was being a little paranoid," Maria said.

What was that? Whenever I had accused my father of being paranoid, Maria blamed me, or repeated her favorite mantra: things aren't always what they seem to be. I looked at Maria. "If I had said that, you'd be all over me."

"I would not, if it was true," Maria said.

"Well it is true," I said. "Gran, I'm at my wit's end with Dad. I don't know why he has to be so difficult. I'm sure Jerry was embarrassed for Roberta."

"Oh, Roberta understands the situation," Granny said. "We've discussed it at length."

"You have?"

"Yes. Jerry and Roberta have been spending quite a bit of time at the house since the jade plant began growing strangely."

"Why don't they take the plant to the lab?"

"Oh, they don't need to. They're growing hundreds of their own."

"So why are they spending so much time at your house?"

"They're going through your grandfather's notebooks. Something Jerry said about his research sounded very familiar. I remembered Stanley discussing a mathematical model with me years ago, about anti-gravity. I suggested to Jerry that Poppy's notes might be of some help in solving a problem he was having."

"Oh," I said. "But getting back to Dad: what did you mean when you said his paranoia was reaching critical mass?"

"Your father has never resolved his paranoia that people are out to get him. What he fails to realize is that he is out to get himself."

"That's crazy. Why would he be out to get himself?"

"Because he has not fulfilled his life's dream. He is approaching the age of regret, and realizes his life is not what he hoped it would be."

"But his life hasn't been that bad."

"In our eyes it hasn't, but in his eyes, he has failed. He has not followed his heart. Every soul has a destiny that it seeks, and your father abandoned his destiny because of the death of hope. It's as simple as that."

"And he is projecting the anger he feels toward himself onto his family," Maria added.

"Exactly," Granny said. "There is nothing worse in life than the death of hope. It ruins more families than even greed or alcoholism."

"So what do you think Dad's destiny was, Gran?"

"I think he was born to be an artist, a sculptor, actually. Don't you remember years ago how your father spent all those hours locked-up in the basement sculpting soap?"

"Yeah, I do." I replied. "So why didn't he stick with it?"

"I could be wrong, but I think he was just impatient. When he didn't become Rodin overnight, he gave up. He perceived himself as a failure, and he assumed everyone else thought that as well."

"So it became a self-fulfilling prophecy," Maria added.

"Exactly," Granny said. "He has become his own worst enemy. It's been going on for a very long time, for as long as I've known him."

"How have you managed to keep your cool all these years?" I asked.

"It's been a rough road. There were times when I could have choked him to death, but my faith kept me from actually doing it. Underneath our personalities we're all the same, and we each have our own set of personal challenges. Just because we can rise above our own problems doesn't mean we have the right to belittle someone who has not summoned the strength or the courage to tackle his," Granny said solemnly.

Maria looked at me. "Granny's right."

I said nothing and exited the Schuylkill.

We rode the rest of the way in silence. Maybe I had been too hard on my father. After all, he had suffered the death of hope.

I kept thinking about my conversation with Margaret earlier; I felt guilty about misjudging her. Perhaps I hadn't taken Mom seriously enough either. I didn't know what to think anymore. Our family dynamics were so complex, they defied rational explanation.

Finally, we pulled into Granny's driveway.

"Oh, look!" Maria said. "The house looks magnificent!" Thousands of white lights illuminated Granny's house, casting a surrealistic glow on the stone exterior. It was as though a fine glitter had dusted the house. Was it pixie dust?

"Aren't you coming in to see the jade plant?" Granny asked.

"Yes," I said, "We're coming."

We walked to the door. Granny opened it and magic spilled out. Maria and I walked in, spellbound by visions of sugarplums. All Granny's plants were lit and decorated; some wore strings of pearls, others wore crystal garlands and white velvet bows. There were pots of pink poinsettias everywhere.

"The house looks beautiful, Granny," Maria said.

"Thanks, honey. A friend of Ivan's did the decorating. He did a wonderful job, didn't he?"

"Wonderful does not even begin to describe it."

"Come into the dining room so I can show you the jade plant," Granny said. We followed her.

"Here it is," she said, pointing to the jade plant next to the window. It did look strange.

"You'll notice the older leaves and the newest growth are normal. But look at these leaves, the ones that grew when the rotator went crazy. Apparently the spinning affected the leaves' shape. After Jerry fixed the motor and slowed it down, they started growing normally again. Isn't it strange?"

"Those leaves look like fish—see the tail?" Maria asked.

I looked more closely at the leaves. They did look like fish. The tails were a bit on the long side, though.

"Don't they look like little ponytails?" Granny asked.

They did. They weren't fish tails, they were ponytails. "They do look like ponytails!"

For several minutes we stood examining the jade plant that had grown ponytails. I then remembered Jerry's ponytail: was he spinning too fast as well?

"Well, Gran, as much as we hate to, we have to get on the road," Maria said.

"Yeah, Gran. We have a lot of work to do tomorrow."

"You kids drive safely. And Tony, don't be too upset by what happened with your father. I have a feeling that things are going to change soon."

"Why do you say that?"

"Because when you're at rock-bottom, there's a fifty-fifty chance that you might go up."

That was true. I could always count on Granny to look on the bright side.

One more kiss and we were on our way. Pulling away from Granny's house, I looked one more time into the rear-view mirror. Maybe I'd decorate the apartment next year, I thought.

Maria and I rode in silence for quite a few miles. I pondered what Granny had said about my father. I wanted to know why Maria *suddenly* had a professional opinion to voice. Whenever I'd asked her for one, she had no comment.

"Maria, can I ask you a question?"

"Sure, Tony. What is it?"

"Why is it that tonight you were able to diagnose my father's neurosis, whereas you normally try to pin everything on me?" I blurted.

"I do not always pin everything on you. What are you talking about?"

"Your response to me is always that things are not what they seem to be. But all of a sudden, with Granny in the car, you're full of input. When we're alone it's almost as though you won't commit yourself by taking a stance."

I suddenly realized I had plagiarized Margaret.

"That's not true, Tony," Maria said. "I didn't know the whole story until tonight. I didn't know that your father was a soap sculptor."

"That one piece of information changes everything?"

"Well, yes. It does. You're always asking me to give you the whole picture when I don't have all the facts. How can I make sense of things when I always feel as though I'm missing chapter one of the story?"

That's what was going on? Maria couldn't help me because she hadn't read chapter one?

The truth was, I had withheld chapter one. Chapter one encompassed my fear, paranoia and self-doubt, the things I couldn't share. Maria wanted to help; I wouldn't let her. It had nothing to do with the hourly rate I wasn't paying. I really was a jerk. I wouldn't say another word until I solved the enigma, even if it meant an eternity of silence.

I looked at Maria. She was sleeping. My constant babbling exhausted her, just as Jerry's had always tired me. How could I be forty-one years old and so ignorant?

As I exited the turnpike, I prayed to God. "Please, dear God, help me to straighten out my life when I get back to New York. I promise, I'll never ask for one more thing. I really mean it this time."

Three

The bleakness of January descended, and so had my spirit. With the joyless passing of the holiday season, I settled into the New Year devoid of resolution. My languid soul was desperately seeking emancipation from melancholy; how had I sunk so low? I prayed that our trip to D.C. the next day would clear the cobwebs and stir some inspiration for the last year of the millennium.

I *needed* a break from work. How could I teach a computer to think when my own thinking was so garbled? I imagined artificial intelligence gone mad with the first mentally ill computer. My name would be forever associated with the first robot to be straitjacketed and institutionalized. SuperSoft would be tossing me out on my butt.

Why would I have such thoughts? I had just gotten a raise; I was doing a fine job of separating my personal affairs from my professional life. Why was I beating myself? The somber music that had been a backdrop to my thoughts couldn't be helping. I decided to play something more lively.

I looked at the clock on the CD player. It was 7:00 p.m. and Maria wasn't home from work. It wasn't like her to be late and not call. I decided to call her office.

There was no answer; she'd left already. But not necessarily, I thought. Maybe Maria was still there and couldn't get to the phone. Maybe her four o'clock flipped out and tied her to the filing cabinets in her office. Why had it never occurred to me that Maria worked in a dangerous profession? And why didn't I drop her cell phone at her office that morning when I'd noticed that she'd forgotten it?

It was 7:10, and still no word. What if Maria was dead? Perhaps some crazed maniac shot her as she hailed a cab in front of her office building. Why didn't I take the ten extra minutes to deliver her phone? How could I have left Maria so vulnerable? I was such a jerk.

The fear of losing Maria made me realize how much I loved her—how had I ever doubted it? They say you never know what you have until you lose it, I thought. They were right.

It was 7:15. There would be no trip to D.C. the next day. I'd be making the funeral arrangements for my poor wife. Why wasn't I kinder? I'd never really shown how much I loved her, and I'd never have the opportunity. Any minute the police would be knocking at the door to give me the horrific news. She couldn't be dead; I had to go and look for her. I went to get my coat.

I was startled by a knock at the door. I looked through the peephole; my whole body quivered in response to the fish-eye view of the two policemen. I had to be dreaming. It couldn't be happening.

They knocked again, harder. I looked through the peephole again, hoping to get an idea of the gravity of the situation from the expression on the officers' faces. It was grim. Their demeanor told me that they had just witnessed the ugliest of crimes. At that instant I knew beyond doubt that Maria was dead. I took a deep breath and opened the door.

"Are you Mr. Anthony Vitello?" the officer asked.

"Yes I am," I said, my voice shaking.

Well, we regret to inform you that we found your wife in the street a few blocks from here. She was run over pretty badly—she's almost unrecognizable. I'm afraid you'll have to get a new one.

"What?" I asked, holding on to the door jamb for support.

"Mr. Vitello, we found your license plate a few blocks from here. It was run over so many times that it's almost unrecognizable. I'm afraid you'll have to go to Motor Vehicles and get a new one," the policeman said, handing me the battered remains of my license plate. "We just wanted to inform you of the situation."

"Well, that's great news," I said. That explained the clanking noise I'd heard when I hit that pothole on the corner of fifty-third. "I don't know how to thank you. Here I thought you were going to tell me that my wife was dead."

I couldn't believe I had said that.

The two policemen looked strangely at me. "Mr. Vitello, do you have reason to believe that your wife may be in danger?"

Was he insinuating that I looked capable of dangerous behavior?

"Oh no," I replied. "She's just a little late getting home from work. You know how your imagination can run away from you."

"Oh," the policeman said, looking at his partner. "Just get down to Motor Vehicles as soon as possible and apply for new plates."

"Will do," I said, nodding at the officers.

"Have a good evening," they said, and were on their way.

I closed the door and stood quietly for a moment. Why did that always happen to me? My worst fears seemed to be realized, only to find that God had played a practical joke. If that was how God operated, then maybe he had too much time on his hands.

I looked at the clock on the mantel. It was 7:35 and Maria still hadn't arrived. I went to get my coat. I was half-way to the closet when another knock at the door sounded. Oh no, I thought—God is going to get back at me for my sarcastic comment; this time he won't be kidding.

I looked through the peephole. It was Maria, alive and well! I unlocked the door and grabbed Maria. "Oh my God—I'm so glad it's you!" I held her tightly.

"Who else would it be?"

"I don't know. Why were you knocking?"

"I was having trouble with my key. When are you going to grease the locks?"

"Oh, I'm sorry. I'll do it first thing in the morning."

"Can we go in?"

"Yes," I said, releasing my grip on her.

We walked into our apartment and Maria put her briefcase in the office.

"Why are you so late? I was worried sick."

"Oh, Tony. You wouldn't believe the day I've had. My four o'clock kept going on and on. Finally, at 5:15 I got her to wrap things up."

"So where have you been for the last two hours?"

"You're not going to believe it. I got downstairs, and my four o'clock still hadn't found a cab. Hundreds passed us, but they were occupied. After twenty minutes a cab finally stopped, and my four o'clock offered to share it with me. I had my reservations, but I was freezing and didn't want to wait any longer."

"And?"

"Well, she was despondent. When we pulled up to her apartment building she seemed manic. I couldn't let her leave in that condition, so I told the driver to go around the block a few times. That was a mistake. It took me another hour and a half to get her stabilized."

"So you rode around the block for an hour and a half?"

"Yes. Can you believe it? Oh my God! The cab driver! He's waiting downstairs to be paid. I almost forgot!"

"You have to pay?"

"Well, I couldn't very well ask my four o'clock to cough up a hundred and twenty dollars, in her condition. When she was finally ready to get out of the cab, I didn't want to do anything to jeopardize my escape. Will you go down and pay the cab driver? He's holding my watch."

"You let him hold your watch?" I asked, reaching into my pocket to make sure I had enough cash.

"Well, I guess he wanted some collateral in case I decided to stick him for the fare. Don't forget to give him a tip—I'll order Chinese food while you're downstairs."

Riding down the elevator, I felt mixed emotions. While I was glad that Maria was alive, I couldn't believe she had allowed herself to be held hostage for two hours by a deranged patient. Weren't they paying her to take control?

Outside, there were two cabs parked in front of our building. As I began to wonder which one had driven Maria, I saw one of the drivers wave Maria's watch in the air.

I walked up to him. "How much do I owe you?"

"A hundred and thirty-one fifty."

"What? My wife told me that it was a hundred and twenty."

"Yeah, that was fifteen minutes ago." The driver seemed disgruntled, so I didn't argue.

"Here you go." I handed him a hundred and forty dollars. "Keep the change. I'm sure it was one hell of a ride."

"Yeah, talk about driving you crazy. It was no joyride, let me tell you. I'm getting the hell out of here." He got into his cab and pulled away.

I stood there for a minute and watched the cab turn left at the corner. He seemed to be in a hurry. I couldn't blame him; he must have gotten an earful.

I went back into the building. I stepped onto the elevator, wondering if Maria had remembered to order the Chinese food—I was starving! It had to be getting late. I looked down at my watch. It wasn't there, I had taken it off already. Oh my God! *Maria's watch!* I had forgotten to get it from the cabby! No wonder he was in such a hurry. How could I have been so stupid?

How was I going to explain the situation to Maria? Her mobile shrink session cost her not only a hundred and forty dollars in travel expenses, but also her six-hundred dollar watch. I was such a jerk; she was going to kill me.

I thought about going back downstairs, but realized it was pointless. The cab was probably twenty blocks away by then. I couldn't believe my luck, or rather my stupidity.

I got off the elevator and walked to our front door. I unlocked it and entered the living room. Good, Maria was in the shower. I'd have a few minutes to ponder an excuse.

I sat on the sofa and tried to fabricate a good story. It was useless; it had been stupidity, plain and simple. There was no rational explanation for being a numskull.

Maria entered the living room wearing her bathrobe. "The Chinese food will be here in ten minutes. Will you get the door when it comes? I had to get out of those clothes."

"Sure, honey."

Maria sat next to me on the sofa. "You know, Tony, I was really touched by the way you greeted me at the door tonight. It made me realize how much you love me. It was sweet." She kissed me softly on the cheek.

"Of course I love you, Maria. How could you ever doubt it?"

"I didn't say that I doubted it; after my day, I really needed a hug."

"What was your four o'clock so worked up about?" I hoped Maria would forget about her watch if we became engrossed in another topic. I had become my mother!

"Oh, Tony. She has me stumped. She has an obsessive-compulsive disorder wrapped up in a host of other disorders. Basically, she spends all her time making lists of things to do, and never does anything because she's always making lists. She then suffers depression over her lack of accomplishment. If only I could get her to do something on her list."

"That's odd."

"Tell me about it. And since she's doing nothing, her list of things to do has evolved into her list of failures. She not only has a fear of failure, she has a fear of her list of failures."

"So she never has time to do anything because of her list-making?"

"Yes. The only thing she manages to do is shop for stationery, you know, those long, skinny, to-do pads. Some with magnets, some without."

"Is that activity on her list?"

"I don't know, I guess it is," Maria laughed.

"Well then, she's accomplished something on her list. Why not tell her that she's not a complete failure, since she keeps herself stocked with the raw materials of her obsession?"

"I know. Isn't it crazy?"

"Well, you had to know that crazy might inevitably rear its head in your line of work."

"Oh, Tony. Don't get me going. I don't think this is ethical, sitting around joking about my patients' neuroses. I'm supposed to be helping them."

"And you are. Your four o'clock is now resting comfortably, while you, on the other hand, have literally been driven nuts."

"Enough about work. What happened to our license plate? It looks crunched."

"It must have fallen off the car. The police found it and dropped it off a little while ago, just before you got home."

"Do you think it will be O.K. to drive to D.C. with only one plate?"

"Yeah. I'll put the mangled one on the dashboard for now."

"Speaking of Washington, I have some bad news," Maria said.

"What? Did the *Omni* cancel our reservations?"

"Oh, no. Nothing like that. Your mother called me at work today. They're going with us," Maria said, burrowing into the sofa in fear of my response.

"What?" I asked in disbelief. "You mean to Washington?"

"Yes, Tony, to Washington."

"They can't go with us. Dad has to work. He can't take any time off."

"Yes he can. The plant is closing for a week because of a glut of product. Apparently globes aren't moving."

"Why would you invite my parents? You knew how I was looking forward to this trip. We were going to relax and have a good time, not to be tortured by my father. Are you crazy? Tell me you're kidding."

"Tony, calm down. I'm not kidding. But I didn't invite them. They more or less invited themselves."

"How the hell did this all come about?"

"Don't yell at me. What was I supposed to do? Come right out and tell them that they weren't welcome?"

"Yes. They'd get over it, eventually."

"Oh, come on, Tony. I couldn't be blatantly rude to your mother. Besides, I think this may be your father's way of making peace. I think he feels badly about what happened at Christmas."

"Well, he should feel badly. He acted like a complete fool, which is why I don't want to spend an entire week with him!"

"Well, there's nothing we can do about it now. They've already made reservations. We're supposed to pick them up in the morning."

"I can't believe this. Why did you even tell them that we were going?"

"What was I supposed to do? Your mother called and said your father was off for a week, and they were going to drive up for a visit. I had to tell them that we weren't going to be here."

"So much for a nice, relaxing trip."

"Well, maybe it won't be that bad. I'm sure your father doesn't have any ulterior motives. I think he just thought it would be nice to spend some time together."

"Yeah, I guess." Where the hell had she been for the last ten years?

There was a knock at the door. "That must be our dinner. Do you have any money left?" Maria asked.

"I think so," I said, digging into my pockets again. "Yeah, I have forty bucks left." I walked to the door and opened it. A young oriental man was smiling at me.

"Your dinner, Sir. That will be twenty-seven dollars and forty cents, please."

I handed the young man three tens and told him to keep the change.

I walked into the kitchen with the food. Maria was putting out plates and silverware. "Do you want fried rice or plain?" she asked.

"I'll take plain."

There was another knock at the door. Maria looked at me. "Who could that be?"

"I don't know. I'll get it." I looked through the peephole and saw the young oriental man carrying a small bag. I opened the door.

"Your fortune cookies, Sir. Almost forgot them—and my boss says *never ever* forget the fortune cookies. Here you go." He handed me the bag.

"Thank you," I said, and closed the door.

"Who was it?" Maria asked.

"It was the delivery boy. He forgot to give us the fortune cookies."

"That was nice of him."

"Yes it was."

We began to eat our meal, which I tried to enjoy despite the fact that my upcoming vacation was ruined. "I can't believe they're going with us," I said, pushing rice around my plate.

"Oh, Tony. Will you let it go? There's nothing we can do about it now. Besides, have you ever considered the possibility that you and your father might have a good time together?"

"Where have you been? When have my father and I ever had a good time together?"

"That's just my point. You expect the worst, and that's what you always get. You might try changing your belief system. Try thinking that you might have a good time, and maybe you will."

"Why do I get the feeling that you always think it's me? Do you really fail to see the absurdity of my father's behavior?"

"Oh, Tony. Things are not always what they seem to be. You're over-analyzing the situation. Can we please end this conversation? I've had an awful day."

Maria looked beaten, and who knew what had transpired prior to four o'clock? Poor Maria, I never gave her a break. One minute I was brimming with gratitude that she was alive, and the next I was torturing her with my off-hours need for psychotherapy.

"I'm sorry. You're right. I'm going to change my belief system," I lied, clearing away our plates.

"Let's have a fortune cookie and see what's in store for us," Maria said.

"O.K."

Maria handed me my fate, sealed in a cellophane wrapper. "You go first."

I unwrapped my fate and broke it in half. I removed the little piece of paper and silently read the message: *Time Waits for No Man.* Thank God Maria hadn't gotten that fortune; she'd be reminded of her watch, and I still hadn't come up with a good enough excuse as to why I didn't have it.

"What does it say?" Maria asked.

I thought for a moment. "It says love and luck are in your future."

"Oh, that's good. O.K., it's my turn." Maria unwrapped her cookie and read her fortune aloud: "Time Waits for No Man."

She got the very same message? How could that be? "Let me see," I said, reaching for her fortune.

"Here," Maria said, "and speaking of time, where did you put my watch?"

Her watch. How was I going to tell her that I had allowed that lousy thief of a cab driver to take off with it?

"Tony—where did you put my watch?"

"Your watch?" I asked again, stalling for time.

"Tony! What is wrong with you?"

My lips began uttering a story so well constructed that I shocked myself. "Well, Maria, you're not going to believe what happened. But as you know quite well, things happen that are unbelievable."

"What happened?"

"Well, I went downstairs to pay the cab driver like you asked me, and even gave him a nice tip. He gave me your watch, thanked me, and was on his way."

"So where is it? What are you trying to say?"

"What I'm trying to say is that I walked toward the lobby door and from the corner of my eye noticed a well-dressed man. He appeared to be lost."

"What was it that made him appear lost?"

What? I hadn't thought that far. Why did Maria always have to jump ahead of me? Couldn't she just accept it on faith, that the man I invented appeared to be lost?

"Tony!"

"What?"

"You're spacing out again. You start telling me a story and stop in mid-sentence."

"I am not telling a story!"

"Not at the moment. But I wish you would continue. What does the well-dressed, lost man have to do with my watch?"

With little conscious effort on my part, I continued an impromptu discussion of an event that had absolutely no basis in physical reality. "Well, I could tell he was lost because he was carrying a street map and wore a perplexed expression."

"And then what happened?"

"Well, we made eye contact, and he approached me. At the time I didn't feel the least bit intimidated because I really believed he was lost."

Maria interrupted. "You mean he wasn't really lost?"

"No, he wasn't. It was all part of a scam." My heart began racing. What the hell was I doing? Had I lost all sense of morality? Was it better to be a liar and cover up my incompetence, or to look like an incompetent in the eyes of my ultra-competent wife? I chose to be a liar.

"So then what happened?" Maria asked, with a guilt-provoking amount of concern.

"He approached me and asked if I knew where the Buford Building was. He was carrying a briefcase and looked perfectly legitimate, so I told him how to get there. Out of nowhere, a kid on a bicycle was coming right at us! We couldn't get out of the way quickly enough, and he crashed right into us."

Maria interrupted me. "Oh my God. What did you do?"

"I fell to the ground, quite disoriented."

Maria interrupted me again. "Then what did you do?"

"I tried to regain my composure and pulled the map off my head. I looked up the street, and there was the well-dressed man, riding on the handlebars of the kid's bike, with his briefcase and his feet in the basket. Before I knew it, they were gone, and so were our watches." My heart was beating even more rapidly—who was I? I hadn't just said that.

"Oh my God, Tony, you were mugged! Do you think it was a father and son team? Oh, never mind. The important thing is that you weren't hurt—were you?"

"Well, I got a nasty brush burn from the bicycle tire, but I'm all right."

"Why didn't you tell me earlier? This is unbelievable."

"It's the truth! I didn't want to ruin your dinner, and besides, you were dealing with your own crisis."

"We should call the police. Those two are probably pulling that scam all over town."

"I thought about that, but I was so startled by the whole thing that I can't remember what the guy looked like. And that kid on the bike came at me so quickly, I never got a good look at him. I wouldn't be able to identify either one, so what's the sense?"

"You should report it anyhow. The police should be aware of what's happening. I can't believe it. I'm just glad that you're all right."

"Thanks, honey. But I really don't want to waste the rest of the night at the police station. I just want to forget about the whole thing." Wasn't it a felony to make a false statement to the police?

"Well, at least you weren't hurt. Watches can be replaced," Maria said sympathetically.

"Sorry, Maria."

"Don't be sorry, Tony. Unfortunately this world is full of psychopaths who thrive on lies and deception. You have nothing to be sorry about; you were the victim. I understand, though. It's a normal reaction to being victimized: you wonder if you were in any way responsible. Don't fall into that trap, honey. And don't ever worry about ruining my dinner."

Ruin her dinner? More like ruin her life, I thought. Maria was trying to make me feel better when I had just wittingly fed her a pack of lies. The shame that I began to feel was far worse than any embarrassment that might have resulted from my telling the truth. I began to feel nauseous.

"Oh, Tony, you're as white as a ghost. I see this whole thing has really taken a toll on you. Why don't you *lie* down on the sofa and do some deep breathing? It will make you feel better."

"No, I don't want to *lie* around and dwell on it. I think I need to keep busy. Why don't you go in and rest and let me clean up the kitchen?" I needed to get Maria out of the kitchen because I couldn't bear to look her in the eye.

"Are you sure? Are you sure you don't need to *lie* down?"

"I'm positive. Don't worry about me. I'm fine."

"All right, if you're sure that you don't need to *lie* down."

Was it my imagination or was Maria putting an awful lot of emphasis on the word *lie*?

"You go and relax, and don't worry about me."

Maria left the kitchen and I was alone with my conscience. What had I done? Not only had I lied to my wife, I had constructed a web of lies so calculated that for a minute, I believed them myself. I was sick!

As I wiped the counter I caught a glimpse of my reflection in the toaster. So that's what the face of a liar looks like, I thought. How could Maria ever trust me again?

Could I sink any lower? Yes. I remembered that my watch, which had been reported stolen, was on the dresser in the bedroom. I looked into the living room and saw Maria resting comfortably on the sofa. I had to get rid of that watch.

I walked into the bedroom; my watch was right where I had left it. I quickly put it into my pocket. I had to get rid of it; if Maria found it, she would discover the truth: I was a no-good, lying sack of animal waste. I couldn't risk that. I went to the hall closet and got my coat.

"Where are you going?" Maria asked.

"I'm going over to the garage to check the car. I want to make sure that none of the exhaust pipes were knocked loose when I went through that pothole." I was lying again. I was really going to duct-tape my watch to the underside of the trunk of the car so Maria wouldn't find it. I couldn't believe how things were snowballing.

"Oh, Tony, are you sure you want to? Why don't you check it in the morning?"

"I'm O.K."

"Are you sure? You still look a little pale. Maybe you should *lie* down."

"What?"

"I said, maybe you should *lie* down. You still look a little pale."

"No, I'm O.K. I'll be back in a few minutes," I said, without looking Maria in the eye. How could I ever look her in the eyes again?

"You seem a little shifty-eyed. One of the symptoms of Post-Traumatic Stress Syndrome is the inability to focus," Maria said clinically.

"I can focus! I'll be right back." I opened the door and slithered out. I closed the door behind me, wondering if I had acted suspiciously. Maria seemed to be looking at me as though she thought I was up to something.

Riding down the elevator, I wondered how I had created such a mess. I didn't mean to lie, I just didn't want Maria to doubt my competence, again. She had sent me downstairs for her watch and I forgot it? I was always forgetting things, as Maria pointed out. Also, I was always spacing-out, being paranoid, or over-analyzing, the early signs of obsessive disorder. Already discontented with my psychological profile, I'd then added habitual liar to my bag of tricks. How could Maria stand me? I could barely stand to be conscious myself.

It felt good to be outside in the fresh air. I decided to continue walking past the garage a few blocks. As I turned the corner onto 73rd Street, I noticed a neon cigarette in one of the shop windows. I could go for a cigarette, I thought.

What was I, nuts? I hadn't had a cigarette in almost twenty years. But if I had just one and threw the pack away, it wouldn't really count. Besides, I needed something for my nerves. Just one for medicinal reasons wouldn't classify me as a smoker again.

I crossed the street and went into the store. Within seconds I emerged with a pack of no-name cigarettes and a roll of breath mints for a chaser. I was armed and dangerous.

Wondering how I could ever lie to my dear, sweet wife, I opened the pack of cigarettes and removed one. I lit it and took a deep drag. I became a little dizzy. I took another drag; I became very dizzy. Why hadn't I remembered that effect? With utter disgust I threw the cigarette into the gutter and had to stop walking for a second to regain my equilibrium. I had a hard time regaining it; I had to lean against a telephone pole and close my eyes for a minute.

My quest for composure was interrupted by a tap on my shoulder, which scared the hell out of me. I opened my eyes to see a man and a woman staring at me.

"Tony, are you all right?" the man asked.

"Yes, I'm fine," I said, wondering how he knew my name.

"Tony, it's Al Steinbright, and my wife Marcia. We had dinner together last year; don't you remember? We're friends of Maria's."

Yes. How could I forget the Steinbrights, whose psychiatric practice was on the fourth floor in Maria's building? I wondered if they saw me smoking. What was I thinking? The smoking was the least of my worries; what about my stumbling to a telephone pole for support and having them find me there with my eyes closed? Those people were wired to detect abnormal behavior.

"Tony, don't you remember us?"

"Of course, Al. How are you both?" I asked timidly.

"We're fine, but you didn't look too well just now; are you O.K.?" Marcia asked.

"Oh, I'm fine. Just a little dizzy spell. Must be low blood sugar; I haven't had dinner yet." Another *lie.*

"Well, why don't you eat one of those mints that you're holding?" Marcia said. "It will raise your blood sugar a bit until you get something to eat. We'll walk you home. C'mon."

"Oh, that's not necessary, Marcia. I'm perfectly fine."

"It's no trouble," Al insisted. "We're going right by your building anyway."

I was in trouble. I had a roll of duct tape and my watch in one pocket, and a pack of cigarettes in the other pocket. I couldn't very well stop at the garage and duct tape my watch into hiding with the Steinbrights tailing me. I was going home with even more to hide than when I'd left. And I was being forced to make small talk with not one but a team of psychiatrists. God had my punishment well-constructed.

"I get low blood sugar once in a while too," Marcia said, "but I don't think I've ever had it *that bad.*"

That bad? I was in big trouble. Marcia was qualifying how bad I was. Things didn't look good for me.

"Before we realized it was you, we thought it was some *drunk* or *junkie* looking for a leaning post," Al laughed.

They were exaggerating; it was only two puffs on a cigarette. Besides, they're professionals—shouldn't they be using the term *substance abuser*? Where did they get off?

"Tony!" Marcia yelled. "Are you O.K.?"

"Oh, I'm sorry, Marcia. Of course I am."

"For a minute there, you *scared* me, the way you were *spacing out.* We have to get you home so you can eat. Al, why don't you hail a cab? I don't think he can make it the rest of the way."

"I'm fine. Of course I can make it," I insisted.

"Nonsense, Tony. It's no trouble at all. We don't want you *passing out* on us," Al said, walking towards the street.

What was happening? How had the situation evolved to where a team of psychiatrists was using words like junkie, spacing out, and passing out to describe my condition?

I began to feel angry at that SOB of a cab driver who was responsible for it all. My faith in humanity was shattered: all it took was one thief to start a chain reaction of evil. Well, at least I was *just* a liar, and not a thief.

Within seconds a cab pulled over.

"C'mon, Tony," Al said, guiding me by the arm.

Oh no—he had to help me into a cab! I made a mental list: junkie, passed out, helped him into a cab. How was it going to sound when they reported to Maria? I then remembered that Marcia and Al wouldn't see Maria all week because we were going to D.C. What were the chances that they'd remember this ten days from now? Right, I thought.

Because I was so deep in thought, I didn't notice the soda can in the gutter, which threw my ankle off balance and sent me barreling into the back seat of the cab as though I was a drunk falling in.

"Tony, are you O.K.?" Marcia asked me for the umpteenth time, as she slid into the cab next to me.

Al got in next to Marcia and looked at the driver. "Madison and 68th, please."

"Really?" the driver asked.

"What do you mean, really?" Al asked.

"Well, that's a coincidence," the driver said. "I was just heading there myself."

Something was very familiar about the driver.

"Oh," Al said, at a loss for any other response.

"Yeah," the driver continued, "I forgot to give some guy his wife's watch, so I'm taking it there now. Poor guy, probably thought I robbed him. There are a lot of low lives out there, but I'm not one of them."

The driver looked into his rear-view mirror as he spoke. Suddenly a light went on in his head. "Hey mister, you're the guy! This is more of a coincidence than I thought. I'm on my way over to a guy's apartment to give him something, and I pick him up on the way. This has gotta mean something. It must be one of those things they call divine intervention," he chuckled.

Yeah, it meant something all right: I was truly and deeply busted.

"His name is Tony Vitello," Marcia was saying.

Why was she telling him my name? No one said anything; I suddenly became very psychic. I realized I hadn't heard the driver ask me my name because I was in shock over having just been busted. So Marcia could also say I didn't even know who I was. And she would be right; I didn't know who I was anymore. I'd thought I was just mildly psychotic, but it seemed clear that deviant with no conscience was a better fit.

"Well, it's nice to meet you, Mr. Vitello. Here's your wife's watch. I'm sorry I forgot about it before. I think I was just dizzy from driving around in circles," he said, handing me Maria's watch.

"Thank you for being so honest," I said.

"Tony," Marcia said, "I didn't know that you smoked."

"I don't."

"Oh—I thought I smelled cigarette smoke on your coat. It must be the driver."

"Oh no," the cabby said, "ain't me, I quit almost twenty years ago."

"I must be mistaken," Marcia said, sniffing like a bunny.

Finally, we were pulling up to my building. The four-block ride was an incident of bent space-time—it happened in an instant, yet seemed an eternity.

"Tell Maria we said hello, and get yourself something to eat," Al said, as I got out of the cab.

"Oh, I'll be sure to," I said, removing what little cash I had left to pay the driver.

"Oh no," the driver said. "This one's on me. I was going to your place anyhow."

I walked around the cab and was about to wave goodbye when Al rolled down the window. "Tony!"

"What is it, Al?"

"You dropped your cigarettes when you got out," he said, handing me the no-names through the open window.

"Oh," I said, taking the pack.

As the cab pulled away, I wondered if what had just happened had really happened, or if I had hallucinated it. Was it possible that my conscience had just constructed the scenario to punish itself? No, my conscience wasn't that clever. I had indeed indicted myself on all counts in front of Maria's colleagues. And, I would be suffering grave consequences in the very near future.

Riding up the elevator, I began to feel sick. What was I going to do? When the elevator stopped on the eighth floor, I didn't get off. I decided to go down and hide on the sixth floor until I could come up with a plan.

I got off on the sixth floor and began aimlessly wandering the hall. When I reached the end of the corridor I threw the pack of no-names into the trash receptacle. What could I do with the watches?

I had to tell Maria the truth about her watch. The Steinbrights would eventually mention our little meeting and the cabby's honesty. She would then know that I had originally forgotten the watch. But she would be so excited to have it back, it wouldn't be a big deal.

But what about the mugging? I told her the watch had been stolen.

O.K., what really happened: I was so shaken by the mugging, I hadn't realized I'd forgotten her watch from the cabby. I assumed it had been stolen, but they only took mine. Even better, I was so shaken that I forgot I had taken off my watch earlier. The assailants had fled empty-handed. So why the hell did I even invent a mugging? No, that wouldn't work; the muggers *did* get my watch.

I didn't know how I was going to remember everything. Hopefully Maria would be happy to have her watch back and that would be the end of it. I walked to the elevator, confident that I had my story straight and could pull off the whole thing.

As I rode the two flights, I prayed that Maria had fallen asleep on the sofa. Then I'd be offstage for the rest of the evening and could deal with the whole mess in the morning.

The elevator doors opened and I jumped. "Maria! You scared the hell out of me!"

"Oh honey, come off the elevator. I'll help you into the apartment," Maria said, in a soothing, almost hypnotic tone of voice.

"Where were you going?"

"I was going to look for you. Mrs. Brown from the sixth floor called and said you were wandering around down there like you were lost. Then it dawned on me: the mugging was more disturbing to you than you would admit. You know, Tony, Post-Traumatic Stress is not a sign of weakness," Maria said, as though she was talking to one of her patients.

"Oh no, Maria, I'm perfectly fine. I got off by mistake on the sixth floor because I was so excited. Look, I got your watch back!" Why couldn't these nosy neighbors mind their own business?

"How did you get my watch back?"

"Well, you're not going to believe it. I'd never gotten it from the cab driver. I thought I had, but I hadn't. So the muggers only got mine."

"How did you get it back from the cab driver?"

"He gave me a lift home."

"You took a cab from the garage? It's only two blocks away."

"Well, actually, it was such a crisp night that I decided to walk a few more blocks. I ran into the cabby on 73rd."

"Oh."

Oh? That was all? I was getting off that easy?

"So what kind of condition was the car in? Was the exhaust system O.K.?"

Car? Oh no. I'd never checked the car. "Well, it was hard to tell in the dark, but it looked all right." *Liar!*

"Wasn't the garage lit? It's usually bright as daylight down there."

"You know, Maria, I think you're right. I think the mugging was more disturbing to me than I realized. I'm having a hard time remembering anything."

"See! I told you. You shouldn't have gone out; although if you hadn't, I wouldn't have my watch right now. But still, you need to relax. You've been through an awful ordeal."

She was right, but she had absolutely no idea of its magnitude.

"Come on, let's go in and relax. Do you want to talk about it?"

"No, honey. I think I'll go in and take a hot shower. That will make me feel better."

"All right. Let me know if you need anything. Why don't you light a candle in the bathroom? It will help you relax."

"Sounds good." I walked down the hallway to the bathroom. I hung my jacket on the back of the door and locked it. I still had to figure out what to do with my watch. I decided to take a bath instead of a shower so I could *lie* down while I thought about it.

I lay back in the water and tried to relax, but it was pointless. As I stared toward the ceiling, an idea came to me: I could remove one of the ceiling tiles and duct-tape my watch to the back of it, and forget this night ever happened. On the way to Philadelphia the next day I would casually mention that I ran into the Steinbrights and that we shared a cab. All would be well. Finally I was beginning to relax.

Suddenly I heard the telephone ringing in the other room. It was probably my father, reminding Maria not to forget him in the morning.

I dried myself and stood on the edge of the tub to dislodge the ceiling tile; it came down with no problem. I cut some duct tape with Maria's manicure scissors, which were poised conveniently nearby. I then proceeded to tape my watch to the ceiling tile and fit everything back into place. I was having a hard time getting the ceiling tile to lie plumb, so I really had to give it a shove. As I did, I slid across the ledge of the bathtub and pulled the muscle in my groin that had been weak. It figured; I had a long drive the next day, and braking would be agony. But at least the ceiling was nice and tight.

I wrapped myself in a towel and prepared for the dash to the bedroom. I opened the door and headed toward the bedroom.

Maria interrupted my jaunt. "Tony, the Steinbrights just called me."

"They did?" I asked casually.

"Yes, they did. They told me what happened. I knew you were suffering Post-Traumatic Stress. Marcia said that you were so disoriented that you practically fell into the cab and couldn't even remember your name."

"Oh, she's exaggerating, Maria. I'm perfectly fine."

"No you're not, Tony. Why don't you let me give you something to ease the anxiety?"

She wanted to medicate me. I knew the day would come when I'd finally break, and my wife would have to drug me to protect me from myself. "O.K.," I found myself saying.

Maria walked to the hall closet and removed a sleeve of purple tablets. "Here. I want you to take both of these. They'll help you sleep."

Sleep sounded good. As I reached to take the pills from Maria, my towel fell. Too bad the Steinbrights weren't there. I could hear Marcia: "We found him naked and disoriented, the poor thing." The Steinbrights might think they knew what they'd seen, but they were sadly mistaken. And Marcia, exaggerating like that, I thought.

"Tony!"

"What?"

"Aren't you going to pick up your towel? It's too cold to be standing around naked. You're going to catch a chill."

I picked up the towel and entered the bedroom. Maria followed me with a glass of water. "Here, take those pills. They'll help."

I did as I was told.

"I'm going to finish packing in the morning," Maria said. "I'm exhausted."

"I am too." I threw on some sweat shorts and a T-shirt and got into bed.

Maria went into the bathroom to wash up. All the while, I prayed the ceiling didn't come crashing down on her.

How had my life become such a lie? Because I didn't want Maria to think I was an air-head, I became a liar and a psychopath. What really troubled me was that I had lied with such grace: a natural born liar. Natural born liar, that's how I'd be remembered.

I heard music and realized it was coming from our clock-radio; it was 6 A.M.. I was glad to be awake; what a horrible dream I'd had! Maria was stirring next to me. "Maria, are you awake?" I whispered.

"I'm getting there."

"You're not going to believe the nightmare I had. I was mugged in front of our building and went crazy. The Steinbrights took me to a mental hospital in a cab."

"Tony, that wasn't a nightmare. Don't you remember last night? Except the Steinbrights didn't take you to a mental hospital. They brought you home."

Reality descended on me with such force, I felt as if I'd eaten a bar of plutonium. A sick, heavy feeling ran through me as I realized the full nature of my predicament. And, it was *day one* of vacation with my father.

Maria and I had a quick bite to eat and finished packing for our trip. As I folded a shirt to put in the suitcase, I prayed Maria would forget about my alleged mugging and that it would be ancient history by the time we left. I didn't want to dig my hole any deeper.

"Tony," Maria said, "do you have something up your sleeve?"

Oh my God. She'd found me out. What did I do to give myself away?

"Of course I don't," I snapped. "What could I possibly have up my sleeve?"

"A dryer sheet," Maria said matter-of-factly. "It's sticking out of the cuff of that shirt."

"Oh." Another one of God's practical jokes.

"I'll be right back. I need my cuticle scissors from the bathroom."

Did I remember to return her scissors when I cut the duct tape last night? I hoped so; I couldn't remember.

I did. Maria was walking into the bedroom carrying them. "Tony, did you use my scissors to cut something sticky? They're all stuck together."

"No, not that I remember." *Another lie.*

"Well, that's odd. I wonder what happened to them? I'm going to get my nail polish remover and clean them."

A few seconds later, Maria returned with clean scissors. "I'll be right back. I'm going to get the broom. There's a spider on the bathroom ceiling again."

All I needed was for Maria to be poking around the bathroom ceiling. I met Maria in the hallway and grabbed the broom from her. "Here, I'll take care of it. I'm taller."

"There he is, Tony. Do you see him?"

"Yes, I see him." The damn arachnid just happened to be parked on the same ceiling tile as my watch. I gingerly tried to brush the spider away; after three unsuccessful attempts, Maria grabbed the broom.

"Tony," Maria yelled, "you have to hit it harder!" As she spoke she gave the ceiling tile a good shove with the broom. She hit it hard enough to dislodge the ceiling tile, but luckily it didn't give way. We did, however, begin to hear a beeping noise.

"What the hell is that?" Maria asked.

"What?" I responded, as if I hadn't heard the alarm on my watch sounding.

"That beeping noise," Maria said, giving the ceiling tile another shove. God's hand held the ceiling tile at just the critical angle necessary to allow my watch to slide down and hit me smack on top of the head. I managed to get out of the line of fire in time to avoid the tile, which fell into the tub duct tape side-up.

Without thinking I yelled. "I thought duct tape held everything?" With the utterance of only six words I incriminated myself on all counts.

"I thought your watch was stolen last night during the mugging? What the hell is this?"

I couldn't think of a thing to say, so I said nothing.

"Tony, I don't understand. Why did you *lie* to me and tell me your watch was stolen?"

Maria deserved to know the truth—that she was married to a natural born liar who couldn't even cover his own tail. "There was no mugging," I said sheepishly.

"If there was no mugging, then why did you tell me there was one?"

"I lied."

"Obviously. Let me rephrase my question. Why would you invent a story like that? Are you nuts?"

Why had I? Was I?

"Tony, don't you have anything to say?"

"I'm sorry, Maria," was all I could say.

Because I offered no explanation, Maria assumed the worst. "Tony, what were you going to do? Sell our watches? Have you gotten us into some kind of financial trouble?"

"Of course not."

"Then what the hell is going on?"

"I don't know."

"How can you not know? You've been acting very strangely lately. Oh my God—you're not doing drugs, are you?"

"No, of course I'm not doing drugs—are you crazy?"

"Am I crazy?"

Our conversation went nowhere. I decided it was time to confess, and hoped that Maria would accept some kind of plea bargain. I told Maria the whole wretched story, while she stood there listening in disbelief.

"You expect me to believe that hair-brained story? You are on drugs!"

What was going on? A lie was believable but the truth was unbelievable?

"I don't know what you were thinking, but your behavior is beginning to scare me." Maria walked away, leaving me to clean up the mess.

As I fitted the ceiling tile back into place, I wondered what kind of a weekend was in store for me. Maybe Maria would brush it off as another psychotic outburst on my part. What did she expect? She knew what I was like.

I walked into the kitchen to put the broom away and noticed Maria putting a full sleeve of purple sedatives into her purse. I couldn't believe her; she probably had a straitjacket in her suitcase too.

"Why are you packing those pills?" I asked, knowing exactly why Maria was arming herself with pharmaceutics.

"I'm not sure, why do *you* think?"

It wasn't like Maria to be so sarcastic. I obviously brought out the worst in her.

I looked Maria right in the eye. "Honey, can you ever forgive me? I felt foolish for forgetting your watch, and I didn't want to look like a fool in your eyes. I thought if it hadn't looked like my fault, you wouldn't think I was such a loser."

"Is that what you think, Tony? That I think you're a loser?"

"No, not a loser: a crazed lunatic. I don't know—I'm never sure how you're going to diagnose me."

"What do you mean, diagnose you? Don't you think I do enough of that at work? You're my husband. I wouldn't have married you if I had thought you were a lunatic."

"Really?"

"What do you mean, really? Is that what you honestly think, that I think you're crazy?"

A shrink was asking me if I thought that she thought I was crazy. Why did Maria always have to answer a question with a question? How did I know what she'd thought?

"Don't be so paranoid, Tony. Let's just forget about this whole farce and go to Washington and have a good time. I'm tired of all this nonsense; why can't our life be easier? I don't get it." There was a tone of disgust in Maria's plea.

Of course our life could be easier. I vowed from that moment forward to forget my wife was a shrink and relate to her as though she didn't have fifteen years of clinical experience under her belt. Of course we could forget the whole farce and have a good time, couldn't we?

While riding the elevator to the lobby, Maria began laughing.

"What's so funny?"

"Nothing," Maria said, trying to contain her amusement.

"What?"

Maria looked at me seriously. "I wish I'd been a fly on the wall when that cab driver handed you my watch."

"What? You get pleasure in watching me squirm?"

"Of course not. But you have to admit it was funny. What were the chances of that happening?"

"Exactly. It's what I've been telling you all along. Too many things happen to me that are weird coincidences. Now do you believe me?"

"Whatever you say, Tony. If that's what you believe, then go right ahead and believe it. I just think it's comical," she said, stepping off the elevator.

"You stay here with the bags. I'll go get the car."

"O.K., Tony. I'll wait inside the door."

Walking to the parking garage, I wondered if I was really off the hook. Was it so easy for Maria to forgive the fact that I'd lied to her? I imagined Maria hailing a cab at that very moment in an effort to disappear without a trace. Perhaps she would flee to Argentina to live in seclusion, under the constant threat of being stalked by the lunatic to whom she used to be married.

I drove to the front door and saw Maria hadn't fled. I got out of the car to get our bags. "All set?" I asked.

"Yes, and I'm driving!"

Driving out of Manhattan, Maria had nothing to say to me. It wasn't until we were on the Turnpike that she finally broke the silence. "You know, Tony, I think you need to go back to your journal writing. When you were writing every day, it seemed to keep you together."

"And now you think I'm coming apart?"

"I didn't say that. I just think it was good therapy for you."

Therapy? I wondered if Maria had been sneaking around and reading my journal. Why would she use the word therapy if she hadn't known anything? I had to burn that journal—if Maria ever found out about Mildred and Martin, she'd have me locked up. Why did I ever bring them home with me? I should have left them on the beach in 1969 where they belonged. But I needed some kind of support. I couldn't get any from anyone real.

Mildred and Martin had been a part of my psyche for so long, I'd come to think of them as my imaginary aunt and uncle. They were my independent observers who enabled me to step outside myself, whenever I wondered what was really going on. The fact that I rarely knew what was going on and that I spent a good portion of my life in group therapy with an imaginary aunt and uncle couldn't be good: it could be used as evidence against me, couldn't it?

It was Maria's fault. Mildred and Martin had existed only in my head until Maria suggested that I start keeping a journal. Written evidence of my certifiability, I thought. Wait a minute, had Maria set the whole thing up?

I imagined a court hearing that had been set up to determine if I was of sound mind and body. "Your honor," Maria said, "I'd like to present exhibit A." Maria held up my purple notebook, my most incriminating body of work.

Wait a minute, where was my lawyer? My wife was defending me? I then realized that Maria was the prosecuting attorney: I was dead.

"Mr. Vitello," the judge said, "are you sure you want to waive your right to an attorney?"

I didn't remember waiving my right to an attorney. I wasn't in my right mind; how could they let me make a decision like that?

"Tony, to whom are you waving ?" Maria asked.

"What?"

"To whom are you waving?"

"No one."

"You were waving to no one?"

"I'm sorry, Maria. I was lost in thought."

"Oh. What were you thinking about?"

What was I thinking about? Could I tell a psychiatrist what I had just been thinking? "I don't know," I *lied*. "I forget. I'm kind of tired."

I sat back and closed my eyes. I wondered what would happen if I told Maria what I was really thinking? Not only what I'd been thinking just then, but what I'd been thinking all my life? It was sad that I couldn't communicate with my wife on that deepest level, but she was a shrink. Maybe if Maria was in a different profession it would be easier for me to bare my soul. Perhaps if Maria wasn't a shrink and I didn't think I was crazy, our relationship would be different. It was not that far-fetched to say, had Maria been a biochemist or an English professor, we wouldn't be in that position. But we were. After eight years of marriage, I felt our bond crumbling.

I didn't know what to think anymore. I did wonder, though, if I'd have worried as much about my grammar, had Maria been an English professor. So why did I fear that my wife would think I was crazy? Probably because my world seemed crazy, and she had the power and the authority to have me locked-up.

Why in hell did I ever say that I was mugged? That was low. In an effort to save face, my ego constructed that farce against my will; I couldn't believe I had actually uttered the words. I had really lost it. But at least I felt guilt; I could have been a mongrel without a conscience. Instead, I was just a dog. I hoped Maria realized I was just a dog.

I opened my eyes and looked at Maria.

"Did you have a nice nap?"

"Yes," I *lied.* I was actually trying to sort through the mess in my head with my eyes closed. If I didn't close my eyes, I was accused of spacing out. I'd rather be thought of as a narcoleptic than a zombie.

"Maria, have you forgiven me? I don't know what I was thinking."

"I don't know either, Tony. The truth wouldn't have been so bad. Sometimes I wonder where our relationship is going."

"What do you mean?"

"Well, it seems as if you're wrapped up in your own little world, and there's no room for me. You seem reluctant to share your feelings anymore."

How could I share my feelings with Maria, of all people? Surely she would have our marriage annulled on the grounds she didn't know I was psychotic when she married me.

The truth was, I had been hiding my deepest fear, that life with my family had made a maniac of me. I'd always grown up with the hope that maybe I was the sane one of the group. But as I grew older, I found more and more evidence of craziness in my own personality. I was no better, I was just as crazy as the rest of them.

What was the worst thing that could happen if I related my innermost fears to Maria? It couldn't be any worse than the private hell I'd locked myself into.

"Maria?"

"What is it, Tony?"

"Did you ever wonder if you were just as crazy as the rest of your family?"

"What the hell is that supposed to mean?"

"Oh, I wasn't talking about you. It's me. Sometimes I wonder if I'm just as nuts as the rest of my family."

"Right," Maria said. "Just because you're feeling low doesn't mean you have to go dredging into my past. And anyhow, I thought we had resolved the issue of the bathroom reading material?"

"I wasn't referring to the toilet brainwashing. I wasn't even talking about your family."

"It wasn't brainwashing! All I did was open them up to a new paradigm. I had to do something—you have no idea what they were like twenty years ago."

I wasn't trying to dredge up Maria's past. Why was she being so defensive?

It was hard for me to believe that Maria's family had been as vile and abusive as she claimed. In their present form, they were gentle as a docile herd of baby lambs. Maria's clan was hooked on a feeling. Actually they were hooked on feeling feelings. Their *raison d'être* was to feel, and to feel how everyone else was feeling. Their feelings were the result of an experiment gone awry, an experiment by a young pre-med student who was sick and tired of all the bickering.

As Maria studied the efficacy of different treatment modalities, namely brainwashing, she had an insight. For a new behavioral pattern to be imprinted, the subject needed to be in a state of complete relaxation. But Maria's family was never relaxed.

Luckily Maria was also studying physiology in preparation for medical school, and she was aware of the fact that it was impossible to have a bowel movement without being completely relaxed. Maria seized the opportunity for change in her family's private moments. She left baskets of self-help books poised conveniently near the toilet, and in a very short time she had created a bunch of monsters. But they were good monsters, if that was possible.

Apparently Maria hadn't considered that her experiment could go the other way. Her family members were then *too* in touch with their feelings, and they were borderline obnoxious—forget I said borderline.

At family get-togethers there was an awful lot of hugging and asking of the question "How are you, *really*?" Because they were so obsessed with their feelings, they were oblivious to everything else that went on.

"Tony!" Maria yelled. "I said, it was *not* brainwashing! I hate when you refer to it as that, as though I'm no different than Hitler."

"I never compared you to Hitler."

Maria thought for a moment. "You're right, Tony. I over-reacted because you opened the conversation with 'Do you ever think you're as crazy as the rest of them,' and I became defensive. I guess deep down inside my worst fear is that I am as crazy as the rest of them."

A shrink was admitting that? Once I was through being stunned by the statement itself, I began to examine it on a deeper level: Maria and I had the very same worst fear. How about that? The difference was, Maria had the guts to admit it, and I hid behind the lie of silence. I was still a dog.

I couldn't bring myself to admit to Maria that I had the very same worst fear, so I said nothing. Poor Maria, she deserved someone honest. But would she be so honest if I was the shrink? I'd say the stakes were a little different. Maybe I was being too hard on myself.

"Well, do you?" Maria asked.

"Do I what?"

"Do you think that I'm as crazy as the rest of them?" She repeated.

"Of course not."

"Well, thank you. It took you long enough to ponder the issue."

What was God doing to me? I wondered if I was just as crazy as the rest of them, and it turned into Maria asking me the very same question about herself. What was God trying to tell me? Loud and clear, a voice inside of my head said: "Relax and enjoy the ride."

Maria said what I had been thinking; God had said what Maria usually said. Maybe I should start listening to Maria, I thought.

"So you've never equated me with Hitler?"

Did I say I should start listening to the woman who asked me *that* question?

"Of course not," I said, to Maria and to myself.

"Well then, let's relax and enjoy the ride. You don't mention the word brainwashing, and I won't mention the word mugging."

A plea bargain evolved from a simple misunderstanding; I hadn't been referring Maria *or* her family. Should I have felt guilty? I had gotten off rather neatly at the expense of Maria's insecurity. She would forget about my crazy *indiscretion* if I kept my mouth shut about her mind-control guilt. I decided not to feel guilty, and accepted it as a gift from God—*a get out of jail free card.*

Maria and I, the air having been cleared, relaxed and enjoyed the ride. While Maria transported us safely, I looked at the interesting cloud formations in the sky. I began to imagine that I was floating on one of those clouds, soaring through the sky on a magic wad of cotton, my quasi-magic carpet. I looked down at the earth below me and noticed how interesting center city appeared.

From that perspective, the people walking downtown looked like the workers in Jerry's old ant farm. I liked floating on clouds; I hadn't done that since I was a little kid. And the cotton smelled *so* good.

I decided to travel to the suburbs to view the landscape. There was no air traffic, so I took the long way. The grid below me began to thin out as I left the city limits. Soon there were fields below me, and from the corner of my eye I saw the color purple: I was approaching a lavender field. Wait a minute, that doesn't look like Bucks County, I thought. It wasn't. I was back in Provence. How did I get *there*?

"How did you get *where*?" Maria asked.

Oh my God, I had said that aloud? I thought I was asleep.

"How did you get where? In the car?"

I thought fast. "No. I said how did we get here so quickly?"

"Oh. I guess you must have fallen asleep again."

"Yeah, I guess so."

"You know, Tony, you take a lot of naps. Why do you suppose you're always so tired?"

"Oh, I don't know. It's probably that subtle nuances project; I've been working like mad to teach that damned machine to recognize inflections," I said. "Or maybe it's that purple stuff you drugged me with last night."

"I did not drug you," Maria said defensively.

Oh my God, I was thinking aloud again. What was wrong with me? I had to be losing it. "I'm just kidding, Maria."

"Well, I hope so," Maria said. "Let's just forget that yesterday ever happened."

We turned the corner onto my parents' street. Space-time was bent again; the ride from Manhattan had gone by in a flash. It was almost as though we had traveled to Philadelphia on a light beam.

"We're here!" Maria announced. She turned off the car and put on the brake. Before we could even get out of the car, my parents were coming out the front door with their suitcases.

We said a rather strained hello, and my mother then looked strangely at Maria. "Honey, would you mind stepping inside for a second? I'd like to get your opinion of the dress I bought for Bobby Taylor's wedding."

"Oh sure, Mom." Maria looked at me. "I'll be right back."

My father looked at me and then at the crunched license plate resting on the dashboard. "That figures," he said. "Leona, wait for me. I'm coming too."

That was strange. What figured? And why was my father following Mom into the house, as if he had even the remotest interest in her new dress? I looked at the clock on the dashboard. It was 10:50, and we hadn't even left Philadelphia. Couldn't the dress have waited?

At 11:00 I began to get impatient, and decided to see what was keeping them. As I opened the car door, my cell phone began ringing.

"Hello?"

"Tony? It's Margaret. Where are you?"

"I'm in our parents' driveway. Why?"

"Well, I just wanted to warn you: Mom and Dad are going to D.C. to confront you on your alleged drug problem."

"What drug problem? Are they nuts?"

"Dad claims he found a bag of heroin in your room after you left on Christmas."

"That's ridiculous! I wouldn't even know what heroin looked like. What the hell is going on?"

"I don't know what is going on, but I have to go—I've got someone under the dryer. Call me later; I'm dying to hear this one."

I hung up the phone. I was stunned; who would have planted a bag of heroin under my bed? I thought back to the documentary I had seen on TV the previous week, about heroin being the drug of choice on Wall Street. I then remembered what heroin looked like: it was a white powder resembling cocaine. A Baggie full of white powder? I thought. I suddenly remembered Maria and I dumping the baking soda into a Baggie on Christmas morning. What did I do with the Baggie? I then remembered that I had carried it upstairs when I went to look for Maria. It must have fallen and gotten kicked under the bed.

I imagined the look on my father's face when he'd discovered his son was a heroin addict. I began laughing uncontrollably—he was going to Washington for an intervention! I laughed so hard I almost wet myself, so hard that I hadn't noticed Maria and my parents standing next to the car.

My father opened the car door. "C'mon, Tony. Get in the house! I don't want the neighbors to see you like this," he ordered.

Seeing the expression on my father's face, I began to laugh uncontrollably again. I looked at Maria. She stared back at me in disbelief. "And to think I believed that cockamamie story about our watches. You were going to sell them for drug money, weren't you?!"

I suddenly realized there was no new dress. My parents had ushered Maria into the house to brief her on my ugly habit. It was insane! I began laughing again, occasionally spewing guttural snorts.

"And now he's going to puke all over the lawn in broad daylight," my father said, walking toward the house. The sound of the door slamming made me realize I had better compose myself.

"C'mon, Tony," Mom said, leading me by the arm to the front door. "We can help you."

I looked at Maria. "Why, Tony? Is your life so bad that you had to turn to drugs?"

I tried to wipe the grin from my face. In a sick sort of way I was looking forward to my father's imminent intervention. His logic never ceased to amaze me, even when it implicated me. I couldn't wait to see the look on his face when his logic crumbled.

Everyone took a seat in the living room. All eyes were on me, and I began laughing again.

My father began his speech. "So you think this is funny, do you? You think it is funny to break your mother's heart and destroy your wife's life? How have you sank so low? Do you know what an embarrassment this is going to be if it gets out? I suggest that you wipe that shit-eating grin off your face and take a good look in the mirror at what you've become."

"Oh, Anthony," Mom said, "don't be so hard on him. It's an illness; it's not his fault."

"Don't tell me what to do, Leona!" Dad yelled. "It most certainly is his fault. No one forced him to start shooting up!"

Maria began to cry. Poor, sweet Maria—look what my father had done. I forgot how amusing the whole thing was when I saw the hurt in Maria's eyes.

" Maria," I said, moving to sit next to her on the sofa. "Do you really think for one minute that I would do heroin?"

Before Maria could say anything, my father had to pat himself on the back. "I knew it was heroin! What did I tell you, Leona? It's a good thing I saw that documentary on channel twelve last week. I knew I was right!"

I looked at my father. "Let me ask you a question, Dad. For what reason do you assume that I'm a heroin junkie?"

"What do you mean, assume? I have plenty of hard evidence. Don't try to twist things around so you can get off the hook!"

"All right," I said. "I'm all ears. I'd like you to tell everyone in this room, including me, just what your evidence is." I looked at Maria. Thank God she had stopped crying.

"I don't think anyone in this room needs to be reminded of your behavior at Christmas. You were so out of it that you were hallucinating—but I guess you wouldn't remember swatting your *imaginary* flies and splashing gravy all the hell over me!"

I looked over at Maria. "Maria, are things always what they seem to be?"

"No, absolutely not."

"Mom," I said, "didn't you tell me you had mistakenly thought that Mr. Thomas had committed suicide?"

"Oh, that's right, honey. We were talking about how our eyes could play tricks on us."

"Let me ask you another question, Mom. Were you on heroin when you made that mistake?"

"What are you talking about, Tony? Of course I wasn't."

"What the hell is your point?" My father growled.

"My point is that my eyes had played a trick on me, and it was an assumption on your part that I was on drugs."

"How the hell long are you going to remain in denial? Why can't you just face up to your problem like a man? The evidence is stacked against you—you may as well face it!"

"What is the rest of your evidence? I'd really like to hear it."

"You want to hear it? Then I'm going to give it to you. You waltzed around here on Christmas flushed as an Irish drunk! Your face was so damned red, it looked as if someone had been slapping you around. And you were sweating like a pig, so badly that your sleeves were wet from your armpits down to your cuffs. And then, the god-damned fuss over Russia—you went on and on like a lunatic."

I looked at Maria and Mom. "Do you remember the lipstick Aunt Vicky was wearing on Christmas?"

"I do," Mom said. "How could I forget it? Of course I don't mean any disrespect to Vicky; she certainly has to advertise her products. But I do think it was a bit much. Not that she looked that bad…"

Maria interrupted. "How does Aunt Vicky's lipstick fit into this scenario?"

"When Aunt Vicky kissed me hello, she transferred half of her lipstick to my cheek. Then she tried to rub it off and smeared it all over my face. Don't you remember my going upstairs to wash my face?"

A light went on in Maria's head. "Yes, I do remember."

"So," I continued, "her lipstick was so waxy that even after scrubbing my face, my cheeks were still red. And in the process of washing my face, water rolled down both my arms and wet my sleeves." I looked at my father. "So, Dad, that explains why I looked like a sweating Irish drunk."

"Well," Mom said, "I guess Vicky would be happy to know her lipstick has so much staying power."

Dad glared at Mom. "Vicky's god-damned lipstick is irrelevant. You're going to accept his lame excuses? I think you're in denial too," he said, walking into the kitchen.

"I am not, Anthony. I just think we should listen to what Tony has to say. Maybe you're wrong."

"You think you can come up with a god-damned excuse for everything? Here!" Dad yelled, throwing the Baggie of baking soda onto the coffee table. "Explain this. I'd say this is hard evidence!"

"Tony," Maria said, "what is it?"

"Remember we were worried about a grease fire when the turkey was cooking?"

That was the only cue Maria needed. "Oh my God!" she laughed. "It's the baking soda!"

"What baking soda?" Mom asked.

"When you went to the Taylors' and asked me to watch the turkey, Tony and I decided to have some baking soda handy in case of a grease fire," Maria explained.

"Why the Baggie?" Mom asked.

"I hooked the box on the cupboard handle and ripped it; we transferred it to a Baggie so it wouldn't spill all over." I said.

"Oh. Well, everything makes perfect sense now. Oh boy, I'm so relieved. I told your father the whole thing was ridiculous. I knew you'd never resort to hard drugs, Tony. You're much too smart for that," Mom said.

Dad was ready to blow. "Well, you were singing a god-damned different tune an hour ago! 'Oh my poor son, where did I go wrong? Not Tony, a junkie, boo-hoo'," Dad mimicked.

"What the hell was I supposed to think? You showed me a bag of white powder and told me it was heroin. How was I supposed to know that it was baking soda?" Mom said, defiantly.

Maria put her arms around me. "Oh Tony, I'm so relieved. After what happened last night, it all seemed to make sense."

"What happened last night?" Mom asked.

"Nothing!" Maria and I yelled in unison.

"Oh," Mom said. She then turned to my father. "Anthony, aren't you relieved that you were wrong? Tony doesn't have a drug problem. It looks as though you've made some faulty assumptions, *again*."

Dad said nothing. It was obvious that he'd rather I was a heroin junkie than admit he was wrong.

"Well, now that things are settled, would anyone like some coffee before we go?" Mom asked.

"We're not going anywhere," Dad said.

Yes, I thought. God was on my side!

"What do you mean, Anthony? We're not going to the Smithsonian? Our bags are already packed and in the car."

Please don't argue, Mom, I silently begged.

"Well, we'll solve that problem," Dad said, walking out the front door. Within seconds he returned with the suitcases.

"I guess we're not going," Mom said with disappointment.

Dad put the suitcases at the bottom of the steps, still not saying a word. He walked to the coffee table and picked up the bag of baking soda. Was it my imagination or was my father not breathing?

Finally he spoke. "Well, I guess you won't be needing this," he snickered, walking toward the kitchen.

"Anthony!" Mom yelled. "Don't throw it away—maybe I'll make a cake tomorrow!"

I wasn't sure if Dad heard her, but I'm sure it wound up in the trash, regardless.

"Well, you two should be running along," Mom said, as Dad re-entered the living room. "You don't want to hit the late-afternoon traffic in Washington."

"Yeah, Mom. You're right." I turned to Maria. "Are you ready to go?"

"Yes, I'm ready," she said. Maria looked at my Mother. "Didn't you want to show me a dress, Mom?"

"No, Maria. There was no dress. That was just a story Anthony concocted to get you into the house without Tony."

"Jee-Zus Christ, Leona. You never know when to keep your mouth shut. You always have to get in one last dig. You and the rest of this god-damned family must take a lot of pleasure in rubbing my nose in my god-damned mistakes. I've never seen anything like it!"

"You two. Get going!" Mom said, ushering us toward the front door. Dad was still mouthing off as Mom kissed us goodbye on the front steps.

We got into the car and I started the engine. I guess I was a little over-eager to make my getaway, because I'd let my foot off the clutch a little too fast and hit the gas pedal a little too hard. I left a pretty good set of skid marks on the driveway, not to mention the horrible screeching noise, which I'm sure had infuriated my father.

Maria's reaction surprised me. "What an exit!" she yelled excitedly.

As we turned the corner and headed towards I-95, Maria turned to me. "I am so relieved, Tony. Not that I thought for one minute that you were really a heroin addict. I do have one question, though. Why were you laughing so hysterically when we came outside to get you?"

I looked at Maria. "I had just hung up with Margaret. She called to tell me that Dad had found my bag of dope."

"You knew, and you let me go on thinking the worst? Didn't you see how upset I was? I'll kill you!"

"I'm sorry, Maria. What was I supposed to do? I had to let Dad present his evidence so I could refute it," I argued.

"I suppose so. You know, the whole thing is so absurd, it's funny. In all my years of practicing psychiatry, I've never seen anything like it."

"I rest my case. My father needs his head examined."

"Well, Tony, maybe we shouldn't be so hard on him. Remember what Granny said?"

"Yeah, I remember. But it's hard for me to feel sorry for him when I am under constant attack. He is pushing this death of hope thing a little too far. And besides, it's the honest truth: there is something wrong inside his head."

"Well, I do think it was a little strange; he actually seemed disappointed that you weren't on heroin."

"Yes, because my being clean meant he was wrong. He'd rather see me go to the dogs than admit he was wrong."

"Well, at least it's over. Let's just go to Washington and have a good time. Boy, it's been one long, strange week."

As I drove I-95 South, I struggled to reconcile my feelings. Why had it taken eight years for Maria to finally see what I had always known? My father's behavior was steeped in irrationality; I was really the sane one. He pushed his own buttons—he didn't need me, or anyone else, to unravel his insanity. It flowed on its own, like a river. A river couldn't be stopped. Yes it could, with a dam. Perhaps a psychological dam could be built to thwart my father's antics.

I was about to ask Maria what she thought, but she was asleep. How could she have slept after that fiasco?

In desperation, I summoned help from Mildred and Martin, who were always there for me.

I looked at the back seat. "Mildred, what do you think of the idea? Could some type of psychological dam be built to keep my father's insanity from spilling over?"

"Well, Tony," Mildred answered, "I'm no shrink, but I think it could backfire on us; I suspect it would be better to develop another approach. I think we have to learn to remain afloat in the floodwaters. Putting a damn on your father's insanity would only bottle it up, and our suffering would be of a much greater magnitude when the bottle inevitably popped."

"I have to agree with Mildred," Martin said. "I prefer the idea of some type of life preserver so that we don't drown in big Anthony's insanity. Better for us to tread water than to be responsible for a flood of epic proportions."

"Well, Martin," Mildred said, "I don't know where you've been, but I think we're already talking epic proportions. I think we need something more than a life preserver. We've already seen Tony's lifesaver spring a leak—don't you remember the summer of '69? I was thinking of something more like an ark."

"Oh yeah," Martin said, "that's right. I think you may be on to something. An ark sounds like a pretty good idea."

"I think it's Tony's only hope. It may be the only way to save his soul."

"Well, Mildred. Looks like we'd better start stockpiling some wood and some animals."

"Oh, Martin, for crying out loud. Why do you always have to take everything I say so literally? I was referring to a metaphorical ark."

I wanted to tell Mildred and Martin that I understood, but I couldn't get a word in edge-wise. Mildred was intent on spelling things out to Martin.

"What I was trying to say, dummy, was that Tony needs to build a metaphorical ark in his mind, built on the strength of his own convictions. He needs to trust himself and his own feelings, and he'll be all right. One's feeling of sanity is a natural by-product of sane thinking. He doesn't need Maria, or any other psychiatrist, for that matter, to validate his sanity. There is nothing wrong with Tony, except that he has allowed his father to erode his self-confidence. The ark that will save Tony from drowning in external idiosyncrasies is the realization that he doesn't have to look outside himself for validation. How he sees himself is all that matters."

"So no animals?" Martin asked.

"Oh, Martin, you numskull. Of course there are no animals. You better watch yourself, or you're going to be written out of this story."

"All right, Mildred. You don't have to threaten me. I think it's time to go anyhow. Maria is stirring; I think she's waking. We'd better get out of here before she realizes that she's been replaced with a figment of Tony's imagination."

"Don't forget what I said," Mildred shouted, as she disappeared from my mind. I looked in the back seat, and they were gone.

"What are you looking for?" Maria asked, stretching her muscles into wakefulness.

"Oh, nothing. Did you have a nice nap?"

"Yes. I hadn't realized how draining these last few days have been. I hope we have a good time in Washington. I really need to relax."

"Don't worry, honey. We are going to have a wonderful time. Simply wonderful."

"Well, you sound confident. I'm glad you haven't allowed the ordeal with your father to taint your mood."

"Me too."

As we entered the Beltway around D.C., a strange feeling came over me; maybe I had made a huge breakthrough. Maybe my life was finally going to change. All I could do was hope; maybe one day I would lead a normal life. Maybe I'd even be able to stand on my own two feet and could let go of Mildred and Martin.

But where would they go? I was pondering their fate—was I nuts? Mildred and Martin were tentacles of my ego.

I remembered something Granny had said. She claimed the greatest thing we could do for ourselves was to banish our egos. So *how* would I let go of Mildred and Martin? Would they disappear without a trace? It seemed a more likely scenario that they would be murdered by my father. Their fate uncertain, I realized the day would come when it would be time to say goodbye.

I imagined the memorial service I'd attend for my dearly departed aunt and uncle. Parting is such sweet sorrow, I would proclaim, as I scattered their ashes at sea. I would say goodbye from the safety of my well-constructed ark. And I would have animals if I wanted.

Those were crazy thoughts; I couldn't stand alone. "Don't go, I need you!" I yelled, the words echoing in the cavern of my mind.

"Oh, Tony," Maria said. "I need you too."

For once, my habit of thinking aloud hadn't gotten me into trouble. I *was* making a breakthrough. My life was *finally* turning around.

I took it as an omen that I didn't miss my exit; on my last trip, I had driven around the Beltway in circles. Finally, I knew where to get off! Things were looking up.

Four

Maria walked into the kitchen and opened the refrigerator. As usual, it was empty. "What are you hungry for?" she asked.

I was hungry for peace of mind, marital accord, and job satisfaction; but Maria had been referring to dinner.

"Oh, I don't know. Whatever you want is fine with me."

"Why does it always have to be my decision?" Maria asked, as though I had a lot of nerve, being so flexible.

"Let me get this straight, Maria. There are millions of women out there complaining because they actually have to cook dinner. You're complaining because you have to make the decision as to what is delivered to your door—do I have that right?"

Maria laughed. "You're right, Tony. But you knew cooking wasn't my forte when you married me. I made that perfectly clear!"

"Yes, you did. I'm not the one complaining, you are."

"O.K., Tony. I'll make the decision, again," Maria said, walking toward the cupboard next to the refrigerator.

"I don't know what you expect to find in there. The cupboard is bare."

"I know. I put our file of take-out menus in there last night," she said, removing the folder. She began rummaging through the menus. "How about Thai?"

"Anything but Thai. I don't know what it is, but I can't get used to the idea of peanut butter and chicken. Peanut butter goes with jelly, not fowl."

"That's expansive thinking. Peanut butter can only go with jelly for what reason?"

"Because we live in America, not Thailand."

"All right. We're having pizza again, whether you like it or not," Maria said sarcastically.

"That's a good idea. We can order it from Angelina's and I'll pick it up. I can stop at Radio Hut for the cables I need."

"Fine. Angelina's it is."

"Give me a ten minute lead, then call and order it," I instructed, walking toward the closet to retrieve my coat.

"I'll turn the oven on to preheat it."

"If it's not too much trouble," I joked. "I don't want you to feel that pre-heating the oven is *always* your responsibility."

"O.K., Tony. Bye-bye now."

I kissed Maria goodbye and walked out the door.

It was a nice night for a walk. It was unseasonably mild for late January, and the sky was sprinkled with stars. The crisp evening air stimulated my appetite; I couldn't wait to bite into a slice of Angelina's pizza. It was the best in the city, provided it was cooked properly. Every once in a while you got a pie that was underdone, in which case the pizza was a disappointment resembling a cheesy rubber pancake. I hoped Maria remembered to specify well-done.

Turning the corner, I was relieved to find Radio Hut still open. I crossed the street and went in. I'd headed toward the back of the store for the printer cables, but was distracted by a color monitor that appeared to be greeting me.

"Hello there!" the monitor said in its monotonous dialect. "Please type in your name so I can greet you in a more personal way."

I looked around the store. The one salesperson was helping another customer choose a portable stereo system, so I decided to type my name and see what the computer had to say. I keyed in my name and pressed enter.

"Hello, Tony. Welcome to Radio Hut. I will take care of you while you wait for a salesperson to become available. While you wait, why not tell me what you want to purchase today? I can tell you if it is in stock. Please type in the item you have come for now," demanded my digital salesperson.

I typed in the words "printer cables" and pressed enter.

"You need printer cables," the computer said. "Please wait while I access inventory to see if they are currently in stock."

I looked toward the back of the store and saw that the salesperson was still trying to sell a boom box.

"Congratulations," the monitor said. "Printer cables are in stock. They are located on the back wall, third rack down, fourth row from the left. Please walk to the back of the store to retrieve your item now."

I was about to do just that when I felt a tap on my shoulder. I turned around; no one was there.

"Having pizza for dinner tonight?" The monitor asked.

What? That was crazy. I walked back to the keyboard and typed , "Yeah, how did you know?" and pressed enter.

"I did not know," the monitor said. "That is why I asked you. Our marketing department is interested in knowing more about you. They would like to know if you came into the store with the intention to purchase, or if you are just killing time while you wait for Angelina's to cook your pizza."

Oh, I thought. How clever of the marketing department. I decided to see where it could go. I typed, "So what if I am just killing time," and pressed enter.

"Killing time is fine," the monitor responded. "It will give me the opportunity to introduce you to the range of products and services that we offer. Please enter your date of birth and annual salary so I may present a range of products and services that would be of most interest to you personally."

I typed my birth date, along with my annual salary padded by 20K, and pressed enter.

"Congratulations. You can afford to buy anything in the store. I will now alert the salesperson with a high-pitched sound, so you may receive prompt attention!"

Sure enough, the monitor whistled a high-pitched sound, and the salesman excused himself from the boom-box sale that had been in progress. As the salesman approached, the computer introduced us.

"Marvin, this is Tony. Money is no object," the monitor seemed to whisper.

"It's nice to meet you, Tony. Are you looking for a new system?"

"No, I'm just here to pick up some new printer cables," I replied.

"Oh," Marvin replied, disappointed. "The monitor seemed to indicate that your transaction would be high-end. I'm afraid you'll have to wait until I'm finished with the customer whom I'm presently helping. I'll be with you as soon as possible." Marvin gave me a dirty look and walked away.

"Do not be angry with Marvin," the monitor said. "He is only trying to earn a living."

What was that? Artificial intelligence gone smart-assed? I walked back to the keyboard and started typing.

"You don't know who you're messing with," I typed. "It so happens that I've designed a similar program that could run circles around you!" I hit enter with gusto.

"I do know with *whom* I am messing, Tony. You are forty-one years old and you earn $132K annually. You need printer cables."

I waited for the monitor to mention the program I designed, but it didn't. So I typed on the keyboard: "I said, my program is better than your program!" and pressed enter.

Suddenly the computer got my drift. "You must be the Tony who works for SuperSoft."

I was stunned. How could this sorry heap of artificial intelligence possibly know where I worked?

"Yeah," I typed, "how did you know?" I slammed enter.

"I did not know. That is why I asked you. I ask you pre-programmed questions so I can learn about you."

"So SuperSoft was just a lucky guess?" I pressed enter.

"I ask all of the computer geeks if they work at SuperSoft. If they answer no, then I go to the next biggest software firm in the fifty-mile radius. If they answer no more than three times, then I go to the question: Where do you work?"

What the hell was wrong with me? The *if then, go to* command was the most infantile in programming logic. I had been outwitted by that stupid *machine.*

I hit the keys sharply: "I don't think it is any of your business where I work!" ENTER!

"Knowing the customer is our business. Our marketing department wants to learn about you so they may better serve you."

"Right," I typed back. "Like your marketing department gives a hoot about anything except how much money I'm going to drop before I walk out the door!" ENTER!

"Tony," the monitor said, "I think you had better go now. Your pizza is getting cold. You have been here for thirteen minutes and have failed to make a purchase. I repeat: your pizza is waiting."

I couldn't believe it: that *machine* was trying to get rid of me. I looked toward the check-out counter; there was Marvin, waving the printer cables and shrugging his shoulders. "Yes, I want them," I yelled. As I walked away, the monitor snickered, "Nice talking with you, Tony."

I had better start working harder; I couldn't get my machines to snicker. It looked as if I needed a review of the basics, too. I couldn't believe that obnoxious machine had gotten me on such a simple command.

"That will be twenty-two twenty," Marvin said. I handed him forty dollars and he gave me my change.

"You know," I said, "that talking monitor over there is a real smart-ass."

"I know, Mister. I just work here. I told my manager that it was a jerk, but he doesn't listen to me. I don't think he anticipated what a quick learner it was going to be—I can't believe some of the things it says. All I know is, those guys who sit around designing these programs must have a screw loose."

I was tempted to tell Marvin that I was one of those guys with a screw loose, but I didn't. I put away my change and kept my mouth shut. As the monitor had reminded me, I had a pizza waiting.

I turned to leave the store; as I passed the talking monitor, it snickered again and said something under its breath. I kept walking; I wasn't going to allow that machine to get the best of me. I left and crossed the street to Angelina's.

Finally, I thought, walking into Angelina's. I went to the counter and gave the girl my name. A few seconds later she returned to the counter empty-handed. "I'm sorry, but I don't have anything for Vitello."

"Are you sure?"

"I'm positive," the girl said. "Could it be under a different name?"

"Maybe. Perhaps my wife used my first name—Tony."

The counter girl disappeared and returned, still without a pizza. "Nothing under Tony. Maybe your wife called our midtown store?"

"Excuse me for a minute while I call her," I replied.

I took out my cell phone and called home. It rang three times before Maria picked up.

"Hello?"

"Maria, it's me. Which Angelina's did you call?"

"Oh my God! I forgot to call. I'm sorry, Tony." After a second of silence, she added, "You're just getting there now?"

"Yeah, I got tied up in Radio Hut. Hold on a minute." I made eye contact with the counter girl. "How long will it be for a large pie?"

"About forty minutes." The girl replied.

I got back on the line with Maria. "It's going to be another forty minutes."

"Oh, Tony, I'm so sorry. I started reading and totally forgot. Do you feel like waiting?"

"What else can we do? I'll see you in about forty-five minutes," I said, and hung up. I returned to the counter and placed my order. "Please make sure it is well-done! I'll be back in forty minutes."

I couldn't believe Maria forgot to call; I had forty minutes to kill. I looked down the street and saw the Uptown Gallery still open. I decided to browse while the pizza was cooking.

I entered the gallery and a man in his early fifties appeared immediately. He was wearing the skinniest tie I had ever seen. "Good evening, Sir. Are you looking for anything in particular this evening?"

"No," I replied. "I'm just browsing."

"Very well, then. If I can be of any service whatsoever, please do not hesitate to call upon me. I'll be at my desk."

"Don't worry," I said, "should I need you, I won't hesitate to call." I began roaming the gallery. I came upon an interesting still life; I might have purchased it had it not measured six by eight feet. It was much too large for our dining room. Still, it was interesting; the lemons looked so real.

"Quite an interesting piece, isn't it?" the skinny-tie man asked. I jumped. I was so engrossed in the painting, I hadn't heard him sneak up on me.

"Yes, it is," I replied.

"Would you like me to wrap it up for you? At sixteen thousand it's a steal," he said.

"Oh, no. I don't have the wall space for it. It's much too large for my apartment." Wrap it up for me? What did he think, I had a truck waiting? The painting was huge.

"Oh," skinny-tie said. "That piece does require an important wall. Perhaps I can show you something less important?"

Was it my imagination or was skinny-tie being condescending? Two could play his game.

"No," I said. "Something less important won't do. I need something just as important, only scaled down sixty-five percent."

"Scaled down in price, or size?"

"In size, of course," I said. Suddenly a small watercolor caught my eye; the woman in the piece looked so familiar. I then realized that she looked just like Maria! The resemblance was uncanny. And, by George, the man in the painting looked just like me! It was a portrait of the two of us, looking pensively out over a balcony, to a garden below. Maria wore a long blue dress; her golden hair fell loosely to her shoulders. I had to say that I looked rather dapper in my gentleman's suit. How could that be? I was stunned.

"Oh, I see you like the Hagan watercolor. It's a beauty, isn't it?" skinny-tie asked. "The one thing I can't figure is why the artist portrayed that beautiful woman with a man who looks like such a schmuck, pardon my French."

"I don't see that at all," I said. "I see a man who is kind but misunderstood. He is not a schmuck at all; he is being wrongly accused, as usual."

"I believe you're right. Now I see it; that woman looks much too bright to be hanging out with a schmuck. He's a perfectly fine gentleman. Shall I wrap it up for you?"

I looked at the price tag. Seventeen hundred dollars for a painting that was fourteen inches square, but it was the perfect Valentine's Day gift for Maria. What were the chances of ever finding something that perfect? I had to get it for her. The couple looked just like us.

"Yes," I said to skinny-tie. "Wrap it up. Do you have Valentine's paper?"

"We certainly do. Would you like elegant hearts or cutesy hearts?"

I thought for a moment. A seventeen hundred dollar painting deserved elegant hearts. "I'll take elegant hearts."

"Very well," skinny-tie said. "I'll have your package waiting at the front desk."

Skinny-tie disappeared with my painting. What had I done? I'd made a seventeen hundred dollar decision on a whim. I hoped Maria would like it. What if she didn't even see the resemblance?

Of course she would. That couple was the spitting image of us. I took out my credit card.

"Thank you very much," skinny-tie said, handing me my package. "I hope your wife likes it, because remember, sale items are non-returnable."

"My watercolor was on sale?"

"Yes, I'm afraid it was. The original price was thirty-two hundred, but we marked it down because it didn't move. I still think people had a problem with the man in the picture—he just seems a little, I don't know, off. But I'm glad you could look past that, because it really is a beautiful piece."

"She's going to love it," I said. I took my package and walked out the front door.

The pizza had to be ready—I had never been that hungry in my life. Crossing the street to Angelina's, I wondered how I was going to sneak in Maria's present. As I opened the door to the pizza shop, an idea came to me.

"Vitello," I said to the counter girl.

"Oh yeah," she said. "You're ready."

"Could you do me a favor?" I asked the counter girl. "Could you sell me an extra pizza box? I bought this painting as a surprise for my wife and I want to get it into the house without her seeing it."

"Sure, Mister," the counter girl said. "That's so romantic. No charge for the box. Here, let me help you put it in." The girl opened the box and I put the painting inside. It was a perfect fit. We closed the box and the counter girl sat the real pizza on top. I paid her and was on my way.

I walked home with a spring in my step—I had a secret! Hopefully I'd be able to wait until Valentine's Day to give it to Maria. I couldn't wait to see the expression on her face when she realized that the couple in the painting looked just like us.

Finally I arrived at our building. I rode the elevator to the eighth floor and got off. I walked into our apartment; Maria was waiting for me in the living room.

"Oh, Tony, I'm sorry about the mix-up. I can't believe I forgot to call. I'm sorry you had to wait all that time." She then noticed I was holding two pizzas. "Why did you get two pizzas?"

"It was buy one, get one free tonight. Some kind of special promotion."

"Oh, that's nice. But what are we going to do with two pizzas?"

"We'll freeze one."

"Good idea. Here, give me one and I'll wrap it."

"No!" I said, rather abruptly.

"Why not?"

"Because you've had a long day. You just relax and read your book. I'll bring the pizza to you," I ordered.

"All right. But I feel bad, your waiting on me, after the way I screwed up."

"Just relax, Maria." I walked into the kitchen with the two boxes. I'd have to put the painting into the freezer for a couple hours until Maria went to bed. Once she was safely tucked in, I'd retrieve it and hide the painting under our bed.

I opened the freezer, which was empty except for six ice cube trays. I thought for a moment. What if Maria decided to peek into the pizza box, just out of curiosity ? Now why would she do that? I was being paranoid. Just in case, I slid the pizza box into the freezer and arranged the ice cube trays on top, so it would be too inconvenient to peek inside. I closed the freezer and walked toward the counter to serve the real pizza.

I opened the box, and a wave of disappointment moved through me: we were having a cheesy rubber pancake for dinner. I told them to make it well-done! "Damn" I said. As I did, Maria walked into the kitchen.

"What's the matter, Tony?"

"Oh, nothing. I'm just a little annoyed; I specifically asked them to cook this well-done, and it's a half-baked mess."

"Oh," Maria said. "Well, let's check the other one to see if it's any better." Maria approached the freezer.

"No!" I shouted.

Maria looked stunned. "Why not?" she said, opening the freezer door.

"Because it's already much too cold."

Maria stood there perplexed, obviously wondering why I had arranged the six ice cube trays into such an intricate pile on top of the pizza box.

"The oven is already pre-heated anyhow," I said. "I'll just put this one in to crisp up. Ten minutes should do it. Can you wait that long? You must be starving by now."

"No, I can wait. I ate a carton of yogurt while you were gone."

"Now you don't have anything to take to the office for lunch tomorrow," I said. C'mon, close the freezer door, I thought.

Maria received my telepathy and closed the freezer door. "Somehow that didn't seem important an hour ago when I was faint from hunger," she said.

"It won't take long," I told Maria. "I turned the oven up to 500 degrees so it will cook faster."

"Isn't that too hot?"

"Oh, no. I think industrial pizza ovens are set at six or seven hundred degrees."

"Really? I didn't know that."

"There's a lot you don't know about ovens and cooking in general," I joked, putting the pizza into the oven.

"Very funny, as though you're the *Galloping Gourmet.* I'm sure I could run circles around you in the kitchen."

"Oh, come on, Maria. All you know how to make is toast."

"Look who's talking—your specialty is instant pudding."

"All right, I've had enough of your insults. Why don't you run along and finish reading? I'll call you when dinner's ready."

Maria laughed and hugged me. "I'm sorry. I shouldn't bite the hand that feeds me."

"You're darn right—now go to your room."

Maria left the kitchen. When I saw that she was reasonably engrossed in her book, I walked back to the freezer. I opened the door and peeked inside to make sure the situation was still under control; it was. The ice cube trays were lying in the same configuration. I closed the freezer door and went to sit at the kitchen table.

As I waited for the pizza to cook, I looked with anticipation toward Valentine's Day and the "unveiling". Wouldn't Maria be surprised when she saw our nineteenth century counterparts? Life was full of bizarre coincidences. Had Maria remembered to order our pizza, I'd never have walked into the Uptown Gallery and discovered the painting. It was destiny!

I then remembered skinny-tie calling my counterpart a schmuck. I'm sure it had been jealousy on his part; he only wished he had the style and grace that my look-alike exuded. It had to be jealousy. He had seemed the jealous type.

I had a disturbing thought: what if the whole thing had been my imagination? What if the couple in the painting bore absolutely no resemblance to Maria and myself? Maria would think I had lost it. I wouldn't even mention the resemblance: I'd wait for Maria to notice it herself. If by some small chance she saw no resemblance, I wouldn't even bring it up. No harm done. Maria would love the painting anyhow; it was so romantic of me, wasn't it?

I still thought the resemblance was uncanny. How anyone else could not see it was beyond me.

"I think the resemblance is uncanny, too," Martin said.

"Martin! You startled me." Martin was perched on the kitchen counter next to the refrigerator.

"I'm sorry, Tony. I just thought you might like another opinion."

"Well, yeah, I would. So you see it, too? You think they look just like us?"

"Absolutely," Martin said. "Don't listen to skinny-tie; he doesn't know what he's talking about. He only wishes he had one speck of the class that your twin has."

"That's exactly what I thought. Where's Mildred? I'd like to get a woman's opinion."

"She'll be here in a minute. She's powdering her nose."

"Powdering her nose? Why would a figment of my imagination need to powder her nose?"

"Oh, c'mon Tony, how would I know? We're your constructs. Perhaps you have a vain streak?"

"Of course I don't. Do I?"

"Let's ask Mildred. Here she comes now."

"You'd better put that cigarette out, Martin. You know how Mildred hates your smoking. And besides, you're going to set off our smoke alarm."

"Tony!" Maria yelled. "Didn't you smell the smoke in here? The pizza is burning! What did you do, forget about it?"

"Oh my God," I yelled, running toward the stove. I turned the oven off and the exhaust fan on. "Where are the pot holders?"

"I don't know," Maria yelled, rummaging through the drawer next to the stove. "Here they are!"

I opened the oven door; smoke poured out. I removed the pizza from the oven and placed it on the stove, so the fan could exhaust the smoke. Suddenly a high-pitched shrill sounded.

"Damn!" I said. "It set off the smoke alarm."

"No kidding," Maria said. "You stay here, I'll get the step-ladder so you can disconnect the battery."

While Maria was gone, I realized I was in trouble. The next logical step in the whole farce was to start again, with our back-up pizza and a more watchful eye. The only thing missing from the equation was a back-up pizza. I was busted.

Maria was talking as she handed me the step-ladder, but I couldn't hear her over the background shrill.

"What?" I asked.

Maria repeated herself, but I still couldn't hear. "Wait a minute," I yelled, stepping onto the ladder to remove the casing from the smoke alarm. I pulled out the battery; the mercy of silence descended.

"That was loud," Maria said.

"Ear-splitting," I said. "What were you trying to tell me?"

"I said you were damn lucky."

"Oh, I know. I could have burned down the whole kitchen. Good thing you walked in when you did."

"No," Maria said. "I was referring to the fact that it was buy one, get one free tonight. How lucky was that?"

So much for the surprise. I was then saved by the bell. The telephone rang and Maria went to answer it.

"Oh, no," Maria said, "everything's fine. We just burned a pizza. No, we won't forget to re-activate the smoke alarm once the air has cleared. Thanks for calling." She hung up the phone. "That was security."

"I figured as much. You know, honey, I was thinking while you were on the phone. We have a loaf of bread in the refrigerator. Do you want to have peanut butter toast for dinner? I'm starving, and that other pizza is probably half-frozen by now."

"Fine with me. The yogurt filled me up anyhow. But I'm making it. I don't want you setting off the alarm again!"

"Fine," I said. "Toast is your specialty anyhow."

At nine-thirty we finally sat down to eat. As I spread peanut butter over a slice of toast, I looked at Maria.

"What?"

"I was just thinking. It looks as if you got your way, after all; we are having Thai," I joked.

"Very funny. You're just lucky that we had a loaf of bread in the house."

The telephone was ringing again. "Who could that be, at this hour," I asked.

"Oh, it's probably security, reminding us to re-activate the smoke alarm," Maria said, getting up to answer the phone.

"Hello?"

"Oh hi, Margaret. No, you're not interrupting anything. We were just finishing dinner."

"Thai," Maria said, winking at me.

"Are you kidding? That's wonderful. When?"

"What a great location. When do you think you'll open?"

"That's great. I thought you didn't want to take a business loan, though?"

Maria listened intently, and I scrutinized Maria's facial expressions, groping for clues that could help me make sense of the half-chat.

"You're kidding?" Maria asked, eyebrows raised. "They were going to sue him? Then what happened?"

My curiosity was mounting. Who was suing whom? And more importantly, was my father involved?

"I imagine they were shocked. I had no idea they were polyester; they *looked like* wood." Maria was shaking her head in disbelief.

What was polyester?

"He paid you how much?" Maria gasped. "What? Are you kidding? It's like winning the lottery!" Maria's jaw dropped.

What, except for actually winning the lottery, could be like winning the lottery? I couldn't wait for Maria to hang up so she could fill me in on the other half of that bizarre conversation. I looked at Maria quizzically. She held up a finger—"just a minute."

"Uh-huh. I don't see why not. What day? A Sunday? Hold on for a minute, Margaret. Let me ask Tony."

Maria looked at me. "Margaret's having a Valentine's party on Sunday the fourteenth. Can we make it?"

"I don't see a problem. What's going on?"

"Wait a minute," Maria said to me. "Yes, we can, Margaret. Sure. That's no problem. Can we bring anything?"

"Yeah, I'm thrilled for you."

"It is unbelievable."

"So you had to return everything?"

"Yeah, I'm dying to see your new place."

"You're kidding?"

"Dental Moldings too?"

"I'll tell him the whole story."

"O.K."

"O.K."

"O.K."

"O.K."

"O.K."

"O.K."

O.K. what? I was trying to be patient, but on the sixth O.K. I lost it and started shouting, "What?!"

"O.K., Margaret, I've gotta go. I think the suspense is killing your brother. Call me if you need anything."

"O.K."

"O.K."

"Goodbye, Margaret."

Finally!

"You're not going to believe this one. Hold onto your hat," Maria said to me.

"What?"

"Margaret's opening her own salon!"

"What's so unbelievable about that? She's been wanting to open her own business for years."

"The unbelievable part is how she came up with the money. Remember the woodwork in Margaret's old apartment?"

"Yes."

"It wasn't real."

"What do you mean, it wasn't real? How could it not be real?" I was confused.

"It wasn't real wood, it was polyester. It wasn't even nailed down. Margaret attached it to the walls with Velcro."

"What? I've never heard of polyester woodwork. What are you talking about?"

"Apparently a friend of Margaret's does injection molding, and he and Margaret worked a barter: she cut his kids' hair for a year and he supplied her with some architectural detail made of extruded polyester foam."

"But it looked like hand-carved wood," I said. "I've never heard of such a thing. Why would Margaret want polyester woodwork?"

"Well, I imagine she'd prefer the real thing, if given a choice. She claimed the apartment was barren of detail, but didn't want to make upgrades that weren't portable."

How silly of me. I assumed Margaret's woodwork had been a fixture in her apartment; I was wrong again. Only my sister would pack up the woodwork and take it with her.

"You mean to tell me everything was held into place with Velcro? Even the Corinthian capitals?"

"Yes. Margaret said *everything* was fake."

"I still don't understand. What do the polyester capitals have to do with her start-up capital? What did she do, sell them?" I joked.

"Yes. That's the ironic part. Let me finish the story. Anyhow, when Margaret told the landlord she was moving, he made arrangements to show the apartment to prospective tenants. They just happened to have a fetish for classic embellishments, and signed a five-year lease."

"So they bought the woodwork?"

"No. So anyhow, the landlord was thrilled, and thanked Margaret for taking such good care of the place. Naturally he assumed the leasehold improvements were permanent—who wouldn't? So Margaret moved out and took the woodwork with her. It never dawned on her that the landlord or the new tenants would think it was staying."

"So then what happened?" I asked, still confused.

"The new tenants moved in, and were stunned to find the place devoid of detail. The woodwork had sold them on the place, after all. They had no interest in moving in at that point; Margaret said they even called the place an architectural wasteland. They were so mad, they hired a lawyer and filed charges against the landlord."

"Filed what charges? What kind of case could they possibly have?"

"Breech of contract, misrepresentation, pain and suffering."

"Pain and suffering? What pain and suffering?" I asked, in disbelief.

"Apparently the pain of living in an architectural wasteland; the judge ruled in their favor. He determined that they were entitled to the embellishments present at the time of lease-signing. The judge ordered the landlord to do an immediate classical revival. Can you imagine?"

"No, I can't imagine, but it doesn't surprised me. I am surprised, however, that the judge didn't subpoena Margaret, since she was indirectly responsible for the illusion."

"She was subpoenaed," Maria said, "but the fact that the woodwork had never been nailed down failed to qualify it as a permanent fixture. The judge ruled that Margaret held no liability; the landlord had been at fault for not checking to see if the improvements were actually nailed down."

I laughed. "So Velcro got Margaret off the hook?"

"Yes. To go on with the story, the landlord had some contractors come in to give estimates, and it turned out that the carpentry work was going to cost upwards of seventy thousand dollars."

"Why doesn't he hire Margaret's friend and get polyester?"

"It turned out that the company discontinued the line because of liability issues. Apparently the polyester foam gives off toxic fumes if it burns."

"I guess that rules out the possibility of any polyester detail in our kitchen," I laughed. "So what was the end result?"

"The end result was that the landlord's lawyer advised him to settle; he offered Margaret thirty-five thousand for the whole lot."

"Thirty-five thousand dollars?"

"You got it."

"But what about the toxic fumes? You mean to tell me that a lawyer advised his client to make a settlement that carried obvious liability risks, just to save money?"

"Yes."

Why wasn't I surprised? "So Margaret is getting thirty-five thousand dollars to restore an illusion?"

"Not getting. She already has the check in hand. She got it yesterday after she and Ivan Velcroed everything back into place."

"What about her new apartment?"

"Luckily it's fully loaded, circa 1920. Besides, after reading the flammability reports, Margaret was too paranoid to use it. So now she has the start-up money for her salon."

"How ionic," I said. "It could only happen to Margaret."

"No, they were Corinthian. Ionic is a Greek design. Anyhow, Margaret's having a party on Valentine's Day to celebrate. She's found a location and hopes to be open in six to eight weeks. I'm really happy for her," Maria said.

"I am too. You know, Granny's been wanting to give Margaret the money for years, but Margaret always refused. She wanted to do it on her own. Who would have thought that she'd get the funds by accident?"

"I think it's great. I can't wait to see her new place. It has twelve-foot ceilings."

"Did Margaret mention who else would be at the party?"

"No, but I assume the whole family will be there."

Whole family—that included big Anthony. I hadn't seen my father since my heroin intervention three weeks earlier; I was certain he was still erupting over his mistake. I entertained a fantasy of showing up on Valentine's Day with short sleeves and a bunch of needle marks created with a red felt-tipped marker. Perhaps my red dots would even coalesce into the spelling of an obscenity. I laughed.

"What's so funny?" Maria asked.

For once, I decided to tell Maria what was so funny, and I shared my perverse artistic vision.

"Tony!" Maria scolded. "See? You just like to push his buttons. Why can't you ignore him? You're always looking for ways to incite him; sometimes I wonder about you."

"Oh, c'mon, Maria. It was just a fantasy. I wouldn't actually do it. It was a joke," I said.

"Well, sometimes a person's fantasies are an expression of a subconscious desire. Has it ever occurred to you that maybe you enjoy seeing your father go off?" Maria asked, accusingly.

"I can't believe it, Maria," I retorted. "You know what my father is like. You saw how disappointed he was that I wasn't on heroin. What kind of father would think that way? Do you think for one minute that I instigated that whole scenario? He built the whole thing on his own faulty logic."

"You're right, Tony. I shouldn't have pointed the finger at you. Joking is your way of dealing with the whole mess, and I guess it's better than crying. I just took you too seriously; it's been a hell of a day. I think I'll take a hot bath."

As Maria left the room, I snickered quietly to myself. See what I got for sharing my thoughts? I was better off keeping my mouth shut.

I decided to change into something more comfortable. I was exhausted too. I cleaned the toast crumbs from the counter and left the kitchen.

I opened my closet door: Martin was hanging from the clothes pole. "Martin, why the hell are you always sneaking up on me? You're going to give me a heart attack one of these days."

"I come back to help you, and that's the greeting I get?" Martin asked sarcastically, jumping from the pole.

"Help me what?" I asked, slipping into my sweatpants.

"Aren't you forgetting something?"

"Oh, c'mon, Martin. I'm too tired for guessing games. What am I forgetting?"

"I'll give you a hint, it's in the freezer."

Oh my God, how could I have forgotten Maria's gift? It was a good thing Martin had reminded me. If the frame had frozen solid, the corners might have split open.

"Thanks, Martin," I said, walking back to the kitchen. I breathed a sigh of relief as I passed the bathroom and heard Maria still splashing in the tub.

I opened the freezer and piled the six ice cube trays in my left hand while I maneuvered the pizza box with my right hand. Unfortunately, the wood, glass and paper were heavier than a thin-crusted pizza, and my wrist gave way. I was successful in saving the pizza box, but the six ice cubes trays fell, sending a hundred ice cubes skating across the kitchen floor. Why couldn't my life ever be easy?

I removed the broom from the closet and quickly swept the ice cubes into a pile in the middle of the floor. I could hear Maria blow-drying her hair in the bathroom. Any minute she'd be coming out. I decided to leave the ice on the floor and abscond with the pizza box immediately.

I ran down the hall with it and quickly slid it under the bed. Safe. It was back to the ice. I left the bedroom, my heart falling as I saw Maria entering the kitchen. I then heard a thump followed by a scream. I ran to help her.

Maria was down. I helped her up and kicked my mind into high gear: I had to come up with a story, pronto.

"Tony, why is there ice all over the floor?" Maria yelled.

"Oh, honey. Are you all right? You're not hurt?"

"No, I'm fine. Just a little startled. What the hell happened in here?"

"Come here," I said, stalling for time. "You have some ice cubes sticking to the side of your nightgown."

I picked three ice cubes from Maria's side; she again asked me for an explanation. I had no choice but to tap into my experience as a natural-born liar. I couldn't ruin the surprise.

"Well," I said, "The toast didn't cut it, so I decided to nuke a slice of pizza." That lie established that there was indeed a pizza in the freezer.

"You were going to nuke pizza? You know that pizza microwaves badly. What were you thinking?"

"I don't know what I was thinking," I said. "Anyhow, when I went to get the pizza, I dropped the ice cube trays."

"So why did you leave them? Where were you?"

I gingerly uttered a lie that would kill two birds with one stone: "Can you believe the other pizza was covered with anchovies? I decided to take it to the trash receptacle—I didn't want it stinking up the kitchen."

"Why didn't you just put it back in the freezer and wait until tomorrow to throw it away? You shouldn't be walking the halls in your pajamas."

"What are you talking about? These are sweatpants; people wear sweatpants in public."

"Not ones that have a big hole in the crotch."

I looked down at my sweatpants. Sure enough, they were torn. "So what? No one saw me."

"I don't understand why you had to rush out in your pajamas; you should have cleaned up first. Why didn't you?"

Why hadn't I? Because I knew that time was running out.

"The anchovy stench was so overwhelming, it seemed more pressing. I thought you were still in the tub. I didn't know you'd go to the kitchen."

"This is crazy; I've heard enough. I'm going to bed." Maria turned to leave the kitchen.

"Wait a minute," I said.

"What?" Maria snapped.

"There's one more ice cube sticking to your nightgown." I had missed one.

"For God's sake, Tony," Maria said, removing the ice cube from her back. "I'm going to bed."

"I'll be there in a minute," I said. "As soon as I finish sweeping the ice."

"Take your time," Maria said sarcastically, leaving the room. "So much for buy one, get one free," I heard echo off the hall.

I swept the ice cubes into a pile again, and awkwardly tried to push them into the dustpan.

"Here," Mildred said, "you hold the dustpan and I'll sweep them in. You look tired."

"Can you blame me?" I asked. "My night has been a comedy of errors."

"Poor thing, and to top it off, Maria looked as if she wanted to smack you," Mildred said.

"No, she didn't. She's tired too!"

"Tired of all the bull. Do you have any idea what it's like to live with you?"

"Live with me?" I asked. "None of this would have happened if Maria had remembered to order the pizza."

"It's no wonder she forgot. Between you and her patients, I'm surprised she can remember her own name."

"It's always me, isn't it?" I asked defensively.

"You said that, I didn't," Mildred replied.

"I can't believe this. You're supposed to be helping me."

"I am," Mildred said. "Martin tells me you need a woman's opinion of Maria's Valentine's gift?"

"Yes," I said. "Don't you think the couple in the painting looks just like us?"

"Well, at one time I think they did, but now, I'm not so sure," Mildred replied.

"What do you mean by that?"

"Let's just wait until Valentine's Day. I can't even remember what the painting looks like."

Suddenly I heard running water. It was Martin, filling the ice cube trays.

"Don't use tap water," I yelled. "It tastes like it's piped in from the river. There's spring water in the refrigerator."

"Sorry," Martin said. "How was I supposed to know?"

"I'm sorry I yelled, Martin."

"Don't be standing here apologizing to us," Mildred said. "You'd better go and smooth things over with your wife. Why don't you do something to make her laugh? That always works."

Mildred was right. I thought for a moment, and something brilliant occurred to me. I walked towards the hall closet, wondering if *they* were there. No, nothing. I then remembered where *they* were.

I entered the bedroom; Maria was getting into bed. She closed her eyes without saying a word to me. I opened my closet door. Sure enough, there *they* were, in a box on the floor.

I approached the bed with my arms behind me, hiding my prank. "Maria," I whispered, "are you awake?"

"Yes, Tony. What is it?"

"I have something for you," I said.

"What are you holding? What is it?"

"I want you to have these in case you need anything from the kitchen in the middle of the night." I handed Maria my ice skates.

Maria looked at me and laughed. Mission accomplished.

"Come here," she said. "Lie down and talk to me."

I dropped the skates and slid under the covers.

"I'm sorry I jumped down your throat, Tony. I've been feeling stressed lately."

"What's wrong?" I asked, stroking Maria's hair.

"Oh, it's work. Sometimes I wonder if I'm really cut out for psychiatry. I really doubt my expertise as a diagnostician sometimes—I don't know."

"Don't doubt yourself, honey. You're a wonderful psychiatrist." How would I know? I thought.

"I don't know, Tony. I used to be so good at reading people, but anymore, I'm full of doubt."

"Does any patient in particular have you stumped?"

"A lot of them have me stumped, but I guess it's my two o'clock that I'm worried about. I can't figure out if he's for real, or if he has a hidden agenda."

"What kind of hidden agenda could he have? You don't think he's really sick?"

"Oh, he's sick. But I don't know if he's a multiple personality or not. I suspect he's using me to testify at his upcoming divorce hearing."

"How?" I asked.

"Well, he claims he hasn't cheated on his wife, that one of his other personalities is the adulterer. He claims to have no conscious knowledge of the affair. My gut instinct tells me he's lying, but how do I really know? Who am I to say that someone is lying or telling the truth? I hate testifying; what if I'm wrong?"

"Well," I said, "what evidence do you have that indicates he might be lying?"

"None. It's just a feeling. That's the problem, my uncertainty. It's not just my two o'clock. My eleven o'clock has me stumped as well."

"Is she the list-maker?" I asked.

"No, she's a he. He claims he needs six months on land and six at sea to feel whole."

"What's the problem? Tell him to get a boat."

"He gets sea-sick," Maria replied. "How do I possibly respond to that?"

"I don't know, but I'm sure you'll figure it out; you always do."

"I guess you're right, Tony. Anyhow, I'm sorry I jumped at you before. I'm just uneasy about tomorrow."

"Maybe it's a scheduling problem," I said. "Has it ever occurred to you to stagger the really far-gone cases? You don't need them all showing up on the same day."

"You know, you're right. Maybe I am being too hard on myself. From now on, I'm going to have Marian schedule differently. I don't need this kind of pressure."

"See?" I said, "Things aren't so bad."

"Thanks, Tony. Would you turn off the bathroom light for me? I forgot to."

"Sure, doll," I said, pulling the covers back. I sprang out of bed and saw stars. "Oh my God," I yelled.

"Tony, what's the matter?"

"I cut my foot."

"What did you cut your foot on?"

"On the blade of the ice skate!" I had forgotten that I dropped the skates at the foot of the bed.

"You better put some peroxide on it while you're in the bathroom."

"I will," I replied, picking up the ice skates and limping to the bathroom.

My foot was throbbing, but sleep wouldn't be a problem. I could rest assured there were at least two other people in the world who were more screwed-up than I was. Make that three, counting my father, I thought.

I lay down, wondering if I could keep the secret until Valentine's Day—it was two and a half weeks away.

No problem, I thought. I was certain the insanity of my everyday affairs would keep me preoccupied. Why should the next two and a half weeks be any different than what I'd been used to?

Five

"You wanted to see me?" I asked, walking into Rich Cardile's office.

Rich was one of SuperSoft's top project managers. He headed *ThinkBig*, the artificial intelligence program my team had been working on.

"Yes, Tony. Have a seat. I'll be with you in a minute," Rich said, shuffling papers on his desk.

I had no idea why Rich had wanted to see me, but the mood in the room suggested I wasn't there for another raise.

"Well," Rich began, "It's been brought to my attention that your work on *ThinkBig* is riddled with some serious design flaws."

"What are you talking about, Rich? Things are moving right along. I'm not aware of any glitches."

"Exactly, Tony. I don't know how to say this, so I'm going to be direct. That you are *unaware* of the glitches *is* the problem."

"What are you saying, Rich? Am I being kicked-off the project?" I asked nervously.

"Kicked-off is a strong phrase; you're not being kicked off. Upper management simply feels your talents would be better utilized in another position."

"Forgive me Rich, but aren't you upper management?"

"Right, Tony. Look, you don't have to take it so personally. We've tried to give you slack, thinking you were having personal problems. The truth is, we can't ignore the situation any longer. SuperSoft has the reputation of being number one, and we don't intend to become a runner-up because of incompetence in our staff. It's not good business."

"What are these glitches you're referring to? You owe me the opportunity to correct them," I said defensively.

"The problem is, you're teaching the computer to think just like yourself. And I'm sorry, but your thinking is seriously flawed."

"What are you talking about, Rich? My thinking is not flawed!"

"Initially, we didn't think so either, but I think we were in denial. We had a false sense of confidence in you because you seemed to come from such good stock." Rich looked away.

"Good stock?"

"You know, your grandfather a noted mathematician, your brother one of the most respected physicists at Princeton. It was a natural assumption that maybe you had a lot going on upstairs too. But you know what they say about assuming," Rich said nonchalantly.

"I can't believe this! I've been working like mad on *ThinkBig*!"

"*Exactly*, Tony. And your program thinks like a madman. I've never seen anything like it! How a computer could become so psychotic so quickly is beyond me. But you know what upper-management says," Rich chuckled.

"What does upper-management say?!" I demanded.

"The mind of a computer is only as good as the mind that programs it; I regret to inform you that your computer has lost its mind. They had to take it away this morning."

"Take it where?"

"To the funny farm."

"To a psychiatric hospital?" I asked, dumbfounded.

"Oh, come on, Tony. The funny farm is a slang term for the basement. They took your computer there to disassemble it for parts. Psychiatric hospital? Have you gone off the deep end?" Rich spoke cold-heartedly.

I sat there in disbelief. I had devoted my whole professional life to SuperSoft, and they were sending me to the basement. There went my hope of upward mobility.

"So, Rich, what are you saying? Am I being let go?"

"No, Tony. We're not that stupid. We realize you'd slap us with a lawsuit and waste years of our time in litigation. We don't have time to waste; we have robots to design. We won't allow a madman to put us behind in the market," Rich said. "We're prepared to cut you a deal, but it would mean re-locating to Philadelphia."

"Philadelphia?"

"Yes, Tony. You know, that city in Pennsylvania where you grew up. Does liberty ring a bell?"

"For God's sake, Larry, I know where Philadelphia is. SuperSoft doesn't have a division in Philadelphia."

"I wasn't referring to SuperSoft Software. We own a small company in Northeast Philadelphia, SuperSoft Pretzels. There's a job open in twisting, and we're offering you the position," Rich said. "We know how skilled you are at twisting things, and we think you're perfect for the job."

"Twisting?" What the hell was Rich talking about?

"Don't sweat it, pretzels aren't twisted by hand anymore. A machine does it, but don't worry, it's pre-programmed. Anybody with half a brain could do it. What do you say?" Larry asked.

"I say you're nuts! I can't believe you'd even consider shipping me off to Philadelphia to twist pretzels—I'm a god-damned software engineer!"

"You don't have to take the Lord's name in vain, Tony. You're beginning to sound just like your father."

"You've never even met my father!" I yelled.

"Yes we have, Tony. We consulted him last year when your work began slipping."

"What?" I couldn't believe him.

"Our meeting was very eye-opening. It made us realize what we could be looking at in twenty-five years. We all voted not to go there."

"I guess the transfer will mean a drop in salary?" I asked sarcastically.

"Now you are being ridiculous, Tony. Did you honestly think we would pay you $112K to twist pretzels for a year? What do you take us for?"

"You're the crazy one, not me! And, I am *NOT* turning into my father! I am nothing like him; this whole company is nuts! Why don't the rest of you go to Philadelphia, and I'll stay here and turn the company around?"

"You sound like your father to me," Larry said. "Look, it's your choice—take the twisting job or end up spinning globes like your old man. Twisting or spinning. You choose."

I had turned into my father. I began to hear a musical accompaniment to my ordeal: "Dizzy…I'm so dizzy my head is spinning…like a whirlpool in the sky." What would happen next, would I start singing *too*? "Please, Dear God, don't let it happen to me too," I prayed.

I must have been dizzy—I awoke on the floor. I couldn't believe it; I'd never fallen out of bed before. Despite my fear of having suffered head trauma, I felt good. It *was* just a dream, but it seemed so damned *real.*

I looked at the clock: 6:30 a.m., February fourteenth. It was Valentine's Day. I anticipated two things that morning: the unveiling of Maria's gift and the subjection of my father. Perhaps my dream had been my subconscious punishing me in advance for what I was about to subject it to?

I was glad it was Sunday; there was no way I could have gone into work and faced Rich after that dream. Oh my God, I thought, what if it had been a precognitive dream? What if it had been a dress rehearsal for my imminent reality? I was crazy for having thought that; I had received a raise not long before.

I wondered where Maria was; the apartment was awfully quiet. I walked into the living room. "Maria?" I yelled.

There was no answer. I walked into the kitchen; there was a note on the table: "Tony. Went to get bagels. Me."

Good, I thought. I'd have a few minutes to compose myself before my psychiatrist (I meant my wife) returned. I decided to take a quick shower and headed for the bathroom.

While showering, I rehashed my crazy dream. One's mind could certainly create scary things. But wasn't I my mind? Was I scary? I thought some cold water might shock me to sanity, so I adjusted the water temperature. There, that was better. I was starting to think more clearly. Of course I wasn't scary. Those constructs were my pressure valves opening; everyone needed to let off some steam. My dream had been just a mental fart. My confidence slowly trickled back into my psyche.

I tilted my head back to rinse my hair. As I did, I saw a spider on the ceiling. Having been reminded of my duct-tape incident, my psyche shattered. My confidence was sucked down the drain along with the few pieces of sanity that had been clinging desperately to the inside of my skull. I turned off the water so I didn't lose it all.

I dried myself, keeping a watchful eye on the ceiling. I couldn't bear imagining how a spider could slide around on my wet body; I wasn't going to be his amusement park! I vacated before the spider could jump.

While dressing, I heard Maria return. "I'm in here!" I yelled.

Maria entered the bedroom. "Good Morning, Tony. Happy Valentine's Day!" she said, walking over to kiss me.

"Happy Valentine's Day, Maria," I said, kissing her back. "I thought you were going to sleep in this morning?"

"I was, but I awoke early and couldn't get back to sleep. I decided to get bagels and make us a nice breakfast," Maria said. "I thought we'd eat, then exchange gifts."

"Sounds great," I said. "I'll be right there."

"Do you want butter or cream-cheese?" Maria asked.

"We have both?" I asked, surprised. After a few seconds of deliberation, I responded: "Cream cheese, please."

"Would you repeat that twenty times rapidly?" Maria asked.

"What?"

"Never mind," Maria said, leaving the bedroom.

I finished dressing and knelt by the bed. While on my knees, I prayed: "Please, God, let Maria perceive the couple in the painting to be our nineteenth-century counterparts." I slid the pizza box from under the bed and opened it. Removing Maria's gift, I noticed the wrapping appeared rumpled; I hadn't noticed that at the gallery. So what, I thought. What was under the wrapping was all that mattered. Still, skinny-tie had a lot of nerve, using recycled paper. He was jealous and cheap.

I walked proudly into the living room with my well-chosen gift. There was a large box sitting on the sofa, wrapped in cupid paper. I wondered what it was. I laid my gift on the sofa and walked into the kitchen.

"Here you go, Tony," Maria said, handing me my plate.

"What is this?" I asked, looking strangely at my breakfast.

"It's a bagel," Maria said, "but they twisted it into a pretzel shape for people who like crust. I knew you'd like it. See, I do think of you."

What was God doing to me? Why did the strange elements of my dreams always surface in my waking consciousness? Maybe God was giving me a sign that my nightmare was precognitive. Perhaps Rich and the ThinkBig staff were riding the elevator at that very moment, escorting my computer to the basement.

What was I thinking? It was Sunday—Rich was probably skiing.

"What?" Maria asked. "You don't like it? I thought you loved crust?"

"I do," I said. "I was silently saying grace."

"That's nice," Maria said, sitting down across from me. "I didn't know you loved crust that much."

I took a bite of my mutated bagel and tried to swallow it without choking.

"I forgot to tell you," Maria said. "Aunt Vicky called after you went to bed last night."

"Really? What's up?"

"Well, I think she needed to talk to someone. She and Uncle Harry are having problems. I can't tell you more than that, because she was seeking advice as a patient. However, I can tell you that Uncle Harry's been working night and day on a business deal. He wants to create a recycling business."

"Recycling what?"

"Styrofoam peanuts," Maria said. "I think he may be on to something; after all, Styrofoam isn't biodegradable. He wants to establish a center where he can receive peanuts from retail businesses and re-route them to manufacturers, so they don't wind up in landfills."

"I remember Uncle Harry discussing it with Dad at Christmas, but my father just blew him off. I remember thinking the idea had possibilities; it makes a lot of sense to me," I said.

"Of course it does," Maria said. "Why dump all that Styrofoam in landfills only to have to produce a new supply? Uncle Harry's idea will be a wake-up call to big business; he's definitely on to something."

"I wonder if he can raise the starting capital?" I asked.

"That's the problem," Maria said. "He's having a hard time securing the money, but Aunt Vicky said he's determined to find the resources."

"I think that's great," I said. "It's about time Uncle Harry's luck turned. It must be a blow to his ego to be a stock boy at his age."

"That's the funny thing," Maria said. "Had he not been a stock boy, he'd never have come up with the idea. Maybe it's destiny, Uncle Harry being exactly where he was meant to be. Talk about climbing out of a hole!"

Maybe there was a message in the story for me. Maybe it wouldn't be so bad if I wound up in a pretzel factory. Perhaps it could be a springboard to something revolutionary, too. I picked up my bagel and turned it over to study its engineering. I could do this, I thought. It would be a step down, but look at Uncle Harry; he had to pay his dues. What was I talking about? I hadn't really been fired. It was a dream.

"Did I toast your bagel too darkly?" Maria asked. "You're looking at it strangely."

"No," I said. "I was just admiring the ingenuity of its design."

Maria didn't understand; she offered me more coffee to blow it off. She filled my cup, looking toward the living room. "Let's finish eating so we can open the gifts—I'm dying for you to see yours."

"And I'm dying for you to see yours," I repeated.

We finished eating. Approaching the living room, I experienced another episode of doubt. Would Maria see the resemblance, or was my judgment seriously impaired? The torture was about to end; why did I inflict those things upon myself?

"I want you to go first," Maria said, passing the cupid-covered box.

"I wonder what this is," I said, shaking the box to guess its contents. I suddenly heard music emanating from it. I shook the box again, not recognizing the tune. On the third shake, I heard a voice speaking to me: "Danger! Danger! Danger!"

"Oh c'mon, Tony. Stop shaking the box and just open it," Maria said.

"I'm sorry. I didn't expect to hear voices." Perplexed, I opened the box and began laughing. It was the robot from *Lost in Space*. "Where did you ever find it? I love it."

"I found it on the Internet. The control panel is on the side," Maria said, pointing. "It even plays the theme song."

That explained my hearing the theme song to *Lost in Space* back in January; at the time, I'd thought I was losing it. I hadn't been; Maria was playing with my gift.

"You've had it all this time and kept it a secret?" I asked.

"What do you mean, all this time?" Maria asked. "It just arrived on Friday. I was nervous, wondering if it would get here in time."

I had been right the first time: I was losing it. My anticipation of the imminent *unveiling*, however, distracted me from exploring that self-deprecating tangent. I handed Maria her gift. Finally, the moment I'd been waiting for.

"Thank you, honey," Maria said, unwrapping the gift. I began to hear the accompaniment of a drum-roller. Will she or won't she, I thought nervously. She removed the last of the wrapping; the truth was finally out.

Why was Maria wearing such a puzzled expression? She didn't see the resemblance. She didn't like it.

"What's the matter?" I asked. "You don't like it?"

"I love it," Maria said. "I was just wondering why they don't have any faces."

"What?" I yelled.

Maria turned the painting so I could see it. Sure enough, the identities of our nineteenth-century counterparts had been washed away. What the hell had happened? They had faces when I bought it, didn't they? Had I imagined seeing our faces in those two blobs of dripping watercolor? No. I wasn't that creative, was I? I was dumbfounded.

"Maybe it's some new genre," Maria said. "Perhaps part abstract expressionism and part realism? Yeah, that must be it. Or maybe it's a spin-off of *The Scream*?"

I felt like screaming, but I didn't. I was going to get to the bottom of it. No wonder it had been on sale; skinny-tie knew he was selling me a defective painting! I'd been taken for seventeen hundred dollars—I'd show skinny-tie what non-returnable meant! Who was he, ruining my Valentine's Day?

"No, Maria," I said. "It's not some new genre—that couple had faces when I bought the painting. There's something defective about it. Their faces *were* perfectly detailed; in fact, they looked just like us! That was the reason I'd bought it. The artist must have used defective paint; no wonder it was on sale."

"I've heard of disappearing ink, but never disappearing watercolor. But at least you didn't pay full price," Maria said, studying the painting. "Actually, Tony, their faces haven't disappeared—it's more as if they were washed away. As though the artist painted the faces and then dropped water on them to create the illusion of their melting. See what I mean?"

"I see what you mean, but I swear, they had faces when I bought it. The artist had nothing to do with washing their faces." I was totally disgusted. I'd waited three weeks for that day, and our counterparts masqueraded in disguise. Suddenly, I felt a rumbling in my intestines; aggravation had sent my *pretzel* through my digestive tract with lightning speed.

"Where are you going?" Maria asked, as I arose and headed toward the bathroom.

"I've gotta go!" I yelled, running. The urgency of my intestinal dance put a spring in my step.

As I sat on the toilet, my bowels stopped quivering; it had been a false alarm. What was God doing to me? I looked up. There was a spider on the ceiling again. Would I ever be able to see a spider again without it triggering self-disgust? Why were we paying a fee for extermination, anyhow? I was going to call maintenance as soon as I got off the toilet; I wasn't going to put up with that bullshit any longer.

I washed my hands and returned to the living room. I was about to call maintenance when Maria spoke.

"Tony, I think I know what happened to the painting."

"What do you mean?"

"Sit down," Maria said. "I hadn't told you this, but I found the pizza box under the bed a few weeks ago."

"You were snooping?" I asked accusingly.

"I wasn't snooping," Maria said defensively. "I was getting ready for work one morning, and I dropped my earring, that big silver hoop. Anyhow, it went rolling under the bed like a wheel; I bent down to retrieve it, and saw the pizza box under the bed. I opened it, expecting to find a decayed anchovy-pizza, but instead saw the elegant hearts. I put two and two together and realized that buy one, get one free was just a scam to sneak my gift into the house."

"Did they have faces when you found it under the bed?"

"I didn't unwrap it," Maria said. "What do you take me for? I closed the pizza box and slid it back under the bed. I didn't want to ruin your surprise, especially after the production you had staged."

"It was pretty clever, wasn't it?" I asked proudly.

"Yes it was, Tony. But unfortunately you ruined the painting in the process."

"What are you talking about?"

"Well," Maria explained, "you carried a hot pizza on top of the painting on the way home. The heat caused condensation to form on the inside of the glass. You then put it into the freezer and the condensation froze. When you finally put it under the bed, the condensation defrosted and washed away the faces of those two figures. It was simple physics, water freezing and then melting again."

"And by some twist of fate the condensation had to fall on their faces?" I then imagined our nineteenth-century counterparts screaming under our bed as they endured Chinese water-torture. "Why couldn't the condensation have dripped onto the garden below? Those roses under the balcony could have used a good watering."

"It's just a matter of probability," Maria said. "The probability that the garden would have been watered was there, but once that first drop fell, the wave-function collapsed and there was no turning back. It was fate. I don't know why the first drop fell where it did."

Just what I needed, another physics lesson. "All I know is that the couple looked like us until they were smacked in the face with that wave."

"Come on, Tony. It's no big deal."

"Yes it is," I said. "It was a total waste of money."

"It's not as if it was a thousand-dollar mistake. So we're out a few hundred dollars, it's no big deal. Besides, it's interesting just the way it is. I love it."

I wondered if seventeen qualified as a *few*? I had to intercept the next credit-card statement, so Maria wouldn't discover how big of a mistake it had really been.

"If you don't mind, Tony, I'm going to take a nap. You did an awfully lot of tossing and turning last night," Maria said. "Do you remember sitting up in bed and talking about the Liberty Bell?"

"No, I don't remember, and I'm sorry to have disturbed you. But you're smart to take a nap; if this morning is any indication, we're in for one hell of an evening at Margaret's."

"Oh, Tony, don't be so pessimistic. Just ignore your father—who knows? Maybe he'll even apologize for the heroin misunderstanding. You never know."

Poor Maria, gypped of a Valentine's gift and an equal partner in marriage. She deserved better that me; I couldn't even pull off a surprise without physics backfiring on me. "Have a nice nap," I said, as Maria left the room.

I intended to go into the office and write in my journal, but I remembered I had a phone call to make. I sat on the sofa and dialed downstairs. It rang.

"Hello," I said. " This is Tony Vitello in 818. I'd like to report that we're having some…" I went to cross my legs and accidentally kicked the robot. "Danger!" the robot finished my sentence.

"What type of danger?" the woman asked. "You've reached the answering service, but if it's an emergency, I can have someone paged."

"No, we're not in any danger, " I said. "That was our toy robot talking. We're having a spider problem and I'd like to schedule someone to come up and spray."

"You'll have to call back tomorrow, Mr. Vitello," the woman said. "Maintenance takes only emergency calls on Sunday."

"All right," I said. "I'll call back tomorrow." I hung up the phone and headed for the office.

I began moving the bookcase to retrieve my purple notebook. I couldn't believe I had to go to such lengths to assure my privacy. Were my thoughts really so disturbed that I had to hide them behind a whole bookcase of psychiatric journals? What was I thinking? Those textbooks were so heavy that Maria would never be able to move the bookcase herself; my purple notebook would be safe. That's what I'd been thinking.

If Maria ever found my purple notebook, she would have me locked-up. Wouldn't she feel compelled to go public with her findings, for the sake of the advancement of science? Not to mention what it could do for her career; maybe she would get to name a new mental illness after me.

I opened my notebook and wrote the date. "Dear Mildred and Martin," I wrote, summoning them. "I need your help."

"How long are you going to dwell on that stupid painting?" Mildred wrote back. "That's all we've been hearing for weeks. You're beginning to sound like a broken record; don't you hear yourself?"

"But, things like that…"

Martin interrupted my writing, grabbing my pen. "But nothing—get over it! Besides, it's one hell of a conversation piece. Maria said she loved it. Why don't you get over it and get on with things?" he wrote.

"All right," I wrote. "You don't have to refer to me as if I was a numskull."

"Tony's right," Mildred wrote. "He isn't a numskull; he figured us out pretty quickly."

"What are you talking about, Mildred?" I wrote.

"You figured out how to keep us from barging in on you. You didn't like us showing up unexpectedly, so you discovered how to put a stop to it." Mildred finished the sentence with a big flourish.

"I don't understand," I printed legibly.

"Yes you do, Tony. You need to express your feelings, in one way or another. By writing in your journal, you keep Martin and myself in the pages of your book and out of your kitchen or the back seat of your car," Mildred wrote.

"You mean all I have to do to keep you guys from materializing is to write to you?" That time I made a flourish.

"Yes. When you vent on these pages, you don't need to vent everywhere else. Haven't you noticed that you've been writing every day and Martin hasn't been sneaking up on you?" Mildred wrote.

"Yes," I wrote, "I have noticed. Am I making a breakthrough?"

"What do you think?" Mildred wrote back.

"I think I am. What a break; I couldn't even go to the bathroom without Martin driving me crazy," I wrote.

"You drive yourself crazy!!!" Martin wrote back. The three exclamation points were his.

"I do not," I wrote, underlining not.

"You keep forgetting that we don't even exist; how can you blame us for anything?" Martin scribbled.

"Shut-up, Martin," Mildred wrote. "You never know when to stop."

"It's always me!" Martin wrote. "How come you get to call all the shots around here? I'm just as much Tony's construct as you are."

"See what I have to live with?" Mildred wrote. "Anyhow, Tony, just remember what I said, vent in your journal. Sooner or later Maria was bound to catch you talking to thin air; then she'd be nagging you for talking to yourself."

"Why are you telling him that, Mildred?! If Tony writes every day, we'll never get out of these god-forsaken pages. I'll be forced to bust out of here," Martin wrote threateningly.

"Can he do that?" I wrote to Mildred, not in my best handwriting. My hand was shaking at the thought of Martin having so much control.

"Don't listen to Martin," Mildred wrote. "He's just the rebellious side of your ego; he's all talk. Why don't you run along and take a nap with your wife? You'll need to be well-rested for tonight."

"Why?" I wrote. "What's going to happen tonight?"

"I don't know any more than you do," Mildred wrote. "Just go and take a nap. You look tired."

"All right, Mildred. Thanks," I wrote.

"What?" Martin wrote sharply. "Mildred gets all the credit? What about me?" Martin wrote harsh words about his being unappreciated and misunderstood. I was too tired to read his sob-story, so I closed the book on him.

I moved the bookcase from the wall and slid my journal behind it. When everything was neatly in place, I left the office and went to take a nap with Maria.

Maria was sound asleep. I too was weary, so I slid into bed next to her and fell into deep, dreamless sleep.

"Tony?" Maria whispered. "Are you awake?"

"Yeah, what time is it?"

"It's 2:30. We'd better get ready to go," she said. "I'm going to take a quick shower. I won't be long."

"Take your time," I said. "We don't have to leave for another hour; the traffic won't be heavy today."

"Tony, did you really like your present?"

"I loved it," I said. "I'm sorry about your gift."

"Nonsense. It will make a great conversation piece. Let's call it *Anonymity*."

"O.K.," I said, laughing. "*Anonymity* it is."

Maria left the room and I thought about that morning. What were the chances of finding an artist's rendering of Maria and myself, only to have our images disappear as though in the witness protection program? I decided to get over it. The outcome of the whole mess hadn't been that bad. If I could get through the evening at Margaret's, I'd be all right.

The traffic on the Turnpike was manageable: most of it was going the other way. While Maria drove, I thought about Margaret's pending salon. I was happy for her; she certainly worked hard enough at her craft. She deserved the luck that had come her way, but what an absurd settlement! I began pondering what incident had inspired the adage *blind luck*. How absurd could life possibly be?

I looked to make sure Maria was still there, then settled back in my seat for some *spacing-out*. I closed my eyes so Maria wouldn't know that I was thinking; if she thought I was asleep, there would be no interrogation later.

My mind drifted to the conversation I'd had with Margaret on Christmas. I'd misjudged her, and felt guilty. How could I think she was the same girl who had lost her ponytail at sea thirty years ago? Sure, she had been obsessed with her appearance, but what fourteen year-old girl wasn't? It was narrow-minded of me to believe that Margaret had not grown past that.

There was a double-whammy: I was guilty of judging Margaret even then, in 1969. I had assumed Margaret was using me as her personal reality consultant, when she was really reaching out for someone. How had I not seen that? What kind of jerk was I? Margaret reached out for me, and I gave her my hand for a manicure. And she had endured even more absurdity than I, having been the first-born.

What had I done to Margaret? Instead of answering her plea for help, I rehashed everything and made her re-live the nightmare. She gave me a weekly manicure, and got nothing in return. Actually, she had her nose rubbed in absurdity, and I was the one pushing her head down. What kind of brother had I been? What kind was I still?

That Margaret had survived her childhood relatively unscathed made me view her in a new light. There was more to her than the mask; I had never gone any deeper, because I was so shallow.

My revelation: I hadn't helped Margaret because I was locked in my own little world of preconceptions. In hindsight, I was guilty of the same crime that I'd accused my family of committing—obsession. My obsession had been the angst of trying to tie life into a neat little package, in the privacy of my own skull. It was still my obsession, after thirty years. Maybe there was no neat little package; maybe I was a dog chasing its own tail. There I was, the dog again.

I was making a breakthrough. I even felt ready to unbolt my head and throw a little honest feeling towards my psychiatrist. I meant my wife. I had failed my last attempt at honesty; Maria thought I was a nut-case for revealing my red-marker fantasy. But I was ready to try again.

I opened my eyes and looked at Maria.

"Did you have a nice nap?" She asked.

"Actually," I said, "I wasn't sleeping. I was thinking with my eyes closed." The truth hadn't killed me.

"Oh. What were you thinking about?"

"I was thinking about my relationship with Margaret." How bold was I, having been so forthright?

"How so?" Maria asked.

"I think I've misjudged her. For some reason, I could never get past the feeling that Margaret was forever fourteen. Sometimes I forget she's changed, or maybe she hasn't; maybe my perception of her was always too narrow," I said, guiltily.

Suddenly, I imagined the interior of our car to be a confessional; my visualization included a sliding dark window that separated the holy from the schmuck. The white collar peeking from Maria's sweater stuck out like a sore thumb.

"As if you were looking through blinders?" Maria asked.

"Yeah, as though my own obsessions clouded my perceptions. I don't think I've been fair to Margaret; to be honest, I hadn't thought there was much below the surface—as though the cucumber mask was all there was."

"Don't be too hard on yourself, Tony. It's a common problem when siblings grow up and move away from one another. You grow apart and think your sibling is the same person she was twenty years ago. You then discover you really don't know her at all, because you remember her in terms of your own childish judgments. It's nobody's fault. It just happens. A lot. I see it frequently in my patients; they blame themselves or their siblings, when no one is really at fault. You have to get past pinning blame and concentrate on the now, which is building a new relationship," Maria said, compassionately.

I couldn't believe what was transpiring: Maria was giving me free professional advice. All I had to do was be truthful about my feelings and risk sounding like a schmuck.

I needed to keep reminding myself that Maria and I shared the very same worst fear. We both feared that we were crazy; my fear was more pronounced, but she had an oxymoron to endure—she was a psychiatrist. We were both in the same boat. Why had I avoided the truth for so long? I wasn't sure.

I realized I was using the word *we* a lot, rather than *me*. I liked we.

"Maria?" I asked.

"Yeah, Tony?"

"There's something I've been wanting to tell you, but haven't had the guts."

"What is it?"

"Remember last month when we were driving to Philadelphia, on the way to my heroin intervention? We were talking about our families, and you mentioned that your worst fear was that you were just as crazy as the rest of your family," I said.

"I remember," Maria said defiantly. "You're not going to start with those Nazi accusations again, are you?"

"Oh no. What I wanted to say was, we have the very same worst fear. Sometimes I wonder if I'm just as crazy as the rest of my family, too. Only last month, I didn't have the guts to admit it."

"Really?" Maria asked. "I thought I was the only one thinking so crazy—you too?"

"Yes," I answered. "Sometimes I look at my father and fear I'll one day turn into him."

"Please don't," Maria begged. "You know, until last month I'd never really analyzed him. Because of my job, I turn off that part of myself when I leave the office. I'd always known your father was high-strung, but until that heroin thing, I hadn't realized how deep his problems went."

"What do you think his problem is?"

"I think Granny hit the nail on the head: at some point in his life, he lost hope. Once hope is gone, what else is left? He is so angry at himself that his anger naturally spills over and infects everyone else."

"I don't think there has ever been a question that Granny's been unable to answer," I noted.

"I know, Tony. You're lucky to have her; I'd give my right arm to have her as a mentor. I'm always tempted to call her when I'm stumped by a patient, but what would that say about me as a psychiatrist, always running to a lay person for advice?"

"You're a wonderful psychiatrist, Maria. Look at your practice."

"I know. But something is missing. Sometimes I wonder if I became a psychiatrist for the wrong reasons. I was trying so desperately to get an expert opinion of my family dysfunction; maybe I became an expert to get the full scoop. Is that sick?"

"No, it isn't sick," I replied. "I understand completely what it's like to attempt to make sense of nonsense."

"Thanks, Tony," Maria said. "Do you have two dollars for the bridge?"

"Here you go," I said, handing Maria the money.

We rode the rest of the way in silence; Maria pondering her issues, I pondering mine.

I learned two things of importance on the Turnpike that day: I had to come out of my head, and my marriage wouldn't survive unless I did. I had to summon the courage to face the truth; I could no longer hide behind the veil of silence. It was becoming impossible to live in my own skin.

"This must be it," Maria said, parking the car. "Twenty-four nineteen. It's a nice building, isn't it?"

"Yes."

"Tony?"

"Yes?"

"Don't worry about your father tonight. You have Granny and me to protect you."

"Do you have the mace?" I joked.

"One for each of us," Maria joked back.

"Have I told you lately how much I love you?" I asked.

"No, you haven't. I don't think either one of us has been saying that enough lately."

"That's going to change," I said, taking Maria's hand. She squeezed mine.

As we entered Margaret's building, it occurred to me that it was the best Valentine's Day I'd had in a long time. Not even my father could take that away from me.

"Hi Maria," Margaret said, kissing Maria on the cheek.

"I love the place," Maria said, walking in, scanning the room.

"Hi Tony. I'm so glad you guys could come." Margaret hugged me.

"Me too," I said, hugging Margaret back. "I love you, Margaret."

"I love you too, Tony." Margaret looked at me strangely. "Is everything all right?"

"Oh yeah. I'm just glad to see you."

"I'm glad to see you, too. Come in, I'll give you a tour. Jerry and Roberta are in the kitchen. Give me your coats."

Jerry and Roberta came to greet us. "Tony, big brother! How are you?" Jerry hugged me and said: "You remember Roberta."

"Of course. How have you been?"

"Fine," Roberta said. "It's nice to see you again."

"You're awfully brave to come to another of our family get-togethers. I apologize, I hope your Christmas wasn't too ruined by our father's little performance."

"Nonsense," Roberta said. "That was nothing compared to what I'm used to. Why do you think I didn't go home for Christmas?"

Oh my God—what was Roberta used to? "You too?" I asked.

"Yes. When Princeton offered me a professorship, I was on the next plane east. It was a no-brainer."

"Where are you from?"

"The Seattle area."

"That's a pretty good distance."

"Isn't it?"

Margaret walked into the room. "Are you guys ready for a tour?"

"Absolutely," we replied.

"Obviously," Margaret said, "this is the living room. What do you think of the dental molding?"

"I love it," I said. "And by the way, I can't believe your windfall; your woodwork may as well have been gold."

"I didn't believe it at first either," Margaret said. "In fact, I was pretty nervous when I was subpoenaed—thought they were going to charge me with grand larceny. I just about fell over when my landlord's attorney called and wanted to cut a deal."

"I wish it was that easy to get grant money," Jerry said. "And speaking of grant money, did you hear that someone from the EPA has been talking to Uncle Harry?"

"No," I said. "How did the EPA discover Uncle Harry's idea?"

"Apparently one of the loan officers at his bank has a relative who works for the EPA. The relative thought Uncle Harry's idea was genius, and forwarded his business plan to Washington," Jerry said.

"It looks like there are going to be two new businesses in the family," Margaret said.

I asked no further questions; I'd talk to Uncle Harry when he arrived. It was Margaret's night, and she deserved a solo spot in the limelight.

"I can't believe the fireplace mantel," I said to Margaret.

"Isn't it gorgeous?" Margaret asked. "Come into the dining room—wait till you see the built-in cabinetry."

We followed Margaret into the dining room.

"Margaret," Roberta said, "I love your dining room set; the color is wonderful."

"Thanks, Roberta. I bought it second-hand. It was an awful mustard color, so Ivan painted it for me. It's called French blue."

"I love it too," Maria said.

"Ivan just finished it a few days ago, but don't worry, it's dry enough to sit on. The kitchen is this way."

In the kitchen, Roberta noticed four tiny bowls in the corner. "Have a cat?" she asked.

"Four," Margaret said. "They're hiding now, but they'll come around once they get used to the noise."

Margaret turned to Jerry. "Would you show Tony and Maria the rest of the apartment? I have appetizers to put in the oven."

"Right this way," Jerry said. While following Jerry, I noticed his ponytail was even longer than it had been at Christmas.

"I see you still haven't found time for a haircut," I joked. "The old man will have a fit when he sees you."

"He'll have to get over it," Jerry said matter-of-factly.

"I like it," Maria said.

"See?" Jerry said. "Maybe you should cancel your next haircut. Can you imagine the look on big Anthony's face if he walked in and saw both of us with ponytails? Oh, and by the way, I'd have loved to have been a fly on the wall during your drug-bust."

"Can you believe it?" I asked. "But it had a good outcome—big Anthony was so disappointed I wasn't a junkie, he refused to go to D.C. with us!" I made the gesture of wiping sweat from my brow.

We followed Jerry down the hall. "This is Margaret's room," Jerry said. "Beautiful light fixture, isn't it? Oh, there's Pageboy!" Margaret's long-haired cat scurried quickly by and ran into the next room.

We followed him. "This is the guest room," Jerry said. "Would you like to make a reservation? Bouffant will be checking out tomorrow." Margaret's cat Bouffant was lying on the bed, his head resting comfortably on the pillow.

"You're so funny," Roberta said to Jerry, hugging his arm. What was that, a budding romance?

We continued down the hall. "Last but not least, the bathroom," Jerry said.

"Look how big!" Maria said. "And a footed tub like Granny's! I wish we had a footed tub."

The bathroom was big. It had to be, to house Margaret's arsenal of toiletries, God love her! I had meant that with affection, hadn't I?

"Can you imagine?" Jerry said. "Twelve-foot ceilings in the bathroom? Must provide a hell of an echo while singing in the shower."

Roberta hugged Jerry's arm again.

Maria looked at me. "This would never work for us," she said, laughing. "We need a drop-ceiling."

What? Had everyone turned into a comedian?

It had been pretty funny; I was then hugging Maria's arm.

"Private joke?" Jerry asked.

"Yeah," I said, as we returned to the living room. Aunt Vicky, Uncle Harry, and Granny were arriving.

I approached Granny. "Tony, my love, I'm so happy to see you,' she said, hugging me. She then whispered: "I'm glad you've managed to come clean," and winked. We both laughed.

"Tony, how the hell are you?" Uncle Harry asked, shaking my hand with authority. I supposed that the meek, unsure character was gone forever.

"I'm just great," I answered. For once, I wasn't lying. I did feel good; Maria had found my earlier honesty endearing. Her joking about the ceiling was my omen that life was on the upswing. We were growing closer, weren't we?

"Hi Aunt Vicky," I said, my aunt approaching me. The natural-born liar continued: "You may not want to kiss me, I'm coming down with a bit of a sore throat." It was just a little white lie. No harm had been done.

"Oh, you poor thing," Aunt Vicky said, hugging me. "Why don't you go in the bathroom and gargle with salt water? Margaret could mix some for you."

"No," I said. "I'm all right; I just didn't want to give you my germs."

"So thoughtful," Aunt Vicky said, shaking her head solemnly. "You've always been such a thoughtful boy."

"How's Tommy?" I asked. I needed to get off the subject of my virtue; I had just lied.

"Oh, he's doing wonderfully. Had a little tendonitis, but he's better now. He'll be in New York the month of April; you two should get together."

"That would be nice. Tell him to call me when he arrives in New York."

"I certainly will. Excuse me, dear, I want to give Margaret a hand."

Margaret was passing a tray of appetizers. "Honey," Aunt Vicky said, "How can I help you?"

"Thanks, Aunt Vicky. Why don't you get everyone a drink?"

Everyone gave Aunt Vicky their drink order, and she disappeared into the kitchen.

I walked over to Granny. "I've missed you," I said.

"I've missed you, too. How was your trip to D.C.? Did you have a good time?"

"Yes. Once I got over the shock of my alleged drug bust! Can you believe that?"

"I heard. Margaret told me the whole story; you must have been beside yourself."

Margaret interrupted our conversation. "How about a snack?"

"Thanks," I said, taking one. "What are they?"

"They're miniature crab quiches. Take two napkins, they're messy." Margaret handed me three napkins by mistake.

Margaret moved on, and Granny and I continued our conversation.

"So anyhow, Gran, I couldn't believe it," I said, biting into the crab quiche. "Boy, these are good, aren't they?"

"Delicious," Granny said. "Don't worry about your father, he'll get over it."

"I just don't get him."

"Look at it this way: your father is on a different wavelength than the rest of us. We're all watching A&E, and he's watching some low-budget talk show on the lowest tier of cable service. He just doesn't have the wiring to go to a higher tier."

What a great analogy, I thought. Of course, I had to take it one step further. "I'm sure Jerry and I could come up with some kind of auxiliary box for Dad; we'll have Maria wire it into his brain."

"Oh, Tony, you're bad!" Granny said. "But you're right, re-programming is probably just what he needs."

Granny was interrupted by Aunt Vicky. "Here's your Merlot, Mom," she said. Granny took her glass and Aunt Vicky turned to me. "And Tony, this is…"

Aunt Vicky didn't finish her sentence, distracted by the yelling in progress at the front door: "Will you forget about it, Leona? It's over!"

Big Anthony had arrived.

I looked at Granny. "See what I mean?"

"Don't be making yourself sick over it; just ignore him. These crab quiches are awfully salty, aren't they?"

"Yeah," I replied, going for a big swig of lemonade. Why was it so warm? I had been half-way into a big gulp when I began gagging, and heaved into my lemonade glass. There was no holding back: I gagged again and emptied my stomach contents into the glass. While grateful that Margaret had given me three napkins, I was never so humiliated in my life.

"Looks like you've got a floater," Jerry said.

"Oh Lord, are you all right?" Granny asked.

Aunt Vicky approached. "Tony, what the hell are you doing? You didn't drink that, did you?"

"What was it?" Granny asked.

"It was warm salt water," Aunt Vicky replied.

"I asked for lemonade," I said, cloaking my glass with a napkin.

"I know, but I thought you should gargle first. I was about to tell you to go and gargle when Anthony entered the front door screaming," Aunt Vicky said.

"I was not screaming," my father yelled, grimacing. "Leona and I were simply having a disagreement."

"Excuse me," I said, running toward the bathroom.

"I'll go and check on him," Maria said, following me.

We closed the bathroom door. I emptied my glass into the toilet and looked at Maria.

"Tony, what just happened? Why did Aunt Vicky give you salt water to drink?"

"It's my own fault. When she went to kiss me, I told her not to because I was getting a sore throat."

"You have a sore throat?"

"No," I said. "I lied. After the lipstick incident on Christmas, I wanted to stay out of the line of fire."

"Oh God!" Maria yelled, and began laughing. "I thought your father's entrance had induced a sudden bout of projectile vomiting!"

We were both laughing hysterically. As Jerry had earlier predicted, the acoustics in the bathroom were that of an echo chamber. Our laughter bounced from one wall to another, amplified to a roar that was broadcast to the living room.

"Maria, stop it! They're going to hear us!"

"I'm sorry," Maria said, trying to contain herself. "That was so damned funny. I can't help it."

"I'm glad you find humor in my physical trauma," I laughed. "Look at me. I have vomit on my shirt. Now what am I going to do?"

"Maybe Margaret has a T-shirt you can borrow. As soon as I compose myself, I'll go and ask her."

"I guess they were salt-water crab quiches," I joked, rinsing my mouth.

We both began laughing hysterically again.

"Tony, stop it! You're going to make me wet myself!"

"Nonsense," I said, pointing to the toilet. "Have a seat."

We continued laughing. "Here," I said, handing Maria a tissue. "Your mascara is running."

"Oh boy," Maria said, wiping her eyes. "I haven't laughed that hard in a long time."

"Me neither. Now do you believe me? My life is a comedy of errors."

"I believe you," Maria said, moving closer to me. "Why don't we sneak out of here a little early tonight?"

"How about now?" I asked. I began to kiss Maria. "We could say I wasn't feeling well. They'd believe that; I have the vomit on my shirt to prove it."

Maria kissed me back. "We have to stay for dinner. We don't want to hurt Margaret. We'll leave right after dinner."

"Stop talking," I said. "I'm trying to kiss you."

The most passionate kiss that we had shared in months was interrupted by the bathroom door swinging open. "Would you two like to use the guest room?" Margaret asked. "No wonder you didn't hear me knocking. I just wanted to see if you were all right."

"Yeah, we're all right," I replied. "Do you have an old T-shirt I could borrow? I'm wearing your crab quiche."

"You know what? Ivan left a sweatsuit here the other day. I'll get the top for you."

Maria looked at me. "I'll go and get the situation under control."

"Thanks, honey. I'll be out in a minute."

Margaret returned and handed me Ivan's sweatshirt. "Lucky you and Ivan are the same size," she said.

"Thanks," I said, as she left the room.

I changed my shirt, took a deep breath, and returned to the living room.

"Honey, do you feel better?" Mom asked. "You look a little pale."

"Oh, I'm…" I remembered that Maria and I wanted to make an early exit, so I changed my tune: "still feeling a little nauseous." Would another white lie backfire on me?

"Well, take it easy," Mom said.

"See what you did to the poor thing?" Uncle Harry said to Aunt Vicky.

"I was only trying to help him. It was Anthony's fault; he distracted me!"

"Don't blame me," my father yelled. "You were the one who gave him the salt water."

My mother spoke. "Anthony, will you please be quiet and sit down?" Everyone except my father had taken a seat in the living room. He was standing by the mantel.

"I'd rather stand, thank you. I don't want to be wreaking of cat for the next week and a half."

"Don't be ridiculous, Anthony," my mother said. "Margaret's furniture does not smell of cat; they're not even allowed on the furniture."

"They're not?" my father yelled. "Then what is that big fluffy one doing in the bedroom? He looked tucked-in to me." Dad was referring to Bouffant, who was resting amidst the fine linens of Margaret's guest bed.

"Oh, Anthony, don't cause a scene. Will you please come and sit down? We're here to celebrate your daughter's success; it won't kill you to sit down with the rest of us."

In a history-making moment, my father reluctantly did what he was told. He had not sat, however, without mumbling two or three obscenities under his breath.

We began talking about the weather, for lack of anything in common.

"Yes," Roberta said, "it's been an unseasonably mild winter, but it was expected, with El Nino."

"I think El Nino is just a bunch of crap," my father said. "The weather in Chile has nothing to do with the weather in Philadelphia—it's four-thousand friggin miles away! Those god-damned weathermen are just groping for excuses for their bad predictions." My father got that off his chest, along with three or four cat hairs he had intently picked from his shirt.

"You'll have to excuse my father, Roberta," Jerry said. "He didn't mean to be insulting. Did you, Dad?"

"What? Is someone in your family a weatherman? I'm sorry, it was nothing personal, Roberta." Dad moved on to pick cat hair from his pant-legs.

"No harm done," Roberta said. She smiled at the rest of us; I swear her teeth were clenched.

We were saved by the dinner bell. "Come on out, everyone," Margaret yelled from the dining room. "Dinner's ready!"

For a split second I imagined everyone making a mad dash to escape my father's ignorance: a crowd gone unruly, people getting trampled. We were, however, quite civil in our exodus.

We entered the dining room and took our seats. "There are three different kinds of salad dressing," Margaret said, looking around. "Where's Dad?"

"He went to the bathroom to freshen up," Mom said. "We can start without him."

Freshening up, I thought. He was probably rooting in the bathroom for *Lysol* so he could fumigate his clothes. My father hated cats; he claimed they "stink the joint up." I imagined him spraying his butt and whatever other body part had made contact with Margaret's furniture.

"So, Margaret," Jerry asked, "have you found a location for your salon?"

"Yes, it's on the boulevard, not far from here. I sign the lease tomorrow."

"When will you open?" I asked.

"Early to mid-April," Margaret answered. "As soon as the plumbing is done."

"Did Margaret tell you I'll be setting up a counter in her salon?" Aunt Vicky asked everyone.

"No," we replied in unison, looking at Margaret. It was apparent that Margaret wasn't thrilled with the arrangement; her face couldn't lie. Margaret had dropped Aunt Vicky as her mentor a long time ago.

"Yeah," Aunt Vicky said, "I'm sure my sales will go through the roof once I start at Margaret's place."

"What about your teaching position?" Maria asked.

"I don't teach on Saturdays. And during the week, Margaret can keep an eye on it for me," Aunt Vicky said.

"Oh," Maria said.

Margaret rolled her eyes; my father entered the dining room and took his seat.

"I served you some salad, Anthony. What kind of dressing do you want?" Mom asked, sniffing like a bunny. "What's that smell? Are you wearing cologne, Anthony? You never wear cologne."

"No, I am not wearing cologne, Leona. Would you please pass the oil and vinegar?"

Mom passed the cruets and looked strangely at Dad. After forty-five years of marriage, my mother was fed-up. What had taken her so long?

"Well, Anthony," Uncle Harry said, "I have a proposition for you. How would you like to go into business together, equal partners?"

"Oh Harry, not that hair-brained Styrofoam idea—it's nuts! I'm not going to leave a promising career in globe manufacturing for a pipe-dream that's going to flop in one month's time. You're going to wind up on the streets! Thank you, but I don't care to join you."

"It is not going to flop!" Uncle Harry argued. "The Environmental Protection Agency seems to think it's a good idea; someone in Washington is trying to get me a grant as we speak. I quote: 'this could be the simplest answer ever to a most complex waste problem.' The government seems to have a lot of confidence in the idea."

"Then I don't have much confidence in the government. Count me out; the idea is the most lame excuse for a business that I've ever heard," my father growled.

Uncle Harry was mad. He arose from the table and began yelling at my father. "You know what I think, Anthony? I think you're jealous because it wasn't your idea. No idea is ever good enough unless it's yours! I think you're just too stuck in your ways!"

Big Anthony was enraged. He went to rise from his chair too, but nothing happened. He put a little more gusto into the effort, and finally managed to stand, though hunched over with the chair attached to his butt. He was standing, but at a ninety-degree angle.

"Anthony," my mother said, "why is the chair sticking to your ass?"

"How the hell should I know?" Dad said, carefully guiding the chair back to the floor. He then looked at Margaret. "What the hell is in that fabric spray of yours? It's like god-damned glue!"

"What fabric spray?" Margaret asked, perplexed.

"The fabric spray in the god-damned bathroom!"

"I don't have any fabric spray in the bathroom."

"Are you telling me I don't know how to god-damned read?! The bottle said fabric spray, to eliminate odors!"

"All right, Anthony," Mom said. "I'm sick to death of your cursing. Have you any idea how vile you sound? You've taken the Lord's name in vain eighty-seven times since you awoke this morning! Yes, eighty-seven! I've been counting! One more time, and you'll be going home alone tonight, *if* you can get out of that chair!"

Bravo! Mom told him! The tides were turning: my father would drown in the floodwaters of his own hysteria. Mildred and Martin hadn't told me my father would go down glued to a chair.

Margaret returned to the dining room. "Is this what you sprayed yourself with?"

"Yes, read it! What does it say?"

"It isn't fabric spray," Margaret said. "It's hair spray. I took the empty bottle to work and filled it from the drum. Why should I pay retail?"

"Well, why the (pause) didn't you label the (pause) bottle properly?" Dad asked. His self-censored outburst sounded like a car backfiring. I guessed he didn't want to go home alone. You had to give him credit for the effort, however comical.

"Why?" Margaret asked. "I knew it was hair spray. How was I to know you'd be rooting through my stuff?"

"I was not rooting! It was sitting on the (pause) shelf in (pause) plain-view," Dad sputtered. "Leona, help me. Try to yank my pant leg back there. How the (pause) did this happen?"

"Well, Dad," Jerry said, "It looks like a rare bonding between paint that hasn't fully cured and the spray adhesive on your pants. Was the hair spray super-hold, Margaret?"

"Yes, I'm afraid it was."

"So when did you win the (pause), oh, forget it!" Dad yelled. "You mean to tell me that you have us sitting on wet (pause) paint, Margaret?"

"The chairs aren't wet," Margaret said. "Nobody else is stuck to their seat."

"Jerry, help me. Try to pull me out of the chair."

Jerry, like myself, always had to take things one step further. He acted as if he was about to get up and help big Anthony, but that he too was stuck in his chair. Everyone roared.

"That's real funny!" Dad yelled. "Are you going to help me or not?"

"Of course I am." Jerry arose with exaggerated ease and stood next to Dad. "O.K., on the count of three I'm going to lift you under the arms; don't fight me," Jerry laughed.

Nothing happened on the count of three. Obviously the bond was permanent.

"I have an idea," Margaret said. "I'll get a spatula."

Margaret returned with a spatula and began working on Dad.

"Ouch! Watch my (pause) leg," Dad said.

"I'm sorry," Margaret said, looking towards Jerry. "Nail polish remover?"

"No," Jerry said. "He might get some nasty chemical burns."

"But I use nail-polish remover on people's fingers."

"Not mixed with hair spray and partially-cured paint. I think it would be too risky."

Everyone took Jerry's word for it. After all, he was a Professor of Physics, possibly a Nobel Laureate; still, I wondered if Jerry had purposely stymied Dad's freedom.

"What are we going to do?" Mom asked. "He can't sit in that chair forever."

Uncle Harry and the others were muffling their laughter.

Roberta came to the rescue. "Why not cut them off?"

"We can't cut off his legs," Mom said.

"What?!" Dad yelled.

"No, Mrs. Vitello," Roberta said. "I meant cut off his pants."

After a group discussion, we came to the conclusion that Roberta's suggestion was our only recourse. Margaret went to get her haircutting shears.

Margaret returned. "Do you want me to do it?" she asked.

"Somebody just do it!" Dad yelled.

Margaret began clipping. She started at the ankle and worked towards Dad's waist, moving along until she hit a problem area at his hip.

"Watch out!" Dad yelled. "You nipped me."

"I'm sorry!" Margaret replied. "You'll have to remove your belt—no sense in cutting through that."

Dad removed his belt and Margaret made the final snip. One leg was freed. With experience as her guide, Margaret released Dad's other leg with ease.

"There," Margaret said. "You're free."

"We've forgotten one thing," Dad said.

"What?"

"I have no pants to wear."

"No problem," Margaret said. "You can wear the other half of Ivan's sweatsuit." She looked at Dad and me. "I guess you guys are glad Ivan forgot his sweatsuit."

"I will not wear Ivan's sweat pants!" Dad said defiantly.

Of course he wouldn't. Dad wouldn't be caught dead in the pants of a homosexual, even if the homosexual wasn't in them. It was a matter of (pause) principle.

"It looks as if you don't have much choice," Mom said.

"The (pause) I don't," yelled Dad. "Jerry, give me your pants!"

"What? Why can't you just wear Ivan's? I'm not giving you my pants."

"Give me your god-damned pants!" big Anthony demanded.

"You think I was kidding, Anthony?" Mom yelled.

Apparently Jerry had a change of heart. Right there in the dining room, he removed his shoes and belt. With a quick motion of one hand, Jerry's pants fell to his ankles; he stood there in his boxer shorts for a moment before stepping out of his pants and speaking: "Here, Dad, take them."

"I didn't mean to take them off here! What are you, some kind of exhibitionist?" Dad yelled. He then looked at the rest of us. "Do you mind giving me some privacy?"

We again made our mass exodus. Once out of Dad's earshot, I looked at Jerry, who was waiting for Ivan's sweat pants. "What made you decide to give him your pants?" I asked.

"Call me crazy," Jerry said, "but I couldn't resist watching Dad try to pour his forty-inch waist into a pair of thirty-four's."

"You are bad!" I replied.

Dad, looking like a twenty-pound sausage in a ten-pound skin, entered the living room and confronted Uncle Harry. "I hope you're satisfied. This is all your fault!"

"My fault? How is this my fault? You know what, Anthony? You're going to eat your words a year from now when I'm a successful shipping magnate, and you're still checking globes for misspellings! Vicky, get our coats!"

"But we haven't even finished our salads," Aunt Vicky said, walking toward the hall closet. She returned with their coats and looked at Margaret. "I'm sorry, honey. I'll call you."

Uncle Harry flew toward the front door and Aunt Vicky followed in his tail-wind.

My father looked at Jerry. "Are you going to stand there in your underwear all night?"

Jerry reached for Ivan's pants and sat down on the sofa.

"The lasagna is getting cold," Margaret said. "Why don't we go back into the dining room and eat?"

We returned to the dining room and took our seats, everyone except Dad. He had a hard time bending because Jerry's pants were so tight. On his third attempt to sit, everyone broke into laughter.

"That's it!" big Anthony yelled. "I've had enough of your ridicule. I'm leaving. Are you coming, Leona?" He left the room.

Mom thought for a moment. "All right, Anthony!" she yelled.

"But Mom," Jerry said, "he cursed one more time."

"I know. I guess I'll have to make an exception this time. He can't drive; he can't even sit down in those pants. He'll have to lie down in the back seat while I drive. I'm sorry he ruined your celebration, Margaret—I'll call you."

"What am I going to do with all this lasagna?" Margaret asked.

"It freezes well," Mom said.

We kissed Mom goodbye, and they were gone.

As the front door slammed, we began laughing uncontrollably; never were so many tears of laughter shed. When we finally regained our composure, Jerry was the first to speak.

"Margaret, do you have a camera?"

"Yeah. Why?"

"I'd like to get a picture of Tony and myself in Ivan's sweatsuit."

"I'll go and get it."

Granny stopped her. "Margaret, honey, one more thing. Do you have a pair of sweat pants that I could borrow? I'm afraid I've wet myself."

We laughed.

"Just kidding," Granny said.

The flash went off on Margaret's camera as Jerry and I stood hugging one another, holding on for dear life.

"Come on, Margaret," I said, "You get in the picture, too. Would you mind taking a shot, Maria?"

"My pleasure."

If a picture was worth a thousand words, that one was worth a million. The three of us looked happier together than I had ever remembered; not a bad outcome for an evening rooted in such absolute absurdity. Maria didn't even have to tell us to smile; it came naturally that night.

As the flash went off for the final time, that last Valentine's Day of the millennium singed my memory. It was the night that I had established a new camaraderie with my siblings. That our reunion had come at my father's expense was unfortunate, but that was how fate had presented it; we had no choice but to roll with the punches.

Six

Manhattan shed its gray cast of winter, and my own dark thoughts became lighter as well. While spring was rearing its crocus heads, a new sense of trust was sprouting in my marriage. Not that our liaison was perfect. We were, however, moving in the right direction. I had good reason to be hopeful that spring.

I even stopped hiding my journal behind the bookcase in the office. Not that I kept it in plain view; I wasn't that confident. I simply decided that ***private*** executed in bold letters across the front of my journal would have to do.

All right, so some extraneous issues were responsible for my coming out of hiding. If I pulled that muscle in my groin one more time, I was probably facing a hernia repair. I couldn't bear that thought.

Spring had also been good to my brother Jerry. He and Roberta, with the help of Poppy's Fractal Calculus, were on the verge of a scientific breakthrough. The Nobel Prize in Physics seemed a real possibility.

But I was jumping the gun: the winners wouldn't be announced until October. Still, it seemed a sure thing. The rumors were flying at Princeton and in every physics department around the world, since Jerry's last publication in the scientific journals.

I sat back in my chair to do some time-traveling, to an incident that had happened almost thirty years prior—an incident in which Jerry's expertise literally blew up in my father's face.

Jerry and I awoke early one Saturday morning to the smell of burning toast.

"We had better stay in our room until the air clears," Jerry said. He was referring not to the smoke, but to our father's rage. The smallest things would incite his temper; I visualized Dad at that very moment scraping his toast like a madman, unaware that half the black crumbs were not making it into the trash can. When he realized his shoes were covered with black dust, the obscenities would fly like jackknives. We were smart to take cover.

"You're right, Jerr. We'll stay in here until we hear the war planes go down." I was referring to the exhaust fans; there were two.

In addition to the fan over the stove, my mother had insisted on a small exhaust fan in the den. Secondhand cherry-tobacco smoke wasn't the most pleasant olfactory experience, and Dad's pipe-smoking annoyed Mom. "Why can't you smoke outside like Harry does?" Mom would ask. Nevertheless, Dad smoked inside, and we stayed out of the den if the fan was running.

"What do you want to do today?" I asked Jerry.

"Well, I was planning to prepare some slides; do you want to help me?"

"No, that's boring," I said, scratching my left ankle with my right foot.

"How can you think the microscopic world is boring? The most interesting things in the world are the things we can't even see."

"There are enough big things to look at," I said, scratching my other ankle.

"Well that's what I'm going to do. I'll go to the library later if you want."

"Jerry, it's Saturday! I'm not going to spend a nice day cooped up in the library." I pulled the covers away and began scratching my ankles with my fingernails.

"What's the matter?" Jerry asked.

"It's a beautiful day. I want to go outside."

"No," Jerry said, "I mean with your ankles? Why are you digging at them?"

"I don't know. They're driving me nuts."

"Let me see," Jerry said, running to inspect my ankles. "Looks like you have a nasty rash. I hope it's not chiggers."

"What's chiggers?"

"Chiggers are microscopic bugs that attach themselves to skin and feed on the dead cells that constitute the outermost epidermal layer," Jerry said clinically.

I was sorry I had asked. "I have bugs crawling all over me?" I yelled.

"I can't be sure without taking a sample."

"How do you take a sample?"

"Well, I'd wet your leg and take a scraping; then I'd examine the scraping, probably under five-hundred power, to identify the micropest."

I had never heard the word *micropest*, but I wasn't surprised. Jerry had coined dozens of compound words that didn't yet exist in the real world.

"O.K.," I said.

"O.K. what?"

"Do it," I said, my voice quivering at the thought of it.

"All right!" Jerry yelled, exhilarated by the opportunity that had been tossed his way, at my expense.

"We need a butter knife," Jerry said.

"What for?"

"To scrape your leg, silly."

"I'm not going out there," I said. "The fans are still running."

"Well, we need something to scrape your leg with."

I began scouring our room for anything that would serve as a makeshift scraping device. There was nothing. "Jerry, where's the little scalpel that came with your microscope?"

"It's in the den."

"Oh."

After a few minutes of deliberation, an idea came to me. "I know! We'll use one of Margaret's nail files."

"She's still sleeping," Jerry said.

"So, we'll be quiet. Besides, it's perfect. She'll never see us, with her sleeping mask."

"Right," Jerry said. "You go and get it, and I'll set up things in here."

I opened our bedroom door and peeked into the hallway: the coast was clear. I walked quietly into Margaret's bedroom. She was sound asleep. I absconded with a nail file without so much as a stir from my sleeping sister.

"I got it!" I said, entering our bedroom. Jerry was carefully setting up the glass slides on his desk.

"Good," Jerry said. "Now go to the bathroom and get a wet washcloth. Make sure it's a clean one; we don't want to contaminate our samples."

I opened the bedroom door and peered out again. I slipped quietly into the bathroom and got a clean washcloth. I wet it and returned to our bedroom.

"O.K.," Jerry said, taking the washcloth from me. "Lie down on the bed; we're ready to go."

"Why do I have to lie down?"

"Do you want to do this or not?"

I did as I was told and lay down. Jerry proceeded to drape a sheet over my body, exposing only my left leg, from the knee down. He set up his experiment with the skill of a surgeon; finally, I was ready to go under the knife.

Jerry swiped me with the washcloth and dragged the file across my leg. "O.K., you can get up now." Jerry walked to the desk and began smearing the glass slides with the scum he had scraped from my leg. "Looks good," He said.

"Now what?" I asked.

"Now I'm going to put a drop of red dye on each slide that is specific to the exoskeletons of bugs; that way we'll know what we're looking at."

"Exoskeletons?"

"Yeah, you know, exterior skeletons."

I did not know. "What are you talking about, Jerry? What are exoskeletons?"

"Oh," Jerry said. "Obviously you weren't paying attention in science class when they covered entomology. But then why would you? You hate bugs."

"So what are they?" I asked impatiently.

Jerry began his textbook description. "Well, all living organisms need some type of support system for their physical shape. We have a skeleton on the inside to support our flesh. Bugs have evolved a skeleton on the outside, hence exo, Latin for outside. Their skeletons consist of bony plates on the outside of their bodies. The crunch you hear when you step on a bug is its exoskeleton being smashed to smithereens."

I was mortified. "You mean the bugs on my legs are covered with bony plates?" I asked, knowing full well I didn't want to hear the answer.

"We're not even sure that you have bugs," Jerry said. "You may just have a nasty case of dermatitis. Let's take a look."

Jerry put one of the glass slides under the lens of his microscope and turned on the light. He was turning buttons and switching lenses, occasionally uttering proclamations such as "Oh my God!", "Will you look at that!" or "Now I've never seen one that big!"

The suspense was killing me. "What is it? Just tell me!"

Jerry turned off the microscope and sat on the edge of the bed. "Well, it seems my original diagnosis was correct. You have chiggers, and lots of them."

"With exoskeletons?" I cried.

"Of course," Jerry said. "I just told you, *all* bugs have exoskeletons. Weren't you paying attention?"

I began to feel sick. Bugs were attacking my skin at the cellular level, and they were procreating under my fingernails as well. And the sneakers I had worn the day before were in the closet, probably infecting my whole wardrobe. My closet was full of exoskeletons! It would have to be fumigated. My only shred of hope was that Jerry had been playing with my head.

Wait a minute, I thought; maybe the whole thing was a scheme concocted by Jerry to keep me inside with him. That had to be it; he wanted a lab partner in his scientific endeavor, and he reeled me in, using my paranoia as bait.

"O.K., Jerry," I said. "The joke is over."

"What joke?"

"You just wanted me to stay in with you and work on slides. What do you take me for? Boy, for a minute, you really had me going," I laughed.

"Tony, I'm not kidding. Take a look for yourself," He said, pointing toward his desk.

I approached the microscope defiantly. "How do you turn this thing on?"

"Right here," Jerry said, flicking on the light. "Look through the eyepiece."

I leaned forward and looked through the eyepiece. Before my eyes swam a sea of red monsters of the most abominable variety. They were indeed wearing coats of armor. "Oh my God!" I screamed. "They're wearing football helmets!"

"They're not football helmets," Jerry laughed. " They're bony plates that protect their brains. Just like our skulls."

"I'm going to faint. Get Mom!"

"Mom's at the grocery store."

"Brains?" I repeated. "They have brains?"

"Tony, calm down. All living creatures have brains, however primitive. And, all living things need to protect this most crucial part of their anatomy."

"Oh Jerry, shut up!" I said, flailing my legs as if to shake off the scoundrels.

"It's no use, Tony. Didn't you notice those claw-like features at the bottom of their legs? They're holding on for dear life."

They had pairs and pairs of legs: I had seen it with my own eyes! "Jerry, give me the trash can. I'm going to throw up," I yelled.

"You're just hyperventilating, Tony. Here, breathe into this paper bag; it will stabilize your blood gases." Jerry shoved a crumpled paper bag over my head. "C'mon, Tone. In and out, in and out, that's it."

I regained some of my composure and pulled the bag off my head.

"Feeling better?" Jerry asked.

"A little. How do we kill them?"

"Great minds think alike; I was just pondering the very same thing. The way I figure it, we need to isolate a solvent that will either shrivel them or make them imbibe enough water to burst."

I imagined a nuclear holocaust engulfing my lower extremities; bony plates and helmets flying, bug gray matter settling like fallout onto my leg hairs. And the clean up! I imagined Jerry wheeling barrels of toxic waste to the curb on trash day.

"My first guess would be salt," Jerry said, "but chances are, we're not going to get enough of their bodily fluids to leech across the cell membrane. Salt isn't going to work; we'll have to mess with their pH."

"How?"

"We'll have to gather some acids and bases to test my hypothesis. Let's make a list, then we'll gather our solutions. Half our work is done; the slides are already prepared."

I pretended to understand what Jerry was talking about, not wanting my ignorance to stand in the way of the scientific method.

"Let's see," Jerry said. "We'll need some bleach, hydrogen peroxide, baking soda, vinegar, and acetone. I'm certain one of those will work."

"What's acetone?"

"Nail polish remover."

No problem, I thought. *Avon* had just called Margaret a few days earlier.

"O.K.," Jerry continued, "you get the bleach, baking soda and vinegar from the kitchen. I'll get the peroxide and the acetone."

"Sure. You make me go to the kitchen!"

"Do you want to do this or not?"

Of course I did, so I opened the bedroom door to listen for the fans. The kitchen fan was no longer running; the fan in the den was still clanging. My father was probably lost in a cloud of cherry tobacco smoke. He would be so busy huffing and puffing on his decrepit corn-cob pipe that he'd be oblivious to my spin through the kitchen. I held my breath and crept down the hallway. Dad was in a good mood; he was singing: *Smoke Gets in Your Eyes.*

I made it safely to the kitchen and began gathering my chemical arsenal. I retrieved everything on my list and tip-toed back to our bedroom. Jerry was waiting.

"Got everything?"

"Mission accomplished." I lined my bottles on the desk.

Jerry began searching for the magic bullet. After three unsuccessful tries, he spoke: "I can't believe the vinegar didn't work."

"What's left?"

"Bleach and nail polish remover. Let's try bleach first," Jerry said. He put several drops of bleach onto the glass slide. After a few seconds, he began yelling: "Oh, my God!"

"What?"

"Take a look at this," Jerry said, shaking his head in disbelief.

I looked through the eyepiece; within a millisecond, I was yelling "Oh, my God!" too. My chiggers had become morbidly obese; their helmets and suits of armor expanded to accommodate them. They weren't dead, they looked rather content. Was it possible that my parasites had become fat and jolly, drunk with joy on a few minuscule shots of bleach?

"Forget the bleach!" I yelled. All I needed was chiggers with a hearty appetite.

"Cross your fingers," Jerry said, squeezing a few drops of nail polish remover onto another slide. He began to examine the results; after a few seconds, he yelled "eureka!"

"What?"

"It works!"

"Thank you, God! I will never ask you for another thing, as long as I live!" I shouted.

"O.K., Tony. Sit down—let's get to work!"

I sat at the desk chair and Jerry began dousing my legs with nail polish remover. "This stuff stinks!" I said.

"Stop complaining," Jerry said. "It's the only thing that works."

When we felt sufficiently queasy, we had the bright idea to open our bedroom window. "Good," Jerry said. "The wind is moving in the right direction." The wind was blowing in; the acetone vapors were leaving through the crack at the bottom of our bedroom door.

"How are you feeling?" Jerry asked.

"The itching is gone, but my legs feel really cold."

"That's to be expected. Acetone has a high heat of vaporization. Your legs will warm up in a few minutes."

Jerry was right.

"When Mom gets home, I'd go in and take a shower," Jerry said. "Dad will be preoccupied with all the new food, so you'll be safe."

Jerry's cure worked like a charm. What we didn't realize, however, was that the exhaust fan in the den had orchestrated a current of acetone vapors directly past Dad's easy chair. We suddenly heard what sounded like a small explosion, followed by a gut-wrenching scream: "Margaret!"

"What was that?" I asked nervously.

"It was Dad screaming."

"No," I said, "that rumble before the scream."

"I don't know."

The yelling was getting closer and louder. Dad was in the hallway, just outside our bedroom door. We heard Margaret's bedroom door open, so we opened ours.

Margaret was standing in the hall sleepy-eyed, her mask dangling from her neck. "Oh my God!" she said to Dad. "What happened to you?"

"What happened?" Jerry and I yelled.

Our father turned to look at Jerry and me. Dad appeared to have a bad case of sunburn; in addition, his eyebrows were gone and his hairline had receded by one and a quarter inches since the night before.

"I'll tell you what happened!" Dad yelled. "That sister of yours must have spilled a god-damned gallon of nail polish remover! The fumes were so god-damned strong that my corn-cob pipe blew up in my face when I went to light it! I could have been blinded!"

"I didn't spill anything!" Margaret yelled. "I was sleeping!"

Margaret looked at Jerry and me. "Were you guys using my nail polish remover?"

Jerry and I had no choice but to tell the truth; we couldn't allow Margaret to be wrongly accused. Besides, we had a perfectly good explanation.

But our explanation wasn't good enough for my father. He hadn't paid much attention in entomology class either, and swore that Jerry and I had deliberately conspired to bomb his corn-cob pipe. Dad went on and on, until hearing our car pull into the driveway. As Jerry had predicted, he was lured by the new food Mom was unloading. Leaving the hallway, Dad had two last words: "you're grounded!"

I never got to play outside on that beautiful Saturday. And, my father wasn't satisfied with a simple sentence; he compounded it with a day of hard labor. I managed to see the outside world only through the windows, as I vacuumed the thirteen sets of venetian blinds that hung between me and my freedom. Dad always had to pour a glass of water on a drowning man.

Our sentence was so harsh because we had forced Dad to be at the mercy of Margaret's professional expertise. He couldn't play cards with the guys that afternoon with no eyebrows.

Margaret reveled in Dad's makeover like an artist blessed with a divine vision.

"Hurry the hell up, Margaret," Dad yelled. "I'm already late!"

"Do you want an eyebrow that is complementary to your bone structure or not? Sit still!"

I don't know if it was her intention or not, but Margaret painted a permanent expression of shock on my father's face. The expression was exacerbated by the new hairdo that Margaret had created in order to bring Dad's hairline down to a level that was "age-appropriate."

"Jee-Zus Christ!" my father yelled, seeing his reflection in the mirror.

I laughed hysterically, and realized God had been on my side. The vacuum cleaner became my saving grace, muffling the guttural laughter and snorting that I was unable to control.

The sound of the front door brought me back to 1999, and I laughed in retrospect. It hadn't been easy growing up with a future Nobel Laureate and a father with a persecution complex.

"I'm home!" Maria yelled.

"I'm in here," I responded.

Maria walked into the office. "Hi, honey."

"Hi, Maria. Did you have any luck?"

"Yes, and it was on sale! I found shoes to match, too." Maria removed the plastic drape from her dress. "Do you like it?"

"I love it," I replied. "Did you happen to get the mail on the way up?"

"No. I didn't have a free hand. Sorry. I'll go back down if you want me too."

"No, that's O.K. I'll go down in a few minutes."

"Are you expecting something?"

"No. I was just wondering if you picked it up."

"How did you expect me to maneuver the mailbox with all these packages?" Maria asked, slightly disgruntled.

"I didn't expect you to," I defended. "I was just wondering if you did."

"It sounded an awful lot like expectation to me. Are you mad because I went shopping today?"

"Of course I'm not mad. Why are you doing this?"

"I'm not doing anything. It just seems as though whenever I walk into the house with packages, you get that look on your face."

"What look? I said I liked the dress."

"That look like, Oh! You've been shopping *again*?"

"I did not have that look," I defended. "Why do you always feel guilty whenever you spend money on yourself? Then you project it onto me and act as if I'm the one responsible."

"Oh, Tony, don't tell me about projection. I think if I was projecting I'd be able to see it."

"Let's not argue," I said. "This is ridiculous. Things have been going so well between us."

"Yes," Maria said. "This is ridiculous!" She noisily gathered her bags; the sound of crumpling paper filled the room like thunder.

"I do like the dress!" I yelled, as Maria left the room.

That's what I get for counting my chickens before they're hatched, I thought. Just when I thought my life was on the upswing, the pendulum did an about-face. I decided to go downstairs for the mail.

Riding the elevator to the lobby, I began to wonder if I had been deluding myself. Perhaps I had imagined the improvement in our marriage. How could something as trivial as the mail have come between us?

I unlocked the mailbox and removed its contents. More bills had arrived, along with several trade journals and what looked like an Easter card. There was a sticker on the envelope of the card, of a newly-hatched chick. I locked the mailbox and headed back to the elevator.

Riding upstairs, I looked at that Easter chick. A little voice in my head shouted a reminder: don't count your chickens before they're hatched! I looked for a return address; the only person who would use cute little stickers was my mother, and it wasn't her handwriting. There was no return address. I opened the envelope: Easter Greetings, the card read. The elevator stopped on the eighth floor; as the doors opened, I examined the newly-hatched chicks that decorated the card's front. Rub my nose in it, I thought, stepping off the elevator.

I stood in the hallway and opened the card. *Happy Easter* was printed on the inside, along with a hand-written message: "We'll have to get together soon! Fondly, Mildred and Martin."

My heart skipped a few beats and a wave of nausea moved through me. I turned and hit the down button, leaning against the wall for support. Why would Maria play such a sick joke on me? It wasn't bad enough that she breached my privacy; she had to be cunning too. I stumbled onto the elevator and rode downstairs with my heart in my throat.

I returned the mail to our mailbox, keeping the Easter card aside. How could Maria have been so cruel? I decided to head for the park; I had to think things through.

It was a nice day, but not nice enough to be outside without a jacket. I headed toward the men's shop on Madison Avenue. I felt my ass: my wallet was there.

I walked into the store and picked the first cardigan in a size large. I took it to check-out and went for my credit card.

"Don't you want to try this on, Sir?" the salesman asked. "It's a markdown, non-returnable."

"No," I said. The salesman processed my credit card and reached for a bag.

"I don't need a bag," I said. "I'll wear it out."

I put on the sweater. Fittingly, the sleeves were an inch and a half too short. The salesman looked at me blankly. "Would you like me to remove the tag for you?"

"Please." The salesman clipped my tag and I left the store. I headed for the park.

Once there, I took a seat at the first vacant bench. How could she have done that to me? Why couldn't she just confront me? Why did she have to concoct such an under-handed, twisted psychological ploy? I was devastated.

I looked up and noticed a couple walking hand-in-hand. They were laughing together, enjoying the first hints of spring. To my far left was another couple, stuck in a long embrace. Everywhere I looked, love was in the air. What the hell was it, springtime in Paris? I suddenly realized I was the only one in Central Park who was alone. Puppy love was everywhere; I was the only lone dog.

As visions of exaggerated affection bombarded me, I thought to myself: this is what I could have had. Instead, my lover had deliberately pushed me over the cliff of psychosis.

I sat for hours on that bench, searching desperately for answers. I even began to rationalize Maria's sick joke; perhaps she had sent it in my own best interest. Perhaps she was aware that a confrontation would have sent me off the deep end. Who knew what was in a shrink's bag of tricks? Maybe I should be thanking her, I thought.

I removed the Easter card from my pocket and began examining it. I looked at the signature; Maria didn't make her M's like that. What was I thinking? Of course she wouldn't sign the card herself. That meant she had discussed my case with someone, probably one of her colleagues. Unless of course, she had merely disguised her handwriting. I began to pray that Maria had committed forgery; I didn't want my condition leaking out to the rest of the Psychiatric community.

I turned the card over and examined the back of it. Sixty-five cents? Where could you buy a greeting card for sixty-five cents? Maria obviously didn't want to go to any expense. Was that all I was worth to her?

I looked skyward and noticed the sun was approaching the horizon. I decided to go home and face reality. Wait a minute, I thought. I wouldn't give Maria the satisfaction of triumph; I'd pretend I had never received the card. I would let her think it had gotten lost in the mail—that would teach her to play mind games!

I walked home, thinking about Maria's statement: "When I leave the office, I turn off that part of myself." What a bunch of empty talk! She had been psychoanalyzing me all along. Why had I believed her? Why had I thought that things were on the upswing? I had to be crazy.

I took a deep breath and walked into our apartment. Maria was in the shower. Good. It would give me time to compose myself.

I walked into the office and removed my purple notebook from the desk drawer, inserting the sick Easter joke into its pages. "Private—yeah, right," I muttered to myself. I gave the bookcase a good pull from the wall; an excruciating pain shot through my groin. Damn, I thought. After sliding my journal behind it, I moved the bookcase back to the wall, being careful to use only upper-body strength. I turned just as Maria was entering the office.

"Tony! Where have you been? I've been worried sick!"

"I just went for a walk."

"For two and a half hours?"

"Yes."

"I didn't know what to think! Look, I'm sorry about what happened earlier. It was all my fault."

Was she referring to her earlier guilt projection or her sick mind games? "For what?" I asked.

"For the way I jumped down your throat before. You were right; I was projecting. I was on the defensive because of my shopping trip."

"I've told you a million times that you didn't have to feel guilty about spending money on yourself." She had far worse things to feel guilty about.

"I wasn't projecting guilt; I was projecting disgust. I went from a size ten to a twelve. I'm afraid I let my self-loathing color my mood. I didn't mean to take it out on you."

"No problem," I said coldly. "If you'll excuse me, I'm going to take a hot bath. I'm chilled."

"No wonder. You shouldn't have been outside without a jacket." Maria looked at my wrists. "Where did you get that sweater?"

"I've had it," I lied. "It was in the back of my closet."

"You should get a new one; those sleeves are way too short."

"Right," I replied, abruptly.

"Come on, Tony. I said I was sorry. Can't we just forget about what happened earlier? Things have been going so well between us."

"It was just an illusion!" I felt like screaming, but I didn't. I wasn't going to give Maria the satisfaction of knowing how deeply her prank had rocked my soul. "Yeah, we can forget it," I said.

"Not to change the subject, but your Uncle Harry called while you were gone: he got the grant money! The EPA will be financing his recycling business."

"Really? That was quick."

"Tell me about it. He'll be operating by the beginning of April."

"But that's next week."

"I know. It's unbelievable. Whatever happened to bureaucratic red tape? His facility will be located in that industrial park just south of the First Union Center. Aren't you happy for him?"

"I'm thrilled for him." My father, of course, wouldn't be so thrilled.

"What a concept," Maria said. "His slogan is going to be, 'keep 'em moving!' Isn't that clever?"

"Keep what moving?"

"The Styrofoam peanuts. Keep 'em moving and out of landfills."

"Oh. That is clever."

The talk of Uncle Harry's good fortune had momentarily distracted me from my angst. I suddenly remembered it, and my heart sank. I looked at Maria and wondered how she could be so cruel.

"Why are you looking at me like that? Are you still angry?"

"No," I lied. "I'm just tired. And cold."

"Well, go and take a hot bath. Do you want to go out for dinner later?"

"Yeah, sure."

"Tony?"

"Yes?"

"Where did you put the mail?"

"I didn't get the mail."

"Oh. I'll go down and get it. It's no big deal."

No big deal, I thought. Of course it wasn't any big deal to her: she wasn't on the receiving end of hate mail!

I turned and walked toward the bathroom. As the tub filled, I rekindled my suffering. How Maria could have committed such a travesty was beyond me. How could I ever trust her again?

I got into the tub and lay back. The warm smoothness of the water caressed my flesh in a fluid hug. I began to feel a little better, and tried to pump some confidence back into my psyche. Yes, Maria had a lot of gall for sending that card, but I wasn't going to let it destroy me.

That Maria could be so dishonest was the unsettling part; how could she treat me that way when I had never been anything but honest with her? If there was anything I couldn't stand, it was a liar. I slid down in the tub to float on the water. While floating, inky-dinky spider reminded me that I was *the* natural born liar. Maybe Maria wasn't so bad after all?

My logic having crumbled, I could no longer argue with myself. Not knowing what to think, I knew it was time to stop thinking altogether. I lay mindlessly floating in the bathtub until the falling water temperature stirred me to consciousness.

Maria and I never went out to dinner that night. We ordered take-out and went our separate ways. I had mindlessly dressed in pajamas after my bath, and Maria perceived it as a non-verbal cue that dinner was off. I didn't care that my actions had been misconstrued; how could I have made small talk over dinner?

Maria spent that Saturday night reviewing case histories in bed, and I sat staring mindlessly at the television.

The climate that Sunday was just as frigid. Maria tried to coax me out of my shell, but she tried in vain; I was shell-shocked. I didn't know what to say to Maria, so I said nothing. She believed I was carrying a grudge over her guilt-projection on Saturday morning, and was angry at my perceived stubbornness. That things had become so confused scared me.

That Monday morning we sat silently at the breakfast table eating our cereal. I was anxious to leave the house; the emotional climate in our apartment made the days long.

Finally, Maria broke the silence. "We turn the clocks ahead this weekend; it will be nice to have another hour of daylight."

"Yeah," I replied numbly, hiding behind the cereal box.

"Do you have a lot going on at work today?" Maria asked.

"I'm not going to work today," I said sharply. "I told you I was taking the day off to go to Princeton, remember?"

"Oh, that's right. I forgot."

I turned the cereal box to read the side panel.

"Tony, will you please come out from behind that cereal box? I can't believe you're still angry over Saturday morning. I told you I was wrong, and I apologized. Why do you want to keep rubbing my nose in it?"

"I don't. Things aren't always what they seem to be." I had been waiting ten years to throw that line back at her.

"The hell you don't. You've given me the silent treatment all weekend."

"I have not given you the silent treatment. I'm just preoccupied with work," I lied.

"What's going on at work?"

I threw a bunch of technical jargon at Maria so she'd be too confused to question me further.

"It's Greek to me," Maria said, "but I'm sure you'll figure it out."

I'll never be able to figure out how you could have hurt me so deeply, I thought.

"Tony, do you want me to go to Princeton with you? I could call Marian and have her cancel my appointments."

"No, that's all right," I said. "I don't mind going alone." I preferred being alone and lonely to accompanied and lonely. It was less heart-wrenching.

"O.K.," Maria said. There was disappointment in her voice and hurt in her eyes. I wanted to reach out to her, but I didn't. My own hurt feelings hindered any compassion I might have mustered.

As Maria left the kitchen to dress for work, I felt a helplessness far worse than any I had ever experienced. How would our marriage ever survive the web of deceit in which it had become entangled? I had no clue.

Maria and I said a cold goodbye and went our separate ways, again.

I left Manhattan, pondering what a hopeless soul I had become. I prayed for mercy.

Driving by Newark Airport, I wondered how many specks on my windshield were actually jets en route to exotic destinations. I also wondered if Maria or I had ever been mistaken for pieces of dirt by an unwitting Turnpike-driver. Perhaps on our honeymoon flight to Bermuda, someone just like me had tried to flick us away with their windshield wiper; in our post-nuptial joy, we simply brushed it off as mild air turbulence.

Post-nuptial joy—Maria and I were so full of hope back then; could we ever regain those feelings? On Valentine's Day, I was certain we could. What was I saying? On Saturday morning, I was certain we could. Until the mailman arrived.

I decided I needed a break from emotional turmoil and turned on the radio. "Hopelessly devoted to you…" No. "You are my everything…" No. "Have I told you lately that I love you…" No! "My heart will go on…" No it wouldn't! How could it, after the way it had been trampled? I turned off the radio and moved my thoughts to Princeton.

Despite my recent emotional trauma, I was really excited over touring Jerry's lab; a little atom-smashing would help me with my frustration. Within forty-five minutes I would be immersed in the high-tech world of particle accelerators and anti-gravity devices; I'd forget all about my personal problems. Until then, I had forty-five minutes more to torture myself.

I tried to look on the bright side: at least I had my career. Who knows what job prospects will become available to me, as the brother of a Nobel Laureate, I thought. Could I dare mention that on my resume?

I got lost in a fantasy of my life as the brother of a Nobel Laureate; before I knew it, I was entering the Princeton campus, oblivious to the last half-hour of the trip. I had to stop that—did I have a death wish or something?

So this is what Princeton looks like, I thought. I had wanted to go to Princeton too, but wasn't accepted. It was disheartening at the time; perhaps if Jerry had been the eldest, I might have been admitted, as his brother. But Penn was a darn good school, just as much ivy-league as Princeton. Why was I arguing with myself?

"I think you're jealous because Jerry has his own parking place," Martin said.

I looked in the back seat, and there they were. "What are you doing here?"

"You've been ignoring us all weekend," Mildred said. "Sooner or later, we were bound to turn up."

Mildred was right. I was too shaken to write in my journal that weekend. Out of the pages and into the back seat—Mildred had warned me.

"I have not been ignoring you," I said. "I pulled a muscle in my groin and was too weak to pull the bookcase from the wall."

"I can't believe you put us there again; the dust chokes me! You need a cleaning woman," Martin said.

"We do have a cleaning woman," I said. "Doesn't she clean back there?"

"Don't be a rat, Martin," Mildred scolded.

Suddenly a light went on in my head. The cleaning woman! Could Edwina have found my journal? Was she reading me like a book when we were paying her to scrub floors? Maybe she sent the Easter card. Had I wrongly accused Maria? What kind of jerk was I? When I got home I was going to compare Edwina's signature on one of our canceled checks to the penmanship on the Easter card.

"I am not a rat," Martin said.

"Then zip it up," Mildred ordered.

"So, does Edwina move the furniture when she cleans the office?" I demanded.

"I don't know," Mildred said. "How much do you pay her?"

"Why does that matter? I just need to know if she sent that card."

"I'd like to know, too, if there's someone out there forging our signatures; before you know it, they'll be running off with our identities as well," Mildred said.

"What do you mean, your identity? Your identity is my identity—isn't it?" Mildred was distracting me from the question at hand.

"You don't even know who you are anymore," Martin added sarcastically.

"All right, you guys. I *am* looking for help here!"

"All right, then," Mildred said. "Let me ask you a question. Why were you so quick to pin the blame on Maria? I thought things were on the upswing between the two of you?"

"They were."

"Then why would Maria send that card? Maybe it was Edwina. Or maybe it wasn't. How would I know? I've been locked up in your notebook like a pressed flower! Besides, I'm not going to be a rat," Mildred said, wriggling out of any commitment.

But, Mildred had asked me why I was so quick to pin the blame on Maria. She knew something and she wasn't telling: it must have been Edwina!

"Tony!" Martin yelled.

"What?!"

"You just passed the physics buildings," he said, in an uppity tone.

"So, I'll go around the block," I said, turning the corner. I went around the block and pulled into the parking lot. Parking was certainly at a premium; not one spot was available.

"Use Jerry's spot," Martin said. "He always walks to work."

"How do you know that?" I asked.

"Don't you ever really listen, Tony?"

Martin's condescension was beginning to irritate me. "O.K., you can stop talking now."

"He's right, Martin. Shut-up," Mildred said. "Tony needs some peace and quiet; he has to call his wife and apologize for being such a jerk."

"I am not a jerk!" I yelled. But they were gone.

I found Jerry's parking spot. Martin was right: it was vacant. I pulled in and turned off the car, thinking about what had just been said, or rather, what I had just imagined. Mildred was telling me to apologize to Maria; she must have been trying to tell me something—it was Edwina! Why didn't she just say so? Maybe it had something to do with changing the course of history. Maybe there was some unwritten law that forbade your imaginary friends from spying on your real friends. How would I know? I didn't even know who I was.

I reached for my cell phone and dialed Maria's office; Marian answered. There was a lot of static on the line. Must be the particle accelerators, I thought.

"Marian—is Maria there? It's Tony."

"Yes, but she's in the middle of a session, Tony. Can I have her get back to you?"

"It's really important, Marian. Can you break in for me? I really need to talk to her."

"Just a minute," Marian said.

Maria picked up. "Tony, what's the matter? Marian said it was an emergency."

"It's not an emergency. I just wanted to call and apologize."

"For what?"

"I didn't mean to hurt your feelings this morning. I just didn't want to disrupt your whole day. It occurred to me later that maybe you really wanted to go. I didn't mean to sound as if I didn't want you to go."

"What?"

"I'm sorry you didn't come with me."

"Me too. I'm really glad you called, though. And it was very unselfish of you to consider my schedule. Here I thought you were still pining over the argument we had on Saturday morning. I'm sorry I was so silly. Forgive me?"

"Of course," I said, hating myself because she was apologizing to me. What did I expect? My whole life was backwards.

"I'll talk to you when I get home tonight," Maria said. "I've got to run; my ten o'clock has a time-management problem."

"Maria, one more thing. Does Edwina move the furniture

when she cleans our apartment?"

"I don't know. I guess it depends on how heavy the furniture is. Why?"

"Oh, no reason," I said. "I guess my visit to Jerry has me thinking about dust mites."

"Gotta run!" Maria said, hanging up.

I sat in the car for a few more minutes, estimating the weight of the bookcase, pondering Edwina's upper-body strength. She seems pretty robust, I thought. Surely if I could move the bookcase with a hernia about to rupture, she could budge it far enough to slide out my journal. So Edwina was strong enough; was she industrious enough to want to move it? She had better be; we were paying her good money to collect dust. It had to be Edwina!

I approached Jerry's building with a bounce in my step. Maria had not broken my heart—it was the cleaning woman! I opened the door and went in.

I aimlessly wandered the corridors in search of Jerry. Everyone was whizzing by as if they were waves instead of particles; I stopped the first person of a normal velocity. "Do you know where Jerry Vitello's office is?" I asked politely.

The young girl looked at her school-chum and then back at me. "Do you mean Dr. Vitello?" she asked, smiling.

"Yes."

"Make the third right at the end of this hall, and it's the last door on the left," she said, smiling.

"Thank you," I said.

She looked at me strangely; I suppose she saw a family resemblance. "Are you related to Dr. Vitello?" she asked, smiling.

"Yes. I'm his brother."

"Oh!" she said, smiling. She looked at her school-chum.

"Thank you, girls," I said. As I walked away, I heard the girl and her school-chum giggling. What the hell were they laughing at? They didn't even know me.

Approaching Jerry's office, I was mystified by the academic buzz; I had never seen so many lab coats in my life. As I made my right turn, I ran into Roberta.

"Tony! What are you doing here?"

"Jerry's giving me a tour of the lab. It's nice to see you again.

I'm sorry; I almost didn't recognize you."

"Haircut," Roberta said. That was it. Roberta had traded her bob for a much shorter do. "I just don't have time to be messing with my hair in the morning. Gotta run—maybe we can meet for lunch later?"

"Sounds good," I said, as Roberta disappeared around the corner.

How ironic, I thought. Jerry let his hair grow so he wouldn't be bothered by it; Roberta cut hers off for the very same reason. Must be some gender-reversal that happens when you spend too much time in parallel universes, I thought.

I knocked at Jerry's door.

"Enter!"

I opened the door and walked in.

"Tony!" Jerry said. "What are you doing here?"

"You invited me for a tour. Did you forget?"

"Oh, is today Monday? I'm sorry," Jerry said, rising from his desk. Jerry's lab coat was sleeveless, and had a lot more pockets than others I'd seen.

"Is it a bad time? I could come back another day," I said.

"Absolutely not," Jerry said. "I just got my days mixed-up. Sit down, it's good to see you."

"Thanks, Jerr. Boy, there's an awful lot of activity going on here."

"Oh, this is nothing," Jerry said. "There's a lot of absenteeism on Monday, but things will pick up by Wednesday. Then it will be downhill again. Hey, did you hear about Uncle Harry?"

"Yeah, can you believe it?"

"No, I can't. But I'd love to be a fly on the wall when Dad finds out what Uncle Harry has named the company."

"What did he name it?"

"You haven't heard? You're in for a treat."

"What is it?"

"You know how Dad kept telling Uncle Harry that his idea was nuts?"

"Yeah?"

"Uncle Harry named the company 'We R Nuts'."

"What?" I laughed.

"Don't you love it?"

"Come on, Jerry. The government wouldn't fund an operation called 'We R Nuts'. You're kidding, right?"

Jerry just looked at me. He wasn't kidding. "Apropos, isn't it?"

"Keep 'em moving!" I yelled. We began to laugh hysterically.

"Can you imagine Dad's face when he finds out? It will get a rise out of him, if he can get out of his chair!"

Our laughter was interrupted by a knock at the door. "Enter!" Jerry yelled.

A young graduate student entered the room. "Dr. Vitello, I'm afraid there's something wrong with the carousel. The centripetal force factor is off by a factor of ten."

"O.K., Bob," Jerry said. "I'll be right down. Leave it running." Jerry turned to me. "Ready for the tour?"

"Ready," I said.

Walking toward the lab, my attention was again drawn to Jerry's lab coat. Where had I seen a sleeveless lab coat before? Something about it was startlingly familiar. "Interesting lab coat," I said.

"You like it? It's Margaret's creation. I complained to her once about getting my sleeves caught in the equipment, so she altered it. She used the sleeves to make some extra pockets, which really come in handy. It has really caught on; everyone in the physics department wants them. Margaret gets ten bucks a pop."

I looked around and noticed that quite a few lab vests were circulating. Why hadn't I noticed that earlier?

We arrived at the lab and Jerry opened the door. "After you," he said. I walked in and was dumbfounded.

"Where's the particle accelerator?" I asked.

"It's in the building across the street," Jerry said. "This building is nowhere near large enough to house it."

I had expected to see a lot of high-tech gizmos amidst a backdrop of high-frequency light. Instead I saw what looked like an amusement park for wayward plants. Jerry noticed my surprise.

"What's wrong?" he asked.

"I guess it's just not what I expected."

"What did you expect?"

"I thought you were smashing atoms."

"Oh, no," Jerry said. "They do that across the street. What we're doing is studying the effect of different force fields on plant morphology. Come here, I'll show you."

I followed Jerry to a corner of the lab. A rosebush was attached to a machine that bounced it as if on a pogo stick. "This device alters the force field in a very subtle way, and it causes very subtle changes in morphology. Jerry pointed to one of the rose petals. "Look at the venation; it follows a pattern of geocentric spirals instead of a branching chain. This machine has allowed us to elucidate a constant in one of our mathematical models. Gravity acts as a vector force in the unified field in very specific ways."

I pretended to understand what Jerry was saying, even though I didn't.

"This one," Jerry continued, "studies a horizontal vector of the force field. This component of the unified field pushes things skyward. Exaggerating this force makes the plant grow upwards, but never sideways."

A rather tall flowering plant moved back and forth from side to side, the horizontal force causing a jiggle in the plant's mass, about two-thirds down from the top. I began to laugh—the plant looked as if it was dancing the hula. Was it any accident that flowers hung from the top of the lanky plant like a Hawaiian lei? It must have been my imagination. That was too absurd to have been a reality. We walked away.

"Wasn't it strange how the plant flowered in a configuration resembling a necklace?" Jerry asked. It hadn't been my imagination.

"Yeah," I said. I said nothing else, because I was floored. Could Jerry really win the Nobel Prize for getting a plant to do the hula?

We approached the back of the lab, where some of Jerry's plants were enjoying a carousel ride. On further inspection I noticed that there were no horses. Jerry's hi-tech merry-go-round sported six spinning magnetic cups instead. Six euphorbia were euphoric, spinning independently while the carousel spun them as a group. It was no merry-go-round, it was the spinning teacups! The engineering department had copied the design; I had my amusement rides confused.

Jerry qualified the euphorbia's predicament: "This device produces what we call *embedded rotation*: a centripetal force within a centripetal force. It induces a change in morphology at the cellular level; their chloroplasts undergo molecular transfigurations which heighten their ability to photosynthesize. From these changes, we extrapolate a theory explaining the genetic mechanisms involved, and they're incredible! Embedded rotation also causes strange movement in the plant's chromosomes during cell division. Before lining up at opposite poles during mitosis, the chromosomes appear to perform a ritualistic dance, like that of a whirling dervish. It's quite amazing," Jerry said.

Amazing to you, I thought. In an effort to appear interested, I asked Jerry a question. "Why are these changes visible only at the cellular level? That whirling jade plant at Granny's had leaves that looked like ponytails."

"Good question, Tone. The difference is that Granny's plant was only subjected to a singular rotational force; these euphorbia are experiencing embedded rotation. Embedded rotation induces changes at a different level of order."

I was sorry I had asked. "Oh."

"Rotational forces are an important component of the unified field, even when magnetic forces are factored out of the equation," Jerry said, as we continued walking.

"This device has provided us with the most exciting results," Jerry said, pointing to an African Violet that resembled a botanical bungee-jumper. "It has allowed us to observe gravity not only along a single vertical plane, but along a myriad of planes all at once. It never stays in one place for very long; that's the beauty of it."

That was the beauty of it, all right. There was nothing else attractive about the plant; in fact, it looked downright scary. Jerry explained: "The field produced by this device has turned the plant's whole morphological reference system upside-down. There are many things to be learned from this mutant."

Be my guest, I thought. I walked away, and Jerry followed.

"I don't get it," I said. "Why plants?"

"Do you honestly think Animal Rights would let us get away with performing these experiments on animals?" Jerry laughed.

"Why not?" I replied. "Maybe rats would enjoy an afternoon at an amusement park."

"This is serious scientific research," Jerry defended.

"I was just kidding," I said. "I meant, why are you studying plants? That's the forte of Botany; shouldn't you be studying sub-atomic things?"

"Oh," Jerry said. "You don't get it. We're not studying plants;

we're studying what forces do to plants. Newton wasn't studying apples; he was studying what forces did to apples."

Jerry's crude analogy got the point across. I felt dumb; Jerry felt motivated to enlighten me. "You see, Tone, we're faced with a question: what is the unified field? The thing is, we can't actually observe the unified field, we can only observe what it does to things. In this case, we're observing how vectors of the unified field affect morphology. We're actually studying the field bit by bit, isolated vectors at a time. The unified field is the sum of everything."

"So where does Poppy's math figure into all of this?" I asked.

"Well," Jerry said, "the bits of forces we observe add up to a sum that forms strange mathematical patterns when plotted in five dimensions. They form a pattern resembling a snowball rolling downhill. We call it a frosty attractor. It's as though one force fits inside another, and then another, and so on."

"Does sound like things are snow-balling," I joked.

"Exactly," Jerry said. "The unified field is the snowball ad infinitum, and encompasses the mass of all the possible snow in the universe. Poppy had worked out a mathematical model for a similar ripple in space-time. It fits our observations to a T."

"So this snowball theory of yours is really going to win you the Nobel Prize?" I didn't want to be disappointed; I was already counting on his success. If Jerry didn't win, I could hear my father: "He didn't have a snowball's chance in hell of winning!" Jerry had to win; it was fate's justice.

"We hope so," Jerry said. "Just remember, we're not studying plants. We're not really studying forces either; we're studying what forces do."

Jerry sounded as if he knew what he was talking about, but what did I know? I taught non-living machines.

Intellectualism was making me weary, and hungry as well. "I saw Roberta on the way in," I said. "She suggested we have lunch together."

Jerry looked at his watch. "Oh, I can't Tone. I have a lecture to give in ten minutes. I don't know what Roberta was thinking; she's going to be tied up in a meeting all afternoon. She probably didn't realize what day it was. How about a rain check?" Jerry asked.

"Sure," I said. I wouldn't mind getting home a little early anyhow; I had to check for dust balls and psychoanalyze Edwina's motives.

"Walk me to class?" Jerry asked.

"Sure."

Jerry grabbed a pile of books and folders from the table in the lab, and we turned to leave. "Could you hold these for a minute, Tone?" Jerry asked, handing me the books.

Jerry returned to the "carousel" and adjusted some of its settings. "Almost forgot to do that," he said.

I walked Jerry to class, still carrying his books. I was back in sixth grade again; Jerry had always needed help with his books, since he carried so many.

"Here we are," Jerry said. We stopped at the door of a very large auditorium.

"This is your classroom?" I asked. "There must be three-hundred students in there!" A large, legged blackboard stood waiting on stage for Jerry, undoubtedly beckoning him at a pitch that was only audible at his level of order.

"It's an introductory course," Jerry said. "Anyhow, big brother, thanks for coming. I probably won't see you until Granny's birthday party, but give me a call, O.K.?"

"Yeah," I said, handing Jerry his books. Jerry gave me an affectionate pat on the back with his free arm, and entered the auditorium.

I stood watching through the open door, as three hundred physics students stood and gave Jerry a standing ovation as he ran onto stage. What was that? Jerry got a standing ovation just for showing up? He hadn't said a word yet. Their response was related to the Nobel rumors, I supposed.

Jerry picked up the microphone and began speaking. "O.K., thank you; you can take a seat now. Please open your books to the chapter on thermodynamic coupling."

I stood there watching as my brother began his lecture. After witnessing that performance, there was no doubt in my mind that Jerry would be going to Stockholm in December. But, come on—a snowball? I thought.

Driving back to Manhattan, I visualized the image of Jerry running onto stage and grabbing the microphone like a rock musician. That image, which became part of my permanent collection, represented the sum of everything Jerry was: unique.

At least Jerry wouldn't have stage-fright when the King of Sweden handed him the Nobel Prize, I thought.

I accelerated in an attempt to beat Maria home from work that day: I had dust to investigate and a marriage to salvage.

Seven

I was stirred to consciousness by the chirping of songbirds: spring was such a wonderful unfolding!

It was unusual for so many songbirds to have congregated outside my high-rise window; I lay wondering what they were perched upon. There was nothing upon which to perch; they had to be hovering. I was being serenaded by a group of hovering songbirds? I perceived it as a sign from God. There was hope: my life *was* on the upswing.

I then realized the chirping wasn't live: it was pre-recorded. Maria had bought us a gentle new alarm clock. My miracle had been just a pipe-dream; why wasn't I surprised?

As I lay being serenaded, I wondered what day it was. Our new alarm clock, though pleasant, didn't display the day or date, features I'd always found helpful.

I looked across the room to the calendar that hung next to my dresser. Squinting, I tried to read the date. It was pointless. I could just about discern the word May. Had I not known it was May, that would have been a shot in the dark as well.

My attention shifted to my name-tag, which lay amidst the dust collecting on my dresser. I reminded myself not to forget it; I was hosting a job fair at SuperSoft that day. We were hoping to snag the best of the millennium's last graduates. I then remembered that it was Friday, May the seventh.

I also reminded myself to buy some magnetic dust-cloths; my imagined population of dust mites frightened me. Edwina hadn't cleaned our apartment in six weeks, since injuring her back.

Edwina's injury confirmed my suspicion that she indeed had been the sender of that pathetic Easter card. What went around certainly came around: Edwina's snooping landed her flat on her back. What had she been thinking? That bookcase had to weigh three hundred pounds. And how had she even known that my journal was behind it?

I entertained a likely scenario. One windy day, the swaying of our high-rise caused a temperature change in the exterior wall behind the bookcase. The drywall shrank, creating an extra micron of space between the wall and my notebook. Gravity acted; my journal fell an inch, coming to rest at a slight angle, with a tiny triangle of purple exposed against the starkness of our white walls. I imagined Edwina spotting the purple corner of my notebook and moving the bookcase to retrieve it. As Edwina passed hours engrossed in my autobiography, dust collected on her cleaning equipment. Cleaning had taken a back seat.

I didn't know where to go from there. When Edwina recovered, surely Maria would welcome her back. I couldn't have someone in my home who didn't respect my privacy, but I couldn't tell Maria that. Where could I go? How could I ever look Edwina in the eye again? Not only had she invaded my privacy; she knew every wretched detail of my sick rationale. And, my marriage could have suffered as a consequence of her snooping; how had I ever blamed poor, sweet Maria?

The guilt generated by having wrongly accused Maria fueled a six-week campaign of ass-kissing on my part. Ironically, these secret acts of restitution were yielding more than I had anticipated; without realizing it, I was coming out of my head, one small secret at a time. My "sharing" drew Maria and me closer. A merciful God had tossed me another *get out of jail free* card. Not only was my marriage improving; my faith was being restored. My prayers were finally being answered.

I lay in bed for a few more minutes of introspection. It was May the seventh, and spring was in full bloom. Where had the last six weeks gone? I began to suspect that my memory was failing; big chunks of my life seemed to be missing.

Mildred assured me that it was my conscience and not my memory that was at fault. She swore I subconsciously blocked those memories which included my acting like a jerk. What did she know? Mildred just liked to pick on me. My life *was* on the upswing!

The past few weeks had brought welcome changes, both self-induced and spurred by my sessions with Maria. Finally, I was getting the professional help I so desperately needed. Having become increasingly aware of my emotional deficits, I began to grope desperately for change; I could no longer bear to despise my thoughts and actions. Self-doubt was eroding my soul; I needed immediate salvation. I prayed, not for God to fix my life, but to give me the strength to fix it myself. My mother once told me that God helps those who help themselves; perhaps my earlier prayers were too greedy.

Still, my life seemed punctuated by the jerking motions of an inner pendulum that was out of sync. I feared I would one day rock aimlessly, my pendulum swinging erratically to the beat of an atomic clock that had spent its half-life. The details of my fear were courtesy of Jerry.

Why was I always going back and forth? I seemed to acquire a sense of emotional balance, however precarious, only to have it toppled by self-doubt. Mildred and Martin weren't helping, and the bickering between them was getting out of hand. Was it possible that Mildred and Martin had become my demons? I wasn't sure; somehow, our relationship was changing. Our conversations no longer helped; on the contrary, they confused me further. I didn't need that; it was the one thing I could do solo.

It seemed obvious that Mildred was undermining my confidence, and I began to consider writing her out of the story. I gave her a warning: if she didn't knock it the hell off, she would be thrust back to 1969 so fast she wouldn't know what day it was. And Martin would be riding on her coat-tails.

I looked at the clock. Had I really been daydreaming for a half-hour? I had a job fair to host. I wondered about the birds: rather than having roused me, they had led me into a trance. Was that a good feature for an alarm clock? I couldn't say anything, though. Maria loved the clock, and she deserved a perk for working so much over-time at home.

I arose and went to look for Maria. I found her in the office, going through the top desk drawer. "Good morning, honey," I said.

"Good morning," she said. "Don't you love the new alarm clock?'

"Yes," I said, abruptly changing the subject. "What are you looking for?"

"The receipt for Granny's gift. I want to pick it up today."

"I remember," I said. "It's on the bulletin board in the

kitchen."

"That's right," Maria said. "Do you want some coffee?"

"Love some. I'll need to be alert today; I'm hosting that job fair."

"Right. Hopefully you'll find some good prospects."

For a moment, my neurotic side began to surface. Would SuperSoft be so cruel as to set me up to unwittingly find my own replacement? No, I was being paranoid. I followed Maria into the kitchen.

"Do you want cereal or toast?" she asked.

"I'll have cereal; it's easier."

"Good. I have to leave early this morning; I forgot a file last night, and I have to review a case before a patient shows up this morning."

That explained Maria being dressed and ready to go at daybreak. We sat at the kitchen table and began discussing Granny's birthday party.

"I hope the weather holds up," Maria said. "Granny's garden is such a lovely setting for a party."

"Isn't it?"

"Yes. You know, I can't believe how great Granny looks for eighty-five. And I know I've said it a million times, but there is something about her house; I simply adore it. It's almost magical; I just don't know how else to describe it."

"Isn't it?" I asked again. "It's probably my favorite place in the world. Can you imagine how wonderful it would be to grow up in a house like that? I wonder if my mother and Aunt Vicky have any idea how lucky they were?"

"I'm sure they do," Maria said. "I have to go. Are you going to be late tonight?"

"I'm not sure. It depends how the job fair goes. I'll leave a message with Marian when I have some idea."

"Great," Maria said, kissing me goodbye. She left the apartment for work. I was on my own that morning.

I decided to have a second bowl of cereal in case I was too busy to stop for lunch. As I chewed, my thoughts returned to my mother: did she really comprehend how lucky she had been? I wasn't sure. My mother was a hard nut to crack.

I suddenly realized how little I actually knew about my mother.

I didn't even know her favorite color. How could that be?

For so long, my mother had been just a buffer between big Anthony and the rest of us; I'm afraid we never really got to know her. That realization saddened me. What was beneath her surface? I decided it was time to find out. My mother couldn't have grown up without absorbing at least some of the wisdom that spilled from Granny. So why had my mother married someone like big Anthony?

That I even had that thought was strange. It was as though I identified big Anthony only as my mother's husband, that I'd somehow forgotten that I was his son, his namesake. I was in denial that I was his creation; how was that for a twisted psychological mechanism? But I didn't let my perception sink me; there was hope. Like a dog in training, I was learning that help was available if I did the right trick.

The trick my wife (who was quickly becoming my personal shrink) was teaching me: to roll with the truth and play as if I was really alive. When I did that, Maria assured me, on a professional level, that I wasn't nuts. That I needed such external validation was another issue; that Maria gave it to me when she did was nothing short of a miracle, because I was going down, fast. On two occasions I almost drowned in the bathtub after turning myself off. That was my rock-bottom: I was becoming a danger to myself. I knew I needed help.

I began to take one risk at a time, growing bolder in my honesty as I realized that truth would never blow up in my face, like the veil of silence had. I learned that words not spoken could be just as cruel as ones spoken too freely. I also learned that I could lie without uttering a word. The veil of silence had rendered my perceptions dangerously warped; I needed to pull it off my head while I still could.

Having psychoanalyzed my spiritual plight, my thoughts returned to my mother. Why had she accepted big Anthony's behavior? Was it possible that, having lost her father at such a young age and being deprived of a male role-model, she didn't know what to expect from a man? Could she have thought my father's antics fell within the realms of appropriate male behavior? After the arrival of her first-born son, she was probably really groping for answers.

I knew there was more to it than that. I decided to spend some quality time with my mother at Granny's party the following day. Suddenly I was an excavator of truth, and I anticipated a big dig at my grandmother's birthday party.

My paradigm was changing, but it was not a steady course; for every transcendent moment, I experienced four episodes of pandemonium. Luckily, I had Maria and my grandmother to usher me back to sanity; my wings were broken and they each served as a crutch. Having already decided not to go there (near my external validation complex), I distracted myself by looking at the clock. It was getting late! I had a job fair to host.

I was about to leave when I realized I'd forgotten my name tag. I went to the bedroom, picked up my name-tag, blew off the dust, and pinned it to my jacket. I arrived at the elevator to find a car waiting. I got on and adjusted my name-tag.

The elevator stopped on the sixth floor and the doors opened.

"Why, good morning, Tony." It was Mrs. Brown, the building busybody; the same Mrs. Brown who had blown the whistle on me back in January, alerting Maria to my aimless wandering of the sixth-floor corridors. It hadn't been aimless wandering: I was on a mission. After my cab ride with the Steinbrights, I needed to pace and come up with a story.

"Good morning, Mrs. Brown."

"Beautiful day," she said, staring at my chest. "Now that's odd; I never knew your last name was Vitello."

"What's so odd about my last name?" I asked. And, I thought, if she *was* such a busybody, why hadn't she known our last name?

"It's not your last name that's odd," Mrs. Brown said. "What's odd is that another couple named Vitello lived in the building at one time, although I believe they spelled it with two T's. Come to think of it, they lived on the eighth floor too, in 818—isn't that your apartment number?"

"Yes," I replied, interested. "When did they live here?"

"Oh, back in the late seventies. I believe they moved out in eighty-one, or maybe it was eighty-two. When you get to be my age…"

I interrupted Mrs. Brown. "You're kidding? That's a coincidence!"

"Yes it is. I never would have realized it, had you not been wearing that name-tag. To be honest, I'd never known your last name; I only knew the two of you as Tony and Maria. How strange, that two couples by the very same last name should have lived in the very same apartment. Not at the same time, of course; you know what I mean."

The elevator door opened onto the lobby. "Aren't you getting off, Tony?"

"No," I said. "I have to go back upstairs. I forgot something."

The elevator doors closed. I thought: two T's! Had that Easter card been addressed to Mr. and Mrs. A. Vittello? Wouldn't I have noticed the misspelling? Of course not—I was in shock!

"Come on!" I yelled, urging the elevator to accelerate. That would explain the sixty-five cent price tag, I thought. One couldn't buy a greeting card in 1999 for less than two dollars; that card must have been lost in postal limbo for the last twenty years! But how could I explain that it had been signed "Mildred and Martin"? Could that be just a coincidence too?

Finally, the elevator stopped on the eighth floor. I tripped off and approached our door. I was shaking so badly that I could hardly maneuver my key into the lock. I steadied my hand and finally unlocked it. Entering the apartment, I hurled my briefcase haphazardly to free both hands. I ran into the office and braced myself, though not adequately, for what was to come: my wrestle with three hundred pounds of psychiatric journals. Once I had conquered them, I would finally know the truth.

I gave the bookcase my best shot; it wasn't enough. I fell over in pain, pulling the bookcase down onto me. I lay buried in the Annals of Psychiatry, my purple notebook just an inch out of reach. I couldn't move, but I wasn't about to be found that way. With all the gusto I could muster, I budged the bookcase with my knees, sliding to reach for my journal. I had it!

I quickly flipped through the pages to apprehend the card. There it was, looking ancient in contrast to the modern pages of my notebook. How had I not noticed *that*? Bingo! There were two T's!

I struggled to rationalize my discovery: the card must have spent two decades jammed in a postal machine. If so, why wasn't it bent? I assumed that Mildred and Martin, whoever they were, hadn't made sure their card had gone down. Who knew where it had spent the last twenty years? I didn't have time to figure it out; I had to become unburied. But I had one more question. Had my burial been a joke on God's part? Or were his signs so blatant because he was all-knowing about my thickness? I didn't know how to reconcile what had just happened to me.

Fortified in knowing that no one had sent me that Easter card, I gave the bookcase a good shove and released myself. Again, pain seized me. I took a moment to massage my groin, hoping to push my guts back in or get them up—whatever! I lay there, still under the Annals, imagining what Marcia Steinbright would think if she discovered me; surely she'd accuse me of some sexual perversion. What was I thinking? I didn't have time for *what ifs*! I had to get out of there; I was going to be late for the job fair. I pushed the books off me and arose, my groin weak but not defeated.

I lifted the bookcase carefully and began re-shelving the Annals. I put the Easter card back into my notebook and went to hide it. I put it in the bottom desk drawer; I *had to* start trusting people. Mistrust was a sin, punishable by God throwing the book at you—literally! I perceived it as my last chance; one more time and God would be delivering my gurney to a waiting surgical team. I wasn't going there!

Riding down the elevator, I noticed how dirty my hands were; the office was filthy! I'd have to remember to call Edwina to see if she had recovered. When the poor woman came back to work, she was getting a raise. How could I have wrongly accused her? And poor Mrs. Brown, I had unjustly labeled her a busybody. What the hell was wrong with me? Maria had been right: I was paranoid. I took a deep breath and prayed for the strength to change.

Outside, I hailed a cab and headed to work. En route, I realized how emotionally drained I was; too much psychoanalysis early in the morning wasn't good—I was spent. I thought about the job fair: how could I recognize promise when my head needed to take the rest of the day off?

I was fifteen minutes late for work. The SuperSoft hopefuls were already congregated in the conference room off the lobby; I still had to go upstairs to retrieve my materials before meeting with them.

I took the elevator up to my office, stopping anxiously at my secretary's desk on the way in. "Mary, get *Hallmark* headquarters on the phone; find out the price range of their greeting cards in 1980!"

"What?"

"Just do it!" I yelled, heading toward my office.

"I'll get right on it," Mary said, as I flew by her again on my way out.

Riding solo down the elevator, I heard a voice speak to me: "You need more proof? And I thought I was all-knowing!"

As God enlightened me with an awareness of my psycho-foible, I laughed aloud; only a jerk would need more proof. There I go, looking through a veil again, I thought.

Walking into the conference room, I performed an imaginary ritual, lifting the veil from my face. I no longer had to mourn the loss of my soul; it was returning just as it had left, one precious shred at a time. The congregated hopefuls rose to give me a standing ovation. I was taken aback; was it related to my epiphany? Was it a sign that God was saying, "You've finally made it?" No. The explanation was forthcoming: "Finally! We've been waiting almost a half-hour!"

So my standing ovation was rooted in sarcasm. I didn't care; it had been a standing ovation nonetheless. It could be whatever I wanted it to be; I was the one holding the ball.

Mary later told me that Hallmarks went for sixty-five cents to a dollar-seventy five in 1980. I had my confirmation, despite my decision that it was unnecessary.

That night I slept like a baby, grateful that my private annals had been spared the voyeur. My secrets were tucked safely into my skull and the pages of my notebook. I was in recovery; no one needed to know how deeply I had sunk.

I awoke the following morning fully cognizant that the chirping songbirds were just an illusion. I sprang out of bed and headed for the coffee, not wanting to fall into a trance that morning.

"Good morning, love," I said to Maria, who was already dressed and on her second cup of coffee.

"Good morning. You're certainly in a good mood today," Maria said.

"Well, I'm really looking forward to the party today," I said. After a millisecond of deliberation, I footnoted a feeling. "To be honest, I miss my mother."

My sharing of that footnote was well-received. I was fascinated: sharing seemed to be the key to the psychiatrist's office. Or was it the key to Maria's heart? Whenever I opened with, "to be honest," the conversation always closed with a sense of peace. It was comforting.

"Well, that's normal," Maria said.

I thought, look at the validation being thrown my way; how could I have doubted *my* sanity? There was nothing wrong with me, a shrink was confirming it. And, Maria had graduated at the *top* of her class.

"You think?" I asked, needing to have my validation quantified.

"Absolutely."

Absolutely meant without a doubt, didn't it? "Go on," I practically begged.

"Well, you haven't seen your mother since Valentine's Day. You've been avoiding your father, and haven't called the house. Do you ever think that you allow your relationship with your father to come between you and Leona?" Maria set us up with another cup of coffee; it was going to be a long session.

"Funny you should say that," I replied. "I was thinking the very same thing yesterday. I suddenly realized how little I actually know my mother."

"And why do you suppose that is?"

"Well, I'm not sure. But I think it has something to do with the way we were always running for cover. My mother provided shelter from my father's wrath; she was expert at averting the warheads. I'm afraid our survival mission left no time to get to know Mom; as a result, we failed to build a meaningful relationship. The only time I felt any real connection with her was when we'd clean her collection together. My intentions were good; I wanted her to realize that her collection was important, because it was important to her. She deserved some kindness for acting as our ambassador. How absurd is that?"

"It's not at all absurd," Maria said. "You were groping, and quite creatively, for any opportunity to build a bridge to your mother. That the opportunity presented itself in the form of inanimate fruits and vegetables isn't important. What is important is that you were trying to harvest something very real—parental connection. There is nothing absurd about a child wanting to feel connected to a parent, even if that connection is based on something that seems ridiculous in hindsight. Your crop dusting was an archetype for the bridge to parental validation. Can you see that? And if you do, how does it make you feel?"

I thought, was it professional for a shrink to ask more than one question at a time? I answered: "I guess. It just seems so absurd. I could never get past the absurdity."

"How could you? You were just a child. Don't you see that?"

"Now I do. I guess I can't understand how my mother could settle for a life built on a foundation of changing the subject."

"Perhaps she conceived of it as a necessary evil; in sacrificing her own interests, she saved her children. What makes you think she is satisfied with her past? We all have regrets. Can you see that?"

"Yes. And I'm just now realizing what an unselfish woman my mother is. Why am I just now realizing that?"

"Why do you think you are just now realizing it?" Maria threw back at me, with the authority of Freud.

"Perhaps I hadn't looked hard enough, or maybe I was looking through a veil of confusion," I admitted.

"Maybe you're guilty on both counts?"

"Maybe," I said, shamefully.

Maria gave me absolution: "I don't know quite how to say this; you were at fault, but it wasn't really your fault."

"That's a relief."

"You were doing the best you could with what you had to work with," Maria said.

Was that meant as a double entendre?

Maria read my thoughts: "I didn't mean that the way it sounded. Anyhow, it is never too late. Don't beat yourself up about it; move forward in a different direction. You need to see your mother with new eyes." Maria looked at the clock.

I thought: my fifty-five minutes couldn't possibly be up yet. With a deep breath, I came to a more rational conclusion: we had better get ready to go if we wanted to arrive in Philadelphia on time.

"You're right, Maria. Thank you."

"You're welcome. Now that we've settled that, we should get ready to go."

"One more thing," I said. "You should never doubt your abilities as a therapist. I'm sure you're a tremendous help to your patients; you have certainly helped me to see things in a different light."

"Thank you, but don't forget that when we talk, I'm speaking as your wife, not your therapist. Do you mind if I take my shower first?"

"Not at all. Take your time."

While Maria showered, I did some more soul-searching. Our conversation, while bringing me out of solitary confinement, opened up a Pandora's box: I realized how filthy and tightly-woven the fabric of my earlier veil had been.

For years I blamed Maria for being unwilling to help me. I had been projecting; I was unwilling to help myself. I refused to let my guard down, fearful of my soul being judged insane. When I was honest, Maria never judged me. She always told me that my feelings were perfectly normal. We even had the same worst fears. What had I been so afraid of?

Maybe it was even time to view my father in a different light. I always accused him of assuming and jumping to conclusions, when I was no better. I had been quick to indict Maria and Edwina. Perhaps God had sent me that greeting card, to force me to take a good look at what I was becoming.

I resolved to break out of the prison of my own head; I'd try to move past my limitations and see myself and others in a new light. As Granny once told me, beneath our personalities, we're all the same. I was going to stop delighting in my father's foibles and instead feel compassion for his personal struggle. Perhaps there was more to my father than my narrow vision had allowed me to see.

My self-analysis was interrupted by Maria's call from the hallway: "It's all yours!"

It was time; with some of my demons having been exorcised, a cleansing bath was welcome. I washed my coffee cup and headed for the baptismal.

While filling the tub, I looked toward the ceiling. For the first time in months, there wasn't a spider to be found. Was it any accident that clearing the cobwebs in my head had rendered our bathroom pest-free as well? I decided it wasn't an accident. God was presenting a sign in the form of a riddle: either I was getting my act together or maintenance had cleaned up theirs. As I showered, I pondered that profundity.

Maria actually trusted me to drive to Philadelphia. I took the tunnel out of Manhattan for a change, marveling at that feat of human engineering.

As I approached Newark Airport, I realized my consciousness was expanding. Those weren't specks of dirt on my windshield; they were people, just like me, searching for meaning beyond the superficial circumstances their personalities had been confronted with. I couldn't treat people like dirt and expect good will in return; what was the matter with me? I thought those thoughts while keeping a watchful eye on the highway; I didn't want to get killed when things were finally starting to make sense. I wondered what lay on the road ahead.

A jumbo jet was getting ready for take-off on the runway parallel to us. As it taxied, I pondered the symbolism buried in that aircraft; it didn't get *instant* lift. It had to taxi, slowly at first, gradually accelerating and counteracting the forces that kept it grounded. Even upon becoming airborne, its effort was not finished; it had to reach a higher altitude before it could soar. My flight from neurosis to emotional balance would follow a similar course.

As the plane ascended, I became charged with the power of hope. I could soar too; I just needed to counteract the force that kept me from flying: my own fear. I resolved that I would soar into the new millennium; that was my deadline. There would be no shortage of on-board refreshments: my head was full of nuts.

Focusing skyward on the disappearing plane, I veered off the road slightly. I looked at Maria; she hadn't noticed. She was staring out the window, obviously lost in thought.

"What are you thinking about, Maria?"

"I was just thinking about how much power we need to make our personalities soar, much like those aircraft."

"You're kidding."

"No, why?" Maria asked.

"Because I was just thinking the very same thing. I wondered if fear kept us from soaring."

"You've hit the nail right on the head, Tony. Fear is the excess baggage that weighs us down. I think our most important mission as humans is to let go of the fear that stands in the way of our true potential. It's such a huge task."

"I know," I said. "I'm just coming to realize what a load I've been carrying."

"At least you realize it. Watch out!" Maria said.

A car was passing and I had trespassed into his lane. "Sorry," I said.

Maria continued. "The disheartening thing for me as a psychiatrist is to see how many people refuse to face that fact. They look to me to provide a magic bullet in the form of medication; what they don't realize is that their burden hasn't been lifted. They're just too numb to feel it anymore."

"I guess we're better off without magic bullets."

"No. We need to look at it from a broader perspective than that. In some cases, medication is an absolute necessity: when a patient's pain is so deep that it stands in the way of rational thinking. Then drugs can be an effective modality; they allow us to numb the pain temporarily while establishing a line of rationality. Drugs aren't always the answer; on the other hand, sometimes they're the only answer."

I re-examined my black and white perspective. No, we weren't better off without magic bullets; sometimes magic was our only hope. Life wasn't black or white; there were infinite shades of gray.

Maria interrupted my self-examination. "Sometimes medication is imperative, in cases of severe depression or organic brain disorder. The disheartening thing that I was referring to is the case of patients who are perfectly capable of sorting through their problems, but refuse to do so because they are unwilling to take an honest look at themselves."

"Oh," I said. "But you shouldn't feel disheartened; you can't force people to stop lying to themselves."

"It's not so much lying as it is avoiding the truth. What really disheartens me is my oath to first do no harm; justifying the decision to medicate is a tremendous burden, the thing I most dislike about my profession. I don't like having that kind of power;

how do I know I am really qualified to be messing with a person's brain chemistry? I'm not God."

Wow, I thought: what a dissertation! I had never fathomed the burden of Maria's existence, apart from my own role in the ordeal. "Wow," I said.

"Thank you. It's a burden I have to deal with every day when I walk into that office. Lately, I've been asking myself if I want that burden for the rest of my life; I'm not sure that I do."

"You know," I said, "I'll support whatever decision you make. As far as I'm concerned, you can quit your practice tomorrow; I make enough money to support us. So we wouldn't have money to invest for awhile; so what?"

"I appreciate your support, Tony, but I would never make such an important decision impulsively. Still, I have been doing an awful lot of soul-searching lately."

Of course Maria wouldn't be impulsive; I was the impulsive one. I was being bombarded with lessons that day, the most recent having been: look before you leap. God added a footnote: "and for my sake, look without a veil!"

I wanted to move past my "veil" issue; I had gotten the point. I had other questions that needed answering, and Maria was on a roll. "Why do you suppose that people can be so unwilling to face their problems?" I asked Maria.

"Well, what most people don't realize is that they have a relationship with themselves just as much as they have a relationship with others. And that relationship can be based on honesty, or it can be deceitful. Just as a person chooses not to reveal his secrets in a relationship with another person, he can also choose not to reveal his secrets to himself. But secrets are the antithesis of communication; so a relationship either fails to develop, or is eroded by mistrust. A lot of people have poor relationships with themselves, which is why they feel lost; that is the true core of loneliness."

I was fascinated, but I kept my eyes on the highway. I had no idea how complex the human mind really was. Perhaps I needed to get to know my own mind a little better. That was it; I would put an end to my casual affair and find a more meaningful relationship with myself. That was my most important lesson.

There were so many lessons I needed to learn; it was probably just as well that I had never fathered a child. How could I have taught a child about life when I was so baffled by it myself? But there was hope; I just needed to wine and dine myself a little more.

"You know, Tony," Maria said, "I don't know how it happened, but all of a sudden I feel our relationship is entering a new phase."

"How's that?" I asked, playing dumb.

"I don't know; I just feel freer to share my feelings with you. To tell you the truth, I've been keeping some secrets."

"What secrets?" I asked, listening intently.

"Well, for a long time I harbored a secret resentment toward you."

"What did I do?" I asked innocently. What I should have asked: "What haven't I done?"

"It wasn't anything you did; my resentment was totally ungrounded. I felt as if you doubted my professional credibility; but now I see I was just projecting my own feelings of inadequacy onto you."

"Oh," I said. I had picked up a current of resentment from Maria many times in the past, but I'd naturally assumed it was a resentment borne of regret; after all, she had married a madman.

"I'm sorry I was such a madwoman," Maria said. "Until today, I've locked myself in solitary with one of my deepest fears: I'm uncomfortable with the power I have as a psychiatrist. I'm sorry I had wrongly accused you; I was the guilty one. I was projecting again. That seems to be a problem for me."

Was there such a thing as a projected deja vu? I was having one. "Don't blame yourself," I said. "If I wasn't so locked-up in my own head, I would have been there for you. To be quite honest, I resented the power you had as a psychiatrist."

"What? How so?"

"I was afraid you would see how crazy I was, and that you would leave me."

"I never thought you were crazy; confused sometimes, but never crazy."

"Good," I said, "because here's the really crazy part: I resented the fact that you were a psychiatrist and wouldn't help me. Then I realized you were unable to help me because I refused to let you know what was really going on. I think I've lived my whole life in an emotional prison, hiding behind the veil of silence."

"I guess we both have," Maria said. "But it's time we came out of hiding."

"You're right; it can be awfully lonely within the confines of your own skull."

"I know," Maria said. "And your imagination can run so amuck; sometimes our imagined fears are far worse than anything reality can slap us with."

"I know. Can you believe I've even gone so far as to imagine that you'd have me institutionalized and flee to Argentina?"

"I believe it," Maria said. "I've even gone so far as to question my own motives in marrying you: do I really love Tony or did I simply need someone to computerize my patient files?"

"You're kidding?" I asked in disbelief.

"No, but don't worry—I do love you! Those thoughts emerged from paranoid fears about myself; they had nothing to do with you."

"I know you love me, Maria," I said. "I was shocked by your honesty, not by your admission; I've had similar irrational thoughts."

"Like what?"

"At times I wondered if I really loved you, or if I married you because I was screwed up and needed psychotherapy—my own private shrink!"

Maria laughed. "I guess Granny was right; underneath our personalities, we're all the same."

"Yeah," I said. "I'm always surprised to find how much we have in common. I guess I thought as a psychiatrist you were spared those feelings of self-doubt."

"I guess it does seem an oxymoron, but even psychiatrists question their sanity at times; we're no different than anybody else. Boy, what a relief it is to spill my guts about that; we can torture ourselves with silence sometimes."

No truer words had ever been spoken; my relationship with Mildred and Martin had locked me into my own private hell of silence. While we were baring all, I decided to come clean about my imaginary Aunt and Uncle. My revelation might send Maria packing, but I could bear the burden of silence no longer.

I revealed every sordid detail of my secret liaison with my imaginary woman and her husband, including that I had wrongly accused both Maria and Edwina of sending me hate-mail.

Maria just sat there, obviously stunned. I couldn't believe I had unloaded angst of that magnitude while operating heavy machinery. We were both stunned.

After what seemed an eternity of silence, Maria finally spoke: "What a scathingly brilliant idea!"

What? It was brilliant? It wasn't psychotic? "You think so?" I asked sheepishly.

"Absolutely!" Maria exclaimed. "How genius of you to create your own treatment modality. Most people won't even face their problems. Not you; you looked them square in the eye and tackled them head-on!"

"I guess I did," I said, dumbfounded.

"Have you any idea how creative your modality was? You lacked the self-confidence to heed your own advice, but you were with-it enough to realize you'd listen to someone of authority. So you transferred your own authority to an outside source, which was paradoxically on the inside. In effect, you created your own team of impartial observers. How did you ever come up with it, with no psychiatric training?"

"I don't know," I replied.

"So you did it all on a subconscious level—true genius!" Maria exclaimed. "I wish I'd thought of it; this is exactly the kind of fresh insight that contemporary psychotherapy is lacking. This could revolutionize psychiatry as we know it; I want to hear all the details, not that I intend to steal your idea or anything."

"I don't know what to say. They just sort of popped in, unannounced. I was tired of being alone in my head; it was a relief to have someone to talk to. I never fought it."

"The power of your mind is incredible!" Maria said. "You did such an excellent job of creating your characters, that you were even able to manifest physical evidence of their existence, in the form of that Easter card synchronicity."

"The card wasn't intended for us," I said. "Vitello was spelled with two T's."

"I realize that; but nevertheless, you were able to summon that card, telepathically, into the realm of your own physical reality. That is powerful!"

How had I done that? I didn't know what to say; never before had so many exclamation points been used to punctuate my psychological prowess. Was that really happening to me? Had I really been hiding genius behind that dusty old bookcase? I must have been crazy to have thought I was nuts.

"Tony," Maria said, "now that we have no more secrets, would you ever consider allowing me to read your purple notebook?"

"Why would you want to do that?" I asked. "I've already told you everything there is to know."

"What about the subtleties, the nuances of your construction? You couldn't possibly have told me everything in twenty minutes' time," Maria said. "Think of all the poor souls out there whom you could help; they'd realize that they didn't have to be alone either."

"All right," I found myself saying. I could bare my soul, if it meant revolutionizing psychiatry as we knew it. I once feared that a mental illness would be named on my behalf; instead, my name would be linked to a cure.

"But don't worry," Maria said. "You'll get full credit for the idea."

"Maria," I said, "do me a favor; leave my name out of it; I have no credentials. I'm giving you full permission to steal my idea." I didn't want to be blamed for any hidden side-effects that might emerge.

"Oh Tony, you should have more confidence; your ideas are brilliant."

"Thanks honey, but had I not been married to a psychiatrist, I never would have thought of it; the credit is really yours. Besides, now we're even; you gave me the idea for that program command I was having trouble with."

"I guess you're right," Maria said. "It doesn't matter whose idea it was. We're a couple; we do things jointly."

"I like that."

"What?"

"*Jointly*. The wall between us is finally crumbling."

"It is."

My soul felt incredibly light. So light, that had I not been driving, I would have projected myself onto a cloud again. But there was a lot of traffic and I needed to stay behind the wheel. I wasn't going to risk killing us both, not when the pendulum was finally swinging in sync. My new mission was to first do no harm; after all, I was a psychiatrist by marriage.

"Do you have two dollars for the bridge?" I asked.

"Here you go," Maria said, handing me the money. She then placed her hand on my thigh. I felt sparks, not of lust but of love.

For the first time since Valentine's Day, we were connected by a current that was powerful enough to shock us out of our heads and into a mutual mindset. Honestly, lust had also been sparked, but as an undercurrent.

"Tony, would you do me a favor?"

"Sure, what is it?"

"Can we have no more psycho-babble for the rest of the day? I really need at least one day off."

"Me too," I replied. In the last chapter of my life I would have perceived Maria's statement as rejection, and would have pulled my cerebellum into a fetal position. But I was in recovery; I took her statement for what it was worth: therapy was a draining process.

We drove the rest of the way in silence, but it was a good silence. I could read Maria's thoughts and she could read mine; we were both enchanted by the colors of the May landscape. The beauty of spring consummated our re-established union; our love appeared to be in full bloom.

"It looks as if we'll have to park on the street," I said, noticing that Granny's driveway was already full.

"Everything looks so beautiful," Maria said. "It makes me realize what we miss by living in a high-rise. Sometimes I yearn for my own garden."

I looked at Maria. "You know, honey, we could move to Long Island."

"I know," Maria said. "But there's the commute."

"True, but everything's a compromise. We'll think about it." I walked around the car and opened the door for Maria; I was going to start acting like a gentleman.

"Thanks, Tony," Maria said, getting out of the car and planting a kiss on my cheek. Our sentiments were interrupted by the sound of a horn. It was Jerry. Maria and I waited at the curb for Jerry to park his car.

"Who's in the car with Jerry?" Maria asked.

"It's Roberta."

"It doesn't look like Roberta."

"She got a haircut."

"Oh."

Jerry and Roberta got out of the car. It *wasn't* Roberta.

"It's not Roberta," Maria said. "It's a guy."

Jerry and the guy approached us. "Tony!" Jerry yelled.

"Hi Jerry," I said, hugging him. Jerry then hugged Maria. "I'd like you guys to meet Tom Avogadro, a friend of mine from Princeton.

Maria and I shook hands with Tom. "Nice to meet you," I said. "Are you in the Physics Department too?"

"No," Tom said. "I'm in Molecular Genetics."

I secretly wondered if Tom had been in any way involved with the headless rats. "I understand there's a lot going on in your field right now," I said.

"That's an understatement," Tom said. "Tony tells me you're with SuperSoft, in Robotics."

"Yeah, but not in the mechanical division; I'm in artificial intelligence. Right now I'm working on a program that teaches a computer to learn from its mistakes."

"Interesting," Tom said. "If only we could teach the general public that."

"That's Maria's department," Jerry said. "She's a psychiatrist in Manhattan."

"Oh," Tom said, interested. "Would you mind if I picked your brain about an idea?"

"Certainly not," Maria said. She looked at me and shrugged her shoulders. We had already agreed to halt the psycho-babble, but what could Maria do? She couldn't be rude.

Maria squeezed my arm; Tom then led Maria down the driveway.

I looked at Jerry. "Why the briefcase?"

"It's not a briefcase," Jerry said. "It's his sample bag."

"Sample bag?"

"Tom is a bio-musician."

"A what?"

"A bio-musician. He matches the base sequence in a person's DNA to musical tones, with a computer. You've never heard of it?"

"No."

"It's fascinating," Jerry said. "Just as no two people have the same DNA, everyone's song is unique."

"That's what Tom does at Princeton?"

"No. It's just a hobby. He's participating in the Human Genome Project."

"So why did Tom bring his sample bag to Granny's party?" I asked, dumbfounded.

"We thought it would be fun to do a profile on the family. I can bring the tapes to our next party."

"So Tom is going to take blood samples after we cut the cake?"

"No, Tony," Jerry laughed. "Tom only needs a few epithelial cells. Just a little swoosh on the inside of the cheek. Don't worry; it's painless."

I laughed. "That's pretty interesting."

"It is," Jerry said. "He did one for me. I was surprised to hear that my song was rock; I'd have guessed it to be more classical. But you know what they say: we rarely see ourselves as others see us."

I recalled the image of Jerry running onto stage and grabbing the microphone. He was right; I'd have guessed his song was rock even though he hadn't.

"Is the old man here yet?" Jerry asked.

"Must be. I passed his car when I was coming down the street."

"Hopefully he'll behave," Jerry said. "I hear he's up in arms over We R Nuts; we'll have to keep him away from Uncle Harry. I don't want to be breaking up any fights today."

"He's just jealous."

"I know. What do you say? Are you ready to go in and face the music?"

"Yeah. I just have one more question. Have you ever wondered why Mom has stayed with big Anthony all these years?"

"Of course I have," Jerry said. "I think everyone wonders. My guess is that she stayed because of the kids. And, I think she felt sorry for Dad; you know how pathetic he can be."

"I know, but doesn't it sadden you? Don't you think that Mom was shortchanged?"

"Of course it saddens me," Jerry said. "But I try not to dwell on it. Why dwell on the things I cannot change? I've tried to help Dad, but I stopped trying when I realized my efforts were futile. I can't spend my whole life trying to fix Dad; I have a life of my own. And don't worry about Mom, she's learning. Since she went back to school, she's finally starting to take charge of her life."

"You're right," I said. I remembered Valentine's Day, how

Mom had blasted big Anthony about his cursing. Even though she eventually caved in, she had begun on an assertive note.

"Don't worry, Tony," Jerry said. "We have each other."

"Thanks, Jerr. You know, I don't think I've ever told you this, but I always knew I could count on you to stand behind me, no matter what."

"Likewise," Jerry said. "We're brothers; we'll always have each other. And don't forget—one bad apple doesn't spoil the whole bunch! Come on, let's go say hello to Granny."

Jerry and I walked alongside the house to the backyard.

For a minute, it was as though I was twelve and Jerry was nine again.

"Are you driving back tonight?" Jerry asked.

"No, Maria and I are sleeping over."

"You're lucky, Tone."

The party was in full swing. Maria and Tom the bio-musician were engrossed in conversation, adjacent to the lilac bush. Margaret was giving instructions to the help, probably briefing them on how to set-up a proper display. From the corner of my eye I caught a glimpse of my father: he was sitting alone at one of the picnic benches. I looked at Jerry.

"We should probably go over and say hello," Jerry said. "Come on; we'll do it together and get it over with."

I took a deep breath and followed Jerry.

"Hello, Dad," Jerry said. I followed with a poorly-uttered greeting.

"Oh," Dad said, "you two must be my sons; I almost didn't recognize you, it's been so long. It wouldn't *kill* you to pick up the phone and call your mother."

"Nice to see you too," Jerry said. "The yard looks great, doesn't it?"

"Why wouldn't it?" Dad snapped. "When money's no object, you can put up a nice front. I see you still haven't had time for a haircut."

"No," Jerry said casually. "Where's Granny?"

"Where do you think she is? She's over there, the center of attention, as usual." Dad pointed to the tent that was set up next to the rose garden.

"Nice seeing you, Dad," Jerry said, as he turned to walk away.

I thought I'd better say something. "See you a little later," I muttered, following Jerry like his shadow.

"He's his usual self," Jerry said, as we approached the tent. I nodded in silent agreement.

Granny looked lovely. She was wearing a pink linen suit that cast a soft glow onto her creamy skin. She didn't look a day over sixty, having the skin of a woman considerably younger. And she moved with such fluidity; Granny was grace personified. I made eye contact with her.

"Tony, my love!" Granny said. "I'm so happy to see you. I've missed you so much." We embraced.

"Happy Birthday, Gran. I've missed you too," I said. "The garden looks wonderful this year."

"And there's my Nobel Laureate," Granny said, turning her attention to Jerry.

"We don't know that yet," Jerry said. "A lot can happen between now and October."

"Nonsense, Jerry. I have a good feeling. I think we'll all be going to Stockholm in December; you wait and see," Granny said. "Why don't you boys get a drink and something to eat?"

"Thanks, Gran," I said, "we will."

I suddenly felt someone hugging me from behind. It was Margaret. "Hi little brother!"

"Hi Margaret," I said, turning. "It's great to see you. How did the grand opening go?"

"Well, it happened a week later than planned, but it went very well," Margaret said.

"Trouble with the plumbing contractors?"

"No, actually I was in the hospital for a few days."

"Hospital? Are you all right? Why didn't you call me?"

"I didn't want to worry you. It was no big deal; just a little freak accident. I guess you could say I was involved in an essential oil spill," Margaret said.

"A what?" I asked, perplexed.

"Well, I was a little stressed out, trying to coordinate the opening; you know how stress can collect in your muscles. I guess I poured a little too much peppermint oil in my therapeutic bath; it sucked all the heat from my body and I went into convulsive chills. Ivan found me shivering uncontrollably and called an ambulance."

"An ambulance? Oh my God—why didn't you call me? I

would have driven down to Philadelphia."

"That's sweet of you, Tony, but I was fine by the following day. It was really no big deal; it just pushed the opening ahead a bit."

"Margaret, promise you'll call me if anything like that ever happens again," I insisted.

"Don't worry, Tone. I'm staying away from the volatile oils; I'm sticking with floral essences from now on. I've learned my lesson—don't worry!"

Thank God Margaret was spared. What if she hadn't survived? We needed her. I hugged Margaret. "I'm just so glad you're all right," I said.

"Thanks, Tony. That means a lot to me. Have you tried the shrimp rolls? They're delicious. Oh, and one more thing, Tone. Don't be taking any drinks from Aunt Vicky; I don't want her slipping you another mickey."

We both laughed. "Believe me," I said, "I've learned my lesson. By the way, where's Mom?"

"She and Aunt Vicky went inside to freshen up."

"Oh. I hadn't realized that Aunt Vicky and Uncle Harry were here already. Where's Uncle Harry?"

"Probably showing off his new *Lincoln* to some poor guest."

"He got a *Lincoln*?"

"Yes. I quote: 'A shipping magnate cannot be driving around in a *Ford* that is twelve years old'." Margaret rolled her eyes.

"I see," I said, laughing. I noticed Mom and Aunt descending the back steps; I went to greet them.

"Tony!" my mother yelled.

"Hi Mom. Hi Aunt Vicky," I responded. Aunt Vicky was wearing pink that day too, but on her lips.

Both women hugged me.

"I'm going to blow you a kiss, honey," Aunt Vicky said. "I just fixed my make-up."

Thank God. Aunt Vicky puckered up and exhaled into the spring air. "Catch it," she said.

"Got it, Aunt Vicky." I really *was* twelve years old again.

"How was your trip, dear?" my mother asked.

"It was great," I replied. I went to say more, but stopped. Great was sufficient; I didn't need to mention that my trip was really twenty years of psychotherapy and eight years of marriage counseling squeezed into a two-hour drive down the Turnpike, not to mention the several exorcisms.

"That's wonderful," Mom said. "I've missed you, Tony."

"I've missed you too, Mom."

"Did you see Harry's new Lincoln?" Aunt Vicky asked, pointing her hyacinth-colored fingernail toward the street.

"No, but I'll be sure to take a look at it," I responded.

"Oh, there's Ivan!" Aunt Vicky said. "Ivan!" she screamed, shuffling carefully away, not to lose her backless shoes as she ran toward him.

"Good," Mom said. "I needed to talk with you about something, Tony. Do you want to take a little walk?"

"How little?"

"Oh, Tony, you always were so silly."

"What do you want to talk about?" I asked, as we walked toward the front of the house.

"Well," Mom said, "I met a man, an artist. I met him at a writing workshop I took last month. He has propositioned me."

"Oh my God, Mom. Are you having an affair?"

"Of course not, Tony. I didn't mean that kind of proposition. Les is a minimalist artist, although he's seeking to expand into a more loaded genre. Les Izmore is his name; have you ever heard of him?"

"No," I said. "Is that his real name?"

"I suppose so. Why would he lie to me about his name?"

"I wasn't implying that he had lied. It just seems a coincidence; I thought maybe that was his professional name, since he's a minimalist."

"Well, like I said, he's trying to expand beyond minimalism. Anyhow, he's working on a new project, an exhibit for the Guggenheim. Les calls it a living sculpture. It's some new twist, a cross between The Last Supper and the first Thanksgiving. Les is calling it *The Last Thanksgiving.*"

I laughed. "That's interesting."

"I didn't think so at first," Mom said, "but after Les explained his rationale, I realized he was on to something."

"Maybe he is," I said. "But what does Les' sculpture have to do with you?"

"Well, I don't know how to tell you this, so I'm going to come right out with it: Les needs my dishes!"

"He needs your dishes?" I asked, confused.

"Yes, but before you say anything, hear me out. I know how much those dishes mean to you; believe me, I had every intention of leaving them to you. But this is *art*, Tony. And where would you store them? Besides, you and Maria don't even cook. Believe me, I'm not doing this for the money."

"How much money?" I asked.

"Ten thousand dollars," Mom said. "After all, most of them are signed and numbered."

"Sold!" I yelled.

"You don't mind?"

"Of course I don't mind; after all, we're talking about *art*," I said, half-laughing.

"I'm so relieved," Mom said. "I'll be able to use the money for tuition; I was accepted into the writing program at Penn."

"What? That's great. I didn't know you had applied at Penn."

"I didn't want to say anything in case I didn't get in."

"Congratulations, Mom. I never knew you wanted to be a writer."

"Oh, yes, since I was a little girl. When your grandmother would read those letters in her hatboxes, I would make up stories about the senders."

"So why didn't you pursue it when you were younger?"

"Well, in those days women didn't want anything for themselves; we were supposed to be content with raising our families. Still, I yearned to be a writer. But your father wouldn't hear of it; he didn't think I had what it took to make any money at it. It was easier to remain silent; you know how your father can go off." Mom stared down the street as if searching for something that had slipped out of her reach a long time ago.

"I don't get it," I said. "With all due respect, Mom, I don't know why the hell you stayed with him."

"Sometimes I wonder the same thing myself," Mom said sadly. "But what could I do? I couldn't support three children on the dream of becoming a writer. And I guess I felt sorry for your father."

"Why?"

"Well, the circumstances regarding your father's immigration were very unsettling to him, and I've always tried to be compassionate."

"What circumstances?"

"Your grandparents in Sicily bought your father his ticket to America, and practically forced him to get on the boat."

"So? They just wanted him to have a better life. A lot of families wanted that for their children—America was the land of opportunity."

"You don't understand, Tony. The Vitello's were one of the wealthiest families in Sicily; they ran your father out of the country, because he didn't fit in with the rest of them."

"Fit in how?"

"How do you think?"

"Oh."

"Anyhow," Mom said, "if I left him, then he'd have been abandoned by everyone; I just couldn't find it in my heart to do that to him."

"That's because you're so unselfish, Mom. But it's a very admirable trait."

"You think so?"

"Yes," I said, kissing my mother on the forehead, just above her illusory question marks.

"Thank you, Tony. You know, it feels good to have gotten this off my chest; I've been carrying it for too long. You were always the one whom I could talk to; that's why it was such a difficult decision to make, my selling the dishes to Les. I kept remembering your childhood, how you'd come running into the dining room when you heard the china closet doors open, always so eager to help. I know how those dishes fascinated you; it is very unselfish of you to let go of them. I'm so glad that you don't mind."

"It's for art," I said. "Don't worry, Mom. You sell those dishes and go to Penn; I'm behind you every step of the way."

"I love you dear," Mom said. "You've always been so sweet—my saving grace. Do me a favor, sweetie; don't mention your father's exile to anyone. If he found out I'd discussed it with anyone, well, you know. I can't deal with that kind of distraction right now; I'm really involved in my work. " She squeezed my hand.

I had been someone's saving grace? What else would I discover about myself before the day was over? "What do you say? Are you ready to party?" I asked.

"I've never been more ready in my life," Mom said.

We walked into the backyard to find a crowd had gathered around Tom Avogadro; people were lined-up, eager for their cheek scrapings. I did a double take—my father was in line! Ivan was acting as Tom's assistant, handing Tom a fresh popsicle stick for each scraping.

"Shall we get something to eat?" I asked my mother.

"Yes. I'm starving."

We walked to the tent arm-in-arm.

"There you are!" Maria said. "I was looking all over for you."

"Oh, we just went for a little walk," Mom said. "Tony can tell you about it later."

I sat down to eat, sandwiched between the two women in my life. My emotional appetite having been satisfied, I filled up on the banquet that Margaret had so skillfully directed. It was appealing to the eye and the stomach, and I feasted with a sense of fulfillment.

"Come on, Tone," Jerry said, coming at me with a popsicle stick. "They're playing our song!"

"All right, Jerry." I rinsed my mouth with the gin and tonic that was at my disposal. I secretly hoped that the gin didn't alter my cheek DNA in any way; I didn't want my theme song to be laced with any slurs or bloopers.

"Open wide," Jerry ordered. I did, and he confiscated my genes in one foul swoop. Jerry walked away with my DNA, to pack it for the return trip to Princeton.

I turned to Maria. "I hope they don't do anything illicit with our DNA; I don't want to be vacationing in Rio one day and run into a gang of boys who are, shall I say, the spitting image of me."

Maria laughed. "I don't know, Tom does look like Gregory Peck."

Mom heard only the last part of our conversation. "Do you think so, kids? I don't see it; I think he resembles our Tommy a bit."

It had been so long, I couldn't even remember what *our* Tommy looked like. I then remembered that Tommy was supposed to call me the month before when he was on Broadway. "Aunt Vicky," I yelled. "Was Tommy in New York last month? He never called me."

Aunt Vicky approached. "He said he was. He was probably too busy with practice and everything. I specifically told him to call you. I don't know what's wrong with him sometimes; if I didn't know better, I'd swear he was avoiding us."

I hadn't meant to get Tommy in trouble. "He was probably extremely busy."

"I hope that's all it was," Aunt Vicky said.

Aunt Vicky's hope didn't sound very convincing. I wasn't surprised; Tommy hadn't been to a family function in almost four years. Maybe he *was* avoiding us.

"There you are, Tony," Uncle Harry said. "Ready for a little spin around the block?"

"Sure," I said, finishing my gin and tonic in one long, desperate gulp.

We walked to the street; approaching the Lincoln, Uncle Harry unlocked its doors with a remote-control.

"Isn't she a beauty?" Uncle Harry asked proudly.

"She certainly is."

"I always knew I'd be driving a Lincoln one day," he said, as we got into the car. "Doesn't it smell good in here? So new! I love the smell of a new car."

"It smells great," I said, as we pulled away.

"I had to get out of there for a few minutes," Uncle Harry said. "Your father's jealousy was becoming intolerable. He still believes We R Nuts is going to flop; we're busier than a candy store on Valentine's Day!"

"That's great, Uncle Harry. I had no doubt you would succeed; it was a great idea."

"It was, wasn't it? I'm so glad to be away from that job at the Giant Mart. I was setting myself up for a herniated disc; some of those cartons weighed a ton. But that's all in the past now, Tony."

"Good," I said. "Are things better between you and Aunt Vicky?"

"I guess. She still maintains she didn't know my speech impediment was contractual. Maybe she didn't; an awful lot seems to go over her head. Still, she's no dummy. But I got tired of arguing about it; I have an empire to build."

"Yes you do."

"Can you believe how powerful this baby is? Look, she still

goes, even when you have your foot on the brake—can't keep her down!"

I looked toward the floor and saw that Uncle Harry was utilizing both feet. "Don't do that, Uncle Harry, you'll ruin your transmission!"

"Nothing wrong with this baby's transmission, she's geared for power."

Not for long, I thought.

We came to Granny's street and Uncle Harry turned the corner. "Damn!" he said. "Can you believe someone pulled into my spot that fast?"

We found another spot up the block, and walked back to the party. Margaret was putting candles on the cake. "Come on, everyone," she yelled. "It's time to sing!"

Granny, surrounded by everyone except my parents, sat down in her seat of honor. The cake was beautiful. Ivan, who was advanced in the art of cake decorating, had adorned it with hundreds of buttercream flowers, all Granny's favorites.

"Where's Mom and Dad?" I asked Margaret.

"They're in the bathroom. Dad claims he has a splinter in his mouth. You should have heard what he called Tom under his breath; you know, the usual vulgarities."

We began to sing. Granny, illuminated by firelight, looked radiant. As she blew out the candles, I made a wish: that she lived to be at least a hundred and twenty. I did some mental math; that would make me in the neighborhood of seventy-seven. I couldn't imagine myself at seventy-seven. I made one more wish, that my mother make it big as a writer. Everyone began shouting and clapping madly.

The party went on, well into the evening. I had a good time despite the growing sadness I was beginning to feel for my father. That he had allowed his demons to control him caused a dichotomy of feelings in me. On one hand was sadness for what he had lost; on the other, hope, for *I* was free to choose the direction of *my* fate.

Catching a glimpse of my father from across the yard motivated me to pray for his salvation, that he might one day entertain a better relationship with himself. The contempt in his eyes was really aimed at himself; we just served to bounce it back to him. In some strange way, he was at fault, but it wasn't really his fault.

When the last of the guests had departed and the catering crew finished their clean-up, Granny joined Maria and me under the tent.

"It was a wonderful party, wasn't it?" Granny asked.

"Yes," Maria and I answered in unison.

"I will never forget it as long as I live," Granny said. "To cap a perfectly wonderful day, I received a letter this afternoon from an old friend in Germany. It was so heart-warming that I've kept it right here," Granny said, patting her heart. Would you like me to read it to you?"

"Certainly," we said.

Granny reached into her jacket and pulled the letter from her chest pocket. She began to read:

Dear Rose,

Well, it seems as though we have out-lived the rest of our group. Who would have thought that one day it would be just the two of us?

I am writing not only to wish you a happy birthday, but to tell you of a conversation that I recently overheard at the University.

I had been invited to speak at a banquet, and rumors were flying that some young lad from Princeton was poised to win the Nobel Prize. When I realized the lad was your grandson Jerry, tears came to my eyes. How proud Stanley would be, although I'm sure he has played a hand in this, on some divine level. That our years of hard work should be consummated by Stanley's grandson is no accident; it is surely God's will, fate falling into place at that laboratory in Princeton.

Perhaps we will all meet in Stockholm in December. For now, I wish you a happy birthday, and the best of luck to your grandson.

With much love,
Walter Water

"That was so beautiful," Maria said.

I was speechless.

"On that note," Granny said, "I say we get tucked in for the evening."

Maria and I hugged Granny and said a teary goodnight. We retired to the bedroom that Mom and Aunt Vicky had shared in their youth.

As we lay, Maria and I held each other in silence, clinging not only to each other but to the hope that had unfolded on that beautiful spring day.

While drifting to sleep, I heard the faint echo of Bach emanating from Granny's office down the hall. The sweetest harmony capped my day, and I fell gently into the night as my lullaby sounded.

Eight

After learning of my father's deportation from Sicily, my inner landscape underwent some radical shifts. Those shifts unearthed more about my own character than my father's: in some perverse valley of my psyche, I harbored a secret delight in my father's perturbations. What kind of person would poke fun at a man who had been exiled by his own parents? The dig into my own tectonics surfaced a revelation: I too was at fault.

I remembered something Granny had said a long time ago: we need to show compassion toward all people, even the obnoxious ones. My father, certainly fitting the bill, deserved more kindness.

After Maria had scoured my journal (my case history), we began having regular therapy sessions. Maria's prognosis? My soul would never be free until I healed the rift with my father.

I even mustered the nerve to call my father. He couldn't talk, didn't want to tie-up the line in case an important call was trying to get through. I hung-up discouraged but not defeated. I was determined to heal the rift by the end of the millennium; that was my deadline.

I looked at the clock on the stove. It was early, so Maria and I would have time to squeeze in one more session before I saw my father at the Fourth of July barbecue that night.

Maria walked into the kitchen wearing a red blouse. "You look nice today, honey," I said.

"Thanks. I bought this on sale last year at the end of the season; almost forgot I had it." Maria opened the refrigerator.

"Nothing in there," I said. "Why don't we go out to breakfast?"

"Sounds great. Let me grab my purse."

We left our climate-controlled apartment to find that summer had descended with a vengeance. Manhattan's glass boxes were sweating; condensation evaporated as it dripped to the sweltering pavements below. The atmosphere was steamy.

"Early for a heat wave, isn't it?" Maria asked.

Maria looked hot in red. As she tugged at her blouse, I noticed how attractive she looked, with bare arms and her chiseled form wrapped ever so lusciously in red. I then realized how long it had been since we'd made love. I wondered if our doctor-patient relationship was interfering with our sexual one; after all, a taboo existed. Our relationship had become quite professional: we were entrenched, quite obsessively, in therapy. That had to explain Maria's lack of interest. Our professional relationship was thwarting our sexual one.

"Isn't it?" Maria repeated.

"Yes, but we can get past it if we try hard enough," I answered Maria and myself, while hailing a cab. I was making a breakthrough; I had simultaneously orchestrated three separate events. Prior to therapy, I couldn't walk and chew gum at the same time. I grew more confident.

We poured into the cool chamber of the restaurant. "It feels great in here," Maria said. "I love a restaurant with a good cooling system."

"I know. The food is awful but at least discomfort won't add to our misery."

"Very funny."

We approached the hostess. "Two?" she asked.

I turned to the couple who had poured in behind us. "Will you be joining us today?" They said nothing, looking at me as though my straitjacket had come undone.

"I guess it will just be the two of us," I said.

Maria elbowed me as the hostess led us to a table. "I can't believe you just did that; what if they'd said yes and we were forced to make small talk over breakfast?"

"Worse than that," I said, "what if they were poor conversationalists? We'd be forced to endure an hour of throat-clearing and awkward silences."

Maria and I laughed. The heat had obviously fried our brains; we weren't normally so silly.

The hostess glared at me while handing me my menu; I began to laugh again, and Maria followed.

"I *said*," the hostess yelled, "Would you like coffee?!"

I was laughing too hard to answer her, so Maria spoke for us both. "Yes, please. We'll both have coffee." Maria then continued laughing.

The hostess spun on her heels and was gone.

"She needn't be concerned about a future canonization," I said.

"It's the heat," Maria said. "The heat has a way of bringing out the worst in people, except in you. You're in rare form today; I'm glad you're in such high spirits."

"Well," I said, "I've been thinking a lot about our session yesterday."

"Our session? Tony, I'd be a little more comfortable if you referred to it as our conversation. It would be unethical for me to treat my husband; besides, you don't need a shrink, you need a sounding board. I'm sorry if I appeared to speak as your psychiatrist; I didn't mean to. To tell you the truth, I'm confused: am I treating you?" she asked in a muffled whisper. Maria scanned the dining room suspiciously before continuing: "If I've failed to separate my professional opinion from my private one, please forgive me. I told myself I was never going to fall into that trap; I hope I haven't placed you in an uncomfortable position."

"Not at all," I reassured Maria. I needed her to fall into that trap; how else would I make a full recovery? "I know that you're speaking on a personal level." She was; it wasn't a completely false statement. But it wasn't entirely true, and I had promised myself that the game-playing was over.

Maria perceived my undercurrent. "What? You sound as if you don't really believe yourself."

"I don't."

"What do you believe?"

"I believe that I do need and want your professional help; without it, I may not survive my neurosis. I think the new phase of our relationship that you've made reference to is really just the eye of the storm."

"I appreciate succinctness in a patient. I would be happy to help you weather the storm; it would be unethical to refuse. For the sake of my conscience, can we call our sessions *conversations*? I hate internal debates with myself."

"Consider it done."

"So," Maria asked, "which *conversation* were you referring to, the one regarding your major demon or your minor one?"

"My major one," I answered. "I'm going to treat my father with more compassion; maybe that will turn him around."

"I'm not trying to squelch your hope, but what seems to motivate your compassion is the goal of receiving an expected response: your father changing. That may or may not happen; true compassion has to come from the gut, not the head. The only thing you can hope to accomplish through compassion is a sense of your own inner peace. If your father happens to be enlightened in the process, that's icing on the cake. You have half the equation right; you realize the need to change your own behavior. Just don't expect your behavior to change someone else; true change can only come from within. Can you see that you really need to question the intentions behind your motivations?" Maria asked.

Before I could answer, the waitress appeared at our table with coffee. "Good morning. My name is Clotilde, and I'll be your server today. Would you like to order now?"

I looked at Maria. She nodded. "We'll both have a western omelet, rye toast, butter on the side." I handed Clotilde our menus and she was gone.

"Not to change the subject," I said, "but have you noticed that kids don't have ordinary names anymore? Are we the last Tony and Maria on the planet?"

"I've noticed it," Maria said, "and my theory is this: A Matilda tries to spare her daughter the perceived social awkwardness of a *different* name, and calls her Mary. Mary grows up wanting a more unique name for her daughter, and calls her Matilda. Name-calling gets shuffled like a recessive trait."

"Interesting theory. Anyhow, returning to our earlier conversation, does the possibility exist that my father may never change?"

"Of course it does; you have to confront that possibility. Do you understand how important it is to confront that?"

"How could I? Wouldn't that be the death of hope?"

"No," Maria insisted. "It might be the death of hope for your father, but not for you. The death of hope for you would be to believe that your own happiness depends on the behavior of your father."

"Oh my God—you're right! Why had I thought that?"

"That was my next question."

"I don't know why. Why do you think I thought that?"

"You were obviously confused; this is a huge issue for you. You need to discover why you still let your father's behavior rattle you; you alone have control over your thoughts and feelings."

"You're right, Maria," I said, reflecting on my earlier, illogical rationale.

We sat in silence for a few minutes. The hard thing about therapy was the constant admission of my guilt. The very nature of therapy might have magnified my inferiority complex, had it not been for Maria's constant reassurance: I was at fault, but it wasn't really my fault.

"Well," Maria said, "I think we can wrap things up on that note."

That was fine with me; I had endured enough excavation on an empty stomach.

"And, with perfect timing," Maria said. "Here comes our breakfast."

Clotilde served our food. "Will there be anything else?"

I looked at Maria; she nodded. "That will be all," I said.

We began eating and I changed the subject. "So how about my mother hooking up with that artist?"

"Speaking of whom, I forgot to tell you something. One of my colleagues is on the board of the Guggenheim; this exhibit is a really big deal. Apparently Les Izmore has quite a strong following. Want some jelly?"

"No, thank you. I wonder what he was doing in Mom's creative writing course?"

"It's not so unusual," Maria said. "A lot of artists seek other modes of expression. Will you pass the salt?"

"You know, I just about died when Mom told me she had intended to leave the dishes to me. It was sweet in an absurd kind of way."

"It was. I guess you can consider *The Last Thanksgiving* your endowment to the arts."

"I guess so."

"Well, I think it's great that your mother is following her dreams. The sad part is the lost years; Granny said she would have gladly financed your mother's education. But I guess everything happens in its own time."

"You have to remember," I said, "that my mother was never allowed to accept financial help from Granny; if big Anthony couldn't provide it, Leona didn't need it. Poor logic, but that was law as declared by my father."

"It doesn't surprise me," Maria said. "I see that trend all the time in my practice. Any hope of happiness is swallowed up by irrationality on the part of one or both parties."

"Isn't that the truth?"

"Yes. It's a shame that we didn't meet earlier in life, when I was *brainwashing* my family. We could have recycled the baskets and tried to toilet-train your father."

I laughed. "I see you're letting go of your guilt."

"I think I am," Maria said. "I'm sorry I always projected my guilt onto you; it was always an ethics thing."

We finished our meal and decided on another cup of coffee. Neither one of us was anxious to brave the heat.

"So, do you really think Jerry's going to win?" Maria asked.

"I'm not sure, but the rumors are flying, if Walter Water heard them in Munich."

"You sound as if you're having doubts."

"It's not that I doubt Jerry's expertise; I know how bright he is. Something seems so primitive about his experiments; I guess I expected something a little more sophisticated than plants doing the hula. It seems so, I don't know, so Physics 101. It's probably my own ignorance, but it doesn't wreak of Nobel Prize to me. It's more like *The Little Shop of Horrors*," I said guiltily, not wanting to sound as if I was undermining Jerry's work—I wasn't. It *had to be* more than an amusement park for thrill-seeking plants.

"Well," Maria said, "some of the most important scientific discoveries are made by accident. And, some of the most complex thought in scientific reasoning has been extrapolated from seemingly simple experiments. I'm sure Jerry knows what he's talking about."

"I'm sure he does, too," I said. "The sum of everything just seems a little too simplistic.

"I'm sure the mathematics behind it isn't so simple. Jerry was probably presenting his results at a level he thought you would comprehend."

"Simplistic?"

"I didn't mean it like that."

"I know. Like I said, I'm probably looking at the whole thing through a filter of ignorance. I barely passed physics in college, even with Jerry's help. What do I know?"

"You know a lot. Just because your expertise lies outside the realm of physics is no reason to undermine yourself. I'm sure Jerry wouldn't have a clue about programming a computer."

"I'm not so sure about that; Jerry would figure it out if he dwelled on it long enough."

"You're right. I don't know what I was thinking," Maria said. "I guess the string theorists are going to be disappointed."

"The what?"

"The string theorists."

"Who are the string theorists?"

"You don't know what string theory is?"

I scanned my memory for anything related to string, thread, yarn, whatever. There was no mental file. "I'm sorry, but I don't," I said.

"String theory says that subatomic particles like electrons and quarks are not particles at all; they are really vibrating loops of string."

"So why are the string theorists going to be disappointed?" I asked.

"From what I hear, they're poised for the Nobel Prize as well. Apparently they have their own unified field theory, but I guess Jerry and Einstein were right."

"What do you mean?"

"Well, Einstein believed that gravity and electromagnetism were really manifestations of some unknown, grander force, the unified field. Isn't that what Jerry's suggesting?"

I thought for a minute. I didn't know if Jerry was suggesting that or not. "I'm not sure."

"Well, think about it. Jerry claims that the unified field is the sum of everything, that forces like gravity are a metaphorical vector of the grand force. And just as the unified field is the sum of many vectors, each individual force is also a summation. That's what Jerry's doing in the lab; he's studying the component vectors of the unified field and extrapolating a theory that explains how forces are imbedded within other forces, and so on and so on. Didn't he tell you about the frosty attractor?"

That *did* ring a bell. "Yes, he did. But come on, a snowball? That's what I mean by simplistic."

"There's nothing simplistic about things snow-balling. Everything increases: mass, momentum, power…"

I interrupted Maria. "It sounds as though you had quite a discussion with Jerry. When did he tell you all of this?"

"He didn't. I read it in the *Science Times* last week."

Jerry was in the *Science Times* last week?"

"Yes. They did a big spread on him. Don't you remember?"

I didn't remember, but I had a clue as to why not. I usually read the paper on my lunch break; last Tuesday I had gone out to lunch with colleagues. I must have missed the paper that day. "I missed the paper that day," I said.

"Tony, you don't remember me saying that I was taking the article to the framer's?" Maria had a puzzled expression.

Maria's tone implied that I had better remember. My expression probably screamed ignorance; look away, I ordered Maria telepathically. I brought the coffee to my lips, hoping to hide behind the mug.

"Don't you remember?" Maria asked again.

"No." I had to be honest, even though I felt the natural-born liar stirring within me.

"How could you forget? The framing job is costing six hundred dollars!"

"We're paying six hundred dollars to have a newspaper article framed?"

"Tony, this is history! Besides, it was a long article, and it needs to be preserved. The framer guarantees that the paper won't rot until at least 2379."

"The year?"

"Yes."

I was tempted to explore the validity of that claim, but another tangent seemed more pressing: a big chunk of my life was missing in action. Why hadn't I recalled that conversation? Not wanting to believe that I had heard it and that I was experiencing irrevocable memory-loss, I chose to assume I had not been listening.

"Tony? Aren't you listening?"

"What?"

" I asked you if you want to have a copy framed for your parents, as a gift," Maria said.

I felt better. There was nothing wrong with my memory; I just didn't give people the courtesy of really listening. I was lost in my head, examining my deficits, while conversations continued without me. I had to stop that; it was rude to others and detrimental to my self-esteem. What the hell was wrong with me? I silently screamed at myself to stop; I did. What had been Maria's last question? Luckily, it came to me. "That would be a nice gift for my parents," I said, "but I don't think theirs needs to be preserved for that length of time."

"Good. Now getting back to the meat of the article, I was just wondering if Jerry's theory and string theory have to be mutually exclusive. After all, relativity and quantum theory existed together for all those years, even though they were diametrically opposed. Perhaps the sum of everything and string theory could share the stage too," Maria said, reaching for her coffee mug.

I began wondering if Maria was also hiding behind her coffee mug, or if it was an innocent gesture. "Stop!" I screamed silently to myself.

"In Stockholm?" I asked. I prayed she didn't mean Stockholm. Sharing the prize would discredit Jerry's achievement in my father's eyes. I almost went where I promised myself I wouldn't go: to the pettiness of paternal bashing. Instead, I silently screamed at myself to pay attention to my present reality. When the screams stopped reverberating, I realized I had missed another chunk of conversation.

"Don't you agree?" Maria asked.

I wasn't about to let things snowball. "Would you mind explaining that one more time? I'm weak in physics."

Maria repeated herself. Having heard her statement, I still had no response. It was true: I *was* weak in physics. "I'm really not qualified to give an opinion, Maria. I'm afraid physics makes my head spin."

"I'm sorry, Tony. I didn't mean to frustrate you. I assumed you had read the article."

I thought quickly; I needed to stop the silent screaming and spinning of my head. I changed the subject. "Well, anyhow, all we can do is hope. Jerry has certainly devoted his whole life to solving the mysteries of the universe. He deserves to win the Nobel Prize."

"You must be so proud," Maria said, "to have a brother on the same level as Newton and Copernicus."

"I am." I suddenly realized that my psyche had not absorbed the full impact of the development. I had been obsessed with Jerry's winning the Nobel Prize as a backlash to my father's condescension; I never stopped to think about the full ramifications. My brother could revolutionize the world as we knew it, solving a riddle that had mystified scientists for centuries. For the first time since the rumors began, the full glory of the situation descended upon me like a wave, sending ripples of shock through my previously ignorant perspective.

"You look shocked."

"I am. I guess I never went below the surface. This is big!"

"Big?" Maria asked. "This is huge! Jerry's accomplishment will bring honor not only to our family but also to our country and the global physics community; not to mention the technology that will emerge. Jerry is rocking the world! It's hard to fathom."

"It is," I said, visualizing Jerry the rock star. "I guess we'll find out in October. The waiting and wondering is probably killing Jerry. I can't wait to talk with him tonight."

"Me too. Do you think we should get the check? We don't know what the traffic on the Turnpike is going to be like."

"Yes." I motioned to Clotilde, scribbling on my hand with an imaginary pen.

We paid the check and left the restaurant to hail a cab.

"So much for patriotism," Maria said, riding back to our apartment. "My blouse is soaked; I'm going to have to change before we leave."

I looked at Maria's blouse. It was clinging rather tightly to her form. "Let me know if you need any help," I said aloud, having believed at the time that I was merely thinking.

"What?"

"Nothing."

We pulled up to our building; the cab driver turned to announce our fare. "Four-eighty," he said, looking me right in the eye. "Say! Aren't you that guy—you are! And you're the lady shrink! What a coincidence. Don't you remember me? I'm the one that returned your watch."

"Oh, that's right," I said, handing him six dollars.

"Thank you," Maria said. "It was very honest of you to return it. Tony bought me that watch for our fifth anniversary."

"My pleasure," the cabby said. "Happy Independence Day."

We left the cab and I walked quickly to the entrance of our building. The last thing I needed was to be reminded of my past. That was a long time ago; I was a different man. Six months *was* a long time, I assured myself.

Riding the elevator, Maria spoke. "That was a coincidence. You know, he is a very nice man."

"Yes he is," I said, as we left the elevator.

We entered the coolness of our apartment. "I'm a little sleepy," I said. "I guess I ate too much."

"No problem," Maria said. "I'll drive to Philadelphia and you can take a nap. It's going to be a long day."

"Thanks, honey. I'll get changed and go down to the garage for the car."

"I'm just going to freshen up a bit. I'll meet you downstairs in ten minutes."

I changed my shirt and gave myself a spritz of cologne. "Maria?" I yelled, "can I brush my teeth before you get settled in there?"

"Sure!" Maria yelled back. She walked into the bedroom. "It's all yours."

While brushing my teeth, I thought about our uncanny reunion with the cab driver. I rinsed my mouth and took a shot of mouthwash; leaning back to gargle, I thought I glimpsed a spider on the ceiling, but it was my imagination. Seeing that cab driver had rekindled the paranoia that my past was creeping up on me. I spit into the sink and left the bathroom. "I'll see you downstairs," I yelled.

"O.K.," Maria yelled from her closet.

I left our apartment and the building and went to get the car.

When I returned, Maria was waiting. The red blouse had been replaced with something less form fitting. Disappointed, I got out of the car and held the door while Maria slid into the driver's seat. Her bare legs safely inside, I closed the car door and walked around to the passenger side. I got in and we were off to Philadelphia.

"The traffic isn't too bad," Maria said, keeping her eyes on the road.

"It isn't. I guess everyone has already arrived at their destinations.

"I'm looking forward to the fireworks tonight," Maria said.

"Me too." The whole family was driving to Penn's Landing after the barbecue that day. I was busy staring at the runways of Newark Airport. "Not much action on the runways today either."

"No."

We rode in silence for a few more miles, and then Maria spoke: "I was thinking about our earlier conversation, about you being the brother of a Nobel Laureate—well, almost. What was it like, growing up with Jerry? Did you know when you were a kid that Jerry was different?"

"Of course I knew he was different," I said. "But at the time I didn't recognize it as genius. I guess I thought he was strange but very good-hearted. His intelligence was certainly a thorn in my father's side; Jerry was always correcting Dad. It wasn't a game of one-upmanship on Jerry's part; he simply didn't want Dad to be misinformed. I'll never forget Dad's lecture on the facts of life. " I laughed.

"What happened?" Maria asked curiously.

"When Dad began his lecture, he was unaware that Jerry had already assembled enough information to do a thesis on mammalian fertilization enzymes. Jerry corrected every other word of Dad's speech; Dad was infuriated, to be upstaged by a nine year-old. Jerry was babbling about the second cell-division when Dad threw a Family Planning pamphlet at him."

After recounting the story, I realized that Jerry and I shared a common experience: we both had the book thrown at us. I wondered if it was a coincidence.

"Your father's reaction doesn't surprise me. What about your mother? How did she appear to perceive Jerry?"

"Well, Mom always felt as if Jerry needed extra protection. She couldn't understand why Jerry never learned to stop pushing Dad's buttons; I think she then conceived of Jerry as being mildly retarded or something. Looking back, Mom did a lot of hovering over Jerry, in an effort to protect him from himself. Jerry was a seeker of truth, and not even my father's rage could make him stray from that path. It's ironic, that a child who was once thought to be a bit mentally challenged should grow up to win the Nobel Prize."

"Believe me," Maria said, "stranger things have happened. Your mother's intentions were good; it's fortunate that Jerry didn't allow others' beliefs to color his self-image. That would have been disastrous; physics would be at a stalemate right now."

"I guess you're right."

"So tell me," Maria said. "Was Jerry the typical child scientist, blowing things up with his chemistry set?"

"I don't know how typical Jerry was," I said. I was tempted to tell Maria about my chigger episode, but that memory was too painful to rehash again. Instead, Dad's brown corduroy pants came to mind. Did I dare tell a psychiatrist that we had used our unwitting father as an experimental subject? Why not, I laughed.

"What's so funny?'

"I just remembered something that happened a long time ago, one of Jerry's first controlled experiments. I can't believe he got me to go along with it."

"Tell me," Maria said. "I find this fascinating."

"O.K.," I said. I got comfortable and time-traveled to 1969.

"Hey Tone. Why do you suppose Dad is so charged up today?" Jerry asked with concern.

"He's charged up every day. It's just his nature."

"I know that, Tony. But today he seems super-charged."

Jerry was right. It wasn't good enough to use a plain old adjective to describe our father. Dad's adjectives needed to be quantified and qualified. Dad was always pissed off—but to what degree and for what reason?

When I didn't respond, Jerry spoke again. "Don't you notice that he's a little worse today?"

"He's a lot worse today; how could I not notice? I'd have to be deaf, dumb and blind not to notice."

"Well, I think I see a correlation here," Jerry said matter-of-factly.

"A cora what?"

"A correlation," Jerry said. "A method to his madness."

"Oh," I said. "What do you mean?"

"Well," Jerry began, "I've noticed something unusual: every

time Dad wears those brown corduroy pants, he's super-charged."

"Oh, come on, Jerry. How could his pants make him act like a jerk?"

"Well, think about it. Dad's initially irritated and then wears something that irritates him even more."

"Why would he wear a pair of pants that irritates him?"

"How should I know? That's a whole other story. Just assume that the pants are irritating in this experiment," Jerry said.

"What experiment?" I wondered if I had missed something.

"Let's plot a graph, mood as a function of pant style, to see if there's any statistically significant correlation between the two," Jerry said, as if it was a completely normal idea.

Normal or not, Jerry convinced me to spy on Dad. We met twice a day; in the morning to record pant style and color, and again in the evening to rate Dad's attitude that day. Jerry was in charge of recording the variables; he delegated to me the task of gathering physical evidence.

One Monday night while Dad was out bowling, I examined his pants for anything out of the ordinary, perhaps a leg sewn on backwards or a rough patch of fabric in the wrong place. The pants came through negative. They appeared to be fine, yet we had statistically significant evidence that Dad became super-charged when he wore the brown corduroys. We had hit a wall.

Apparently we had overlooked the obvious. One morning Dad walked into the kitchen wearing the well-documented pants; Mom looked at him strangely. "Anthony, don't you think those pants are a little too tight? They're like a tourniquet."

"I have not gained an ounce!" Dad retorted.

"I didn't say you had; those pants have never fit properly."

Jerry and I looked at one another and communicated telepathically. "Restricted circulation to the brain," I nodded.

"Eureka!" Jerry acknowledged, rolling his eyes.

The following week my mother accidentally spilled bleach on the brown corduroys and had to throw them away. Dad bought a new pair of pants, which seemed to accommodate him nicely—or so I thought.

I noticed Jerry looking analytically at Dad's new pants. He waited until Dad left the room to voice his concern: "Do you think those pants are a little too short-waisted for Dad?"

"Oh, come on, Jerry. I'm tired of this game. It's getting old."

"But how is Dad going to act if he has a perpetual wedgie?"

"He's going to act like he always does, Jerry," I laughed.

My laughing shocked my consciousness to the present. Maria looked puzzled. "What's the matter? You don't think our experiment was funny?" I asked.

"How would I know?" Maria said. "You haven't told the story yet. Is something wrong? You were spacing-out."

Something was wrong, dangerously backwards. Many times in the past I said things aloud while under the delusion that I had been silently thinking. Never before had I silently thought something while being under the delusion that I had spoken aloud. Perhaps I was having too much therapy, too soon? There was a kink in my brain.

"Are you going to tell me, or not?" Maria asked impatiently, eyes still on the road.

"Yes." I rehashed the entire story, pausing intermittently to check that I was actually speaking aloud. I must have been, because Maria was reacting.

"That is such a funny story," Maria said. "You two sounded like quite a team."

"That's an understatement. That story is only one of many; one day when you aren't driving, I'll really blow your mind."

"You're lucky to have all those good memories," Maria said. "At least you and Jerry had one another; that must have been a buffer to the absurdity."

"It was," I said. "Even though I often felt that Jerry was off his rocker, I always knew I could count on him."

"That is wonderful," Maria said.

"Do you?" Maria asked.

"Do I what?" I answered.

"Do you have two dollars for the bridge?"

"Oh my God, we're here already?" I had been lost in another wrinkle of space-time, oblivious to the big chunk of silence that had transpired.

"We made good time today," Maria said.

We crossed the bridge to Philadelphia. While Maria paid careful attention to the highway, I stared intently at the sky: wispy clouds floated against a backdrop of the most magnificent silvery-blue.

The humidity was lifting. The luminescent blue beckoned me to cloud nine; I sailed magically on my ship of pure, soft white, seeing the cars on River Drive below as if they were my toys. I scanned the grid below me—what was that? Was that Uncle Harry's *Lincoln* broken down on the side of the road? With that thought, I was drawn back to the passenger seat of our *Lexus*. My fantasy was over; we had arrived.

"We're here!" Maria announced, pulling into Granny's driveway beside Uncle Harry's Lincoln. Seeing his car made me realize that my fantasy had in fact been a fantasy and not an out-of-body experience. It shocked my consciousness to ordinary reality just as the midwife's slap roused the newborn. That slap was strangely reassuring, especially so after my earlier foible of having non-verbally recounted the corduroy incident to Maria: I wasn't totally disconnected after all. Still, I wondered if there was any credence to that old saying: sometimes things get worse before they get better. Would I lose my mind before re-claiming it? Before I could examine that possibility, Maria jostled my arm.

"Tony?"

"Yeah?"

"It's getting hot in the car."

I became fully aware and left the car to open the door for Maria.

"Thank you," Maria said, taking my arm.

We walked arm-in-arm to the front door, which was flanked by two rose bushes that had climbed to meet in the middle, forming an arch of the most luscious hue of pink and green. "Are these rose bushes new this year?" I asked Maria.

"No. They've always been here—don't tell me you've never noticed them. Don't you remember the one early bloom on the day of your grandmother's birthday party?"

Apparently another chunk of life had gone over my head. I cowardly uttered, "no."

Maria looked at me as though sympathetic to my tunnel-vision; that she showed compassion rather that critical judgment allowed me to move forward without berating myself.

I looked closely at the archway; how had I overlooked its

reverberating hue? Were my senses just then coming to life?

We crossed the fragrant threshold separating the ordinary from the enchanted: that which existed behind the wood and fairy-glass of Granny's front door. I was home again; how could a *place* speak to me in such a colorful tongue?

Inside, the house was still. "Everyone is outside," Maria said. "Let's go."

"Wait a minute," I said. "Do you hear something?"

"No. What do you hear?"

"Water cascading."

"I don't hear it."

Huh, I thought.

I followed Maria through the kitchen and out the back door. Walking down the steps, Maria spoke: "Tony, look!"

I looked up to see cascading water: there was a fountain standing in front of the garden wall separating the patio from the rose garden. It was a cement angel that spurted water from a copper trumpet.

"Isn't it beautiful?" Maria asked.

Before I could answer, Granny shouted, "Tony!"

I approached Granny and we embraced. "I see you've noticed the fountain. What do you think?" she asked.

"I think it's beautiful. When did you get it?"

"Last month," Granny said. "I've been wanting one all my life. Finally I said to myself, Rose, you're eighty-five years old—what are you waiting for? Isn't it lovely?"

"It's incredible," Maria said. "I've never seen anything like it."

That angel represented an intellectual paradox: while realizing it was brand-new, it was as if it had always been there. My sister Margaret prevented me from exploring that paradox.

"Tony!"

"Hi Margaret," I said, hugging her. "You look great; I see you've been laying off the peppermint."

"Absolutely. You're not looking so bad yourself. Did you change something? You look good."

I made a conscious effort not to perceive Margaret's question as loaded. "Thanks. How's business going?" I asked.

"It's great. I've picked up a lot of new heads. Can't complain."

"How's it working out with Aunt Vicky?" I asked, scrunching my face in mock empathy.

"She's not with me anymore. I had to let her go," Margaret said, breathing a sigh of relief.

"You fired Aunt Vicky?"

"It wasn't as though she was on my payroll or anything; she just *worked* her counter, if you know what I mean. I had to let her go; my suppliers saw it as a conflict of interest. What could I do? They supplied my signage and capes; I had no choice!" Margaret said.

"What was Aunt Vicky's reaction?"

"I don't think she was too disappointed; she missed having her Saturdays free. One weekend she didn't even show up. Of course that was the day there was a public outcry for *Avon*. I thought the day would never end."

"What a *daymare*," I said.

"Tell me about it," Margaret said, her facial expression changing. "Here she comes."

"Aunt Vicky, Uncle Harry," I said, with exaggerated enthusiasm. "How are you?"

The lipstick was coming at me; there was no time to react—smack!

"We're just fine," Aunt Vicky said, retreating from my cheek. "Oh dear; I'm afraid I've smudged a bit of lipstick on your cheek. Here you go," she said, handing me a cocktail napkin.

"Damn, Vicky! I told you to blot," Uncle Harry scolded. "I'm sure poor Tony doesn't want to walk around all day with Patriot Red stamped on his cheek, Independence Day or not."

"It's no big deal," I white-lied. Why did Aunt Vicky and Uncle Harry always have to refer to me as *poor Tony*? That was almost as annoying as the lipstick transfer. I changed the subject: "How's Tommy? Haven't heard from him."

"Don't feel bad," Aunt Vicky said. "He never calls us either. I guess that's a dancer's life for you, always on the road."

Something was strange about the way Tommy had just dropped out of the family four years earlier. If I hadn't known better, I might have suspected my Aunt and Uncle of foul play: was Tommy their feral child, kept locked in the attic?

"Here comes Leona and big Anthony," Aunt Vicky squealed.

I turned to look. Sure enough, my parents were entering through the back gate. I instinctively headed in the opposite direction. I had earlier conceived of our visit as an opportunity to practice compassion, but my preconceptions went over the fence when I saw my father in the flesh. I just needed a little more time to muster my courage—where was Jerry?

"Who wants to help me husk the corn?" Margaret asked.

"I do!" I yelled. I had drawn attention to myself with the enthusiasm of my outburst; my father looked at me. It was now or never, I threatened myself; I approached my parents.

"Hi Mom," I said, hugging her. "How are you?"

"I'm doing just fine," Mom said unconvincingly. There was a subtle tone of despair in her response.

"Dad," I said, extending my hand.

"Hello," my father grunted, ignoring my hand, suspended in mid-air between us.

"Aren't you going to shake hands with your son?" my mother asked.

"Oh Leona, will you get off my case? Of course I am," Dad said, taking my hand. He shook my hand, digging his thumbnail into the fleshy delta that connected my thumb to the rest of my hand: the spot that was apparently teeming with nerve-endings. I escaped Dad's clutch, perplexed. How could he be so cunningly mean?

"Are you going to help me or not?" Margaret yelled, saving me.

"I'm coming!" I yelled. I walked away, massaging my delta.

"I'll help you guys too," Maria said, joining us at the picnic table.

I looked at Maria. "Can you believe what my father just did to me?" I asked, showing Maria the impression that Dad had left on me. There was a red arc on my delta where Dad's claw had penetrated.

"Oh my God," Maria said. "Why did he do that?"

"Apparently he has some hostility toward me," I said, "and he's not doing a very good job of keeping it under wraps."

"That's unbelievable," Maria said, handing me an ear of corn. "Will your injury affect your ability to husk?"

"Not at all."

Maria was about to say something else, but was interrupted by Margaret. "Am I the only one husking?"

"No, we have just now begun to husk," I said. Maria and Margaret laughed; our folly kept my mind off my delta. I added a footnote: "doesn't the corn silk remind you of *Barbie* hair?"

"It does," Margaret said. "Why didn't I notice that before?"

"Maybe all your *Barbies* were brunettes or redheads?"

"No, I had a blonde," Margaret said. "Don't you remember? Jerry cut off her ponytail to examine it under the microscope when he was studying synthetics. Don't you remember how upset I was?"

"I don't, but it must have been traumatic."

"It was. Speak of the devil!" Margaret said.

Jerry and Roberta were entering the backyard.

"Hey everyone!" Jerry said. His ponytail had grown longer since May, and Roberta's hair was even shorter than when I had seen her at Princeton.

"Hi, Roberta!"

"Hi, Tony! Sorry we couldn't have lunch when you were at Princeton; I was tied up in a meeting all afternoon."

"No problem," I said. "We'll do it another time."

Mom approached our picnic table. "Jerry, dear," she said, hugging Jerry. Mom stepped back, staring at Jerry's chest. "Jerry, who is that on the front of your T-shirt?"

You'd think that $E=mc^2$ would have given it away; apparently Mom hadn't done the math.

"It's Einstein, Mom. Why?" Jerry asked.

"Because you look just like him, Jerry. Tony, doesn't Jerry look like Einstein?"

I examined Jerry's chest, then his face; he did look like Einstein. Why had I never noticed that before? "He does," I said in disbelief.

My father approached us from behind and commented: "But of course Einstein had a respectable hairdo, and your brother here has the ponytail of a fruit. "

It was the first time in history that anyone had accused Einstein of having a respectable hairdo.

"Well, I can fix that," Margaret said, approaching Jerry with a ponytail fashioned of corn silk. She held the mock ponytail to his chest: the resemblance was uncanny.

"I give up on you people," my father muttered, walking away.

Granny joined us. "That is remarkable," she said. "Jerry looks like Einstein with a ponytail. I never noticed it before; how can one not, with their faces in a vertical line-up?"

Everyone laughed.

"O.K.," Jerry said. "The fun is over. You can remove the corn silk from my chest now, Margaret."

We laughed again; our laughter was part amusement, part shock. The resemblance was scary; even scarier was that none of us had noticed it before. It was so obvious.

"What's with the boom-box, Jerry?" I asked.

"Rich Avogadro sent the bio-musicals."

"How did they turn out?"

"I don't know. I haven't had time to listen to them."

"I can't wait; I find the concept fascinating."

"After dinner," Margaret ordered. "We still have a lot of corn to husk."

We finished husking the corn. I carried the pot to the stove; Maria and Margaret swept the *Barbie* hair from the picnic table.

Meanwhile, Uncle Harry had donned his apron and was taking orders: "O.K., that's six medium, four well, two rare, three medium well, a Pittsburgh rare, and four toasted buns. Who wants dogs?" I wondered if he would remember all that, or if we would all get medium and like it.

There was a time when my father would have assisted in the grilling, but he was pretending not to know Uncle Harry. After their argument on Valentine's Day, Uncle Harry became a stranger. When Uncle Harry pulled up in a Lincoln, Dad hated that stranger.

I looked toward my father: he was looking pensively at Granny's new fountain. He was alone in a crowd, the worst kind of alone. I looked down at my delta: my flesh had expanded and the impression was hardly visible. Maybe it had been an accident, I thought. I was sure he hadn't intentionally clawed me. In a moment of unbridled compassion, I found myself walking toward my father.

"Nice fountain, isn't it?" I asked.

"Real nice. A little ostentatious, but I guess if you've got it, flaunt it."

"Flaunt what?" I asked.

"Flaunt your wealth; that's what your grandmother is up to. She loves to rub my nose in the fact that she has more money than she'll ever be able to spend. I take that back," Dad said. "She doesn't just flaunt it; she announces it with a god-damned trumpet."

I visually located my mother to see if she was within earshot, secretly hoping she was and that she'd heard Dad curse. "How can you say that about Granny? She has never rubbed anyone's nose in anything," I said.

"Believe what you want; you have always worn blinders when it comes to Rose. What you see is not always what you get—remember that! One day your eyes will be *pulled* wide-open, just as mine have been; *mark my words*," Dad said with contempt.

"I don't know what you're talking about. Granny doesn't need to flaunt anything; she's the most honest woman I know."

"One day you'll wake up from your god-damned dream world and see things for what the hell they are."

Dad was pushing the wrong buttons. How dare he talk about my grandmother that way, I thought. Even the heavens were appalled; water stopped cascading from the angel's trumpet and began burping and spurting intermittently. Big Anthony was enough to make an angel choke.

"I'm tired of the way you talk about my grandmother, and I'm sick to death of your cursing. Do you have any idea how vile you sound? You can't complete one sentence without throwing in a few obscenities. Why don't you go back to compulsive singing? It was the only time you censored yourself!"

"I've had enough of your self-righteous bullshit," Dad yelled.

"Good. And I'm sure that God has had enough of yours. If I were you I'd clean up my act; things aren't looking so good for you at the pearly gates."

"I always knew you were god-damned trouble, from the minute you were born!"

The angel stopped burping and started furiously shooting water; Dad was in the line of fire. God was pushed to his last resort, forced to control an unruly crowd of one with a fire-hose. For a second my father was unable to move, paralyzed by shock and anger. By the time he regained his motor skills, he was soaking wet.

A crowd had assembled to witness God's divine intervention.

"Jerry! Get your father a towel!" Mom ordered.

"What happened?" Granny asked.

"I'll tell you what happened," big Anthony growled, "that friggin angel of yours just hosed me down!" My father then stomped away, toward the house.

"Apparently there was air in the line," I said to Granny. "The angel burped a few times, then shot water madly."

My mother looked at me and winked. The crowd dispersed;

everyone returned to what they had been doing before God's hand intervened.

Margaret approached me. "I guess Dad will start bringing a change of clothes to family parties," she laughed.

Joining Margaret in laughter, I remembered my earlier pact with myself: I was going to stop delighting in my father's antics. But that had been before he cursed the day I was born. I was laughing, but wrenching inside; I needed a father, and realized I would never have one. And, I had allowed his behavior to make me react, violating a moral pact with myself.

Margaret looked into my eyes. "What's wrong?"

"I told myself that I was going to show more compassion toward Dad, and here I am, laughing at him again."

"Oh Tony," Margaret said, putting her arm around me, "Dad would push the buttons of a saint. Don't beat yourself up for being human. If you weren't laughing, you'd be crying."

"I know," I said. "It's just that I wonder if I'm really a creep for taking pleasure in something so pathetic."

"You aren't a creep. You're not laughing at Dad; you're laughing to vent the anger and frustration that his behavior incites in you. Laughing and crying serve the same end; they're both pressure valves."

I had no idea that Margaret was so well-versed in matters of the psyche. "How do you know so much?" I asked.

"Because I had this very same conversation with Maria two months ago," Margaret laughed.

"Right from the mouth of a shrink; I should have known."

"Come on," Margaret said, taking me by the arm. "Let's join the others."

The party was in full swing; the only thing missing was the smell of barbecuing food. Uncle Harry was having trouble getting the grill lit.

"Need a hand, Uncle Harry?" Jerry yelled.

"No," he replied. "I need another pack of matches." Four empty matchbooks littered the grass next to the barbecue pit. Jerry went to Uncle Harry's rescue.

From the corner of my eye I noticed my father had returned; he was sitting in a sunny spot, nostrils still flared.

Mom approached me. "What was that all about?" she asked.

"The usual," I replied. " He was mouthing off about everyone in the family. I try to be patient, but sometimes he's impossible."

"I know," Mom said. "And he's really ripe today. Just ignore him; that's what I'm learning to do."

"By the way, Mom, how's the writing going?"

"Great. I have some good news—I won a contest!"

"You did? What kind of contest?"

"Children's fiction. I wrote a story called *The PonyTale*. Won first prize, fifty dollars. Not a lot of money, but it really made me feel good, as if I might have some talent after all."

"Of course you have talent," I assured Mom. "I'd love to read your story."

"You would?"

"Of course I would; why do you sound so surprised?"

"Because I know how busy you are."

"I'm never too busy for you, Mom."

"Oh Tony, your heart is so big. Even after the disappointment of losing my collection, you're still there for me. I was blessed the day you were born," Mom said, squeezing my hand.

Mom's sentiment balanced the sting of my father's proclamation, and I was at emotional ground-zero again. I squeezed my mother's hand, in gratitude. "Mail me a copy, O.K.?"

"I will," Mom said. "First thing Tuesday morning. The post office is closed on Monday since the holiday fell on a Sunday."

"Good," I said. "I'll be looking forward to it."

Our moment of tenderness was interrupted by Margaret's announcement: "Dinner is going to be a while yet, so we're going to listen to our bio-songs now."

"Come on, Mom," I said, taking her hand. Everyone was excited, eagerly anticipating the playing of their song. Even Dad was moving his lawn chair to be within earshot.

"All right," Jerry said. "First up is Granny." Jerry popped in the tape and pressed play.

We listened intently to the sound of Granny's soul. It was a beautiful score, not surprisingly in the classical genre.

"That is beautiful," Maria said. Everyone agreed, mesmerized by Granny's vibrating DNA. We didn't want the song to end, but the tapes were only ninety seconds long; it was all Avogadro had time for.

"O.K.," Jerry said, "next up is Mom."

Mom's song was cute, comparable to the theme song of a children's show—no wonder Mom won that prize! Her song was upbeat and happy; you almost wanted to sing along, chanting your ABC's as you marched in time to the band of Mom's complementary base-pairs.

My reaction to the first two songs was awe; how had Avogadro come up with the idea?

"O.K., Tony," Jerry shouted, "this is your life!"

As I listened to my vibrating strings, I had a deja vu. The song sounded familiar; it resembled the theme song to *Lost in Space*. The tune was fresh in my mind; I had played with my toy robot the day before. Those ninety seconds were the longest of my life.

"Next up, Uncle Harry," Jerry yelled.

Uncle Harry's song was somewhat garbled; could music stutter in its reverberation?

"That can't be mine," Uncle Harry said. "I don't sound like that anymore!" His song played on, advancing and then retracting. I looked at the boom-box. It appeared to be expanding and contracting.

"Turn it off!" Uncle Harry yelled. "There must be something wrong with the tape," Uncle Harry said, walking back to the barbecue.

"Dad, this one's for you!" Jerry said, pushing the button.

There was no song; rather than music, we were forced to endure what sounded like a wire brush being dragged across a chalkboard. The screeching was ear-piercing.

"Turn it off!" Margaret yelled.

Everyone begged Jerry to turn off Dad's song. If only it was as easy as pressing a button, I thought. "I can't!" Jerry yelled. "The button is jammed!"

The screeching boom-box sounded Dad's song until Jerry removed its batteries.

"Thank God!" everyone cried in unison. Uncle Harry added: "*That* was horrifying!"

"I'll tell you what's horrifying," Dad yelled, "is that my own son would go to such lengths to make a fool of me."

"What are you talking about?" Jerry asked.

"Anthony, don't be blaming Jerry," Mom said. "Obviously there's something wrong with the machine; it's not Jerry's fault."

We were saved by Uncle Harry's ring of the dinner bell: "Come and get it!"

The smell of food momentarily distracted Dad from the horror encoded in his DNA.

"Let's just forget about it and eat," Mom said. "The rest of you can take your tapes home and listen to them."

We sat down and tried to eat a civilized meal. No one said another word about the bio-musicals, not wanting to light my father's fuse.

"I would like to propose a toast," Granny said, "to the last Independence Day of the millennium."

Everyone shouted and raised their glasses.

"Tony," Uncle Harry said, "what's all this I hear about Y2K glitches? Anything I need to worry about? I don't need any problems down at the plant."

"No, you don't have to worry," I said. "Your system was recently designed; you're safe."

Aunt Vicky expressed her concern: "Could store shelves really be empty on New Year's Day?"

"I believe it's a bunch of hype, sensationalism aimed at generating mass hysteria. Don't worry; computers are smarter than that. Sometimes I think they have a mind of their own."

"Especially the ones you work with," Jerry said. "Better watch out; one day one of those computers is liable to start programming you. You don't want to wake up one day with a mouse wired into your brain!"

"Very funny, Einstein. Do me a favor, click that bowl of coleslaw over to me."

"I'll take some of that when you're through," Maria said.

"The food is delicious," Roberta said. "There's nothing like a summer barbecue."

"Yeah," Dad said, "It's about time I get a decent meal. Ever since Leona here went back to school, she hasn't made anything that can't be cooked in a paper towel. She even sold her dishes, have you heard?"

"I have heard," Roberta said, "and I think it's wonderful that Leona has gone back to school."

"Wonderful for whom?" Dad blurted. "It isn't wonderful for me; I didn't even have a clean shirt to wear to work yesterday. Can you imagine how I felt, showing up for work in a polo-shirt? I was mortified."

"Perhaps you should go back to school, Anthony, to learn how to operate a washer and dryer; there's really nothing to it," Mom said sarcastically.

"What? I have to eat dinner three nights a week with truckers at some greasy spoon, and do my own wash too? I don't think so!"

"Then it looks as though you'd better buy plenty of shirts," Mom said.

"There's a great sale going on right now," Aunt Vicky said, "over at..."

Dad interrupted Aunt Vicky. "I think you had better watch how you talk to me, Leona. You're forgetting that I'm your meal-ticket; I don't have to take this shit from you!"

"Not now, Anthony. We're at a party," Mom said. "We'll discuss this later."

"I don't care where the hell we are, Leona. I'm not going to sit here and have my own wife insult me!"

"I didn't insult you; I merely suggested that you might want to learn some new skills."

"Mom's right," Jerry said. "Come on, Dad. Calm down."

"Don't tell me to calm down, you god-damned sorry excuse for a man, wearing a friggin ponytail like some kind of fruit! I'm sick of you people!"

"Don't you dare talk to your son that way—he's a Nobel Laureate. He can wear his hair as he pleases!" Mom yelled.

"Laureate, smaureate! I'll believe that when I god-damned see it!"

Dad's nostrils flared to a dangerous diameter. Is there a doctor in the house? I thought. Any minute Dad's nose would require an episiotomy: his face was about to split open.

"I think you should leave, Anthony!" Mom ordered.

Dad rose to leave. "I'll tell you one thing, Leona. I will never forgive you for this. You're lucky I don't move to an efficiency near the globe plant."

"Do whatever you have to do," Mom replied.

"What did you say, Leona?"

"I said, do whatever you have to do."

"That's it!" big Anthony yelled. With a fist of rage, Dad picked up a pickle and flung it across the table at my mother. The pickle hit Mom just under her left eye before landing in her lap.

"Get off my property!" Granny yelled. It was the first time in forty-two years I had heard Granny raise her voice.

Big Anthony reached for another pickle, probably intended for Granny, but was intercepted by Uncle Harry, who had grabbed Dad by the wrist in a stronghold.

"Put the pickle down," Uncle Harry said. "You heard Rose—it's time for you to leave!"

"Get your god-damned hands off me, Harry. You know what? You picked a great name for your business—you are nuts!" Uncle Harry released Dad, and my father walked toward the back gate, shaking his head.

My mother just sat there in shock, a tear of pickle juice running down her left cheek. I went to sit by her. "Are you all right Mom?"

"I'm fine," Mom said, "but look what he's done to my new skirt."

I looked at my mother's white skirt. Forensic evidence of my father's assault remained: a green, gherkin-shaped stain. "Don't worry, Mom. I'll buy you a new skirt if the stain doesn't come out." Mom said nothing, squeezing my hand.

"What has gotten into that man?" Granny asked. "I've never witnessed behavior so vile, not in a grown man."

"I think Anthony's on the verge of a breakdown," Mom said to Granny.

"Verge? Leona, honey, face it, he's already gone over the edge."

"Granny's right," Jerry said. "He needs help. What would trigger such a maniacal outburst? Is he that upset by your going back to school?"

"That's only part of it," Mom said. "I'm afraid that your father received some very upsetting news this week."

"What?" we asked.

"His elderly parents were killed in an automobile accident last month in Sicily," Mom said.

"Oh," Jerry said. "But he hasn't spoken to them in over forty years; their death hit Dad that hard?"

"It wasn't their death that was such a blow," Mom said. "It was the fact that they left their entire fortune to their butler and silver maid."

"What's a silver maid?" Margaret asked.

"A maid who polishes silver," Maria answered.

"Dad's parents had a butler *and* a silver maid?" Jerry asked. "I thought they were poor?"

"No, Jerry. They were far from poor; they owned practically every olive orchard in Sicily," Mom said.

"But Dad told me they were poor, that they sent him to America in search of a better life," Jerry said.

"It was all a facade. Your father came to America because he was exiled; apparently your Sicilian grandparents were well-connected, if you know what I mean."

"Were they mobsters?"

"I don't know the facts, only what your father has implied."

"This is unbelievable," Jerry said.

Mom continued. "As their only child, your father stood to inherit a fortune. But now, the butler and silver maid are sitting pretty, and your father feels cheated."

"It's his own fault," I said. "He never attempted to make amends with his parents. He let forty years slip by without so much as a hello."

"You're right, Tony. It was your father's own stubbornness that blew up in his face," Mom said.

"Wow," Aunt Vicky said. "What a story! It's like winning the lottery and realizing that you threw your ticket away in the garbage. No wonder Anthony's such a madman."

"I have a question, Mom," Jerry said. "I remember at one time getting a birthday card from the Vitello's. Why do you suppose they stopped sending them?"

"They didn't stop," Mom said sadly. "Not at first. Your father began confiscating the cards and had them returned, marked deceased. After a while, the cards just stopped coming. I assume they believed you were dead."

"Let me get this right," Margaret said. "Are you telling us that we could have been next in line for the throne, had our grandparents not thought we were dead?"

"It looks that way," Mom said.

"Why did you let him get away with it?" Margaret asked.

"What could I do?" Mom said. "Your father was young and arrogant; I tried to convince him that he was making a mistake, but he wouldn't listen to reason. Eventually his little secret got swept under the rug, and we never discussed it again. It was easier that way; if I hadn't let it go, our lives would have been intolerable."

"Why did you tolerate that kind of abuse, Leona? You could have brought the children here to live," Granny said.

If history had taken that course, how different our lives would have been!

"I guess I couldn't bear that I had gone against your advice and made such an awful mistake. I was ashamed, and I guess I figured my life with Anthony was punishment for having made a decision based on faulty judgment. I'm sorry if I did the wrong thing by not leaving; I'm afraid the emotional turmoil left me weak, unable to make a rational decision. I could barely manage to get through each day."

"We're not blaming you," I said. "We all know what he is like."

"He's right, Leona," Granny said. "We're not blaming you. I just wish I had known the true nature of your ordeal. Anyhow, why don't you stay here for a few days to think things through? Things need to settle down."

"Thanks, Mom. I think I will," my mother said. "And I'm very sorry that Anthony ruined the party for everyone."

"Nonsense," Jerry said. "The day is still young."

No one else knew what to say. Our family secrets exposed, we cleaned up the aftermath as best we could, in silence.

Needing a few minutes alone, I walked to the garden wall to ponder the whole mess. I looked at the angel, which was shooting a gentle stream of water from its trumpet. How untimely that the angel should have blasted its trumpet in my father's ear at the exact moment he had cursed my birth. Maybe it had been more than just a coincidence; maybe it was a sign from God that I wasn't such a schmuck. The rage of an angel had to be a sign.

I felt a hand on my shoulder. It was Maria. "Some day," she said.

"I'll say. How could a day that began with such hope have fallen so quickly into pandemonium?"

"I don't know. Maybe this is some kind of test," Maria said.

"How so?"

"Maybe it's a test to see how far we can reach into our own souls for compassion."

"Toward my father?"

"Maybe."

"I want to be compassionate, Maria. But I don't know if I have it in me. He is capable of stirring the worst kind of rage in me; not to mention how his behavior has affected the rest of the family.

Sometimes I wonder what our lives would have been, had my father been a different kind of man, if we hadn't always felt that we were on the front line of battle."

"That's perfectly understandable," Maria said. "Although, in being your father's son you were able to develop your character in ways that wouldn't have been possible otherwise. Perhaps if your road had been different, you wouldn't be the man you are today: the man I love."

"I know," I said. "It's hard to think positive when you've just been beaten down."

"That's how strength develops," Maria said. "Every time you pick yourself up and blow yourself off, you're a different man."

"Thank you for trying to make me feel better. I do appreciate you."

"I know. Just remember that fate unfolds in mysterious ways; had Anthony been a different kind of father, you wouldn't be who you are today. Sometimes greatness evolves from the sorriest of circumstances."

"Lately, Maria, I'm really beginning to appreciate the goodness in life. We are surrounded by so much beauty; why can't my father see any good in the world?"

"I don't know," Maria said, "but it is a travesty. It is a lost soul who cannot marvel in the beauty of our world; we who can need to feel compassion for those who cannot."

"You're absolutely right, honey. I just wish I could carry the enchantment that I feel at Granny's house with me into the rest of my life. When I'm here, I feel that miracles are possible."

"Miracles are possible everywhere, if we know how to look."

"In a strange way my life is beginning to make sense. I doubt I'd have reached this point if it weren't for you. Maybe all our lives are interconnected is some fateful way; I know I wouldn't be the man I am without your love."

"The same is true for me, Tony. Every day I learn something new about myself by seeing myself through your eyes."

"Really?"

"Really."

Maria's revelation stirred a new sense of meaning in my existence. If we were all interconnected, each having an impact on the life of the rest, I wanted to make certain my impact was a positive one. I was grateful for the marvelous influence Granny and

Maria had had on me. Even my father's impact had not been entirely negative: his behavior taught me what not to become.

"Let's go away," I said.

"Right now?"

"No, but soon. Let's go away for a weekend, somewhere woodsy, far from the city."

"O.K.," Maria said. "Are you ready for the fireworks now?"

"I'm ready."

The fireworks exploding into bursts of color against the curtain of night mimicked the realizations illuminating my own dark curtain. My day, which had gone from hope to despair and back to hope again, became my own personal Independence Day. It was a day of paradox, my independence having been gained in the realization of how dependent on one another we really were.

I learned that isolation is not the natural order of things. I saw proof of that in the sky: the majesty of a singular burst of color was dwarfed by the collective grandeur of multiple sparks exploding in unison. That is how life should be lived, I thought, as my gaze turned earthward to the faces joined in awe and wonder. While the heavens were still ablaze, I prayed that my father would one day learn that lesson as well. All my compassion had not gone down with that pickle.

Although darkness inevitably fell, I was able to carry some of the sparks from that experience as a flicker of hope in my memory.

The Fourth of July was just the beginning of my awakening; I was still far short of my destiny. That I was able to move forward with hope was my personal miracle; everything had not been taken from me.

Those were the things I pondered as I passed Newark Airport that night on the way home. I would never give up my dream of flying: it was my birthright.

Driving into Manhattan, I realized how much my consciousness had changed in so little time. The concept of time continued to baffle me, but I was certain of one thing: my life *was* on the upswing.

Nine

Believing I had experienced enlightenment during the Fourth of July fireworks, I thought my life would automatically take a turn for the better. Both beliefs were delusions: I had experienced only a faint flicker of enlightenment and the turns my life took were circular.

Maria assured me that my spiritual plight was normal; enlightenment would occur one flicker at a time, eventually snowballing into a sense of inner peace. I prayed she was right; after experiencing random episodes of pure contentment, I became greedy for more. How had I lived any other way?

Between flickers of enlightenment existed my usual state of affairs: family dysfunction, self doubt, memory-loss and guilt. Had it not been for Maria and Granny, my snowball would have melted. While Maria got the ball rolling with psychotherapy, Granny nudged me with the wit of Twain: "Don't kick a bad habit down the stairs; coax it down gently, one step at a time."

My bad habit was the self-torture of circular thinking. At one time, I had resented Maria for being unwilling to treat me as a patient; when I became her patient, I felt guilty about placing such a load on her. Why couldn't I just be happy? That's why I was in psychotherapy. Hopefully an answer would be forthcoming; self-doubt and guilt hindered my momentum.

I couldn't decide if I had a real memory problem or if my perception of time had become altered. I struggled to remember recent transpirings as if they were in the distant past; individual days passed in seconds but weeks seemed an eternity. Suddenly everything seemed a paradox; I began questioning not only my neuroses, but all of life. That old adage *was* true: sometimes things got worse before they got better.

My family dysfunction was escalating: my parents had separated after the pickle incident on Independence Day. My father moved out of the house and into a small efficiency near the globe plant. For almost three months, he contacted no one in the family except Margaret; she gave Dad ironing lessons. Margaret saw it as a glimmer of hope that Dad was learning, if only to starch a shirt.

Though I bounced erratically toward enlightenment, I bounced in the right direction. The void created by my fleeing neuroses was slowly being filled with new thought patterns. My life became a period of discovery; like civilization, I too could leave the Dark Ages and experience Renaissance. History became my inspiration.

Hope seemed alive and well for everyone in my family that autumn. I was coming out of my head, and my marriage was thriving. My mother was enjoying success in her writing endeavors, and her tableware was about to make its debut at the Guggenheim. After inventing a new hairstyle, Margaret increased her business threefold. We R Nuts hit the country by storm, pushing Uncle Harry closer to his dream of being a magnate. Any day the Nobel Laureates would be announced; while the string theorists posed some threat, I was certain Jerry would win. Perhaps there was even hope for my father: in losing it, maybe he would realize what he'd had.

I looked at the clock: Maria would be home any minute. While waiting, I thought about the Nobel Prize. We should have heard something by now; what was taking so long? I prayed the Swedish Academy wasn't having second thoughts about Jerry; had the string theorists taken the lead?

I thought about the similarity between the race for the Nobel Prize and the race for political office. Why weren't the Nobel candidates on TV slandering one another?

I imagined Jerry on a televised debate, the intellectual race having become a political one: "What makes my theory better than string theory is that I've never been married, and therefore have never committed adultery. I'm concerned purely with science; my opponent, Dr. Ball, is concerned purely with vagrancy. Who do you want as your Nobel Laureate? Someone better than that slug, or a slug who uses string during illicit sexual acts with his graduate students?" Jerry then pointed to a raised hand in the audience.

"But Dr. Vitello, you haven't told us exactly what your theory is," a young woman asked.

"My theory?" Jerry asked. "I'm afraid I've forgotten what my theory is. But it isn't really important. Just take my word for it; it has to be better than anything this jerk could formulate. Can you believe him?" Jerry pointed to another raised hand.

An older woman stood. "For the record, Dr. Vitello, are you saying that the Swedish Academy should vote for you because you say you are better than Dr. Ball without telling us why you are better?"

"Absolutely. Just trust me—I have family values," Jerry said.

It was Dr. Ball's turn at the podium, but I didn't have time to produce the end of my imaginary press conference—the front door to our apartment opened: Maria was home.

"Hi Honey! How was your day?" I asked.

Maria leaned her briefcase against the sofa. "It was great. My two o'clock is making great strides, thanks to you."

"Really?" I asked, kissing Maria. What a relief! Since Maria began her clinical trial of my imaginary group therapy, I'd become paranoid over hidden side-effects. I was certain that something dire would emerge, rendering the genius of my purple notebook null and void. My paranoia was ungrounded; my genius was sound.

"Why do you sound so surprised?" Maria asked. "The new modality is working like a charm, although my two o'clock has deviated slightly from your prototype. She's created an imaginary trinity; felt she needed a bit more input than a couple could provide. Her fantasy is very well-constructed; she's in group therapy with a set of identical triplets who look alike but think very differently."

"How creative," I said.

"It's more than creative," Maria said. "It's amazing. It has really expanded her consciousness; she's now seeing the world through eight eyes instead of two."

"Maria," I said nervously, "you don't think there's any danger of this little fantasy triggering multiple personality disorder, do you?"

"Of course not," Maria assured me. "I've given my patients very suggestive instructions on how to construct their ego projections. They're fully aware that the reality they're creating is just an illusion. Don't worry."

"Good," I said. "I'd hate to think that I was pushing anyone over the edge."

"Oh, Tony. You really need to have more confidence in your ideas. I've never seen such rapid progress in my patients; it's been a magic bullet for the Steinbrights, too."

"You didn't let them read my journal, did you?" I hadn't spoken very highly of the Steinbrights in my pages.

"Of course not. Do you really think I would violate the oath of confidentiality between us?"

"No. I'm just being paranoid."

Maria changed the subject. "Did you call your mother today?"

"Yes," I said. "She's doing wonderfully. One of her professors is urging her to propose *The PonyTale* to a children's publisher."

"That's great. I'm so happy for your mother; her life is really turning around. Let's read her story again after dinner."

"O.K.," I said. "I'd love to. It's a shame that my father can't be there to share in her success."

"Who knows, Tony. Maybe this separation will turn your father around. You know what they say: you never know what you have until you lose it."

"That's the truth." I learned that lesson during the gray days of January; luckily I had lost only my license plate.

"What do you want for dinner?" Maria asked.

"How about Thai? That new place on 63rd Street delivers." I was learning not only to compromise but to expand my dietary horizon.

"Great. Will you call and order while I take a shower?"

"I will."

I called the Thai Kitchen and ordered dinner. I hung up the phone, and it began ringing. It was Margaret.

"Hi Margaret! How's it going?"

"I'm fine, but Dad's not. I had to bail him out of jail last night."

"What? Why? What the hell did he do?"

"Are you sitting down?"

"Yes."

"He was arrested for cocaine possession."

"What? Dad's on drugs?"

"No, it was all a misunderstanding. The charges are going to be dropped after the court hearing tomorrow."

"What kind of misunderstanding?"

"I didn't know it," Margaret said, "but apparently one-dollar bills are just seething with cocaine."

"They are? How?"

"People roll them up and use them to snort cocaine. Residual powder gets trapped in the fibers of the money, and clings to them even after the bills are back in circulation."

"Really?"

"I guess so. That's what the lawyer said today."

"I don't get it. Why was Dad arrested? Surely the amount of cocaine trapped in a one-dollar bill wasn't enough to indict him."

"You're right, Tony, but you're forgetting Dad's habit of carrying a hundred of them."

"Huh?"

"Apparently," Margaret said, "the collective amount of cocaine in Dad's bankroll was enough to alert a drug-sniffing dog."

"Where?" I asked.

"Some greasy spoon where a lot of cops have dinner. One of the drug-sniffing K-9's went nuts and pinned Dad down to the counter where he was eating. The dog finished off Dad's meatloaf, too."

"Oh my God!" I yelled, laughing.

"Tell me about it," Margaret said.

"Is he all right?"

"He is now, after talking to his lawyer today. But he was a mess last night; you know how he feels about large dogs."

"I didn't know they allowed dogs in restaurants."

"I guess only seeing-eye dogs and K-9's," Margaret said. "Anyhow, we're talking about some greasy spoon, not *The Russian Tea Room*."

"Oh. So Dad's O.K., then?"

"Yeah," Margaret said. "In some absurd way I think the experience did him some good. It was very humbling for him to be locked in a prison cell for all those hours."

"How many hours?"

"About seven," Margaret answered. "I didn't get home until midnight."

"Wow," I said, imagining my father as a member of the lower element.

"You know, Tony, I think this is going to be the thing that turns Dad around. For the first time, Dad was actually able to share feelings of vulnerability with me. He told me that his whole life flashed before his eyes as he lay pressed to the counter under the weight of that dog."

"It must have been horrifying," I said.

"What? His whole life flashing before his eyes?"

"No," I said. "I meant being pinned down by a vicious dog."

"Oh, yeah."

"So I guess Dad will be laundering his money from now on."

"Exactly what I was thinking," Margaret said. "Isn't the whole thing absurd? Who'd have thought that Dad's little quirk could get him into so much trouble? Anyhow, I have to run. Ivan's here; we're going out to dinner."

"O.K., Margaret. Thanks for calling. I'll talk to you soon."

I was stunned. What went around certainly came around: Dad had wrongly accused me of being a heroin junkie, and he was now facing similar charges. I thought about Margaret's statement: "Who'd have ever thought that Dad's little quirk could get him into so much trouble?"

Suddenly I fell into a mental wormhole, falling toward 1969. I emerged from the wormhole in front of the Wax Museum. Granny was speaking: "One day, Anthony, you'll realize that foolish games can get you into trouble."

I blinked and returned to present reality, mentally answering Margaret's question: Granny knew Dad's quirk would get him into trouble; she had warned him thirty years ago. I was stunned. Not only were people interconnected in our journey through space-time; events were too. I realized that many bizarre events of my childhood were culminating in the present day: could it really take thirty years for an event to come full-circle?

Even more perplexing was the paradox embedded in these culminations. Could an event with seemingly absurd beginnings be an agent of positive change in disguise? Could Dad's game, the false illusion of wealth, in the end be responsible for shattering his other, far-reaching illusions?

I came to the conclusion that life was far too complex to be understood by the intellect. The web of irony in which my life was embedded had no explanation in ordinary language. I decided it was time to give up trying to understand life; I needed to sit back and marvel in the paradox. Maria was right; miracles were everywhere if you knew how to look. After forty-two years, I was finally beginning to see clearly. I began to laugh.

"What's so funny?" Maria asked, entering the living room.

"Did you know that paper money was riddled with cocaine?"

"Yes," Maria said. "That's why I hate carrying cash. Not only is it seething with cocaine; it's laden with bacteria. Haven't you ever heard the expression that money is the dirtiest thing around?"

"Well, yeah, but I had no idea it was harboring anything illegal."

"Who called?" Maria asked.

"It was Margaret. She called to tell me that our father had been busted."

"What?"

I told Maria the whole sordid tale, including Margaret's prognosis that there would be a positive outcome.

"That is unbelievable," Maria said. "Who knows? Maybe Margaret is right; sometimes it takes something shocking to initiate change. Maybe your father will reflect on his life and move forward in a different direction."

There was a knock at the door. "Must be our dinner," I said. I was right; it was the delivery boy from the Thai Kitchen.

"Twenty-seven seventy-two," he said, handing me the bags. I placed them on the hall table and reached into my pocket. I had only a fifty. "Maria? Do you have any change? I only have a fifty."

"No, I don't have any cash."

"Can you change a fifty?" I asked the delivery boy.

"No problem," he said. "But I'll have to give you all one's." He started counting.

"You can stop when you get to eighteen," I said.

"Thank you, sir. You're very kind. Have a good evening." The delivery boy walked away and I was left holding the money.

"You'd better go and wash your hands," Maria said. "And use the antibacterial soap."

Maria and I sat down to our fragrant dinner. "Did Margaret mention if Jerry had heard anything?" Maria asked.

"No, and I never thought to ask her. I'm sure she would have mentioned something if there was any news."

"We should be hearing something any day; it's already October the seventh."

"Any time now," I added.

We continued eating without much conversation; we were hungry.

"I'm really looking forward to our trip tomorrow, honey," Maria said. "Did the B&B call to confirm our reservations?"

"Yes, they did. This time tomorrow we'll be enjoying the colors of fall from our private balcony. I can't wait; Manhattan is getting that gray cast again. If it weren't for Central Park I'd go nuts."

Maria had a funny look on her face. Was it something I said? "What's the matter?" I asked.

"Oh, it's that darn ringing in my ears again; I must have gotten water in my ears when I went swimming yesterday. I forgot my ear plugs."

"Maybe you should see a doctor," I suggested.

"No, I'm O.K.. I just need to remember my ear plugs. Anyhow, have you thought about touring Scandinavia in December if we go to Stockholm?"

"Yes, I have, but I'm afraid it doesn't look too good. It's the timing; SuperSoft needs me to be on call in case any unforeseen Y2K glitches emerge. I'll be lucky to get a few days off."

"That's a shame," Maria said. "I was hoping to take that ferry across the Baltic Sea to Oslo."

"I know. But we don't even know if we're going to Stockholm yet. You know, the suspense is really starting to grate at me."

"Me too," Maria said. "I can only imagine how Jerry must feel."

"Knowing Jerry, he's preoccupied with his work and hasn't yet realized that it *is* October."

"You're right."

"So what do you want to do? Do you want to watch a movie?" I asked.

"No. I'd like to read your mother's story again. Why don't we sit and read it together?"

"O.K. I'll take care of the dishes. Mom's manuscript is on the bookshelf in the office; I'll meet you on the sofa."

"Thanks for cleaning up again, honey," Maria said, as she left the room.

As I washed the dishes, I began worrying about Maria's ear. I wish she'd remember her earplugs, I thought.

Maria and I snuggled on the sofa and examined my mother's cover page. "Isn't it funny how Mom spelled her name in upper and lower case letters? I guess she wanted to add some flair to her name," I said.

"I don't think so, Tony. Look, the capital letters spell *love*. How clever."

It was clever; why hadn't I noticed that?

"Will you read it aloud, Tony?"

"Sure," I said, grounding myself in space-time. Paying close attention to where I was and what I was doing, I looked down at my mother's pages and began reading aloud:

The Pony Tale
A Children's Story
by
LeOna VitEllo

Once upon a time, there lived a boy named Sammy. Sammy was different from the other boys his age. While Sammy's friends were playing and riding their bicycles, he was running errands and doing chores for the neighborhood women. Sammy worked hard; he was saving his money for something very special.

Every Saturday, Sammy went downtown to gaze into the shop window that held his treasure. His treasure was a small black box with a glass hole: it was a camera.

One day, Sammy counted his money—he finally had enough! His hard work had finally paid off. Sammy ran downtown to buy his little black box.

Sammy reached the shop and ran to the

window excitedly. His heart sank—the camera was gone! Sammy ran into the store. "Sorry," the clerk said, "it was the last one."

Sammy walked sadly home, heartbroken over his lost dream.

When Sammy got home, his mother saw that he was troubled. "Don't look so sad, son," she said. "Go and see your Poppy."

Sammy's father was sitting in his chair, reading the newspaper. Sammy noticed a package sitting on the table next to his Poppy. It was decorated gaily with blue and yellow ribbons.

"Don't be so sad, son," his Poppy said. "I have a present for you."

Sammy thanked Poppy and began opening his present. He tore off the last of the wrapping and opened the box: it was something black. "It's the camera, Poppy!" Sammy shouted. "I've been wanting it for so long! Thank you Poppy!"

Sammy loved his camera. The first thing he did was engrave his initials on the bottom of it.

Everywhere he went, Sammy took his camera and snapped pictures. He pinned his pictures to the wall of his bedroom. Every night before he went to sleep, Sammy looked at the pictures of his friends and family. Pretty soon his walls were covered with pictures.

Sammy's little black camera was his favorite thing in the whole world. He believed the camera was a magic box: how else could it capture his life on paper? It had to be magic.

Sammy lived in his magical world until one day, when he came home from school and found his mother crying. "Why are you so sad, Momma?"

Sammy asked.

"I am sad because Poppy will not be coming home today: he has gone to heaven," she said.

Sammy was so sad that he dropped his camera and ran to his bedroom. He lay sobbing on his bed for a very long time. Suddenly, Sammy looked up and saw something through his tears: a picture of his Poppy, smiling at him.

"Thank you, Poppy," Sammy said silently. He had an idea. He emptied the coins from his bank and ran downtown.

Sammy scoured the albums until he found the perfect one: it was filled with black pages and had a smooth leather front. There was a place on the cover to write an inscription. He paid for the album and ran home.

Sammy went upstairs to his bedroom and went to work. Sammy took every picture of his Poppy from his bedroom wall, except one, and placed each of them carefully in his new album. When he was finished, he wrote on the cover in his best handwriting: "Our Poppy."

Sammy opened a drawer, where he had been saving the pretty paper and blue and yellow ribbons. He wrapped his album and ran downstairs.

Sammy's mother was making a pot of soup in the kitchen. Tears flowed into the pot. She was heartbroken.

"Don't be so sad, Momma," Sammy said. "I have a present for you."

Sammy's mother dried her tears and looked at her little boy. "That is so sweet of you, Sammy." Sammy handed the gift to his mother and she unwrapped it. "Oh," she cried, "it is the best gift anyone has ever given me."

But Sammy's mother was crying even harder. "I didn't mean to make you sad," Sammy said.

"I am not sad," Sammy's mother said. "These are tears of joy."

Every night Sammy and his mother would look through the album and cry tears of joy together.

Many months passed and times grew tough. Sammy and his mother barely had enough food to eat, because they had so little money. Little by little, Sammy's mother sold her belongings, until their house was bare and only one treasure remained: the cuckoo clock Poppy had given Momma on their wedding day.

Sammy couldn't let his mother sell that clock, so he worked harder. He ran more errands and did more chores. But it wasn't enough.

Sammy did what he had to do: he took his little magic box downtown. The storekeeper gave Sammy nine dollars for his camera.

Sammy walked sadly home. He had lost his Poppy and his camera, but at least he could buy food for his mother. And, the little bird would still give his mother pleasure as it announced the hour.

When Sammy gave the money to his mother, she was saddened because he had sold his treasure, but was happy to have such a thoughtful son.

Things began to get better, and more money came to them, enough to keep the household running. Momma hoped to buy Sammy a new camera, but her wish never came true. Sammy was happy anyhow; he had already taken the best pictures: the ones in their special album.

Many years passed, and Sammy grew into a man. One day he married a woman and they moved into a house of their own.

Sammy and his wife waited for God to send them a baby, but a baby never came. That saddened Sammy, because he loved children and wanted some of his very own.

Sammy watched the neighborhood children playing in the alley and prayed even harder for a child. Still, no child came.

Sammy was sad and lonely: he had lost his Poppy, his camera, and his dream of a child.

One night Sammy was so sad that he sat down on his back steps and wept. He held his head in his hands and cried for everything he had lost. Suddenly, he heard a strange noise: clip-clop, clip-clop, clip-clop.

Sammy looked up saw a pony! He was shocked—the pony was wearing a camera around his neck! It was just like the camera Poppy had given him when he was a little boy.

"What are you doing here?" Sammy asked the pony.

"God sent me to you," the pony said. "He's sorry that he couldn't send you a baby. He sent me instead."

Sammy thought it was odd that a pony could talk, but after all, the pony had been heaven-sent. It was the most beautiful pony Sammy had ever seen. At the base of his ponytail was a small pink rosebud.

"Why are you wearing a rosebud on your ponytail?" Sammy asked the pony.

"It is a symbol of your new fate," the pony said. "From now on, there will be only roses—no more tears." The pony leaned down so Sammy could take the camera from him. "This is a special camera," the pony said. "Anyone who has his picture taken with this camera will be blessed with magic."

Sammy took the camera and examined its bottom. There were his initials, which he had scratched into the black leather so long ago.

Sammy sat on the steps and cried tears of joy. "But I sold this camera a long time ago," he cried.

"You were its rightful owner, and it found its way back to you. When you sold your camera to help your mother, God blessed it with magic. That magic brought it back to you," the pony said.

A little boy interrupted Sammy and the pony: "Mister, could you take a picture of me on your pony?"

"Hop on," Sammy said. Sammy looked through the lens of his camera, shocked by what he saw: a rainbow of colored light dancing above the boy's head. When he looked away from the camera, the rainbow was gone.

Everywhere that Sammy and his pony went, they were surrounded by children and the magical light.

Sammy built a stable in his backyard for the pony, and the neighborhood children took turns feeding the pony and brushing his long, thick ponytail. The children loved the pony so much that they came to Sammy's house every day. The children didn't know it, but they had been blessed by the magic that was crystallized in Sammy's little black camera.

The pony never spoke another word after that first night, and Sammy believed God had spoken to him through the pony.

One day Sammy and his wife sat on their back steps watching the children play with the pony. Suddenly, Sammy realized all his dreams had come true. He had his beloved camera, and God had sent him not one child, but three dozen.

It didn't matter to Sammy that the children weren't his very own: he loved them anyway.

Sammy looked at his little black camera, which was a symbol of his Poppy's love, Sammy's love for his mother, and the magic of love for all children. "Thank you, my dear pony," Sammy said.

The pony looked at Sammy but didn't speak; he swung his ponytail in a happy gesture and nuzzled the children who were hugging his gentle soul.

The End

"That is such a sweet story," Maria said. "It's amazing how your mother has used that story to reconcile grief over her own father's death."

"How so?" I asked.

"Well, a horse took her father's life, and instead of her loss festering into an equestrian hatred, she has substituted mysticism for her anger. The horse no longer symbolizes darkness; it becomes an agent of hope, shrouded in magic. It is a story about healing," Maria said authoritatively.

"Wow," I said. "You read a lot into it. I hadn't thought about it that way, but you know, you're probably right. It probably also explains Mom's curio cabinet full of porcelain ponies."

"Absolutely," Maria said. "And the fact that your mother had the courage to put her own children on a horse for a portrait—that was a true act of forgiveness!"

As absurd as it sounded, I believed Maria was right. So what could explain the recurring "ponytail incidents" which had occurred in our family? Were they in any way related to the loss of my own Poppy? "You know, Maria, I wonder something: Margaret lost her pride when her ponytail was swept out to sea; my father lost his when he was slapped in the face by the tail of the diving horse; Dad is trying to destroy Jerry's pride because of a ponytail—what could all this mean?"

"It means your mother is trying to heal the shame of their ponytail incidents by suggesting that a ponytail not be equated with doom. Your mother's ponytail incident has a good outcome, and she is trying to convince others that their own ponytail incidents can be reconciled as well."

"She is?" It sounded ridiculous, but Maria was a skilled diagnostician, and I believed her. Still, why would something as absurd as a ponytail become a symbol of lost pride in our family?

Although Maria made an interesting point, she had misunderstood my question. I wasn't questioning my mother's symbolic intentions: I wondered if the ponytail incidents were my dead grandfather's way of trying to communicate with us.

"Don't you agree?" Maria asked.

"Agree with what?" I missed something.

"That she's expressed her message at the level of myth so even children can comprehend it?" Maria repeated.

"I guess so," I answered, my mind jumping to another tangent: neither Granny nor I had experienced a ponytail incident. I perceived it as a sign; Granny and I had a special connection. We had both been spared the brush of the ponytail.

"The story isn't over yet," I thought Maria said.

"What?" I asked.

"Tony, will you pay attention? *I said*, you hate to see the story end," Maria repeated.

"I know. You'll have to forgive me, Maria. I'm really tired," I said.

"Why don't you go to bed? I'll be in shortly; I want to read *The PonyTale* again."

"If you don't mind," I said, kissing Maria.

"Of course I don't mind. Go to sleep if you're tired."

While undressing for bed, I reviewed Maria's analysis of my mother's story. Could something as baffling and arcane as a ponytail really be an icon of pride in our family's story?

The more deeply I analyzed life, the more absurd it appeared. I fell asleep realizing I would never be able to express the mystery of life in intellectual terms: the language didn't exist. I remembered that Jerry had coined his own words when lacking an existing word; I would explore that option when I was more rested. Exhausted, I succumbed to sleep.

I rolled into wakefulness with the sound of waves splashing against the shore. I listened to the periodicity of my beckoning: first a powerful surge of water, then a gentle foaming. A surge, then a foaming. I began to doze off again, hypnotized by the ocean's rhythmic chant.

I looked toward the water's edge; dozens of sandpipers were tip-toeing in synchrony to an inaudible beat. Under the newly-risen sun, the ocean's color became a magnificent hue of robins' egg blue. I marveled in the beauty of the new day, suddenly feeling a deep connection with everything that ever was and everything that ever would be. I was one with the universe: I became the waves that pounded my feet and the birds that flew overhead.

I was especially connected with the birds: one had used my head as a target. With a plop and a splat, I awoke.

Maria lay in bed next to me. "You were talking in your sleep again, Tony. You kept saying 'Did you have to use my head?'. Are you all right? Did you have a bad dream?"

"Actually," I said, "it was a really good dream, until a bird crapped on my head."

"What's that in your hair?" Maria asked.

"Where?" I asked, running my fingers through my disheveled mane.

"Got you!" Maria said, laughing.

I laughed and looked at the alarm clock. "Did you turn off the alarm?" I asked Maria.

"Yes. You didn't even hear it."

"The strange thing is, I did hear it, and it was somehow incorporated into my dream. I was on the beach at sunrise having a religious experience when a seagull brought me back to ordinary reality with his wet little gift."

"That seagull was just one of your fear demons," Maria said. "Your life is getting better; you subconsciously wonder when things will begin unraveling again. It's a typical response to forward growth; you fear the uncharted territory that lies ahead, so your subconscious manifests a fear demon to keep you from going there."

"Really?" I asked. I'd thought my head was just in the wrong place at the wrong time. Was there really so much subconscious meaning symbolized in my dream?

"You mean I subconsciously willed that bird to crap on me?" I asked.

"Yes," Maria replied with conviction. "The wet shock of that seagull excrement prevented you from moving deeper into non-ordinary reality, because you were afraid of what you would find there."

"Afraid of finding what?"

"Your deepest feelings about yourself. You're afraid that those feelings will send you catapulting backwards; concurrently, another force, the antithesis of fear, drives your soul forward, searching for the truth about yourself. You have to let go of your fear."

"I had no idea that dreams meant so much," I said. "I thought they were simply the downloadings of a tired mind."

"Oh no," Maria said. "Your subconscious assigns a meaning to each of your dream elements. The ocean is a symbol of the unknown, in all its power and vastness. Birds are your thoughts, sometimes flying in circles, sometimes crapping on you. The multitude of colors reflected on the surface of the water is the spectrum of your mood, which reflects the deeper, hidden agenda of your subconscious."

Psychoanalysis was hard to swallow so early in the morning, but I was grateful for Maria's help. That Maria could spurt forth such intense analysis upon awakening deepened my professional faith in her; I moved forward with even greater hope. My hope and gratitude were interrupted by the ringing of the telephone. I looked at Maria. "Who could it be, at this hour?" I asked.

"I don't know," Maria said, sitting up in bed.

I answered the telephone. It was Margaret.

"Tony," Margaret screamed, "he's in!"

"Who? Dad?"

"No, Jerry. He won!"

"Jerry won!" I screamed to Maria.

"When did he find out?" I asked Margaret.

"Late last night. The Royal Academy called him late last night. Can you believe it? Our brother won the Nobel Prize in physics!" Margaret screamed.

The three of us squealed in excitement. "Oh my God," I said, "where is Jerry now? I have to call him."

"He's at home," Margaret said.

"How is he?" I asked.

"He's shocked. I don't think it ever really occurred to him that he would actually win; he's totally oblivious to his own genius. And of course, Jerry is feeling sorry for the string theorists, that they've suffered such a disappointment."

"That sounds like Jerry," I said. "Listen, Margaret, I'll call you right back; I want to call Jerry and congratulate him."

"O.K.. Bye," Margaret said.

"This is so exciting!" Maria said.

I dialed Jerry's number; it was busy. I dialed again; it was still busy. "I'll go in the office and have the computer auto-dial Jerry until we get through," I said.

Running toward the office, I tripped over Maria's briefcase. It triggered a childhood memory of tripping over the molecular models that had littered our bedroom floor. All those stubbed toes were worth it, I thought. No pain, no gain—my brother was a Nobel Laureate! I flew proudly into the office and nervously set-up auto-dial. As the computer called Jerry, I paced anxiously.

Maria entered the office. "Anything yet?"

"No, still busy."

"I'll put the coffee on," Maria said.

After a hundred and thirty-six unsuccessful attempts, auto-dial finally got through. Jerry's line was ringing.

"Hello?" Jerry answered.

"Congratulations, little brother!" I yelled.

"Tony! Thanks. I've been trying to call you for the last forty-five minutes; your line's been busy."

"He's been trying to call us," I said to Maria.

"I've had the computer on auto-dial, trying to get through to you. Tell me: how does it feel?" I asked.

"It feels like a dream," Jerry said. "I still can't believe it. Would you believe I entertained the thought that the call from the Swedish Academy was a figment of my imagination? I even pressed star sixty-nine after we hung up; my caller ID was off," Jerry laughed.

"I guess it must seem pretty unreal," I said.

"It does. Anyhow, Tone, thanks for calling, but I have to run; I have a press conference at nine."

"Good luck, Jerry."

"One more thing, Tone. Will you go?"

"I don't know if I can be in Princeton by nine, but if it means that much to you, I can try."

"I wasn't referring to the press conference, Tone. I meant Stockholm."

"Oh, absolutely! I wouldn't miss it for the world."

"Thanks, Tone. It would mean absolutely nothing if you weren't there to share it with me."

"Don't worry," I said, my voice cracking. "I'll be there."

"Thanks, Tone."

I hung up the phone. I thought: the bond between Jerry and me meant more to him than the Nobel Prize? He did have family values! I sat down at the desk and cried. I was drowning in joy, from pride and love. At that moment I realized the power of love could revolutionize the world in a way far more earth-shattering than any scientific discovery. I blew my nose and went into the kitchen for another cup of coffee.

"If you want to drive to Princeton today," Maria said, "we could drive to the bed and breakfast later this afternoon."

"Thanks, sweetie, but the press will be stalking Jerry all day; I'm sure he'll be busy. Maybe we'll head back a little early on Sunday and catch Jerry at home."

"Good idea," Maria said. "I wasn't thinking about the press. You're right; they're going to be all over him."

I looked out the kitchen window, the sky was clear and blue. "It looks like we're going to have nice weather for our trip," I said.

"I have a feeling it's going to be a perfect weekend, all the way around," Maria said. "I'm going to start packing; do you want to skip breakfast and stop for an early lunch once we get on the road?"

"That sounds good," I said.

Maria left the kitchen. I stood there, spellbound, trying to reconcile reality. As I stared at the vertical patches of blue through my kitchen window, I thought about the grandfather whom I knew so well but had never met.

Poppy would be so proud, I thought. His labors of love in mathematics were finally bearing Nobel fruit, albeit posthumously. More than a half century later, Poppy's own work was culminating in the vision of his grandson: how could our fates be so inexorably bound? The divine laws governing our destiny were unfathomable to me. Rather than apply logic to the unfathomable, I accepted it as a mystery. Acknowledgment of the deep connection between Jerry and our grandfather further eroded my illusion of separateness, which had begun to crumble on Independence Day.

I walked away from the kitchen window, changed. How had I ever believed my mortal ego could comprehend that which was shrouded in magic? Logic held no place in the realms of the non-ordinary. Eureka: I had been a dog chasing its own tail! I was blessed with another flicker of enlightenment, and filed it in the mental space that had been vacated by my departing ignorance.

Maria and I finished packing and left for our weekend in the country.

We were driving about twenty minutes when the colors of fall began striking our retinas. It was a welcomed explosion of color, filling the void created by the long shadows of Manhattan's skyline.

While the city offered a plethora of cultural and intellectual color, my soul longed for the spectrum of nature. My childhood excursions to PennyPack Park with Granny had stirred such feelings of completeness in me; I longed to be lost there again. It was with eager anticipation that I approached our weekend retreat.

Maria was also hypnotized by the fall landscape; her eyes reflected the golden hues of the trees that beckoned us with their outstretched limbs. Maria shared my lusty fervor for the tapestry of fall.

"What are you thinking about, honey?" I asked.

"I was thinking about your mother's character Sammy, how he longed so for a child of his own. I guess I still haven't come to terms with the fact that we may never have a child of our own."

So much for my intuition; the reflection in Maria's eyes was melancholy, not autumnal bliss. "I know, honey," I said. "I feel that way too."

In eight years of marriage, and despite total disregard for contraception, Maria and I had failed to conceive a child. After every fertility check at their disposal, medical science couldn't provide an answer. There seemed to be no logical reason, physiologically or otherwise, for our infertility. It was a mystery to our doctors and ourselves.

"Are you sorry we didn't pursue in vitro?" I asked Maria.

"No, not really," Maria said. "I kind of left it in God's hands; if it was meant to be, it would have happened. Maybe God will send us a pony instead. Can you imagine, the two of us walking a pony through the lobby of our building?"

"At least you haven't lost your sense of humor," I said.

"No," Maria said, "and I hope I haven't brought you down. Let's dwell on the positive; we were blessed with beautiful weather, and we have a lot to celebrate."

"That's right—we're going to Stockholm!" I yelled. "Do you think it would be in poor taste to throw around the fact that I'm a brother of a Nobel Laureate? I like the sound of it."

"If you've got it, flaunt it!" Maria replied. "Do you want to stop for lunch soon? I'm pretty hungry."

"Me too. I'll pull over at the next restaurant. When we stop, I want to call Granny to see how she's taking the news."

We ate a decent lunch at a small Mom and Pop diner and were back on the road within forty minutes. I was unable to reach Granny. Knowing her, she was off to one of her social engagements; for an eighty-five year old, her calendar was surprisingly full.

Within an hour, we were pulling up to the bed and breakfast. "Look!" Maria said. "They've painted the building since we were last here."

They had. The large Victorian structure, previously a pale yellow, had become a soft shade of pink that dripped with white gingerbread trim. There were pots of white mums everywhere, grouped in three's on the large wrap-around porch. Floral chintz cushions and pillows softened the white wicker furniture. In warmer weather one could dine at a round table, which then displayed some of the strangest-looking gourds I had ever seen.

"We're in heaven," I said.

"It looks like a gingerbread house in the middle of an enchanted forest," Maria added.

I retrieved our bags from the trunk, and Maria and I approached the house. We climbed the porch steps and entered the house through a large set of double doors, each one a marvel in stained glass. A woman sitting at a large desk in the foyer looked up and greeted us.

"Good afternoon, folks," she said, "my name is Christine Cooper. Do you have a reservation?"

"Yes," I said, "Vitello."

"Oh yes," Christine said. "We've been expecting you. Did you have a nice trip?"

"Yes," Maria and I said in unison.

"Good," Christine said. "Before I take you to your room, I'd like to show you around a bit. Our records indicate that you've been here before, but we've changed ownership since then, and there have been a lot of changes."

That explained the new exterior, I thought.

"This is our lounge area," Christine said, pointing to the large room off the foyer. "The bar opens at four, and during happy hour free snacks are served."

We followed Christine down the hall and turned a corner. "This of course, is our dining room, and across the hall we have our new conservatory. It is perfect for quiet reflection or an afternoon sun bath."

I heard trickling water, and scanned the conservatory in search of its origin. "Look, Maria," I said, pointing to the far corner of the glass room. "It's a fountain like Granny's, only smaller."

"It is. What a coincidence," Maria said, looking queerly at me.

"Isn't it lovely?" Christine asked. "Now if you'll follow me back to the foyer, I'll call James and have him take your bags to your room."

We followed Christine to the front desk. She took an imprint of our credit card and called James to help us. Christine then handed me a set of keys to Room 18, another coincidence.

Within seconds, James was turning the corner. Our bellboy certainly was a boy; he couldn't have been more than twelve years old. Christine must have noticed my surprise. "It's a family-run business," she explained.

"Hi Ya," James said, waving.

"James, this is Mr. and Mrs. Vitello; we'll be taking them to Room 18."

The four of us piled into a small elevator and rode up one flight.

"Here we go," Christine said, motioning us down a small hallway. Christine unlocked the door and we followed her into Room 18. It was big and beautiful.

"It is beautiful," Maria said, walking through the room.

It was. Art hung on the walls in large gilded frames; fresh flowers were everywhere. Gold poured through the open balcony doors, steeping the room in the magic of the season. There was a small stepladder to assist one's climb into the huge canopy bed.

"We'll leave you alone to get settled," Christine said. "Come on, James."

James approached me. "Will there be anything else, Sir?" he asked, in a suddenly mature tongue.

"No, thank you," I said. James looked at me. "Oh, here you go," I said, reaching into my pocket and handing him a five-dollar bill.

"Thank you, Sir!" James proclaimed, and they was gone.

"You're right, Tony, we are in heaven!" Maria said, climbing the ladder and falling into the soft chintz garden of a bed. "This bed is great; in fact, I could take a nap right now. That big lunch has me feeling sleepy."

"Don't you want to go for a walk?" I was eager to explore the great outdoors.

"What I'd really like to do is rest for an hour. Then I'll be able to enjoy the rest of the day."

"You don't mind if I go for a walk, do you?"

"Of course not. I'll join you a little later."

I kissed Maria goodbye and left the room. James was in the foyer as I left the building.

"Do you have more bags, Sir?"

"No, thank you," I said.

The air was cool and crisp. I headed toward a wooded area behind the bed and breakfast, where well-established trails cut through the woods. Every few hundred feet was a bench nestled among the trees, the perfect spot to sit and contemplate the fragrance of nature. I was alone that afternoon, but by the next day the trails would be filled with other visitors, some on foot, some on horseback.

I walked for quite a while, listening to the wind moving through the trees and the occasional rustle of leaves as squirrels scurried in their search for acorns. This is bliss, I thought. I approached a bench that was situated conveniently by a small stream, whose babbling called my name. A golden light reflected on the surface of the water, mirroring the foliage of the trees which towered overhead. I walked to the bench and sat down.

I sat back and closed my eyes, enjoying the aroma of pine as the wind stirred it beneath my nose. I became lost in the moment: the elements of nature had captivated my every sense. Soon I had lost all sense of my physical self; I became the soft amber earth beneath my feet and the leaves that blew by me. My heartbeat resonated with the chant of the wind and my breath punctuated the soft stillness of my golden other-world. I suddenly became aware of my body again when the wind brushed the hairs at the nape of my neck. I sat there as nature soothed me.

I became more and more aware of my physical self, and the wind tickled my neck in a more marked fashion. I reached back to touch my neck; my hand was met by a wiry mop of hair. I don't have a ponytail, I thought. Startled, I jumped to my feet and turned; I was looking right at a horse's ass. It wasn't the wind: I had felt the horse's tail brush my neck. There was a small pink rosebud at the base of the horse's tail. I must have fallen asleep; my ponytail incident had to be a dream.

The horse turned, and I almost fell over in shock—there was a box camera dangling from its neck! I had to be dreaming, I reassured myself; it couldn't be the pony from my mother's story.

"I'm sorry to have disturbed you," the horse said.

"What?" I said. "Horses can't talk."

"They can't?" the horse asked. "Then I guess I'm not a horse after all. But the song says, "*A horse is a horse of course of course.*"

"That's the theme song from *Mr. Ed*," I said.

"Don't you love him?" the horse asked. "My master is addicted to TV, so I get to watch the re-runs on *Nick at Night* while he cleans the stables."

"There's a TV in your stable?"

"Oh yeah," the horse replied. "I like to watch the races too. A friend of mine won the Trifecta last week. Took quite a beating though; those damn jockeys keep pushing and pushing."

"This is crazy," I said. "Why are you wearing a camera around your neck?"

"It's my magic camera," the horse said. "Come on, I'll take your picture. The wind's just right; your hair will be blowing nicely off your face just like those dudes in the magazines."

"What?" I asked in disbelief.

"Come on," the horse said. "Just smile."

I obeyed the horse and mustered a smile. The horse chewed the small bulb to release the shutter.

"O.K.," the horse said, "now turn your head a bit to the right, that's it!" *Click!* "Now look into the lens as if you're looking at the hottest babe you've ever seen!" *Click!* "Now loosen up, unzip the jacket a bit, that's good!" *Click!* "You're hot now! Purse your lips a little!" *Click! Click!* "Take off the jacket; throw it over your shoulder and look right into the lens!" *Click! Click! Click!* "That was hot! Now, hands on your hips, one leg bent; you've got it!" *Click! Click!* "You're a natural! Now bend over and fluff up your hair a bit…"

I interrupted the horse. "This is ridiculous!" I yelled. I had actually let the horse boss me around as if he was doing a photo shoot for a magazine.

"What's ridiculous?" The horse asked. "You don't believe in magic?"

"Well, yes," I replied.

"Then do me a favor, will ya?" the horse asked. "Dry this shutter bulb for me. The enzymes in my saliva are tough on the casing."

I dried the shutter bulb on my jacket and put the camera strap around the horse's neck. "One more thing," the horse said. "You wouldn't happen to have any oatmeal cookies on you, would you?"

"You like oatmeal cookies?" I asked.

"Love 'em!" the horse replied.

A gust of cool wind stirred me, and I awoke. My eyes still closed, I laughed at my dream. When I realized I had fallen asleep in public, my vulnerability startled me, and I jumped to my feet. Again, a vision shocked me: there *was* a horse looking me straight in the eye. It was identical to the horse in my dream, except for two features: no camera and no rosebud. I half-expected the horse to talk, but it didn't. What I did hear was a man's voice calling as he approached the bench where the horse and I were standing.

"There you are," the man yelled. He then addressed me: "I hope he didn't startle you; he got away from me at the bottom of the trail."

"Not at all," I lied.

"Sammy Thomas," the man said, extending his hand. "I have the stables down yonder."

"Nice to meet you, Sammy," I said, shaking his hand. "Tony Vitello."

"Are you sure my horse didn't startle you? You look a little shaken."

"No, I'm all right," I said. But I was shaken; it was the most bizarre coincidence I had ever been involved in. I would never again allow myself to fall asleep outside.

Sammy said goodbye and led his horse down the trail toward the stable. When they had advanced about fifty feet, the horse turned and looked at me; I found myself waving to him. The horse turned and continued walking, but not without swinging his tail in a friendly gesture.

I headed in the other direction, toward the B&B. Needing a little introspection, I decided to sit in the conservatory and mull over my ponytail incident.

I entered the building and turned the corner to the conservatory. It was empty: I would be alone with my thoughts. I sat in the overstuffed chair next to Granny's look-alike fountain. As the falling water soothed my jostled soul, I rehashed the ponytail incident that had just unnerved me.

There was no reasonable explanation for the event; it was too uncanny to be brushed off as a mere coincidence. It had to be a sign from God; I just wasn't sure what it meant. I'd need Maria to help me decipher that dream.

Several couples walked into the conservatory and greeted me. I could tell by the sound of cars outside that people were beginning to pour in for the weekend. I decided to go upstairs and freshen up before happy hour. I'd need a few drinks and Maria's expertise to help sort out the weird events that had transpired in the woods.

I ran up the stairs and entered our room. "There you are," Maria said. "Did you have a nice walk?"

"Yes," I said. "Did you have a nice nap?"

"Yes, and I had the strangest dream," Maria said. "I was eight years old again, watching *Mr. Ed* on TV and eating oatmeal cookies. Remember that show?"

"How could I forget that show?" I asked. I was dumbfounded. Not only were people and events interconnected; our dreams were too. Life was an enigma, but an exciting one. Every day, the discoveries made possible by my new vision alerted me to a divine order that was mystifying; life could only be explained by magic.

"Do you want to go to happy hour?" Maria asked.

"Yes. Just let me freshen up a bit; I need to splash some cold water on my face."

Maria and I went downstairs to the lounge. Several other couples were having cocktails, and we introduced ourselves. Wanting to be out of their earshot, I suggested we take a seat at the bar.

"Good idea," Maria said. "Maybe the bartender will turn on the news at five-thirty so we can see if there's coverage on Jerry."

"Good idea," I said, helping Maria onto her barstool.

We sat down and ordered drinks; the bartender served them with a smile. After thanking him, I turned to Maria with my burning questions. I told Maria every detail of my strange experience in the woods that afternoon. I then sat back and waited, rather anxiously, for her psychoanalysis.

"That is strange," Maria said, "that we should both dream about *Mr. Ed* and oatmeal cookies. I'm going to have to ponder that one for a while. But the appearance of the horse in your dream, that's easy to figure: it was another fear manifestation."

"How so?"

"Well," Maria said, "You were approaching a state of ego dissolution in your dream, having become one with your surroundings. But fear of the unknown crept in, and your subconscious had to construct a distraction that was a symbol of comfort and safety: it summoned the pony from your mother's story. It was a distraction that kept you from crossing the line to ego banishment; your psyche is just not ready to go there yet. Do you want some nuts?"

I took a handful of peanuts from the dish. Suddenly, the aroma triggered an olfactory nerve and I fell into the wormhole that emptied into 1969. I was twelve again, standing in front of the Peanut Shoppe with my mother, whose hair had become cotton candy. I began choking on a nut; my wrenching brought me back to the lounge of the B&B.

"Are you O.K.?" Maria asked.

"Yeah, I'm O.K.," I said, "a nut just went down the wormhole the wrong way."

"What?"

"A nut went down my windpipe."

"Oh."

"So tell me, Maria. Is it a sign of psychological weakness to conjure these distraction symbols?" I suspected it was.

"Absolutely not. Only a handful of saints and sages have ever crossed the line to true ego banishment; it comes only after years of mental discipline and practice. We ordinary mortals avoid that place, out of fear. Our soul yearns to go there, but we construct distractions, such as your photo-shooting pony, to bring us back to ordinary reality. Non-physical reality is frightening to someone who hasn't been spiritually primed," Maria said. "Do you want another nut?"

"No thanks." The conversation was getting interesting; I didn't want to miss anything by falling into another wormhole. I concentrated intently on our conversation. "You learn this stuff in medical school? It sounds more like mysticism than psychiatry," I said.

"It is," Maria said. "I didn't learn it in medical school; I learned it from your grandmother."

I wasn't surprised, but I did feel left-out; where had I been during those conversations? "Granny never discussed these things with *me*," I said.

"Perhaps she didn't think you were ready for it, but you've come a long way in a short time. The first step toward ego dissolution is coming out of your own head long enough to shatter the illusion of separateness. Do you want another nut?"

"No, I've had enough nuts. Tell me, how long does it take to reach this state of ego dissolution?"

"Most of us will never get there," Maria said. "We chase enlightenment like a dog chases its own tail."

That metaphor made perfect sense to me, having been there and done that. "Well, that's a paradox," I said. "Where's the logic?"

"There is no logic in the journey, that we can comprehend at the mortal level; that's where faith and trust enter the picture. Enlightenment is a flower; it doesn't have to be in full bloom to appreciate its beauty. Each phase in its cycle holds its own charm. Haven't you ever heard the Buddhist metaphor of the lotus flower?"

"I have, but I didn't know the meaning."

"It's five-thirty," Maria said.

I looked at the bartender. "Would you mind putting the news on?" I asked.

"Not at all," the bartender replied.

Maria and I became glued to the television, listening intently for the key word: Nobel. After a few minutes of local crime coverage, the anchorwoman began Jerry's story.

"That's my brother!" I yelled to the bartender.

The anchorwoman continued: "It was announced late last night by the Swedish Royal Academy of Science that a Princeton physicist would claim the last Nobel Prize of the millennium. The Nobel Prize in Physics will be awarded to Dr. Jerry Vitello, the youngest scientist ever to win a Nobel Prize. We're going live to our anchor in Princeton."

"Thanks Jackie. This is Heather Cooper, reporting live from Princeton University, where the campus is buzzing with the Nobel announcement. With me is Dr. Jerry Vitello, the youngest Nobel Laureate in Physics. Dr. Vitello, how do you feel about winning?"

"He has a ponytail!" The bartender yelled.

"I couldn't be happier," Jerry said. "I'm glad to accept this honor on behalf of Princeton. No man is an island, and the credit should really be given to the whole Physics Department; it was a synergistic effort."

"Can you comment on the rumors that your research was fueled in part by a body of mathematics developed by your late grandfather more than fifty years ago?" the anchor asked.

"The rumor is true," Jerry said. "My late grandfather, Stanley Freeman, had developed a branch of mathematics that he coined

Fractal Calculus. It was a pivotal tool in analyzing our research data. Thanks, Poppy," Jerry said, looking skyward.

"And thank you, Dr. Vitello. Congratulations on your achievement. And now, back to our anchor in Hartford."

"Thank you, Heather, and congratulations to Dr. Vitello and the Physics Department at Princeton. And now, our environmental consultant has a story about a new recycling plant in Philadelphia that has a funny name, but a very serious mission. Amy?"

"Hello. This is Amy Cardile live in Philadelphia at We R Nuts, a recycling center that is revolutionizing waste management along the East coast. We R Nuts is the genius of Harry Mincer, who opened the plant six months ago with a grant from the EPA. Mr. Mincer, how did you ever come up with the idea?"

"While working in retail last year, I witnessed literally tons of Styrofoam peanuts being thrown away. I said to myself, why throw them away? There's nothing wrong with them. We could use them again. Keep 'em moving and out of the landfills!" Uncle Harry said.

"Bravo!" the anchorwoman said. It's about time that manufacturers and retailers took responsibility for their waste. Good luck to you Mr. Mincer. Back to you, Jackie."

"All right, Uncle Harry!" I yelled. The bartender looked at me from the corner of his eye.

The news continued: "And now, to Manhattan, where an exhibit at the Guggenheim is rocking the art world."

"Good evening. This is Mike LaTorre live in Manhattan at the Guggenheim Museum, where crowds have descended to view the opening of an exhibit by the famed artist Les Izmore. His exhibit, entitled *The Last Thanksgiving*, has drawn record-breaking crowds to the Guggenheim. As you can see, Izmore's exhibit is fashioned of inanimate fruits and vegetables, and the crowd is going crazy over them."

"You told me the opening was next Friday," Maria said. "I can't believe we missed it."

"I must have gotten the dates confused."

Maria just looked at me.

"Look!" I said, pointing to the television.

The anchor continued: "More that twenty thousand people are expected to visit the Guggenheim this weekend, and timed tickets only will be sold. Back to you in Hartford, Jackie."

I began nervously eating the peanuts from the dish on the bar.

I became twelve again, wondering if there were really 19,999 women out there as smitten with ceramics as my mother. There were; they were lined up in front of the Guggenheim. I began choking.

"Are you all right?" Maria asked.

"Yes," I said, sipping my drink.

"I can't believe it," Maria said. "What are the chances those three news clips would be aired in succession? I will never forget this moment, as long as I live."

"Me too," I coughed, a nut still stuck.

"We must be dreaming," Maria said.

But we weren't dreaming; we were in ordinary reality, sprinkled with a little magic. Surely the pony in my dream had blessed me with his magic camera during that absurd photo shoot. There was no other explanation for life as I began to see it.

As Maria and I marveled in that afternoon of synchronicity, the bartender looked at us as if we were both nuts.

"I know it sounds crazy," I said to the bartender, "but every word of it is true."

That was it: my life in a nutshell, as uttered to a bartender.

Ten

After our magical weekend in the country, I began to view life differently. Spiritual contentment seemed far more important than any earlier goal to which I had aspired. My new vision filled me with hope: my life could only get better. Unfortunately, my vision lasted only three weeks; by the end of October I had fallen into spiritual despair. Had my progress been just an illusion?

On the afternoon of Mischief Night, I sat pondering my despair while waiting for Maria to return from a shopping trip. I tried to blame my neurotic relapse on the season, but try as I might, I couldn't ignore a truth that had snaked its way into my consciousness: I was no longer satisfied with the lifestyle I had created; it no longer seemed to fit. My life became one long, run-on question.

My work, which at one time had been so rewarding, seemed shallow and mundane. My first day back at the office was great: I was the brother of a Nobel Laureate. But my celebrity status soon fizzled, and I was quickly demoted to ordinary Tony.

Even the prestigious Manhattan address that had once seemed an achievement no longer impressed me; it didn't feel like home. I wanted to live where there were real songbirds, not illusory ones. I wanted roses on my threshold and a trumpeting angel in my backyard.

If the dismal, artificial life that I had created for myself didn't sink me, the psychic guilt generated by my parents' reconciliation would. Most children would be happy to see their parents reunited; that I believed my mother was better off alone generated guilt—what kind of son was I? I was supposed to be developing compassion. My own lotus flower was probably a dried-up seedling that was too weak and spindly to bud.

Big Anthony moved back home after convincing my mother that he was a different man. His near-death experience while being pinned down by the meatloaf-gobbling K-9 had supposedly changed him. My mother took him back, but not without conditions. Dad was to go to confession, to absolve a life-time of cursing; should he ever use the Lord's name in vain again, he would be back in a one-room efficiency so fast his head would spin. I'd say it was my mother who had changed.

If I had been truly compassionate, I would have given my father another chance as well. Instead, I visualized him in the confessional, quantifying his sins in scientific notation. I was just as bad as I accused my father of being.

For months, a new paradigm seemed to offer hope; my thinking was expanding in new directions, and I was finally coming out of my skull. On Mischief Night, my paradigm began shrinking so rapidly that I was left with a black hole between my ears.

I felt a tap on my shoulder. I jumped: it was Mildred! "You scared the daylights out of me! I almost didn't recognize you, it's been so long," I said. "What's that smell?"

"It's lavender," Mildred said. "You seemed to be doing so well on your own that Martin and I decided to get away; we've been vacationing in Provence. Lavender has a calming effect; I thought you could use a souvenir and a good dose."

"Where's Martin?" I asked.

"He's sleeping off his jet lag," Mildred said. "He'll be here momentarily."

"Here I am," Martin said, entering the office. He was wearing a beret.

"So what was so important that you had to summon us on a Saturday afternoon? I was just on my way out to the hairdresser's," Mildred said.

"Yeah," Martin said. "I thought you had it all figured out? By the way, what are you going to be for Halloween?"

"Shut-up, Martin," Mildred ordered, "and let the poor boy talk."

Martin bulged his eyes in defiance and adjusted his beret.

"Well," I said, "I thought I had everything figured out, but suddenly my world seems to be crumbling around me."

"Maybe that's good," Mildred said.

"How could that be good?" I asked.

"If your world is so easily crumbled, maybe you need a better world, one that's not so brittle," Mildred said.

"What are you talking about?" I said. "I can't change the world."

"What world?"

"The real world," I said impatiently.

"There is no real world," Mildred said. "There exists only the world that each of us creates in our own minds; what we perceive as the real world is only an illusion. Haven't you learned anything from Jerry's equation?"

"What equation?" I demanded.

"The sum of everything," Mildred said. "Those four words apply here too."

"How?" I was confused; Mildred seemed to be talking in circles.

"Tony, dear, there is no real world. There is only the sum of all the worlds created by the eight billion minds on the planet. It may seem earth shattering, but it's the truth," Mildred said.

"So what are you saying?"

"I'm saying that your world is no longer in sync with what you really want to create; that's why it's crumbling. It's time to create a new world," Mildred said. "Something that reflects your new spiritual paradigm—something larger."

I had no idea that I had the power to create a new world. While the idea seemed exciting, I hadn't a clue where to begin. "I don't know how to create a new world," I argued.

"Use your feelings as a guide," Mildred said. "You were already on your way; this is just the big bang you needed."

"Big bang?"

"Yes," Mildred said. "The big bang that awakens you and tells you it's time to change."

I began to hear music, the theme song to *Lost in Space.*

"Martin, put that thing down," Mildred scolded. "We're here on a mission, not to play."

Martin put my robot back onto the shelf. "I never get to have any fun," he said.

"Do you see what I have to put up with? And you think you have problems," Mildred said, shaking her head in disgust.

I was having problems. I was trying to become more grounded in reality, and Mildred was telling me that there was no reality. I had created an imaginary friend who was pushing me over the edge. Or was she? Perhaps Mildred was right. I didn't know what to think anymore.

I heard the front door to our apartment open. "You'd better go," I said, rushing Mildred and Martin off. "Here comes Maria; I don't want her to think I'm regressing."

"Hi Honey," Maria said, entering the office. "What smells so good in here? Did you spray something?"

"No."

"Oh. Did you have a nice day?"

"It was all right," I said, scanning the room to make certain no other evidence of Mildred and Martin's visit remained.

"Tony, what's wrong?" Maria asked. "You look upset; you're not mad that I spent the morning shopping, are you?"

"Of course not," I said. But I could no longer hide my despair: the floodgates of my psyche collapsed, deluging Maria with a sick barrage of my twisted thoughts. My *exposé* included my recent haunting by Mildred and Martin.

"You just missed them," I said despondently. "I thought I had laid them to rest months ago, that I was finally able to stand on my own two feet. What is happening to me?"

Maria removed her new shoes from their bag. "Tony, you're hyperventilating. Breathe into this bag; it will stabilize your blood gases." Maria put the bag over my face. "Come on, nice and easy, in and out, in and out, that's good. Everything's going to be all right."

Whenever I reveal my deepest fears, someone always wants to put a bag over my head, I thought.

"Feeling better?" Maria asked.

"Yes," I said. "Just ashamed of my weak character."

"You're not weak, Tony. What you're going through is perfectly normal. It's a necessary part of the spiritual process. We all fear change, because it means venturing into the unknown. Your old world is crumbling because you've outgrown it. It's normal for all these questions to arise; you're building a new world with new values and feelings. We all question our tactics, because we want so desperately to get it right the second time."

"Why do I feel as if I'm having a nervous breakdown?"

"You're *not*, believe me. You're having a spiritual crisis. And you don't need a psychiatrist, you need a spiritual advisor. Have you ever considered spending a few days with your grandmother? She always pulls me through my dark hours."

"Maybe that isn't a bad idea," I said.

"Of course, I'm more than happy to help you," Maria said, "but I'd just be paraphrasing Granny. You'd be better off hearing it right from the horse's mouth."

"Maybe I'll give her a call."

"Why don't you? I'm sure she'd enjoy a visit. It will do you both good."

"I'll call her right now," I said, reaching for the phone.

I dialed Granny's number. "It's ringing," I said. After thirteen rings I hung up the phone disappointedly. "She's not home."

"You can try again later," Maria said. "Let's have a cup of tea; it will make you feel better."

I followed Maria into the kitchen like a lost dog. She filled the kettle and I slumped into a chair.

"Don't be so hard on yourself, Tony. Don't forget what Granny said: underneath our personalities, we're all the same. You're not alone; we're all involved in the same desperate search for meaning."

The kettle was boiling, but it somehow whistled a different tune. "Doesn't the kettle sound funny?" I asked.

"The phone's ringing," Maria said.

"Oh!" I jumped to answer it. "Hello?" I said. "Granny!"

"Hi sweetie. I was outside watering the mums when you called. What's up, dear?"

"I was wondering if you'd like some company tonight."

"Absolutely; I'll make dinner for the three of us."

"No," I said. "Maria won't be joining us; it will just be me."

"Oh?" Granny said. "Everything all right? You sound a little down."

"No, everything's fine."

"Good enough. What time shall I expect you?"

"I should be there by six."

"Good. Do you prefer broccoli or green beans?"

"I don't want you going to any trouble for me."

"It's no trouble. I had a roast defrosting anyhow."

"O.K. then, broccoli."

"Drive carefully," Granny said. "I'll see you this evening."

"O.K., Gran. See you in a little while."

I hung up the phone and looked at Maria. "Are you sure you don't mind if I go?"

"Of course not. It will give me a chance to review some cases; I have a busy month approaching. Pre-holiday depression gets going in November, and I'm already overwhelmed with SAD cases."

"Sad?"

"Seasonal Affective Disorder."

"Oh."

"You know what?" Maria said, "I have a few things of Granny's that you can return for me. I'll gather them while you're packing."

"O.K.," I said, walking toward the bedroom to get a change of clothes.

This is absurd, I said to myself while packing. Running off to grandmother's house, at my age—what the hell is wrong with me? I threw my toothbrush into the bag and walked to the living room.

"Here's Granny's stuff," Maria said.

"In a basket?"

"It's Granny's basket. Please thank her for loaning me the book; tell her it was very enlightening."

I lifted the book from the basket. "Living with a Mentally Ill Spouse?" I asked suspiciously.

"Oh," Maria said, "it's not what it seems. Granny thought it might help me with a patient; it wasn't for my personal use. Granny knows the author."

"Oh," I said, only partially convinced. "All right, honey. I'll probably return sometime tomorrow night. I'll call you in the morning."

"O.K., Tony. And be careful on the Turnpike. I love you."

"I love you too," I said, kissing Maria goodbye.

Walking toward the parking garage, I wondered if my life could grow any more pathetic. Probably not, I thought, realizing that I was off to grandmother's house with a basket! Not only was I an idiot, I looked like one too.

I reached the garage and locked my bag and basket into the trunk of the car. Heading out of Manhattan, I wondered if Maria had any personal epiphanies while reading the book Granny had loaned her.

I entered the Turnpike and set my cruise-control. As I approached Newark Airport, I wondered if my spirit would ever soar. All my old fears and anxieties were creeping back; I would never be airborne. Too much baggage, I thought. How would I ever lift my spirit?

I drove the rest of the way to Philadelphia in contemplation of my sorry life, reaching for any glimmer of hope. Before I knew it, I was reaching into my pocket; I need two dollars for the bridge. My mood took a positive turn when I realized I'd be entering the safe haven of Granny's nest in less than twenty minutes.

At quarter to six I pulled into Granny's driveway; I breathed a sigh of relief. I turned off the car and retrieved the articles from the trunk. Approaching the front door, I noticed a faint glimmer of pink: a few hardy roses had survived the shorter days and colder temperatures. Maybe I would survive too; with hope, I crossed the threshold into Granny's world.

"Tony, love!" Granny said, walking to the front door to greet me. "You made good time. I just put the broccoli on."

"Hi Gran," I said, hugging her. "The traffic was pretty light on the Turnpike."

"Come into the kitchen while I finish dinner," Granny said. "You can put your things upstairs later."

"This is your basket," I said. "Maria sent it. Some of your other things are in here too."

"Just put it at the bottom of the stairs."

I followed Granny into the kitchen. "Something smells good in here," I said. "There's nothing like a home-cooked meal. I miss that."

"That's right," Granny said. "You and Maria don't cook. I guess there isn't time, with the two of you working so hard."

"We manage. There's no shortage of food in Manhattan."

"Speaking of food, did you get to the Guggenheim? What did you think of Les Izmore's exhibit?" Granny asked, as she began preparing a salad.

"It brought back a lot of fond memories," I said. "We never got to meet Les, though. We missed the opening; I had the date confused. We were in Connecticut that weekend."

"On business?" Granny asked, cutting tomatoes precisely into wedges of equal degrees. As she did, I compared her chopping skills to my own; was I a klutz or just lacking her additional forty years' experience?

I imagined myself as an old man at the cutting board, butchering my tomato. A seed flung up and hit me in the eye, and that red stuff on the cutting board wasn't tomato juice. I decided I was a klutz who would never learn. That realization (the death of hope), made it very difficult to be me; I began hyperventilating.

"Tony, dear," Granny said, reaching for a lunch bag, "Are you all right? Breathe into this bag; that's it, nice and easy, nice and easy."

When my blood gases had stabilized, Granny spoke. "Was that brought on by my reference to *The Last Thanksgiving*? I knew those dishes meant a lot to you, but I hadn't realized just how much. You need a distraction, honey. There's some romaine in the refrigerator rolled up in a paper towel. Why don't you pat it dry and tear in into this bowl?"

Paralyzed to say anything, I followed Granny's orders and patted the romaine.

"I saw Jerry and Roberta a few days ago," Granny said. "We went out for a celebration dinner. I am so proud of Jerry. When he spoke of your grandfather on the News, I just about lost it. Stanley would be so proud."

"We all are," I said, tearing the leaves. "You're making the trip to Stockholm, aren't you?"

"Absolutely," Granny said. "And I've decided to go on to Munich and Paris from there. I may as well visit some old friends while I'm in Europe; I don't know when I'll be making *that* trip again. But we could take the same flight to Stockholm."

"Great. You know, Gran, it seems as if things are getting better for some of us. Margaret's business is thriving, Jerry's a Nobel Laureate, Uncle Harry's making it big, and Mom is finally living her dream."

"I'm particularly happy that your mother is finally chasing some of her dreams. She gave up a lot when she married your father."

"I know," I said. "I can't believe she took him back."

"I knew that was going to happen," Granny said. "It's hard to walk away from forty-five years of marriage, even when you are having pickles flung at you. Come and sit down. It's time to eat."

I carried the salad to the table and served it. "Do you think he'll ever change?" I asked.

"I don't know, honey. All we can ever do is hope, although I must admit, the prospects look a little grim," Granny said. "He hasn't been back in the house three weeks and already he's misbehaving."

"Cursing again?"

"No," Granny said. "Your mother made it clear that she would no longer tolerate that. It's just the same old attitude resurfacing; instead of being proud of Jerry's accomplishment, he's fixated on whether or not Jerry will get a haircut before the prize ceremony."

"Oh, that," I said. "Margaret told me."

"The thing I am grateful for is that he wasn't able to destroy hope in you three kids. That was always my worst fear, but luckily, an ungrounded one. Look how high the three of you have soared."

I was one of the three; was it possible that Granny, whose opinion was just under God's in my book, really believed I had soared?

"You look stunned," Granny said.

"I guess I am."

"Why?"

"I guess I've never thought of myself as the soaring type."

"You really underestimate yourself. Do you really suppose you'd have advanced this far in your career without soaring?"

Granny was right. SuperSoft wasn't paying me $112K to sharpen pencils; maybe I didn't give myself enough credit. But my career success opened another can of worms: I was losing interest in my job. Artificial Intelligence began to seem unreal; why should we be teaching machines to think when a good portion of the human race, including myself, needed such an education?

"To tell you the truth, Gran, I'm beginning to lose the passion I once felt for my work."

"Maybe it's time for a career change."

Could things really be that simple? "Maybe it is," I said, "but I don't know what else I'd do; I've been with SuperSoft all my adult life."

"Well, just look at your Uncle Harry," Granny said. "He's the perfect example of what you can do with a lot of confidence and a simple idea."

"I know. I've never seen anyone turn his life around so quickly. It's amazing."

"It certainly is," Granny said. "On one hand, it seems a shame, all those wasted years. But, everything happens in its own time. Harry had to admit that he had a problem before he could reach out for help."

I wasn't sure to what Granny was referring. "What do you mean, Gran?"

"I mean his speech impediment. All those years it left Harry devoid of confidence. I really respect Harry for taking that first step."

"What step?"

"Speech therapy, Tony. Harry finally came out of denial and met his problem head-on."

I was confused; Uncle Harry had told me he'd conquered his problem at show and tell. He never said anything about speech therapy. "He did?" I thought aloud.

"Of course he did, Tony. His problem didn't just disappear by magic. It must have taken months of therapy to rid Harry of his stuttering."

Must have were the operative words, I thought. I suspected Granny had made an assumption; I fished for affirmation. "Who did Uncle Harry see, someone in Philadelphia?" I asked.

"I don't know any of the specifics. Vicky and Harry don't talk about it; they never have. But I know one thing for sure: whoever helped Harry did one hell of a job. It was the birth of hope for him."

Granny *had* assumed. How had anyone of Granny's level of wisdom not seen that Uncle Harry's problem was contractual? Even I had seen that, as a twelve year-old. The fact that I alone was privy to the origin of Uncle Harry's speech impediment said nothing about Granny, but a lot about myself. I felt something stirring inside me: it was confidence. Granny's oversight boosted my self-confidence; all I then needed was a simple idea.

"Do you want some more broccoli?" Granny asked.

"No, I'm full. Everything was delicious; thank you."

"I'm glad you enjoyed it. Now tell me: what's wrong?"

"What makes you think something is wrong?"

"Why else would you pack your bags and run off to grandmother's house, at your age? And with a basket, nonetheless,"

Granny laughed.

I laughed with her, at myself. Laughing at my own foible was a strange release; it felt good. I chalked it up to confidence.

"Honestly, Gran," I said, " I think I'm having a spiritual crisis. For years I've locked myself into my own head, trying to make sense of the absurdity in my life. I had even convinced myself that I was psychotic, and felt angry at Maria for not wanting to help me. And then I realized she couldn't help me because I was never honest with her about my feelings."

"Of course Maria would want to help you; she's trained in that sort of thing," Granny assured me.

"I know," I said. "Anyhow, with Maria's help, I was making so much progress. I finally realized that most of my problems stemmed from my illusion of separateness. I was advancing nicely; I even began feeling compassion for my father."

"That is progress. It's a true sign of spiritual growth to feel compassion for our adversaries. Do you want a piece of cake?"

"No thanks."

"So what happened?"

"Just when I was on the verge of a big-bang, everything fell apart."

"How so?" Granny asked.

"My life seems so steeped in absurdity; I wonder if it's me or if the world is really that absurd. Am I nuts?"

"Of course you're not nuts, Tony. What would ever make you think such a thing?" Granny asked, rising from the table and walking toward the cupboard. She returned with a box of chocolates. "Here. Have one of these," Granny said. "It's hard to be sad when you're high on *Godiva*."

"Thanks, Gran," I laughed, removing a heart-shaped piece of chocolate. I took a bite; how apropos that it was cherry-filled—a bleeding heart, just like mine.

"So anyhow," Granny said, "why would you think it was you?" She pushed the chocolates toward me, and I took another.

"Well," I said, chewing the oyster shell, "it's just that the pieces of the puzzle never add up to a whole picture that makes sense."

"I think your answer lies there, in that statement," Granny said. "Have another chocolate."

I took a dark chocolate flower. "Where?" I asked.

"In your statement, 'the whole picture doesn't make sense.'

Why do you assume that the whole picture should make sense? Hasn't it ever occurred to you that life is, among other things, absurd? Why do you blame your own perceptions?"

"Is life supposed to be absurd?" I asked.

"Life isn't supposed to be anything," Granny said. "Life just is. If life appears absurd, why not just laugh?"

Granny was right. Why had I taken life so seriously? "I don't know if our polishing off a box of chocolates has anything to do with it, but the absurdity is pretty darned funny," I said.

"They're not gone yet. Here, you take the one with nuts," Granny said, pushing the gold box within my reach.

"Take Valentines Day," I argued. "I bought Maria a watercolor of a couple who looked like our twins. For two weeks I lived in suspense, wondering if Maria would find the resemblance as uncanny as I had. She opened the gift to find that condensation had washed away their faces. It was a scream."

"Now that is funny," Granny laughed. "Perhaps you should be recording these absurdities; it would be great material for a book."

It would, I thought.

"Remember Walter Water, that dear man who sent me the letter on my birthday? He wrote your grandfather a letter about absurdity many years ago. I should read it to you; it will shed some light on the subject," Granny said, looking at the empty gold box. "For the love of chocolate, what have we done?"

I laughed. "You're right, Gran. It is hard to be sad when you're high on *Godiva*."

"Come upstairs to my office," Granny said. "I'll read Walter's letter to you."

I followed Granny upstairs, noticing something strange. After climbing the steps, I was mildly out of breath from the effort. On the contrary, Granny had floated up the stairs like a newly-spawned fish swimming gracefully upstream. Besides having relapsed into neurosis, I was coming undone physically as well.

We walked into Granny's office. "Sit on the couch while I get the letter," she said. "I know exactly where it is." Granny opened the top hatbox and removed Walter's letter.

"Before I read it to you, let me give you a little background on Walter. Like Jerry, he was a physicist, one of the grandfathers of Quantum Mechanics. Walter had set up very elaborate models of the order of the cosmos. He spent his whole life trying to prove that the universe was like an onion, with order built upon order upon order, just like the layers of that bulb vegetable."

Prior to our conversation, the words Quantum Mechanics had seemed intimidating, but it didn't take an Einstein to understand an onion. I needed to let go of my assumptions and preconceptions.

Granny began:

> Dear Stanley,
>
> I hope all is well for you in Philadelphia. Although an ocean separates us, I always feel we are tightly connected. If it weren't for your mathematical model of embedded order, my theory would be nothing but a testament to my weakness in mathematics. How can I ever thank you for your insight? That a mathematician of your caliber had come along when I was sorely in need of a good mathematician was nothing short of a miracle. It was no accident that we met in Munich last year; it was destiny that our paths should cross.
>
> The purpose of my letter today is to share with you an idea that my comrades and I formulated last night. I thought you would find it interesting.
>
> We finished work at six-thirty, and a group of us from the department decided to visit the local beer garden for a few brews. Needless to say, a few brews turned into who knows how many; at midnight I found myself engrossed in a most absurd philosophical debate with my drunken colleagues.
>
> Karl Thyme, the head of the department, was responsible for the madness. He asked us to entertain the idea that life's absurdities were actually ripples in space-time caused by God's laughter. Karl postulated that God's humor was an action; the equal and opposite reaction was perturbations in the multi-dimensional fabric of the universe, comparable to the shaking of your chair during a good belly-laugh. Be it the brew or not, by early morning Thyme had us all convinced that

God's jest was sending informational ripples through the cosmos, manifesting absurdity in different intersections of space-time.

What do you think of this nonsense? Was it the brew, or could we be on to something? I am anxious to hear your views, since I hold your opinion in the highest regard. Does the remotest possibility exist that God's laughter could be expressed as a mathematical model? Perhaps you will tell me to keep the department out of the beer gardens, in which case I will heed your sound advice. My best to you and Rose.

Sincerely,
Walter Water

Granny looked at me. "What do you think of that?" she asked, folding the letter carefully.

I was speechless. I didn't know what to say. On one hand I was shocked, having assumed that physicists sat around writing textbooks in their spare time. As far as the content of his letter, it sounded far-fetched but seemed exciting. "I guess anything is possible," I said. "What did Poppy think?"

"He immediately ran upstairs to his blackboard and began working out the mathematics. When he finished, he sent a copy to Walter and Karl Thyme. They were so excited that they sailed to America at the end of the semester and showed up at your grandfather's office one afternoon. They spent the first few weeks of summer refining the theory. They were a wild group," Granny said.

"Wild how?"

"Well, you'd think men who spent so much time immersed in science and religion might be lacking in the fun department. Not them; it was almost as though they were privy to some divine comedy the rest of us were overlooking. By the time Walter and Karl left, I was convinced their lives were such fun because they laughed *with* God. What better way to live?" Granny asked.

"Unbelievable," I said. I then wondered: how did one become privy to that divine comedy? How did one laugh with God? Suddenly, I fell into another wormhole and became juxtaposed in space-time. I emerged from the wormhole in a German beer garden: Poppy was sitting next to me at the bar.

Poppy raised his mug: "I would like to propose a toast to God's thirty-year sneeze, which is just completing its cycle."

"How could a sneeze last thirty years?" I asked.

"Tony, my dear lad," Poppy said sympathetically, "have I taught you nothing about the new physics? You know that time ceases to have meaning at the level of order in which God exists. God's sneeze is instantaneous in his dimension, yet it can take thirty years before the dimension of our universe settles."

"Can I conclude that a second of divine time is approximately equal to thirty years of earthly time?" I asked.

"I'm afraid not, Tony," Poppy said. "There are no relationships between time in the different levels of order; the concept of time is a construct of the human mind, not God's mind. We just invented time to help us make sense of our own level of order. Time doesn't even exist."

"It doesn't?" I asked, reaching for my mug.

"No, it doesn't. Think about it, lad. How else could we be sitting here having a beer together when I died twenty years before you were even born?" Poppy asked.

"You're right," I said. "So finish telling me about God's thirty-year sneeze."

"Well," Poppy said, "Back in 1969, for one reason or another, God began to sneeze. You just happened to be situated at an intersection of space-time where you were bound to feel the perturbations. While that may have initially shaken your life quite a bit, once everything settles, magic will begin to unfold. The perturbations may have seemed an inconvenience, but in hindsight you will realize that God has blown a higher order into your life. A good sneeze by God can manifest more than a hundred miracles."

"It can?" I asked, stunned.

"Oh, I don't know, lad. Perhaps it's just a mathematicians pipe-dream, but it sounds good, doesn't it?"

Poppy was so funny. "It sure does," I said. "So everything's going to work out for me, then?"

"Everything's going to be just fine," Poppy said. "Just remember: the perturbations may have seemed an inconvenience, but you are about to experience the joy of a higher order. It's just God's way; he's a real mover and shaker. You'll see."

"I will?" I asked excitedly.

"Yes, you will. I am absolutely certain of it, because I have already seen your future," Poppy said.

"You have? What's going to happen?"

"Oh, lad, settle down. I would never rob you of the mystery of your life. You need to experience the magic of waking up every morning and wondering where your life is going to take you, what discoveries you are going to make. To experience wonder is to look into the eyes of God," Poppy said.

"I never realized how interwoven science and religion really were. It's almost as though you can't have one without the other," I noted.

"A lot of mortals don't realize that, but I was lucky enough to have had that during my lifetime, with a little help from my friends," Poppy said. "When you study the mysteries of the universe, you are witnessing the core of magic, and it is this vision which allows you to enter the kingdom of God while still on earth." Suddenly, it felt as though the bar was shaking beneath us. "What's happening, Poppy?"

"You're doing a lot of tossing and turning; you're about to awaken," Poppy said. "If I were you, I'd chug-a-lug. No sense in wasting that cold one."

"What do you mean, awaken? Is God enlightening me?"

"Perhaps, but I meant literally awaken. You're dreaming," Poppy said.

"I am?" I yelled, as the bar shook with even greater fervor.

"Yes, Tony, you are. And I have to tell you one more thing, so hold on for a minute! Tell your grandmother that the *Swiss Army Knife* was intended for Jerry; she'll know what I mean. No offense, lad—you can have Mark Twain!" Poppy yelled, disappearing from view.

"Poppy!" I yelled. "Poppy, come back!" I fell out of the wormhole and landed on the couch in Granny's office. I was cocooned tightly in several cotton blankets and a patchwork quilt. I had fallen asleep, and Granny had tucked-in her big baby for the night.

I wondered what time it was. I rolled over and saw the silver notes of Bach. Playing the notes in my mind, I realized how much I missed my dear, sweet Maria. Magic was about to unfold in my life, and I wanted Maria there to share in it.

I arose from the couch and looked at the clock on Granny's desk: it was three o'clock in the morning. I stared at the clock, remembering Poppy's words: time has no meaning at the level of order in which God exists. If that was so, it wouldn't really matter if I drove back to Manhattan in the middle of the night. I could be home before Maria awoke; it was perfect.

I wondered if it was rude, to flee and have Granny awaken to find me gone. No, I decided; Granny would understand. I would leave her a note.

I walked quietly across the room and sat down at Granny's escritoire. It felt good to sit at her desk; I hadn't done that since I was a child. I took a sheet of paper and began writing:

> Dear Granny,
>
> I can't tell you how grateful I am that you have again saved me from myself. For the first time in thirty years, my life has meaning again, thanks to you and Poppy. I've discovered that my crisis wasn't a crisis at all; it was just God blowing order into my life.
>
> I'm sorry I won't be having breakfast with you; I'll miss you and your orange marmalade. I have to go home and let Maria know that everything's going to be all right.
>
> I will never again look at an onion without thinking of the legacy of love and wonder that you and Poppy have created. Thank you for giving us that.
>
> I'll call you this afternoon. And thank you for sharing your chocolates with me: you were right about them!
>
> All my love,
> Tony XO

I arose quietly to leave the room, but something stopped me—the flower oils on the top shelf of Granny's desk. I removed a small brown bottle of rose absolute; I opened it and took a long whiff. I wanted to remember that night forever: everything was coming up roses. I dabbed a small bit of oil on the cuff of my shirt to take some magic home with me. Before leaving Granny's office, I looked toward the ceiling and listened to *The Joy of Man's Desiring* one more time.

I walked quietly downstairs to the dining room, and left Granny's letter in the spot where she always sat. I then slipped quietly through the threshold into the crisp air of my brand-new world.

Driving toward Manhattan under the twinkling of stars, the smell of roses was burning its mark on my olfactory memory. It was a welcome change; I had been smelling nuts for far too long.

My spirit soared with the pre-dawn jets that were leaving Newark Airport. Finally having learned to fly, I made it to Manhattan in record time.

I slipped quietly into our apartment. It was five after five; I couldn't wake Maria that early on a Sunday morning. I tip-toed down the hall to our bedroom. As Maria lay sleeping, I stood there watching her for a long time, grateful that I had found this angel when our paths crossed at that fateful intersection of space-time ten years ago.

Suddenly sleepy, I got undressed and slipped under the covers next to Maria. Without waking, she nuzzled close to me; we lay there like a pair of silver spoons reflecting the full moon. From the bedroom window I caught a glimpse of a lone star; drifting to sleep, I made a wish and held my angel close to me. The faint aroma of rose mingled with our dream clouds; it was a sound, perfect sleep.

At nine o'clock the bells tolled; Maria must have changed the setting on our alarm clock.

Maria stirred and opened her eyes. "Tony, what are you doing here?"

"Things didn't take as long as I'd expected, so I drove back during the night. I couldn't wait to tell you about my revelations. My life is definitely on the upswing! I can feel it."

Maria listened carefully as I recounted my marvelous dream and chanted excitedly about Walter's letter. I finished my dissertation and waited for Maria's response.

"Life certainly is a paradox!" Maria exclaimed. "That you should finally let go of your demons on the morning of Halloween has to be an omen!"

It was an omen. I ventured into uncharted waters with confidence and a simple idea; what worked for Uncle Harry would certainly work for me. The winds of hope would chart the course of my new adventure.

I did not set sail without first sharing a few hours of passion with my lovely ship-mate. I no longer needed psychotherapy; with the dissolution of our doctor-patient relationship, we were able to resume our sexual one. It wasn't until noon that we disembarked rapture and swam to ordinary reality.

"Do you want to go for a walk in the park after brunch?" Maria asked. "It's a beautiful day."

"I'd love to. You know what? Every day will be a beautiful day, as long as we're together."

Maria's reply was a soft kiss on my cheek.

Maria and I left the building and took a cab to the restaurant, where we enjoyed a leisurely brunch of onion omelets and croissants slathered in orange marmalade. We discussed our hopes and dreams for the future, punctuated by silences that resonated with a still sense of sweetness. Fortified by our morning, we skipped the cab and walked arm-in-arm to the park.

Central Park was teeming with other Manhattanites basking in the crisp, fall afternoon. Maria and I walked for a long time, dodging the awkward maneuverings of small plastic tricycles and listening to athletic shoes as they pounded the earth's crunchy carpet.

We approached an empty bench and sat down. We snuggled close and sat back to do some daydreaming and people-watching. From the corner of my eye, I noticed Maria and I had become the target of some poor soul's gaze.

A man, about my age, was staring at us with eyes that gushed a flood of sadness. His expression of despondency was so heart-wrenching that it pierced the distance between us and stung my heart: I became that man. I watched Maria and myself through his eyes, my pain amplified by the love belonging only to others. I was alone in that crowd of couples, with no one to share in the delight of the beautiful fall day.

Suddenly my gaze was my own again, but my tears belonged to the stranger who was approaching the street. My compassion tied me inexorably to that broken-hearted stranger, whom I recognized as myself in another season of my life.

Maria glanced at me with a questioning expression.

"Tears of joy," I explained. Not only had I reclaimed my soul and rekindled my marriage: I had learned the true meaning of compassion. That moment of intimacy with the stranger in the park was the final blow to my illusion of separateness. I would never again feel alone in a crowd: we were all one, bound in a web of compassion.

I wiped my cheek and looked at Maria. The wind was blowing her hair into tempests of gold around her pink cheeks. "You look cold," I said. "How would you like to trick or treat in front of a roaring fire while sipping fine brandy?"

"You're reading my mind," Maria said. "Let's go."

After lighting a fire and changing into our costumes of leisure-wear, I called Granny to apologize for my premature exit that morning.

"That's O.K., my love," Granny said. "I'm happy that you're feeling better. Tell me about your dream, did your grandfather look well?"

"He looked wonderful, Gran," I said. "And he had a great sense of humor. I was thrilled to spend some time with Poppy, even if only in a dream."

"Never underestimate the power of a dream, Tony. Dreams are the portals that connect us to the other side. And now, I feel better knowing I was right about the *Swiss Army Knife*."

"What was that about?" I asked.

"Well," Granny said, "the last words that your poppy uttered on his deathbed were: 'Give my Swiss Army knife to whomever wins the prize.' At least that's what the Javelle huckster said; I wasn't there."

"The Javelle huckster?"

"The carriage driver. I guess I've never told you the whole story, but it's time I did," Granny said. "Back in the thirties, horse-drawn carriages carried bottles of Javelle Water through the Philadelphia neighborhoods."

"What's Javelle Water?" I interrupted.

"Well, I suppose Javelle Water was the precursor to chlorine bleach. It was a beautiful liquid, an eerie shade of pale, fluorescent green. We used it back then as a laundry additive, to whiten our clothes. Every week the Javelle hucksters would drive their carts up and down the streets shouting: 'Ja-vel-le Water, Ja-vel-le Water,' to alert the housewives; we'd trade our empty glass bottles for a full one, and he'd be on his way. I used Javelle Water to disinfect the toilet, too," Granny said.

"So it was a Javelle carriage that struck Poppy?" I asked.

"Sadly, yes. I guess it was really the horse that pulled the cart. Anyhow, your Poppy was preoccupied, as he often was, and fell off the curb into the street just as a Javelle cart was passing. The horse struck him on the temple, and I'm afraid it was a fatal blow," Granny said.

"He died instantly?" I asked.

"Not quite. As he lay there taking his last breath, he managed to utter his last wishes to the Javelle huckster. And then he was gone."

"I'm sorry, Gran. I didn't mean to make you rehash something so painful."

"That's O.K., love. So anyhow, at least the mystery is solved; I can grant Stanley's last wish. I'm glad I didn't give the knife to your mother when she won first prize in that bake-off contest."

"I don't remember that," I said, switching the phone to my other ear.

"You were just a baby," Granny said. "Leona even had her name mentioned in a local cookbook. It was an exciting time for your mother; she had invented the recipe herself. It was a spice cake with a bourbon frosting. The flavor was so subtle, you'd never imagine there was bourbon in it. It was quite good, but not Nobel Prize material," Granny laughed.

Suddenly I fell through a wormhole: I was a toddler, eating a large slab of my second-birthday cake. Licking the last bit of frosting from my fingers, I became dizzy and fell onto the metal ladder of my shiny new fire truck. I was a big boy—it didn't even hurt! In fact, I couldn't feel anything. I began rolling around on the rubbery floor, entertaining myself whole-heartedly until the big woman picked me up and carried me to bed. I was behind bars again, the painted clouds on my walls coalescing into a twister.

"Tony! Are you there?" I heard Granny yelling through the phone.

"I'm sorry Gran," I said.

"That's O.K., dear. Anyhow, there's the doorbell. The children are here."

"Children?" I asked. No one in the family had children.

"The trick-or-treaters," Granny said.

"Oh! I'll let you go then. Thanks again. Love you!"

"Love you too. If I don't see you before, I'll see you on Thanksgiving. Goodnight."

I hung up the phone and joined Maria in the living room.

"Was Granny all right with your leaving suddenly?" Maria asked.

"Yes. She understood."

"Let's have a toast," Maria said, "to Granny, who has been such an inspiration in our family."

Maria and I brought our snifters together, saluting our one perfect Rose.

"You know," I said, "we should use the fireplace more often. Why don't we?"

"I guess we're always too busy," Maria said. "By the time we get home at night we just settle into the apathy of routine."

"I know. But I'm getting bored with our routine."

"Me too," Maria said. "The world is larger than our careers; perhaps it's time to expand our horizons."

"I'm with you. Last night, I told Granny about my dwindling passion for Artificial Intelligence, and she made an interesting suggestion."

"What was that?"

"She suggested I consider writing, and report on the absurdity of life."

"Life certainly is absurd; I am reminded of that everyday when I look at *Anonymity*. I hung it in the waiting area, by the way. As absurd as it is, that identities could be washed away by pizza condensation, there has been a good outcome. It has really opened my patients' eyes, and my own, to the fact that we sometimes have to wash away our identities and take on new ones. That painting has become a symbol of hope, that change is possible," Maria said.

That magnitude of hope was a bargain at seventeen hundred dollars, I thought.

"So what do you think of the idea?" Maria asked, taking a sip of brandy.

"It intrigues me. But if I don't have the energy to build a fire at night, how could I ever write a book?"

"Do you see yourself at SuperSoft for the rest of your life?" Maria asked.

"Honestly? No."

"Then quit and write a book. Money is no problem; like you once told me, it would just mean fewer investments. So what? We've cleaned up on the Stock Market already, and besides, that kind of growth can't go on forever."

"But what about you?" I asked. "You admitted to reservations about your own career. You couldn't very well go back to school and study another specialty if I wasn't bringing in any money."

"Why not? And who says you wouldn't be bringing in any money? Why couldn't your book be a success?"

It hadn't occurred to me that my book could be a success and bring in money. I remembered Granny's advice: all you need is confidence and a simple idea.

"That's true, Maria, but I would never make a decision like that without giving it a lot of thought." I *was* changing; previously, I had been famous for impulsive action.

"So think about it," Maria said.

"I will."

"Did Granny have any news regarding your father?"

"Yes," I replied. "Seems as though he's put a lid on his cursing, but other than that, he's up to his same old tricks."

"How's that?" Maria asked.

"Begging Jerry to get a haircut before the prize ceremony. You know, a Nobel Laureate cannot have a (pause) ponytail!"

"Oh, that. Margaret told me about it."

"I don't get it," I said. "Where is it written that a Nobel Laureate cannot have a ponytail?"

"In your father's book of stereotypes, limitations, and

preconceptions—the book he lives by."

"Do you think it is in any way related to his getting slapped in the face by the tail of the diving horse years ago?"

"Perhaps," Maria said. "After that incident, your father equated a ponytail with shame, and he fears being publicly humiliated again. He associates a ponytail with being a sissy, and fears the whole world will believe he's raised a sissy, even though in everyone else's reality, he has raised a Nobel Laureate."

"You're probably right. Why does he do that?"

"Faulty logic, and focusing on the what-ifs instead of the givens," Maria said.

"True." I then realized I had spent a good chunk of my life pondering the what-ifs, in the not too distant past. Granny was right: underneath our personalities, we were all the same. My father simply wasn't as lucky as I was; he hadn't had the opportunities of a full-time shrink, a grandmother/mystic, and the blessing of a divine sneeze. I needed to feel compassion for his suffering; all humanity was one.

I looked toward the fireplace: it suddenly became a kitchenette, and I became my father. Our oriental rug was replaced by a low-grade industrial carpet, stained with grit and dirty, flattened pancakes of discarded chewing gum. Dark drapes obscured any light that might be shed on the dismal interior of my new home. If only I hadn't thrown that pickle, I thought. If only I could turn back the hands of time and retrieve that gherkin in mid-air. If only, I would be relaxing at home in my den in front of the fire. So it wasn't a real fire: it was better than this den of inequity. If only I had controlled my rage; why was I so angry? I could have been in Sicily tending to the olives; instead, I was alone in a wasteland with a rusty old toilet and a black and white TV. I missed Leona; why had I started that food fight? My parents had been right in shipping me off to America; I was a sorry excuse for a man.

"What are you thinking about?" Maria asked.

"I was thinking about how my father must have felt while living in that efficiency. It must have been horrible."

"True, but sometimes the horrible can be a portent of change. The horrible has a way of forcing us to examine our lives."

"What can we do to help him?" I asked.

Maria just looked at me.

"What?" I asked.

"That was the first time you have expressed a desire to help your father. True compassion is wanting our adversaries to resolve their struggles so they may experience joy with us."

"So where do we go from here?"

"All we can do is treat your father with compassion, and pray that he one day makes peace with himself. You just have to be careful not to let his antics destroy the inner peace you have cultivated for yourself."

"Thank you."

"For what?" Maria asked.

"For your patience. My road has been a long and hard one, and you never gave up on me."

"You're welcome."

I sat back in my armchair and stared into the fire. The brandy having kicked in, a warm feeling spread through my chest. As I rolled the brandy in my snifter, an idea sprung: a ponytail was a simple idea. A ponytail could be a symbol of hope. Perhaps Jerry, with his ponytail tied to the Nobel Prize, was subconsciously trying to bring hope back into our family. My own brush with a ponytail had certainly been an eye-opener. And hadn't Mom symbolized hope with that gesture of a swinging ponytail?

Yes, I thought, a ponytail was a simple idea. I could write a book about a ponytail, a simple book. Granny was never off the mark. Suddenly her words became a mantra which rang repeatedly in my mind: all you need is a lot of confidence and a simple idea. *A ponytail would be my simple idea.*

I took another sip of brandy and realized how comfortable I had become in my armchair. I could sit and concoct stories for a living, I thought. Maybe I would leave my job at SuperSoft.

I imagined my mother driving me to school. We were classmates in the writing program at Penn, and were carpooling with Les Izmore.

"Did you do your homework last night?" Mom asked. "I don't want to see any C's on your report card!"

"I finished it while watching TV last night. If you don't believe me, see for yourself," I said, showing her the box which held my manuscript.

"Good boy," Mom said.

Les was sitting in the back seat, surrounded by Mom's porcelain ponies. "What are you doing with Mom's ponies?" I asked.

"I've purchased them for my next living sculpture," Les said. "I'm calling it *The Myth of Chincoteaque.* It opens at the Met in April."

Mom pulled up to the Van Pelt Library. "Do you have your lunch money?"

"Got it!" I said, leaving the car.

"Tony!" Mom called.

"Yeah?"

"Get rid of the gum, please."

"Oh Mom, I'm not a little kid anymore!"

"You will always be my little boy," Mom yelled, as she and Les drove off into the sunset.

Eleven

As usual, Maria was right: that I finally released my demons on Halloween was an omen. My hope became indefatigable; my inner pendulum seemed in resonance with some larger cosmic pulse. More important, I felt empowered to change my life. I was extremely grateful for that power; it helped me unravel my last bits of neurosis and bid them farewell.

That my gratitude should reach its peak when we were about to celebrate Thanksgiving—was that an omen too? For the first time in forty-two years, I approached the holiday with genuine meaning. Anxious to begin my four-day weekend, I stepped off the elevator and practically floated to our front door.

I slipped the key into the lock and my holiday began. I immediately went to change my clothes: the ties I had worn for twenty years suddenly felt like a noose around my neck. I donned leisure wear and built a fire.

Taking the last few pieces of firewood, I made a mental note to buy more on the way home from Philadelphia that Friday. A fire ablaze, I headed for the kitchen to start dinner.

Pasta and salad seemed manageable, so I put a pot of water on the stove and washed some romaine. Next on the cutting board was a small, perfect red onion. What a beauty, I thought, slicing through its juicy, purple flesh. If only humanity appreciated the onion for what it symbolized; the whole world would be crying tears of joy with me. My contemplation of the onion was interrupted by the sound of our front door.

"Tony? I'm home," Maria shouted.

I went into the living room to greet her.

"Tony, what's wrong?"

"Nothing, sweetie. I'm cutting an onion for a salad."

"Oh. You're cooking again?" Maria asked, kissing me on the cheek.

"If boiling water for pasta qualifies as cooking, I guess I am," I answered, wiping the tears from my eyes.

"I'll get changed and open a bottle of wine," Maria said, heading down the hall.

I went back into the kitchen. As the water began to boil, I opened a box of linguine.

"What a day," Maria said, walking into the kitchen. "You know my three o'clock, the woman plagued by hallucinations? I finally got to the root of the problem."

"How so?" I asked, waiting for a full, rolling boil.

"She's been treating a sinus infection with herbs, drinking a tea infused with wormwood oil! I couldn't believe it." Maria shook her head in disbelief as she removed the cork from a bottle of Cabernet.

"What's wormwood oil?" I asked, dumping the sticks of linguine into the pot of water. A few got loose and fell to the floor.

"It's the stuff that most likely sent Van Gogh over the edge. Wormwood oil contains hallucinogenic compounds similar to those in lysergic acid diethylamide."

"Similar to what?"

"LSD."

"Van Gogh took LSD? I never knew that."

"No, Tony, LSD didn't exist in nineteenth century Europe. They drank absinthe back then; it was loaded with wormwood oil."

"Never heard of it," I said, examining the floor for runaway linguine.

"No?" Maria asked. "It was popular in Paris during the reign of the French Impressionists. In fact, happy hour was referred to as the *green hour* because absinthe was so celebrated."

"Why did they call it the green hour?" I asked, stirring the linguine.

"Because absinthe was an eerie shade of florescent green. I've seen photos of it in Pharmacology journals."

I stopped stirring the pot. "What did you say?"

"I said that absinthe was an eerie shade of florescent green. Why?"

"That's what I thought you said."

"Why the strange look?" Maria asked.

"Because that's exactly how Granny described Javelle Water to me."

"What water?"

"Javelle Water. The laundry additive that was being carted by the horse that trampled my grandfather."

"Oh, that's right. Well anyhow, absinthe was outlawed in the beginning of the twentieth century when it's chemical formula was elucidated. The government didn't want half the population tripping; after all, look what happened to VanGogh."

I was only listening to Maria with one ear; I kept thinking about absinthe's color: an eerie shade of florescent green. My mind began playing detective.

"Maria, do you think it's possible that Javelle Water was actually a front for bootlegging absinthe? It seems a coincidence that both should be the same eerie shade of green. Maybe the hucksters weren't really pulling bottles of laundry additive; perhaps they were pushing acid."

Maria laughed. "Tony!"

"I'm serious," I said. "No wonder those housewives were so enthralled with the laundry. Perhaps Javelle Water was really the mother's little helper of the day. Granny told me how those women ran when they heard the Javelle hucksters calling; they were probably desperate for a fix."

"Tony, I doubt it."

I started laughing. "Got you!"

"Tony!"

"You had that one coming," I laughed.

"I guess I did," Maria said. "Do you smell something burning?"

"Yeah," I said, walking to the stove. "It's just a piece of linguine that stuck to the burner." I carried the black, smoking noodle to the sink.

"Now you see why I don't cook," Maria said.

"So finish telling me about your three o'clock," I said, extinguishing the linguine.

"Anyhow," Maria said, handing me a glass of wine, "she had a sinus infection and decided on an herbal remedy, namely Artemisia absinthium. Needless to say, her afternoon teas were one long, strange trip. I'm glad I did a thorough history before scouring the DSM; it could have been a diagnostic nightmare. Understandably, she was relieved to discover her hallucinations were drug-induced."

"How did you finally solve the mystery?"

"She said she only hallucinated during sinus infections; it didn't take a rocket scientist to figure it from there," Maria said, topping off my glass of Cabernet.

"O.K.," I said, "coming through with hot stuff." I carried the pot of linguine to the sink and drained it into a colander. I shook the colander a bit; something weird had happened: the linguine was glued together into a ball. I had followed the package directions, so assumed it to be a normal reaction.

Maria sensed trouble. "Can I help you?"

"Yeah, give me a hand here, will you?" I was struggling to separate the forkful of linguine I was trying to serve from that which remained in the colander.

"What happened?" Maria asked. "Did you cook it too long?"

"No. It said fourteen minutes on the box. Here, you hold the colander down," I instructed Maria.

I continued pulling the linguine, but it was useless; it had become one starchy mass, refusing to be apportioned. "Get me the scissors, hon."

Maria opened the kitchen drawer. "Pinking shears all right?"

"Where did they come from?"

"I don't know," Maria said. "I can't find a regular pair of scissors."

"All right, give me the pinking shears."

"I'll wash them," Maria said. "We don't know where they've been." Maria rinsed the pinking shears under hot water and handed them to me.

"There," I said, proceeding to cut portions of linguine in a zig-zag fashion from the mother load. "How many handfuls do you want?" I asked Maria.

"Just one," Maria laughed. "I'll get the salad from the refrigerator."

We sat down and began eating our soggy dinner, cutting the linguine into little pieces to coax it onto our forks. There was little time for conversation; our full attention was concentrated on taming the pasta, then washing it down. I downed Cabernet; Maria chose spring water. As we finished, Maria spoke.

"Tony?"

"Yeah?"

"Remember how you did this. The recipe will come in handy

when we're old and have lost our teeth."

"Very funny. You could be eating pizza again." I then realized we were eating dough, sauce, and cheese.

"I'm only kidding," Maria said. "I really do appreciate your efforts. Cooking isn't a skill that is acquired overnight."

"Well, I'll have you know I'm the son of a woman who once won a bake-off."

"I knew you were well-bred when I first laid eyes on you," Maria joked. "Well, since you cooked, I'll do the clean-up. I'll meet you in front of the fire in ten minutes."

"I'll be there," I said, "digesting the blob."

Maria rose from her chair to remove our plates, and stood motionless for a second, holding onto the back of a chair.

"Too much wine?" I asked.

"No. I only had half a glass. I don't know what it is; I had a dizzy spell yesterday, too."

"Have you been wearing your earplugs?" I asked accusingly.

"No," Maria said. "I need a new pair. Come to think of it, my ear was hurting last night. I'll have to get some ear drops."

"I told you not to swim without earplugs. You don't know what's in that pool with you."

"I know," Maria said. "Problem is, I never remember until I'm in the water."

"I'll get you a pair on Friday. Why don't you go in and sit down? I'll clean up," I said, rising from my chair. I stood motionless for a second, holding onto the back of a chair.

"Swimmer's ear too?" Maria asked.

"No, I have a loaf of bread rising in my gut."

Maria laughed. "Are you sure you don't mind cleaning up?"

"No," I said. "It will only take a few minutes."

It took more than a few minutes to scrub the glue from the cookware. My Cabernet buzz distorted my perception of time: I felt as if I'd been scrubbing most of my adult life. Finally, I thought, rinsing the last bit of starch from the colander and pot. I went to join Maria in front of the fire.

"What are you reading?" I asked Maria.

"Yesterday's *Science Times*," Maria said. "According to this article, Japanese scientists have cloned a clone of a clone."

"A clone of a clone?"

"That's what it says: they've made a copy of a cow-copy."

"I wonder if each successive clone loses some subtle aspect of its cowhood?"

"Tony, have *another* glass of wine," Maria laughed. "Seriously, what would be the relationship of this clone to the original?"

"It would be his clone twice-removed."

"When did you win the (pause) Nobel Prize?" Maria laughed.

"You insult me, after the wonderful vegetarian meal I provided? Tomorrow night, it's a cloned steak *thrice*-removed for you! And it's not going to be the other white meat!"

Maria threw down her newspaper in mock disgust. She was right: I'd had too much wine. She held out her arms, motioning me toward the sofa.

"You know, Tony," Maria said seriously, "we really have a lot to be grateful for this Thanksgiving. Remember how strained our relationship was, this time last year?"

"I do, and I'm sorry to say, most of it was my fault."

"I wasn't trying to place blame. Besides, I was too involved in my own problems to see that you were reaching out for help. Anyhow, I only mentioned it because I'm feeling very grateful for what we now have."

"Me too."

"By the way, did you stop at the travel agency on the way home?"

"Yes, I did," I said. "There are three first-class tickets to Stockholm in my briefcase. I wish Margaret and my parents would have allowed me to buy their tickets; I feel a little guilty, sitting in first class with you and Granny, while they're squashed into coach."

"Don't feel guilty, you offered. When is Jerry leaving?"

"He's leaving on the fourth," I said. "He has press conferences and a slew of informal celebrations to contend with before the actual ceremony."

"I still can't believe it," Maria said. "Have you thought about Jerry's gift?"

"A present or Jerry's intellectual prowess?"

Maria laughed. "A present."

"Yes. What would you think of a gold pocket watch? I thought we could have one engraved. Jerry hates wearing anything on his arms, and he certainly has enough pockets," I laughed.

"That's a great idea. Let's go shopping this weekend."

"It's a date," I said. "You know, I'm really looking forward to seeing everyone tomorrow. We certainly have a lot to celebrate. Isn't it amazing, how things can change in a year's time?"

"It is," Maria said. "Speaking of change, have you come to any decisions about work?"

"Yes and no," I said. "I seem to oscillate in my thinking. One day I think yes, I could make it as a writer. The next day, I'm clutching to the security of my job at SuperSoft."

"That's understandable," Maria said. "It's a big decision. But I really love your ponytail idea; have you elaborated on it at all?"

"Actually, yes," I said. "I've been jotting down ideas as they come to me. In fact, I feel a little guilty about it."

"Why?"

"Because lately, it seems as though I'm spending an awful lot of time at work jotting down ideas; Rich Cardile would have a fit if he knew I was using company time to explore my literary interests. But if I don't write things down, I forget them."

"You're not behind on your project, are you?"

"No," I said. "Not yet. But I will be if I don't regain my focus."

"Maybe your lack of focus is a clue," Maria said. "You seem to be more involved in exploring your literary interests than in digital feedback loops. Not to influence your decision, but I say grab the pony by the tail and go with it."

"We'll see. I'm not doing anything until the Y2K transition. I can't very well leave SuperSoft in the lurch, should any unforeseen problems arise."

"Of course not," Maria said. "You still want to retain your professional reputation."

"It has nothing to do with my reputation," I argued. "It has to do with doing what's right. If I do decide to leave SuperSoft, I owe it to them to make my exit as smooth as possible. I've got to finish what I started on the DFL project and at least be available as a consultant until another team leader is appointed."

Maria looked at me.

"What?" I asked.

"It is very noble to entertain how your actions will affect other people. All day, I deal with people whose only concern is with themselves. They then expect me to clean-up the aftermath of their self-centeredness. I'm really proud of you; I'm sure you're a great team leader, and should you choose to be, you'll be a great soloist."

"Thanks, Maria. But you really should be proud of yourself; I'm just another one of your success stories. If it weren't for you, I'd be cleaning up the aftermath of my self-centeredness too."

Maria just squeezed my hand. We sat together staring into the fire, our hearts ablaze with gratitude. We were grateful not only to have each other, but for our shared vision. At some point during the past year, we made the mutual decision to seize each day; enough precious moments had been wasted. Each new day became an opportunity to live our new philosophy. Besides, I had undoubtedly exhausted my supply of *get out of jail free* cards.

Maria had fallen instantly asleep; as I watched her cherubic face glowing in the soft firelight, I prayed for the strength to become a better person. Maria deserved only the best, and I needed to be great in order to fill that post. It meant nothing to be a good team leader or writer. My greatest achievement would be in giving back to Maria all she had given me—I was a husband first.

On that last Thanksgiving eve of the millennium, I learned the true meaning of gratitude. I was grateful not only for what I had and who I was, but for what I could become. I had finally solved an equation: love plus gratitude plus hope equaled soaring.

The mood that particular Thanksgiving was a weird blend of solemnity and surrealism: I realized that my life had finally come full-circle. That my enlightenment evolved from the same set of circumstances that had originally threatened to push me over the edge was truly a paradox. Nothing had changed in my life, except my perspective. Another thing I learned during the year was that there was only one certainty in the wondrous thing called life: everything is a paradox.

I soared through sleep on the wings of angels. I was in heaven, wasn't I? I was resonating with grace delivered by God himself: everything was soft, pure white; delicate floral fragrances sounded their notes in harmony with those of the gently plucked harp strings. I floated softly on sensations that were both bombarding and soothing.

I then realized that I was *really* floating, and that those sensations were not sensations at all; they were pure thought. I could no longer feel because I had lost my physical self; my only awareness was of my own consciousness. Oh my God, was I dead? With that thought, I stopped floating and began free-falling through space-time at the speed of light, falling too quickly to clutch onto any of the realities I moved through. My consciousness was sinking and folding into and onto itself, contracting to a singular point like a bullet, which penetrated my head on the pillow and exploded into wakefulness.

"Tony, honey, wake up," Maria was saying.

"I have my body back!" I proclaimed. The strong final pluck of a harp string sounded as my exclamation point. I was awake, born again. Maria had changed the setting on the alarm clock so we'd awaken to the sound of angels. I still wasn't sure if that alarm clock was a good thing.

"Were you having a bad dream?" Maria asked.

"I'm not sure what it was," I said. "My mind was floating around without my body, and when I became aware of that fact, my mind accelerated through space like a bullet. I shot myself in the head."

"You committed suicide?" Maria asked, gently stroking the bullet's point of entry on my forehead.

"Not literally—my consciousness *became* a bullet. It was as if I actually saw my sleeping, unsuspecting head on the pillow, and took a nose-dive for it. It was the strangest dream I've ever had."

"Sounds like an out-of-body experience," Maria said. "You haven't been treating a sinus infection, have you?"

"No," I laughed, "and I believe I still have both of my ears."

Maria and I laughed together; I felt my ears, just to be sure.

"Happy Thanksgiving, Tony."

"Happy Thanksgiving to you, sweetie," I said, kissing Maria tenderly. "Tomorrow we'll awaken at Granny's house."

"I know," Maria said. "Do you think we could just move in with Granny?"

"Are you serious?"

"Of course not. I was just kidding." Maria put her hand to her ear.

"How's your ear this morning?"

"Better," Maria said. "The pain's gone. There's just a slight sense of pressure; I'll be fine."

"If you have one more dizzy spell, I want you to see the Ear, Nose and Throat Specialist in your building, do you hear me?"

"What?" Maria shouted.

We laughed and lay there in silence for a few seconds, staring at the ceiling.

"You know," Maria said, "the thing I hate about this building is the no pets rule."

"Still thinking about that pony?"

"No, a cat," Maria said. "You'd think an apartment that goes for eight hundred thousand would offer some freedoms."

"We didn't pay eight hundred thousand for this apartment."

"I know. But that's what they're going for now. The Smiths on the sixth floor just got eight-ten for their place."

"They did?" I had no idea we were sitting on a gold-mine. I was suddenly glad we had opted for a fifteen year mortgage. The place was probably half paid for by now.

"Yes," Maria said, "and their office is smaller than ours."

I began doing the math: whoa! "I like cats too," I said.

"Maybe we should look for a small house in Connecticut, or even in Bergen County; the commute wouldn't be so bad. I'd love to have a garden, maybe even with a fountain like Granny's."

Maria knew which buttons to push. "Yeah," I said, "we could drive into the city together; a commute wouldn't be so bad."

"Let's search the Internet when we get home on Friday. It can't hurt to look."

"No, it can't," I said. I pulled the covers up to my neck and began to think. It was hard to fathom how things could change in a year's time. Maybe we'd awaken in our very own house next Thanksgiving. It would have to have lots of rose bushes, and of course, a fountain. And plenty of windows—I wanted to fill my new house with plants. I would ask Granny to start making some cuttings. A lot could happen in a year. Those cuttings could really take-off!

"I'm going to start packing," Maria said.

"Already?" I asked. As I spoke, I realized Maria had meant to pack for our trip to Philadelphia.

"I'm just eager to start the day."

"Me too," I said, pulling the covers down and stretching my legs. To feel my legs again was such a relief. Although shaken, I was also intrigued by my out-of-body experience. On that note, I got out of bed and walked solidly to the bathroom.

Leaving the building, Maria looked at our bags. "Did you remember the candy?"

"Yes," I said. Our contribution to Thanksgiving dinner was two pounds of *Godiva*. We didn't want to walk in empty-handed, and Granny knew better than to ask us to prepare a vegetable, or worse yet, a pie. Speaking of pie, I wondered about the quality of the Granny Smith harvest; would my mother be bringing a pie?

"You wait here, sweetie. I'll get the car," I said, leaving Maria in the lobby of our building.

I returned with the car and loaded our belongings into the trunk.

"Do you want me to drive?" Maria asked.

"If you want to."

"Sure," Maria said.

It was a relief that Maria had offered; what if my mind became a bullet again while driving the Turnpike? Perhaps Maria had also pondered that *what if*. I slid into the passenger seat, and we were off to Granny's.

"If you don't mind," Maria said, "I think I'll take the tunnel."

"Not at all," I replied, getting comfortable in my seat. As we drove, I fantasized that we were leaving Manhattan after work, commuting to our abode in Bergen County. Goodbye, New York, I thought.

We entered the Holland Tunnel and my eyes began registering the succession of lights as we moved rapidly through the tiled burrow. We seemed to be accelerating.

"Are you in cruise-control?" I asked Maria.

"Yes."

I looked at the speedometer: it was motionless, no change in velocity. Suddenly the dashboard moved further and further from my field of view, and it was gone; so was our car. I was soaring through the tunnel on the wings of my mind, weaving in and out of traffic to avoid the vehicular exhaust, heading straight toward the light of day.

I emerged from the tunnel above the clouds, which obscured my bird's eye view of the Turnpike below. I descended through those angels' pillows and found myself soaring above the runways of Newark Airport. Toy-like, the massive jets were lined-up in single file, waiting for their turn in the sky.

I hovered gently on pockets of air, amazed by my ability to fly. I noticed one of the toy planes inching down the runway in preparation for take-off; I followed suit. I tailed the jet as it accelerated faster and faster through space-time, and became its shadow in the sky as it achieved lift. I ascended in formation with my steel brother, leveling off and maintaining constant altitude once we had maintained an adequate altitude above the clouds.

My thoughts soared: what kind of bird was I, that could fly so high? Surely I am an eagle, I proudly hailed in a wind song. An eagle should be riding on the nose of this plane as a hood ornament, I thought, in proud testament to the glory and power of man.

I accelerated gently and approached the front of the plane; on my second try I landed firmly on its nose. Turning around to peek inside the cockpit, I caught a glimpse of myself in the looking glass of the pilot's window. My reflection startled me: I was a turkey! I couldn't be a turkey—I was a testament to power and glory!

As disillusionment drained my testament, I made eye contact with the pilot. He looked at me and began opening the window of the cockpit. "What are you doing, you fool?" I yelled, "you'll depressurize the cabin!" The roar of the engines muffled my plea; the pilot stood there yelling my name. Why could I hear him? And how did he know my name?

Suddenly the pilot pulled out a shotgun and aimed it directly at me. I tried to fly away, but was paralyzed by fear. The pilot began firing; as the third shot rang, I knew I was dead. With a trail of feathers following, I began free-falling through the sky toward my Thanksgiving fate.

As I approached a hungry earth I began to recognize the landmarks that were becoming larger and larger in my field of view: was that the Statue of Liberty? I should be a hundred miles away by now, I thought. A gust of wind moved me uptown, and I momentarily floated northward on that vector, until I was suddenly in free-fall again. I was making a nose-dive for the Guggenheim; there was no turning back. "God help me!" I yelled, as I impacted the Guggenheim and fell through its glass roof.

I began rolling down around the Guggenheim's corridors; I

quickly gained momentum and became a bowling ball, headed right for Les Izmore's exhibit. I crashed into *The Last Thanksgiving* with a thunderous sound, ceramic shards and feathers flying, as Les stood watching helplessly.

"Tony!" Les screamed, "I knew you would one day reclaim your birthright, but did you have to destroy my masterpiece?" He approached me with a carrot shard and began chasing me with his pointed, mock weapon; I ran uphill as Les dangled the carrot behind me. "I'll get you for this, Tony," he screamed. "Tony, you bastard, Tony!"

I opened my eyes; Maria was gently shaking me. "Tony, honey, wake up."

I came to consciousness and looked around: Maria had pulled into the rest area. My dream had left me speechless; I just looked at Maria.

"Did you have a nice nap? You went out like a light, just as we hit the tunnel."

I looked into the rear-view mirror; I was no longer a turkey, I was a man again. "What a dream," I said.

"I have to use the bathroom. Do you want a cup of coffee or something?"

"O.K.," I said, running my fingers through my tousled hair. I opened the car door and planted my feet firmly on the ground.

Heading toward the building, a wave of contentment moved through me: I was making progress. Rather than let the dream ruffle my feathers, I jotted down a mental note. My dream was stranger that fiction, and I filed it under absurdity for later use. When I finally sat down to write my story, this chapter would come in handy.

"I'll be right back," Maria said. "Would you get me something cold to drink?"

"Certainly." I walked to the counter, reading the menu board for the beverage selections.

"Can I help you?" A woman asked.

I looked around.

"Yes, you," the woman said. "What can I get you?"

I looked intently at the woman who stared at me from behind the counter. Did I know her? Something about her was familiar.

"Call me when you've made up your mind," the woman said, walking away in indifference.

I stared at the counter woman, trying to make some kind of connection. Where had I seen her before? I peered over the counter, listening to the crunch of salt under her feet as she passed the pretzel display. Suddenly, a light went on in my head: she was the counter woman who had threatened to call security last year when I refused to pay for a pretzel that had been manhandled. I stepped back in fear.

As the gruff counter woman retied her apron strings, I felt a cinching of my own waist. A man approached me and ordered a hot dog. I walked bitterly toward the spinning frankfurters, angry that I was working at that lousy counter on yet another holiday. He's never going to stop drinking, I thought, of the husband whom I'd left on the sofa that morning. I should be home cooking a turkey for my kids; they shouldn't be spending another holiday with my brother. But someone has to feed the kids, I thought, putting the hot dog onto a bun. At least I had a job. But somehow that realization didn't lessen the sting of never spending a holiday with my children.

Suddenly I was on the other side of the counter again, my apron gone. No wonder the poor woman is miserable, I thought. Working like a dog while that no-good slug of a husband sleeps off another hangover. I began to admire that woman's strength; to endure the daily rat-race of hot dog slinging so her children could have a better life—she should be canonized!

The woman again approached me, her hair net reflecting the neon light of the signs overhead; it became a halo as she asked me for my order.

"Thank you for being so patient," I said. "I'll have a large coffee and a medium lemonade, please."

"One large coffee, one medium lemonade!" she yelled to her entourage.

"That will be three-sixty," she demanded.

I reached into my pocket and discovered that I had only two fifty-dollar bills. Seeing Grant approach, she became disgruntled: "Don't you people ever carry small bills?" As she grudgingly handed me my change across the counter, we made eye contact.

"No, that's for you," I said.

"But mister, you gave me a fifty."

"I know," I said. "It's Thanksgiving—buy something for the kids."

Her expression of bitterness melted into a smile. "How did you know I have kids?"

"Just a lucky guess," I said, taking my coffee and lemonade. "Happy Thanksgiving."

"And to you too, Mister," she beamed. "Come again soon!"

I walked away from the counter with a warm feeling. So I had just spent fifty bucks for a cup of coffee and a lemonade; so what? The light in that woman's eyes was worth a million bucks. Besides, I was sitting on a gold mine back in Manhattan.

"Thanks, honey," Maria said, taking her lemonade. "Ready to go?"

"Yes," I replied, opening the door for Maria. Before leaving, I turned and looked toward the fast-food counter. My new friend was smiling as she served her next customer. One person can make a difference, I thought, walking out the door.

Exhilarated by my experience and the caffeine, I asked Maria if she would like me to drive.

"Thanks, honey," she said. "I am feeling a little sleepy."

Heading onto the Turnpike, I looked at Maria. "Did you ever feel as though you could actually get into someone else's head?" I asked.

"Every day at the office," Maria answered.

"No," I said, "I mean actually feel what they are feeling, with no motive other than to share their pain or their glory."

"You mean compassion? Of course I've felt compassion. Unfortunately all that I'm feeling right now is fatigue; here's two dollars for the bridge in case I fall asleep."

I took the money and focused on the road ahead and the direction my life was taking. My path was blessed with the landmarks of love, gratitude, hope, and now, compassion. Poppy had been right: my life would be just fine. Everything was coming up roses.

As I moved forward on my journey, I realized that I could no longer be content with the nine-to-five routine of teaching computers how to think. Life was for the living, and I finally reached a well-contemplated decision: I would say goodbye to

SuperSoft once it was guided safely into the new millennium.

As I paid the toll and crossed the bridge into Philadelphia, I looked forward to my new career. What better way to live than to laugh along with God in the garden of life? Poppy would be proud; I was extremely grateful that God had blown a higher order into my life. God's sneeze may have been over, but it was just the beginning for me.

I pulled into Granny's driveway behind my father's car. I turned off the engine and looked at Maria. She was sleeping so peacefully, I hated to wake her. I gently nudged her.

"We're here already?" she asked. "What did you do, fly?"

"Yes, as a matter of fact, I did. You'll notice that your pilot has turned off the seat belt light. You may now disembark the aircraft."

We got out of the car and I removed our bags from the trunk.

"Look," Maria said. "The lights are up."

Thousands of white lights adorned Granny's house, but they weren't twinkling yet. That tradition would happen the following evening, on Black Friday, as the season began with the flick of a switch. Perhaps Granny would allow us to break tradition this year and turn on the magic tonight, I thought.

We walked into Granny's haven and were met by the fragrance of celebration; the air was filled with the enticing aroma of sweets and savories.

"Tony!" my mother yelled, entering the foyer to greet us.

"Hi Mom," I said, hugging her. "Happy Thanksgiving."

"You too, honey," she said, approaching Maria. "Maria honey, are you all right? You look exhausted."

"I'm fine, Mom," Maria said, kissing Mom on the cheek.

"Well, here. Let me take your coats. Your father is in the living room. Why don't you go in and say hello."

I walked somewhat nervously toward the living room; I hadn't seen my father since the pickle incident on the Fourth of July. Although nervous, I was determined to maintain a sense of decency in our interaction.

"Hello, Dad," I said, walking into the living room.

"Oh, hello," Dad said mechanically. I could tell by the tone of his voice he was already stewing over something.

"Where's Granny?" I asked.

"She's in the kitchen," Dad mumbled. "Wait till you get a load of her; she's losing it, I tell you."

I walked toward the kitchen, silently telling myself to calm down. How could he talk about my grandmother that way?

"Tony, my love!" Granny said, approaching me.

My jaw dropped. Granny was losing it all right: it was all gone. Granny was bald! My heart sank; she had been secretly enduring chemo, suffering in silence, not wanting to worry us. "Oh Granny, your hair," I cried softly, hugging her tightly.

"Oh, didn't I mention it?" Granny said casually. "I must have forgotten to."

"How could you not have told me?" I begged Granny. "I would have been here to help you; driven you back and forth."

"Nonsense, Tony," Granny said. "I took the bus. Needless to say, the ride home was interesting; the looks were enough to kill me!"

"Oh Gran, you took the bus home too?" I imagined my poor sweet Granny, anguished in pain, stumbling to find her way from the hospital to the bus stop.

"Of course I did," Granny said. "Why wouldn't I?"

"Weren't you feeling sick?"

"Not at that point," she said. "What I was sick of was all those chemicals. That morning, I awoke and said to myself: Rose, you are eighty-five years old; you don't have to do this any more."

At that point, tears were rolling down my cheeks. Maria walked into the kitchen, seeing Granny's bald head and my tears, and surmised what was happening. Maria put her arm around me. I couldn't bear the thought of losing Granny; I was shocked.

"You can't give up, Granny. Maria, tell her how important it is to keep on going," I pleaded.

"Tony's right, Granny," Maria said. "The outcome of this depends to a large extent on whether or not you surrender your will."

"I will no longer be a slave to those chemicals," Granny said. "With all due respect to the two of you, I don't know why this has become such an issue; it's my life. If I can live with a few weeks of social awkwardness, what's the problem?"

"Maybe you are eighty-five," I said, "but you could have another twenty good years ahead of you."

"That's true," Granny said, "and I don't intend to dye my hair for the next twenty years."

"What? Dye your hair? What are you talking about?"

"I was tired of dyeing my hair," Granny said. "Now love, is this conversation about over? I have another turkey to contend with."

Maria laughed.

"How can you laugh at a time like this?" I chided.

"I think what Granny is trying to say is that she's dying to stop dyeing her hair, Tony," Maria said.

"That is exactly what I was trying to say," Granny laughed. "I took the bus to Margaret's shop for a haircut, and decided to go all the way, give my hair a fresh start. I'd look ridiculous trying to grow out sultry brunette; there is nothing sultry about announcing the fact that you've been trying to hide your age. I'd rather be bald."

I began laughing, and Maria followed. Granny joined us.

Big Anthony walked into the kitchen. "You think her new hairdo is funny? Let's see how funny you think it is when we're the laughing stock of Stockholm, your brother with a ponytail, and your grandmother a skinhead. You won't be laughing then, mark my words."

"Oh Dad," I said, "no one will be concerned with anyone's hair. Jerry has won the Nobel Prize in Physics; no one cares about his hair, or his grandmother's, for that matter."

"If I don't mind being a skinhead, Anthony, why should it matter to anyone else?" Granny asked.

"You people just don't get it," big Anthony mumbled as he left the kitchen.

Ordinarily, I would have entertained a solitary game of one-upmanship with my father. But my life was no longer ordinary; I was becoming compassionate, *and* I was overjoyed that my precious Granny wasn't sick; there had been no stumbling to the bus stop! She was perfectly fine.

"What was that all about?" my mother asked, entering the kitchen.

"Anthony's still grieving over my hair," Granny said. "He's afraid the King and Queen will deny him an audience because of his family's hair."

"Did he *curse*, Mom? Tell me the truth," Leona said.

"No, Leona. He didn't curse. Why don't we change the subject? Have you told Maria and Tony the good news?"

"Not yet."

"What good news, Mom?"

"Well, I sent a proposal for *The PonyTale* to a children's publisher, and I think they're interested. They want to read the whole story; I sent it to them yesterday."

"That's great, Mom."

"Well, just because they liked the proposal doesn't mean it's a done deal. I'm trying not to get my hopes up too high."

"That's nonsense, Leona," Granny said. "Aim high! No one ever accomplished anything of importance without high hopes."

"Granny's right," Maria said. "Your story is wonderful; of course the publishers are going to want it. I'm thrilled for you."

"Thanks, Maria," Mom said.

Mom's pep talk was interrupted by the arrival of Aunt Vicky and Uncle Harry.

"Hello everyone!" Aunt Vicky yelled.

"Happy Thanksgiving to all!" Uncle Harry proclaimed. He was wearing a rather expensive-looking ensemble—was that a cashmere sweater?

"Sorry we're late," Aunt Vicky said. "We couldn't figure out how to get the loaner car started; it won't start unless the seat belts are engaged. We didn't know that."

Aunt Vicky kissed me. "Hello, sweetie. How's everything in New York?"

"Just great," I said. I looked strangely at Aunt Vicky: something was different about her. I felt my cheek; there was no lipstick. I looked at Aunt Vicky's pale, unglossed lips: she looked like a different woman unadorned.

"Tony, good to see you," Uncle Harry said, shaking my hand. It *was* cashmere.

"Good to see you too. Why are you driving a loaner car? Is the Lincoln giving you trouble?"

"Yeah," Uncle Harry sighed. "The transmission is shot, can you believe it? I only had the damned thing six months."

Yes, I could believe it. I was surprised the transmission had lasted that long. "Oh well," I said, "at least it's still under warranty."

The front door opened again. It was Jerry and Roberta.

"Excuse me, Uncle Harry."

"Jerry!" I said, hugging my brother. "So how does it feel?"

"Actually, it feels pretty darned good," Jerry said.

"Hi, Roberta, good to see you!"

"You too, Tony."

Maria walked into the foyer and greeted Jerry and Roberta. "Why don't we go into the living room? Here, Roberta, give me your coats."

We settled into the living room and Granny entered with a tray of snacks. There was another round of hugging and kissing. No one said anything about Granny's hair.

"By the way, Jerry," Uncle Harry said. "Can you give me Avogadro's number? I have to call him; that other tape he sent me was defective too."

"Sure Uncle Harry," Jerry said. "I'll give it to you before you leave."

"So tell me, Harry," my mother said, "how is everything going at the plant? We saw you on the news; it must have been exciting."

My father began choking on a piece of cheese.

"It was exciting," Uncle Harry said. "Everything's going just fine. Some minor kinks to work out, but we'll get through it."

"Tell them about your gymnasium," Aunt Vicky said.

"What gymnasium?" Jerry asked.

"We're putting in a gym down at the plant," Uncle Harry explained. "Our health insurance rates were going through the roof, with so many of my men getting thick around the middle. As you may guess, it's not much of a workout, moving boxes of Styrofoam."

"That, and all the expired cupcakes," Aunt Vicky added.

"What?" I asked.

"Oh," Uncle Harry said, "there's a bakery thrift shop in the industrial park, where you can get cupcakes six for a buck. They're actually pretty good, not a darn thing wrong with them. Seems as though my men are wandering over there at break-time. Between that and the inactivity, well, you get the picture."

"So what type of equipment did you get?" I asked my uncle.

"Oh, a couple of treadmills is all. And then of course, a lot of heavy boxes."

"Heavy boxes?"

"Yeah," Uncle Harry answered. "You know, I got to thinking: what if the regular shippers ever went on strike? We could make a fortune in sub-contracts, but not if my men were too weak to carry the load. So now I require them to spend forty-five minutes a day in the gym, moving the real thing. Your Aunt has even painted a mural on the wall that looks like the back of a rig. We put a steel shelf under the mural. It's very realistic; the guys think they're loading a real truck."

"That is nuts," big Anthony said. "I've never heard anything so crazy."

"Well," Uncle Harry said, "We R Nuts, can't deny that! It's plastered all over the sides of our trucks."

Everyone laughed. My father rose from his chair and went to get his coat. "I'm going for a walk; I've heard enough of this nonsense."

Jerry looked at Uncle Harry. "So tell me, Uncle Harry, what did you do, fill the boxes with weights?"

"Hell, no," Uncle Harry said, as the front door slammed shut behind my father. "Have you any idea how expensive weights are? I said to myself, Harry, what's the heaviest thing you can think of? I then saw my answer, right there in the kitchen sink."

"Huh?" everyone uttered in unison.

"Water," Uncle Harry said. "We just filled the empty boxes with water balloons; very little investment, and a lot of return. No better training than lifting boxes of water."

"What if you get a leaker?" Jerry asked.

"No problem," Uncle Harry said. "There's a drain in the middle of the floor; they used to kill hogs in there. We just stack the leakers in the middle of the room."

I looked at Maria; she was trying to stifle laughter too. "I'm going to give Granny a hand in the kitchen," Maria announced.

"I'll go too," I said, following Maria.

"Wait for us," Jerry said, taking Roberta by the hand.

The four of us piled into the kitchen, closing the door behind us. Our laughter spilled forth uncontrollably.

Jerry looked at me. "Stale cupcakes and water balloons! Can life get any more absurd?"

We both laughed a good belly laugh.

"Another comedy of errors transpiring?" Granny asked.

"Dear God, Gran," I said. "If I didn't know better I'd swear we were on *Candid Camera*."

"Speaking of cameras," Jerry said, "have you heard Mom's

news?"

"Yeah," I said. "Who would have thought Mom would one day become a children's author?"

"I know," Jerry said. "If anyone in the family should become a writer, I'd have guessed you."

"Why do you say that?"

"Come on, Tone. You're the one who's always so obsessed with the nitty-gritty. You must have volumes packed away by now."

"I'm obsessed with the nitty-gritty? That's like the pot calling the kettle black."

We laughed. "I guess it is," Jerry said. "Anyhow, did you get your plane tickets?"

"Yes. We're really looking forward to the trip."

"Thanks, Tone. It means the world to me."

"Don't get sentimental; I'm only going to have an audience with the King and Queen."

Our moment was interrupted by what was transpiring at the kitchen table. Roberta was hovering over Maria. "Are you all right?" Roberta asked with concern.

"I'm fine," Maria said.

"What's the matter, honey?" I asked. "Is it your ear again?"

"I guess so; I'm just feeling a little dizzy."

"She's had an earache," I explained. "Swimming without earplugs again."

"Oh Maria," Jerry said. "You never want to swim in a public pool without earplugs; it's a veritable primordial soup of germs."

"Jerry's right," Roberta said. "I caught a nasty ear infection from a pool once. It threw my equilibrium way off; I felt as if I was walking on ball bearings."

"That's it," I said. "You're going to see a doctor. You have a chronic infection; you can't risk your sense of hearing."

"What?" Maria asked.

"I said, you're going to see a doctor."

"Huh?"

Everyone laughed. "All right," Granny said, "who's going to slice the turkey? Enough fun and games; we have work to do."

"I'll do it," Jerry said.

"Good," Granny said. "Roberta, honey, will you fill the water glasses?"

"What can I do?" I asked Granny.

"You can set up some folding chairs around the dining room table, and then go outside and call your father for dinner."

I went into the dining room and put out a few chairs. I looked into one mirror and saw Uncle Harry talking animatedly to my mother and Aunt Vicky. In another mirror I saw the front door opening. Good, I thought, I won't have to go and look for him. But it was Margaret. I walked to the foyer to greet her.

"Margaret," I said, hugging her. "It's good to see you."

"Hi, Tony. I've missed you. How have you been?"

"I'm fine now," I said, "but I was in shock when I first saw Granny; I thought she was sick."

"Why?"

"Because of her buzz; I thought she had lost her hair to chemo."

"Oh," Margaret said. "I was a little surprised myself, that she wanted to go all the way. But you know Granny; she doesn't give a hoot what anyone thinks."

"I know. By the way, Margaret, why don't you let me buy you a ticket in first class? The money is no big deal. I want you to sit with us."

"Thanks, Tony, but I already bought tickets on the Internet, three ninety-six apiece—can you believe it? I'm going to go say hello to everyone; I'll talk to you later," Margaret said, squeezing my arm.

I couldn't believe it; was it really worth an extra thousand bucks to stretch out? So much for the free cocktails, I thought.

Granny walked into the foyer. "Did you find your father?"

"Not yet, I was just getting my coat."

I walked out the front door and looked up and down the street: there was no sign of my father. I walked around the house to the backyard. I saw Dad standing contemplatively next to the garden wall. I approached him.

"Dad, it's time for dinner."

"Great. Has Harry finished his little speech?"

"What are you talking about?"

"I'm talking about the fact that he has to rub my nose in his success. Isn't it obvious?"

"Dad, Uncle Harry's not rubbing your nose in anything; he's

just excited about his business. Why do you always assume the worst about people?"

"Because everyone seems to enjoy making me the target of their mockery. I'm sick of it."

"Oh Dad, come on. It's all in your head; no one is trying to make a mockery of you. Have you ever considered that maybe you're your own worst enemy?"

"Don't give me a bunch of psycho mumbo-jumbo. Just because you're married to a shrink does not give you the right to psychoanalyze me. It's a bunch of bullshit; Maria hasn't been able to do a thing for you. You're still the same no-good…"

"The same what?" I asked. "Go ahead, Dad, say it. Mom's not here. Why don't you tell me once and for all what you really think of me? Maybe we can get to the bottom of this."

"Why?" Dad snapped. "So you can go running to your grandmother? I'm sick of this bullshit! It's always me. No one in this family will ever admit that I'm right about anything. I'm sick of this whole friggin family!"

"Then why did you come here today?"

"I came for your mother's sake. She hates driving the Schuylkill. Contrary to what everyone says, I can be a nice guy once in a while. I'm not going to have your mother in a pile-up just to spare my own feelings."

"So you're telling me that you're here today only as Mom's chauffeur?"

"Of course not. Someone had to come and talk some sense into that brother of yours. He can't be receiving the Nobel Prize with a ponytail swinging as he walks onto stage. We'll be the laughing stock of Stockholm."

"I see." It was obvious that our conversation would go around in circles forever. I chose to get off the merry-go-round, without the ring. "I'm going in. Dinner's ready."

I walked into the house through the back door. Dad took the long way.

"Everything O.K.?" Jerry asked, carrying the turkey platter toward the dining room.

"Everything's just fine," I said. I wasn't going to let my father's antics ruin another holiday. While my life was coming up roses, it was natural to get pricked by a thorn every now and then. That I had been pricked without getting into a screaming match with my father was progress.

I took my seat at the table, quickly wedging myself into the safety zone between Maria and Roberta.

"Come on, Anthony," Mom yelled.

Everyone looked in the mirror at my father, who was standing in the foyer, groping his crotch like a baseball player getting ready to go up to bat. Luckily, he didn't spit as well. When would he ever learn to behave in Granny's house of mirrors? We were about to eat a meal, after all.

My father walked into the dining room and took a seat at the table.

"Everything looks wonderful, Gran," I said.

"Thank you, dear. Would you like to say grace this year?"

"Certainly." We joined hands, and I began: "Bless these gifts which we are about to receive. In gratitude we receive not only this meal but all of the blessings which have been bestowed upon this family—the love, the prosperity, and last but not least, the Nobel Prize."

"Amen!" everyone shouted.

We began passing the food around the table.

"Did you get to see Les Izmore's exhibit at the Guggenheim?" I asked Jerry and Roberta.

"No, we missed it," Jerry said. "With all the commotion going on at Princeton, we couldn't get away. But I hear it was phenomenal."

"That's an understatement," I said.

"Don't worry, Jerry. It's coming to Philadelphia in the spring. Maybe things will settle down for you by then," Mom said.

"I think Les is a genius," Margaret said. "By the way, Gran, the stuffing is wonderful."

"Yeah," my father said, "and I guess we won't have to worry about finding any stray hairs in it."

"Oh, Anthony, will you forget about my hair? If it will make you feel better, I'll get a wig for the prize ceremony," Granny said.

"I just got some new ones," Margaret said. "There's a pageboy to die for."

"Really?" Aunt Vicky asked. "Did you get anything in an ash blonde? I'm thinking about making a switch. It would be nice to try on the color before actually hitting the bottle."

"That's a good idea, Aunt Vicky. You don't want to pick the wrong shade," Maria said, trying to make conversation.

We sailed through Thanksgiving dinner with a lot of talk, but without much actually being said. I sat quietly eating my meal, taking it all in. I ate everything on my plate except turkey; I skipped that out of compassion for the poor bird. After all, I had flown in his wings before. My Thanksgiving file of absurdities was jam-packed that year.

"Well," Granny said, as we finished eating, "I think we'll dispense with the Black Friday tradition this year and light up the house tonight, in honor of Jerry."

"Thanks, Granny. That's very sweet of you. I'm honored."

"Why doesn't everyone get their coats? I'll throw the switch," Granny said.

Everyone rose from the table and went to the foyer closet to get their coats. My father walked into the living room and sat in front of the fire.

"Aren't you coming, Anthony?" Mom asked.

"I've seen the lights a hundred times. I'm staying right here, where it's warm."

"Suit yourself," Mom said, rolling her eyes.

"Wear your hat!" I ordered Maria. I was really worried about her ear.

"Yes, Sir," she replied.

The whole family, minus my stubborn father, assembled on the front lawn to await the magic of the season. I put my arm around Maria and held her close.

"Everyone ready?" Granny yelled from the front door.

"We're ready."

Granny flicked the switch, and everyone stood spellbound, gazing at Granny's idyllic little mansion, bathed in the light of a thousand stars.

"Isn't it beautiful?" Maria asked. "When we get a house of our own, I want it to look just like this at Christmas."

"Me too," I said, kissing Maria on the cheek.

I stood there and watched the faces of my family, aglow with wonder and excitement. The birth of hope—that was the magic of the season.

I looked at Maria. "Do you want to go for a walk in the garden?"

"I'd love to."

We walked around the side of the house toward the rose garden, which had been cut back for the winter. Maria and I sat next to the trumpeting angel, whose song had also been winterized.

"It's still beautiful," Maria said, "even without the water falling."

"It is," I said, looking up at the night sky. "Do you ever wonder what really lies out there, beyond the stars?"

"Yes," Maria said. "I think space is full of hope. I think all the wished-upon stars reflect hope with their light, beaming our own dreams back to us, blessed with a little celestial magic."

"I like that."

Maria and I sat there on that last Thanksgiving of the millennium, silently pondering the cosmos, wishing upon a star. What we didn't realize was that our fate-wish had already been granted. It had been beamed back to us at the speed of light, as we silently spoke the last words of our dream.

We sat there at that blessed intersection of space-time for a few more minutes, absorbing the pixie dust that was falling with the cosmic rays.

"Wishing upon a star?" Margaret asked, walking toward us.

"Yes," Maria said, as we huddled together to make room for Margaret on the bench.

"Well, my wish has come true," Margaret said. "After forty-five years, I've finally found Mr. Right."

"That's great," I said.

"We're so happy for you," Maria said. "What's his name?"

"I believe you know of him," Margaret said. "His name is Les Izmore. We began dating last month after meeting at his opening."

We were stunned.

"Les?" I asked.

"I know," Margaret said. "We seem to come from two different worlds. But sometimes, when worlds collide, there's a really big bang! And I love his art; it's so revolutionary."

We laughed.

It looks like Mom's dishes might remain in the family after all, I thought. I added that note to my mental file, which was already burgeoning.

"I'm glad that you have found love, Margaret," I said. "It's all there is."

"I know," Margaret said, squeezing my hand. "It's all there is under the heavens. Nothing else seems quite so important anymore."

I liked Margaret's choice of words; I added that one last footnote to my mental file and closed the book for the evening.

We sat there silently, absorbing the impact of our dreams as they were reflected back to us. Our dreams were filled with high hopes, for ourselves and each other.

As I sat there, between my wife and my sister, I beamed my own gratitude up to the heavens. The universe seemed to shout a big "you're welcome!" but I'm sure it was my imagination. Then again, maybe it hadn't been: maybe the stars were speaking to me in the language of light. Who knows what is possible at the level of order in which God exists, I thought.

I chose to believe that God was speaking to me on that starry night. The echo of his voice didn't create perturbations; the evening was soft and still, reverberating only peaceful harmonics. Nothing was more perfect than that night.

Twelve

I sat anxiously in the waiting room of the Ear, Nose and Throat Specialist in Maria's building, shrouded in fear and hope. I feared the loss of Maria's hearing, while I hoped it was a mere case of swimmer's ear.

"You can go in now, Mr. Vitello," the receptionist said. "They're in room three."

I approached room three in silent conversation with God: please don't let Maria go deaf; I promise I'll never ask for another thing, ever!

Maria and Dr. Hamberger were sitting at a large mahogany desk.

"Have a seat," Dr. Hamberger said, sitting back in his chair, pensive with concern. After looking back and forth at Maria and me several times, he *finally* spoke. "You appear to have an inner ear problem, Maria. It could be a simple case of swimmer's ear, or it could be something a lot more serious. I can't tell you anything conclusive until I get some of your test results."

"How serious?" I asked, reaching for Maria's hand.

"I wouldn't worry, Mr. Vitello. It's probably nothing to be concerned about," Dr. Hamberger said. "I'm going to prescribe some ear drops to reduce the inflammation; as a precaution, I'd recommend staying out of swimming pools and airplanes until we know what we're dealing with."

"Airplanes?" I asked.

"Yes," Dr. Hamberger said. "The pressurized cabin could cause the eardrum to burst, should there be a fluid balance problem. But I'm sure it's just a case of swimmer's ear. Don't worry, we'll know for certain in a few days."

"But we're flying to Stockholm in the morning!" I cried.

"Yes," Maria said. "Tony's brother won the Nobel Prize in Physics."

"Really?" Dr. Hamberger asked. "That guy who looks like Einstein is your brother?"

"Yes."

"What a small world. I saw Dr. Vitello on the news; I hear his discovery is going to change the world. How about that?"

"How about the plane ride?" I asked. "Can't you get the lab to push things through? Our flight leaves at 9 a.m. tomorrow."

"I'm afraid not, Mr. Vitello. Some of these cultures need at least forty-eight hours to grow. I really don't know what to tell you. If Maria was my wife, I wouldn't risk a transatlantic flight," Dr. Hamberger said. "I hear CNN will be televising the Nobel ceremonies, if that's any consolation."

It wasn't. I looked at Maria. "Don't worry, Tony," she said. "I'm sure it's nothing to worry about. But Dr. Hamberger is right, I don't want to do anything to jeopardize my hearing."

"If you can't go, then I'm not going either," I said. "I'm not going to leave you alone with an eardrum that could burst."

"Mr. Vitello, there is little chance that Maria's eardrum is going to burst; she's going to be fine. What I said was that her eardrum could burst *if* she has a fluid balance problem and sits for hours in a pressurized airplane cabin. This is just my advice; you can take it or leave it," Dr. Hamberger said. He then addressed Maria: "Now, if you have no further questions, I'll get back to you in a few days when I have your test results."

"Thank you, Dr. Hamberger," Maria said.

"Yes, thank you," I said.

"And congratulations, again, on your brother's feat," Dr. Hamberger said, leaving the room.

"I can't believe it," Maria said. "But Tony, you have to go to Stockholm. Jerry needs you there; it's a once in a lifetime event. I can watch it on *CNN*. You *have to* go. It would destroy Jerry if you weren't there."

I certainly didn't want to destroy Jerry. I did have to go. I remembered Jerry's words as if he had spoken them yesterday: "The Nobel Prize would mean nothing if you weren't there to share it with me."

"I'm so disappointed," I said. "But more than anything, I hope there's nothing seriously wrong with your ear. I couldn't bear it if anything happened to you."

"Don't worry," Maria said. "I'm sure it's nothing serious. Come on, let's go have lunch somewhere. I'm famished."

"O.K.," I said. "Did Marian cancel the rest of your appointments this afternoon?"

"Yes. Now don't look so glum. It could be worse: you could have the earache and be unable to make the trip. At least you're going to be there for Jerry. And you're only going away for four days, with Granny by your side."

That was some consolation, but nowhere near enough to ease the sting of disappointment I felt.

"We can't forget to stop at the jewelers on the way home," Maria said. "We have to pick up Jerry's watch."

"Then why don't we have lunch at that little place down the street from the jewelers, the one that makes that great onion soup."

"The Oasis?"

"Yeah, that's it."

"Great, let's go."

We hailed a cab and were off to lunch. Maria suggested picking up Jerry's watch first, so the cab stopped in front of the jewelry store.

We walked in; the one salesperson was busy with another customer, so we admired the gems on display while waiting.

"Oh my God, Tony, look at this!" Maria said, motioning me to one of the jewelry cases. "Isn't it beautiful?"

Maria was referring to a pendant set in platinum. "I've never seen anything like it," I said. It was the most dazzling amethyst I had ever seen, emerald-cut, surrounded by diamonds of the same shape.

"Can I show you something in the case?" The salesman asked, approaching us.

"No," Maria said. "We're here to pick up a special order; Vitello is the last name."

"Oh yes," the salesman said. "It's in the back. I'll get it."

"Do you want it? It's yours," I said to Maria.

"Tony, no! It's six thousand dollars. Are you crazy?"

"Yes, crazy in love."

"Oh Tony, that's sweet. But let's not go crazy until someone actually makes an offer on our apartment. And don't forget, we're going to be living on one paycheck for awhile."

"Does that scare you?"

"Absolutely not. I think you're doing the right thing. I just don't want to spend six thousand dollars on a piece of jewelry right now. End of discussion, O.K.?"

"O.K."

"Here you are, Mr. and Mrs. Vitello," the salesman said. "Your watch."

I immediately approached the salesman; Maria stopped to admire the amethyst one more time.

"It's a beauty, isn't it?" the salesman asked Maria.

"It's the most beautiful amethyst I've ever seen," Maria said, walking away from the case.

"It's not an amethyst," the salesman said. "It's a purple ruby. You very rarely see them; in fact, it's only the second one I've seen, in twenty years as a gemologist. They're found only in Madagascar."

"Maria, it's an omen," I said. "Granny's Celestine geode came from Madagascar."

"Come on, Tony. Let's look at Jerry's watch," she said, leading me by the arm to the counter.

"It's beautiful," Maria said, looking at Jerry's watch.

I picked it up and turned it over. The engraving was beautifully done: *Time has no meaning at the level of order in which God exists. Love, Tony and Maria 12-10-99.* "Thank you," I said. "Beautiful job."

"Will there be anything else then?" the salesman, or rather the gemologist, asked.

"No," Maria said. "That will be all."

The gemologist processed my credit card and we were off to lunch.

Leaving the jewelry store, we noticed how dark the sky had become. "Looks like it's going to rain," Maria said.

It was about to pour. Maria and I walked quickly to the restaurant, which luckily was only half a block away.

Lunch was in full swing at the Oasis. By the time we got a table, poor Maria was about to faint from hunger.

"I don't know why I'm so famished," Maria said. "I ate half a bagel this morning."

"Your body is fighting an infection," I said. "You need extra nourishment."

The waitress arrived and we ordered lunch.

"There is no onion soup today," the waitress said. "The soup du jour is split pea."

"I'll pass on the soup, then," I said.

At that moment, I didn't give a hoot about soup, or lunch for that matter. All I could think about was that purple ruby from Madagascar. It had been an omen: that gem was meant for Maria. I was going to buy it for her, despite her reservations about the expenditure.

I waited until Maria received her soup before making my exit. "I'll be right back," I said.

"Where are you going?" Maria asked.

"To the bathroom."

"Oh," Maria said, blowing across a spoonful of her soup.

I rose from the table and headed toward the front door. I left the Oasis and ran down the block to the jewelry store. As I did, the sky opened and it began to pour.

Soaking wet, I opened the door and entered the jewelry store. I headed straight for the case that held the purple ruby. My heart sank—it was gone!"

The gemologist appeared from his workspace. "Mr. Vitello. Was there something wrong with the watch?"

"Oh no," I said. "It was fine. Did you sell the purple ruby that quickly?"

"Heavens, no. I moved it to this case," he said, walking to retrieve the ruby."

"Just wrap it up," I said. "I'll take it."

"Very well," the gemologist smiled. "I'm sure Mrs. Vitello will get a great deal of pleasure from it. I'll ring that up for you."

I handed him my credit card. A few minutes later he walked back to the counter with a disappointed expression. "I'm sorry, Mr. Vitello, but your card was denied."

"Here, try this one," I said, handing him another card. Those three first-class tickets to Stockholm had apparently sent my first card over the edge.

The gemologist returned, smiling. "Mission accomplished," he said. "If you'll just sign here."

I signed the receipt. "On second thought," I said, "don't wrap it. I've got to get back to the Oasis; my wife thinks I went to the men's room."

"Here you go, then," the gemologist said. "I thank you, and hope your wife gets years of pleasure from it."

"Thank you," I said, tucking the small box securely into my chest pocket.

Outside, a small monsoon was transpiring, but I had to make a run for it; by then, Maria was surely questioning my whereabouts. I returned to the Oasis dripping wet, and headed for the bathroom.

As fate would have it, there were no paper towels to be found, but there was a wall-hung air dryer. I hit the big chrome disc with my elbow and knelt on the floor to dry my jacket. While the hot air soothed me, I prayed that the purple ruby would be as blessed as Granny's Celestine geode. I stood saying "amen" and then bent over at the waist to dry my hair. When the cycle finished, I moved to look at my full-length reflection: I had fluffy hair and dirty knees, and there wasn't a damn thing I could do about it. I was already late for lunch. I headed back to our table.

"Tony!" Maria said. "What took you so long? I was beginning to think you had fallen in."

"Just a little constipated," I lied.

"Then you should have ordered the split pea. I hope you don't mind that I started eating without you," Maria said, looking at me strangely. "Did you do something different with your hair today?"

"No, why?" I asked, with a forced innocence.

"I don't know. It just looks kind of, I don't know, fluffy or something. But it looks good," Maria said, biting into her Reuben.

"Do you want my pickle?" I asked.

"It depends on whether you intend to throw it at me or hand it to me nicely."

"Poor Dad," I said. "Will he ever be able to live that one down?"

"I'm sure," Maria said. "He'll do something, good or bad, to overshadow the pickle incident. Hopefully it will be something good."

"I just hope he behaves in Stockholm. I can't believe that Granny actually had to buy a wig to put a lid on his needling."

"I know," Maria said. "Not to change the subject, I think you should eat a few prunes when we get home; you don't want irregularity to interfere with your trip. To tell you the truth, honey, you look a little flushed, kind of purple. Are you feeling all right?"

I looked purple? Was energy being emitted from the purple ruby in my chest pocket? I reasoned that my Madagascan gem was indeed blessed. It would bless our lives just as Granny's chunk of ice-blue magic had blessed hers.

I had an epiphany: a year before, I had been locked pitifully into a prison built of my own ill-constructed illusions. I approached the new millennium with new illusions, built on a foundation of magic. Was it insane to believe in magic? I didn't care; I preferred it to the hellish insanity I'd previously cultivated. It was more fun.

"Tony!" Maria yelled.

"I'm sorry, honey," I said.

"Are you feeling all right?"

"Yes, I'm sorry. I was lost in awe for a moment, thinking about the magic of the past year."

I looked at Maria: her eyes were filling up with tears. "What's the matter, honey?"

"I don't know. I'm feeling very emotional today; I guess it's the disappointment of not going to Stockholm with you."

I reached for Maria's hand. "I know. I'm really disappointed too. But what can we do? I would never want to jeopardize your health."

"I know," Maria said. "I know it's crazy, but I used to love it when you went away on business; the solitude was a welcome treat. But I'm really going to miss you this time." The tears flowed.

Our relationship had really changed: we enjoyed one another's company again. My trip to Stockholm would be our first separation since renewing the promise of our relationship. "I'm going to miss you, too," I said, handing Maria my napkin. "But I'll call you every single day."

"O.K.," Maria said, drying her eyes. "Just don't forget about the time difference." She then proceeded to finish her Reuben, just like that.

Poor Maria, I thought. I had never seen her so emotionally up and down. The infection raging in her ear was really weakening her spirit. I was tempted to give Maria the purple ruby at that moment, but her Reuben seemed consolation enough. Besides, I intended to hide her gift in my sock drawer and call her from Stockholm with instructions on where to find it. That was more romantic.

"How's your burger?" Maria asked.

"It's good," I said. "Do you want a bite?"

"O.K.," she said, reaching across the table.

I handed Maria the other half of my cheeseburger. I sat waiting for its return, quickly realizing I was waiting in vain.

"You know," Maria said, "I think I'll take advantage of the next few days; all my appointments have already been canceled. I think I'll have a spa day tomorrow and go to the Met on Friday."

"That sounds good," I said, watching Maria take the final bite of my cheeseburger.

"What?" Maria said, noticing my amusement.

"My sandwich," I said.

"Oh my God, Tony, I'm so sorry. I can't believe all this emotional eating I'm doing. I guess I'm swallowing my disappointment along with everything else on the menu. Before I know it I'll be back to a size twelve again."

"That's all right," I said. "I could go for some dessert anyhow." I motioned to the waitress.

"Yes sir?" she asked.

"I'd like apple pie a la mode. Honey, do you want anything?" I asked Maria.

"Nothing else for me," Maria said. "I'm full."

"That's all," I said to the waitress.

"Remember that little Donna incident last Christmas?" Maria asked.

"How could I forget? I can't even look at an apple pie without visualizing my father scraping the toaster with that spatula."

"I know," Maria said. "I wonder if he ever got over losing that pack of pies?"

I laughed as the waitress returned with my dessert. "Here you go, sir. Your apple pie," she said, setting it in front of me.

Maria and I laughed at the sight of it.

"Is something wrong?" the waitress asked.

"No," I said, "everything's fine."

She looked at us strangely and left our table.

"That looks good," Maria said.

"Do you want a bite?"

"Oh, all right. Maybe just one bite."

I knew better than to pass the plate to Maria; instead, I loaded a forkful and personally fed it to her.

"It's delicious," Maria said. "Thank you."

Proceeding to eat my dessert, I silently wondered what to do with Maria's ticket to Stockholm. "Should I cancel your ticket? We could probably get a refund, with a doctor's excuse."

Maria hadn't heard me; she was intently staring at my pie.

"Why don't you finish this," I said. "I'm full."

"Are you sure?" Maria asked, looking for her fork."

"Absolutely."

Maria motioned to the waitress. "May I have a glass of milk, please?"

"So anyhow," I continued, "what shall I do with your ticket?"

"Why not just upgrade Margaret? You wanted to buy her ticket anyhow," Maria said.

"Thanks, Maria," I said. "That's a great idea." I sat silently watching Maria devour the rest of the apple pie. I had never known Maria to be an emotional eater; I imagined returning from Stockholm to find her swollen with melancholy.

"Do you want anything else?"

"Dear God, no," Maria said.

Thank God, I thought.

As we waited for our check, Maria stared longingly at me. "You know," she said, "whatever you did to your hair this morning, you should do every morning. It looks great with a little lift."

"Thanks, honey," I said, laughing to myself.

It was raining madly; we got soaking wet, walking to the curb to embark our cab. Needless to say, my fluffy new look assumed its previous flatness. Maria seemed disappointed.

"I'm going to get out of these wet clothes," Maria said, entering our apartment.

I picked up the phone to call Margaret. I was about to hang up when she finally answered.

"Hello. Shear Envy, Margaret speaking."

"Margaret, it's Tony. Do you have a minute?"

"Yeah, just a minute though. The shop's been crazy today. I had to take care of all my Saturday heads, since I'm closing this weekend."

"I have bad news; Maria can't go to Stockholm."

"No? Why?"

"It's her ear. Her doctor feels that the pressurized cabin of an airplane could burst her eardrum."

"What a disappointment for her," Margaret said. "I hope she's all right."

"She will be. So anyhow, I want you to sit in First Class with Granny and me."

"I love you, brother. You wouldn't believe how Dad's been torturing me about Jerry's hair. He's been calling twice a day; can you believe he even suggested that I clip Jerry's ponytail while he lay sleeping?"

"Yeah, I believe it. So you'll sit in first class with us?"

"Absolutely. And I owe you, big time. You're sparing me eight hours of grief on the flight. I love you!"

"I love you too. What time are we meeting at the airport?"

"We should be there by seven-thirty. I'm picking up Granny at five-thirty and then swinging by to get Mom and Dad."

"Good. I'll see you in the morning. Are you excited?"

"Immensely, although I'll miss Les."

"I know. I'm going to miss Maria. But it's only four days."

"I know."

"Well, drive safely. The traffic around Kennedy can be nuts."

"I will. Thanks, Tony, for everything."

"My pleasure. See you in the morning."

"Bye, Tony."

I went into the bedroom to get out of my wet clothes. I dressed in a sweat suit and listened outside the bathroom door: Maria was in the shower. I headed down the hall to the office to wrap her gift.

I looked for wrapping paper, but it was pointless. There was none. I caught a glimpse of my old purple notebook lying on the bookshelf. I picked it up and tore an empty page from the back of the book. I wrapped Maria's pendant in the lined paper and fashioned a bow out of four old rubber bands. I then tore another sheet from the notebook and began to write.

Dear Maria,

I know you said not to go crazy until someone actually made an offer on our apartment, but you said that to a crazy man. Besides, how often do you come across a purple ruby from Madagascar?

Please accept this gift as a token of my love and appreciation, for always standing by me. You deserve something, for putting up with all those years of my hiding in my purple note-book. If it weren't for you, I'd be lost in the limbo of those pages for eternity.

I'm sorry you're not with me in Stockholm. Although there is an ocean between us, we are connected.

All my love, Tony

I signed my name, realizing I had plagiarized Walter Water. Sorry, Walter, I thought. I rolled my letter like a thirteenth-century manuscript and secured it to the gift with a rubber band. I quickly carried my token of love to my sock drawer, and nestled it safely in a pair of argyles that had been lying idle for at least five years. For a second I stood wondering if those socks were emitting purple; I hadn't remembered any lavender in those socks. Maria was coming; I closed the drawer just as she entered the bedroom.

"Did you call Margaret?" she asked.

"Yes, and she's extremely grateful," I said. "Seems as though Dad's been torturing her, to give Jerry a clipping."

"That figures," Maria said. "You know, I was thinking in the shower. You should remove the plastic bag from your tux and let it air overnight before you pack it; those dry-cleaning solvents should out-gas for awhile."

"Good idea," I said, walking to the closet.

"Oh, and don't forget the prunes! You don't want to be constipated when you get on that plane tomorrow. The time change will be enough of a shock to your system. You don't want the whole trip to be ruined because you can't go to the bathroom."

"I will," I said. Why was Maria being such a mother hen? I then imagined Maria force-feeding me those prunes, and my spending eight claustrophobic hours in an air-toilet the next day. "I'll go and eat them now," I lied, to spare myself the public restroom embarrassment on the flight to Stockholm. I hated lying to Maria; I knew from experience how things could snowball. But it had been a harmless white-lie, instigated to maintain a surprise. Still, lying had been tossed from my repertoire a long time ago, and I didn't like the unease it stirred. I decided I was over-analyzing and headed for the kitchen.

I opened the cupboard and grabbed the box of prunes. I removed six and stuffed them into my pocket. I headed for the bathroom, leaving the prune box conspicuously on the counter as evidence that I had taken Maria's advice.

I flushed the toilet, probably setting an historical precedent: the first prunes to be flushed undigested. As the prunes went down in history, I felt guilty, for wasting perfectly good food. I began an argument with myself, circular in nature. Realizing I'd never win, I silently screamed: *stop!* I did, and walked innocently from the bathroom.

It was strange to pull into Kennedy Airport, when I was so emotionally tied to Newark. As Maria looked for a parking spot, I looked to the future: in less than two hours I would be nothing more to Maria than a speck of dirt on our windshield. I would become very small in her eyes.

I suddenly realized that the details of my metaphor were courtesy of Jerry; he had taught me to see the paradox of size, that it depended on one's reference point. I was grateful that Jerry had pushed me to assume different reference points, even though relativity seemed to yield the bizarre. The bizarre was becoming more and more attractive to me, fueling my imagination and increasing my awe and wonder quotient. I really loved Jerry for the gift he had given me. Everything began to seem a miracle.

Maria parked the car and I retrieved my luggage from the trunk. We began walking toward the terminal.

"Where are your gloves?" Maria asked. "It will be freezing in Stockholm."

"They're right here," I said, pulling them out of my pocket.

We entered the terminal and I checked my luggage. As we approached our gate, I caught a glimpse of my father, looking nervously at his watch.

"It's about time," he yelled, seeing Maria and me enter the waiting area.

"What are you talking about?" I said. "It's only eight o'clock."

"Well," Dad said, "our tickets distinctly say to arrive an hour and fifteen minutes before scheduled take-off on international flights," Dad grunted.

"Oh Anthony, be quiet," Mom said. "Maria honey, I'm so sorry you won't be going with us. How's your ear?"

"It's fine, Mom," Maria said. "Don't worry."

Margaret hugged me. "Thanks again, my savior," she whispered, handing me her coach ticket.

Granny was wearing a shoulder-length chestnut pageboy; it suited her well. "Love the hair," I said, hugging Granny.

"Thank you, dear. I figured the minor inconvenience of itching would be easier to endure than your father's hounding."

I went to the desk to cancel Maria's flight and upgrade Margaret's. I then went to be with Maria until it was time to board. I sat down and took her hand.

"Call me as soon as you get to the hotel tonight, honey."

I did some mental math. "That should be about six in the evening, New York time."

"But it will be midnight in Stockholm. You'd better try to stay awake on the flight; you want to be able to sleep when you get to the hotel," Maria said.

Maria's concern (eat your prunes, out-gas your tux, wear your gloves, get enough sleep) was endearing. This is what love is, I thought. I then proceeded to calculate how much actual sleep I would get before the Nobel festivities: it wasn't much.

Maria and I sat silently pondering our own thoughts, but our hands were joined. I thought about the promise of the new millennium. Who knows what the future holds, I thought optimistically.

My thoughts were interrupted by an announcement: "Attention passengers. We will now begin boarding Scandinavian Airway Systems flight 713 to Stockholm. Will all passengers holding a first-class ticket please approach the gate and begin boarding the aircraft. I repeat…"

Maria looked at me. "I guess this is it," she said. "I hope you have a wonderful time, Tony. Give my love to Jerry."

I hugged Maria tightly. "I'll call you tonight. I love you," I said, brushing the tears from her cheeks.

"I love you too. Do you have Jerry's watch?"

"Got it," I said, patting my carry-on.

I kissed Maria one more time and approached the gate. I

looked over to my parents. "See you in a bit," I shouted.

Boarding the aircraft, I really did feel like a piece of dirt, leaving my poor, weeping wife behind while I was off to Europe.

Granny took my arm. "Don't worry, sweetie. She'll be all right. Maria's a strong woman."

"Thanks, Granny," I said, as we took our seats in the front of the plane.

"I feel awful for Maria," Margaret said.

"I know," I said, looking out the window toward the terminal. I wrestled my emotions while the rest of the passengers embarked. I swam in the excitement of Jerry's honor, yet sank with the disappointment of leaving Maria behind. Margaret took my one hand and Granny took the other; their compassion helped balance my dichotomous emotions. I sat back and prepared for take-off.

As our plane began taxiing down the runway, I tried sending thought clouds to Maria: I love you…Wish you were here…I'll call you tonight! With Godspeed we were airborne.

Within five minutes a flight attendant was taking our drink orders.

"Let's have champagne," Granny said. "My grandson is receiving the Nobel Prize in Physics tomorrow night," she explained to our attendant.

"Yah?" the attendant asked. "The man who looks like Einstein is your grandson? I saw him on television."

"Yes," Granny said proudly.

"Champagne it is," the attendant said. "It's not everyday that one's grandson wins the Nobel Prize!"

From the corner of my eye, I noticed a man in his early fifties looking at Granny curiously. "Pardon me," he said to Granny. "I couldn't help overhearing; are you Dr. Vitello's grandmother?"

"Yes, I am," Granny said.

"You probably don't remember me, but we met a few years ago in Boston. Roger Turner, from MIT," he said, extending his hand.

"Why, yes. I do remember," Granny said. "Roger! How are you? This is such a coincidence."

"I'm headed to the prize ceremony myself," Roger said. "I was invited by one of my Swedish colleagues. Congratulations on your grandson's feat. You must be very proud."

"Oh, I am," Granny said. "Roger, I'd like you to meet my other grandchildren. This is Tony, Jerry's brother, and their sister Margaret."

"How do you do?" we said.

"It's nice to meet you both," Roger said. "Congratulations on your brother's feat."

"Thank you," we said.

While Granny and Roger became reacquainted, I turned to Margaret. "Isn't it strange, how Granny always runs into someone she knows?"

"It is," Margaret said. "Do you know what else is strange? Every time someone congratulates us on Jerry's feat, I imagine Jerry posing for a picture with his podiatrist."

"Me too," I said. "I guess we're both deranged."

We laughed.

"So how's it going with Les?" I asked.

"It's going wonderfully—he was worth waiting for. To tell you the truth, I guess I never really believed I'd find someone who was worth the sacrifice of my freedom. You never know what the future holds."

"One more glass," Granny was saying to the flight attendant. "Dr. Turner will be joining us."

The attendant returned with a fourth glass, and we toasted Jerry's feat.

As we sipped champagne, Margaret elbowed me and whispered: "Tony, listen." She motioned toward the flight attendants who were within earshot.

"Yah," the blonde attendant said. "Can you believe the likes of that man? I've never met an American so obnoxious. Who does he pretend to be?"

"If he desired so much doting, he should have come up with the extra kronor and bought a ticket in first class," her comrade said.

Margaret and I looked at one another. "Poor Mom," I said.

Margaret looked out the window to the vastness of the ocean below us. Granny was involved in her conversation with Dr. Turner. Alone with my thoughts and a slight champagne buzz, I sat back, and closed my eyes.

As we flew toward the international date line, I did some mental time-traveling of my own. My mind began flipping through the pages of time and I fell into another wormhole.

I emerged from the wormhole to find myself floating on the Atlantic Ocean: it was 1969. I stared toward shore, watching Jerry ponder a world that no one else could see. My olfactory memory conjured the aroma of freshly roasted nuts. Some mild air turbulence stirred the sands of time; as a storm ensued, I became sucked into a water spout and was spit into the future.

It was 1970. Jerry was recording variables as I searched madly through Dad's dresser drawers for slacks gone awry. That memory being doused with acetone vapors, I quickly dove back into the wormhole to avoid asphyxiation.

I emerged next in 1975. While I pulled out my hair, in anguish over Physics 101, Jerry was dressing for the National Honor Society dinner. There were two opposing fragrances attached to my memory: the sweet smell of success and the stench of failure. I wreaked of the latter, and desperately escaped into my future.

My next lay-over was 1980. We were both graduating; Jerry prematurely as valedictorian of Princeton, myself summa cum nothing from Penn. I smelled nuts again!

Lured by the smell of frankincense, I emerged eleven years later at the altar, looking nervously at my watch. The bride *had* shown; we were waiting for the best man. Jerry finally ran into the church, stripping off his lab coat to the beat of Pachelbel's Canon, throwing it into the pew with our parents as he moved to stand by me. I smelled every conceivable variety of flower as Maria marched toward me. As I reached to take her hand, I was back in the wormhole.

It was Valentine's Day, 1999. Jerry was standing in his boxer shorts, his pants around his ankles. The click of the magic camera sounded as fabric freshener masked the aroma of burning nuts, which became the aromatic blend of spring as Jerry ran onto stage and grabbed the microphone.

Soon my trip became a jumbled mess of sights and smells: pickles flying against a backdrop of barbecue smoke as Mom's dishes rolled around the Guggenheim in a fruity blend of thunder. But then, a soothing calm descended, along with the fragrance of roses. Jerry was accepting the Nobel Prize from the King of Sweden, while the Queen looked at me and winked, softly calling my name.

"Tony, wake up," Margaret was saying.

I looked around in a daze. "What year is it?"

"You mean what time is it?" Margaret asked. "It's one o'clock New York time. They're about to serve lunch."

Granny was still conversing with Dr. Turner.

"You'd better try to stay awake for the rest of the flight," Margaret said. "You'll never be able to sleep tonight."

"I know," I replied. "Do me a favor, if you see me nodding off again, give me a little wake up call?"

"Sure thing."

"Attention passengers," a voice announced. "This is your captain speaking. We are currently flying over the Atlantic Ocean at an altitude of thirty-five thousand feet. The weather in Stockholm is a crisp twenty-six degrees, with clear skies. We should be landing at Arland Airport at our scheduled arrival time of 11 p.m. And again, thank you for choosing Scandinavian Airway Systems."

"What time is it in Stockholm now?" Margaret asked.

"Let's see," I said, counting. "It's a little after seven."

"Oh," Margaret said. "Four more hours."

"It will go quickly," I said. "After lunch we can go through some brochures I picked up at the travel agent's."

"Hi honey," Granny said. "Did you have a nice nap?"

"Wonderful," I said, recalling the royal glances that had been bestowed upon me.

A flight attendant approached with our lunch trays.

I surveyed my tray. "What is it?" I asked Granny.

"It's Swedish meatballs and potato kugel."

"Oh," I said, sampling a forkful. "It's good."

We ate our meal, making small talk with Dr. Turner. After an obligatory visit to our parents in coach and to the restrooms, we settled in for the final three hours of flight.

We scoured the brochures and decided on our itineraries for the following day. Margaret would shop the markets in search of the perfect Anna Holfblad sweater; Granny and I would visit the *Tekniska Museet.* We would meet back at the Grand Hotel by three o'clock for a short rest before we were off to *Stockholms Konserthus* on *Hötorget Square.* Following the prize ceremony, of course, we'd attend the gala banquet at City Hall.

"It's going to be a busy day," Granny said, "but the adrenaline generated by the excitement of the city will see us through it."

My own adrenaline was generated not only by the excitement of Nobel Week in Stockholm, but also by what waited for me back in New York: a whole new life. The new millennium would bring a wave of change: a new career, an new home, and whatever other surprises fate would bestow.

The thought of a new career generated dichotomous emotions. I was excited about breaking away from SuperSoft; my heart just wasn't there anymore. But I was scared to death that burning that bridge might lead to my ultimate demise. What if I couldn't make it as a writer? What if my insight was tainted with ignorance and my words minced stupidity?

In quiet desperation, I closed my eyes and summoned the help of my trusty old friends. Despite my plea, Mildred and Martin failed to show. It had been my third unsuccessful attempt to retrieve them—they were no longer dependable. Three strikes and you're out, I thought.

I decided that I could only depend on myself. With two Swedish flight attendants as my unknowing witnesses, I banished Mildred and Martin from my mindscape forever. In an imaginary rite of independence, I sliced through the tentacles by which Mildred and Martin dangled precariously from my ego. I pushed them from me and watched from the window of the plane as my cohorts splashed into the dark, icy waters of the Atlantic. The impact of their crash was felt in every chamber of my psyche, each one spitting sparks of self-reliance into a growing flame that burned a message onto my soul.

That fiery message repeatedly sounded on my heartstrings: let fear not rule my fate and make me my own enemy. Unencumbered by fear, I would finally be free. That was it, my millennium mission. Maybe I wasn't a great writer, but maybe I could become one. Things would come up roses!

I sat there for a long time, pondering positive what ifs. It wasn't until I heard an electronic bell that my thoughts returned to ordinary reality.

"Attention passengers: the pilot has turned on the seat-belt lights. We are approaching Arland Airport and will be landing approximately eight minutes ahead of our scheduled time of arrival. Please remain in your seats with seat belts fastened until further notice."

"Thank God," Margaret said. "I can't wait to get some fresh air."

"How long does it take to get to the hotel from the airport?" I asked Granny.

"About thirty-five minutes," Granny said. "We'll take a taxi down the E-4 Highway. Downtown Stockholm is only about forty kilometers south of the airport."

"Boy," I said, "you remember all that from your last trip?"

"Heavens, no. My memory isn't that good; I've been studying the travel guides."

Our conversation was again interrupted by an electronic bell. "Attention passengers: the aircraft is making its final descent in preparation for landing. Everyone must remain in their seats with seat belts fastened. Please return all food and beverage trays to the upright position, and as always, thank you for choosing Scandinavian Airway Systems."

Within minutes we had touched down and were coming to a grinding halt on the runway of Arland Airport. Everyone breathed a sigh of relief, to be safely on land again.

"Attention passengers: this is your captain speaking. Welcome to Stockholm. The temperature is currently twenty-eight degrees Celsius and the local time is 10:56 p.m. We hope you've enjoyed the flight, and look forward to serving you again on Scandinavian Airway Systems."

"Enough commercials?" Margaret laughed.

As the plane taxied to the terminal, we gathered our personal belongings and braced ourselves for our reunion with big Anthony. We disembarked first and went to wait for our parents at the gate. Within minutes, they emerged, my father running at the mouth.

"Oh Anthony," my mother said, "will you forget it? It was an accident!"

"It was not an accident, I tell you. He was trying to get back at me for taking the last can of ginger ale!"

"What's the problem?" Granny asked.

"The man behind us accidentally hit Anthony on the head with his carry-on while removing it from the overhead compartment," Mom explained. "Anthony swears he did it on purpose."

Margaret looked at me suspiciously. "How much did you pay

him?"

"Margaret!" I laughed.

"You two think it's funny? I won't be so (pause) funny when I lie in the hotel tonight with a (pause) concussion!"

"We weren't laughing at your getting hit on the head, Dad," Margaret said. "We're just a little slap-happy, after being cooped up on that plane for eight hours."

"Oh, it must have been awful," Dad said, "with all that leg room and the fancy drinks. I really feel sorry for you."

"You can stand here and argue if you want," Granny said. "I'm going to get my luggage and find a taxi."

Margaret and I followed Granny.

"Come on, Anthony," Mom yelled.

We retrieved our luggage and went outside to get a taxi. We needed two, so Mom and big Anthony followed us.

"How quaint," Margaret said, viewing Sweden's old world charm from the window of the cab.

"Wait until you see it in the light of day," Granny said.

We rode the rest of the way without speaking, busy absorbing the charm of the lamplit streets and waterways. As Granny had earlier predicted, we pulled up to The Grand Hotel of Stockholm exactly thirty-five minutes after having left the airport.

"Oh my God," Margaret said. "It's even more beautiful than I expected!"

"It's majestic," Granny said.

A bellhop was wheeling a cart toward our cab; my parents' taxi was pulling into the loading zone behind us.

"We're together," I said to the bellhop as he loaded our luggage onto the cart. "You can wait for their bags."

I turned and looked at the hotel. It was majestic, a veritable castle! From the front of the building hung a banner: Welcome Nobel Laureates. At that moment, reality finally pierced the fairy tale my imagination had conjured: my little brother *was* a Nobel Laureate!

I turned to find my father struggling with his bags; if he didn't put them on the cart, he wouldn't be in any way responsible for the bellhop's tip. Although I had fully intended to bear the expense, I said nothing. Granny had once told me that there was a time to speak and a time to be silent; I wasn't about to ruin the magic of the moment with an argument in front of The Grand Hotel.

We entered the lobby and were greeted by the concierge. "Good evening," he said. "Under what name is your reservation?"

"We're the Vitello party," I answered. "My brother is Dr. Vitello, one of the laureates."

"Oh yes," exclaimed the concierge. "Congratulations on your brother's feat. Walk this way."

We followed the concierge to the desk and got our room assignments. While handing us our room keys, the concierge reminded us that we were very special guests and that the entire hotel staff would be at our beck and call.

"How much are these becks and calls gonna cost me?" big Anthony mumbled under his breath.

"Come on, Anthony. Let's go," my mother said. There was a growing sense of impatience in her tone; the eight hour flight with my father must have rattled her.

The bellboy led us to the elevators; we piled in, eager to revel in the sanctity of our (non-adjoining) rooms. It was 6:10 p.m. in New York, and I was dying to call Maria.

"I'm going right to bed," Margaret said. "I'm not going to do my six-hundred dollar gown justice tomorrow night with bags under my eyes."

"You spent six hundred dollars on a dress?" our father asked defiantly.

"Dad, this is a once in a lifetime event!"

"Are you nuts?"

"Leave me alone. I'm tired."

"Yeah, you're tired. At least you don't have a welt the size of a god-damned golf ball on top of your head," Dad said.

Everyone turned to look at Mom; Dad had taken the Lord's name in vain. "Anthony, this is your last chance. If I ever hear that kind of talk again," Mom said, "you'll really be sorry."

My father growled. The bellboy looked frightened. The elevator finally stopped and the doors opened. The bellboy meekly escorted us down the hall to our rooms.

"What time are we meeting for breakfast?" Margaret asked.

"I think Jerry said 7:30," I answered. "I'm going to call him as soon as I get settled."

The bellboy stopped in front of Room 402. "Here we are, Mr. and Mrs. Vitello, your room." He opened the door, motioning my parents to enter.

"Good night," Mom said. "We'll see you bright and early."

"Good night, Mom. Good night, Dad," I said.

"Humpf!" was all my father could muster.

We continued down the hall a hundred feet or so until the bellboy stopped his cart. "Here we are, Ms. Vitello and Mrs. Freeman. You're in Room 413, and Mr. Vitello, you're right across the hall in Room 414."

"Good night, my love," Granny said. "I'm going to call it a night. I have to remove this wig; it's driving me crazy."

"Good night, Gran," I said, kissing her on the cheek.

The bellboy followed Granny into the room with her luggage.

"Good night, little brother," Margaret said. "Tell Maria I said hello when you talk to her."

"I will," I said, following the bellboy into my room.

"Will that be all, then?" he asked.

"Yes. Thank you very much," I said, handing him a ten-dollar bill.

"My pleasure, Sir." And the bellboy was gone.

I surveyed my temporary home. Not bad, I thought. I went into the bathroom to inspect the bathtub and toilet. Very good, I thought. They were devoid of protozoan *Jello*.

I sat down on the bed and picked up the phone, carefully following instructions for international dialing. It began ringing.

"Hello?" Maria answered.

"Honey, it's me."

"Tony! Are you there?"

"Yes, I'm at the hotel, in my room."

"How was your flight?"

"Not bad," I said. "We landed eight minutes ahead of schedule. How's your ear?"

"Much better, but now I'm coming down with a stomach bug. On the way home from Kennedy this morning I had to pull over; needless to say, my day at the spa was nixed. But I'm feeling a little better."

"I'm sorry, Maria. I wish I was there to take care of you."

"I do too, sweetie. But I'm glad you arrived safely. What is

Stockholm like?"

"From what I can see, it's beautiful. Wait until you see the hotel; I'll take plenty of pictures. When we come back for our Scandinavian tour, I'm bringing you here. It's magnificent."

"That's great. Oh, guess what? The Realtor brought a couple to look at our apartment this afternoon. They seemed to like it."

"Great. I don't think we're going to have any trouble selling it."

"I don't either," Maria said. "How's Jerry? Have you talked with him yet?"

"No. I'm going to try his room when we hang up. I'm sure he's still awake; I don't know how he'll sleep tonight, with all the excitement."

Our conversation was interrupted by a knock at my door. "Maria, hold on for a minute. There's someone at the door; it's probably Jerry."

I opened the door. It wasn't Jerry, it was the concierge. "Mr. Vitello, sorry to disturb you. You left this package in the taxi earlier; the driver returned it just now."

Oh my God, I thought. It was Jerry's watch. "Thank you," I said gratefully, reaching into my pocket. "I don't know how to thank you! It's my brother's gift." I went to hand him a twenty dollar bill.

"That isn't necessary," the concierge said. "Don't thank me; thank the honesty of our dedicated taxi drivers here in Stockholm. Good night, Mr. Vitello."

I was floored. I ran back to the phone.

"Maria?"

"Was that Jerry?" she asked.

"No, it was the concierge. You're not going to believe it, but Jerry's gift must have fallen out of my carry-on bag on the cab-ride here. The driver brought it back to the hotel. I can't imagine how it happened," I said in disbelief.

"What is it with you and watches and cab drivers?" Maria laughed. "You must have an angel on your shoulder. That was a miracle."

"It was a miracle," I said. "I would have been devastated had I lost it."

"Thank God for honest cab drivers," Maria said. "So sweetie, give me a call after the ceremony tomorrow."

"I will, and I hope you feel better. I love you."

"I love you too, Tony. Talk to you tomorrow."

"Good night, love. Sweet dreams," I said, and hung up the phone.

I held Jerry's gift, wondering how it could have fallen from my bag. Was it some kind of sign, and if it was, was the operative word watch or cab driver?

Another knock at the door sounded. I opened it and shouted: "Jerry!"

"Big brother! How long have you been here?"

"About twenty minutes," I said.

"Where's Maria?"

"She couldn't come," I explained. I relayed Maria's inner-ear problem to Jerry, along with her regrets.

"That's a darn shame," Jerry said. "But thank you for coming ."

"So tell me," I said. "Are you nervous?"

"Well, I was," Jerry said. "I didn't finish my acceptance speech until this afternoon. I kept stumbling over one paragraph. But I finally got it right."

"Another Einsteinian flash of insight?"

"Actually, no," Jerry said. "It was something that a cab driver said to me this afternoon."

I listened with interest. "What did he say?"

"Well, when I told him I was in a hurry to get to the Royal Academy, he said 'What's the rush? Time has no meaning at the level of order in which God exists.' I thought to myself, that is exactly what I was trying to say in that paragraph of my speech that I kept tripping over."

I looked at Jerry in disbelief.

"What?" he said.

I walked over to the dresser and picked up the small box that the concierge had just delivered. "I was going to give this to you tomorrow, but now seems like the right time. Congratulations, dear brother," I said, handing him the box.

"You didn't have to do this," Jerry said, removing the wrapping. He opened the box and looked at the watch. "Oh, Tony. It's beautiful, and perfect, too. You know how I hate wearing anything on my wrist." Jerry removed the watch from its box to inspect it more carefully.

I just stood there, absorbing the magic and the majesty of that sacred, profound moment.

Jerry turned the watch and read the inscription. "I don't understand," he said, looking at me quizzically. "How could you have known?"

"I don't understand either," I said.

"How did you come up with the inscription?"

"A few months ago I fell asleep in Granny's office and had a dream about Poppy. In the dream we were discussing the concept of time, and Poppy said that time is man's invention, that it has no meaning at the level of order in which God exists," I said.

"This is strange," Jerry said. "I wonder how the cabby came up with that line?"

"I don't know," I said. "Even stranger, your gift fell out of my carry-on bag on the way here from the airport. The cab driver found it and brought it back to the hotel for me."

"What did he look like? Was he middle-aged, blond, with a lot of freckles?"

"Yes," I said, "he was. I wonder if we had the same driver?"

"We must have," Jerry said. "He must have opened the gift and read the inscription."

"Jerry, that cabby took you to the Royal Academy first; at that time your gift was flying across the Atlantic."

"You're right. What the hell am I thinking?"

"I think something divine is going on here; I'm just not sure what it is or how it happened," I said.

"I can't figure it out either," Jerry said. "Why don't we go downstairs to the bar and have a drink. This little mystery deserves a toast."

"Good idea," I said. "Besides, it's only 7:00 according to my inner clock."

"Time has no meaning at the level of order in which God exists," Jerry said, as we left the hotel room.

We walked down the hall, Jerry with his arm over my shoulder, pondering our little miracle of time. Our moment was interrupted by a shout. We turned to find Margaret's head peeking from her door.

"Hey guys! Where are you going?" she yelled down the hall.

"To the bar," we yelled in unison.

"Wait for me! I'll get my shoes!"

So much for my beauty sleep," Margaret said, as we took our seats at the bar.

"Let's order vodka gimlets," Jerry said, "in honor of our old kamikaze days."

I laughed at Jerry's statement. There had been only one kamikaze episode in our history, at my bachelor party. And Jerry had left early, needing to take measurements at the lab.

The bartender served our gimlets, and Margaret led the toast: "to our brother, the mad scientist!" We pushed our glasses together and sipped our drinks.

"Who'd have ever thought we'd be sitting here one day?" I asked rhetorically.

"I did," Jerry said. "I don't know why or how, but ever since I was a kid I dreamed about going to Stockholm. Granny planted the seed in my mind."

"I thought it was Dad," Margaret said.

Jerry laughed. "Can you believe how he used to scream at me, about the *noble* prize? I swear to God, my scientific achievement is not an act of spite. But it is a coincidence, isn't it?"

"Come on, Jerry, you mean to tell me that Dad's condescension didn't spur your determination, in the tiniest way?" Margaret asked.

"Honestly? No," Jerry said.

I believed Jerry, but I wasn't sure that Margaret did.

"Another round?" the bartender asked.

"Yes," Margaret replied.

"We'd better slow down," I said. "We have a big day tomorrow."

But we didn't slow down. After three gimlets each, time ceased to have meaning.

"Let's play a game," Margaret said. "We'll take turns revealing a secret from our childhood."

"All right," I said, "but since it was your idea, you go first."

"O.K.," Margaret said. "Remember that time you guys caused Dad's corncob pipe explosion?"

"Yes," we laughed.

"Well, I purposely gave Dad a bad makeover!"

Jerry and I laughed. "You're bad," I said.

"O.K., Tone, you're next. What's your big secret?"

"Well," I said, "You know how Dad always got pissed off when he couldn't find the TV Guide?"

"Yeah?" Jerry and Margaret said.

"Well, on more than one occasion I tore the TV Guide into pieces and put it down the garbage disposal just to make him crazy."

"You guys are bad," Jerry said. "I'm sorry to disappoint you, but my secret has nothing to do with torturing our father. My secret is that I felt like a cheat all through high school and college."

"What? You had cheat-sheets?" I asked.

"No," Jerry said. "Granny taught mc a memory trick. While I was studying, I would periodically take a whiff of a certain scent—balsam fir was one of my favorites. Come exam time, I'd wear that scent on the cuff of my shirt, and my olfactory memory helped me recall facts. Now I know that it wasn't really cheating, but at the time, I felt guilty. I can only imagine how suspiciously I must have presented myself."

"That's funny, Jerr, because the smell of roasted peanuts has always stirred memories for me. I never thought of using it to my advantage; why didn't you tell me? Maybe I could have been a Nobel Laureate too," I said.

We laughed together at our crazy past. Margaret and I ordered another drink; Jerry had the sense to stop after his third.

So much for being rested for the big day. We sat talking at that bar until the early hours of morning, sharing stories of love, hope and endurance. We were no longer siblings muddling through the common element of a bizarre childhood. We were a Nobel Laureate, a writer, and a businesswoman with a strong following. The absurdities that bound us more than compensated for our lack of mutual interests. Our lives had come full circle.

As I crawled into my strange bed at 4 a.m. Stockholm time, I managed to utter a silent prayer of gratitude before I surrendered to the Absolut (hiccup) vodka. Dear God, I prayed, thank you for sneezing on me. If I had it to do over again (hiccup) I wouldn't change a thing. Thank you most of all for the sum of everything you have done for me.

I met the rest of my family in the lobby with only three hours sleep under my belt, but I felt surprisingly rested. Granny had been right: the adrenaline generated by the excitement was carrying me nicely.

"We're just waiting for Jerry," Mom explained.

"Leona, why don't you and Anthony go in and get us a table?" Granny said. "I want to show Tony and Margaret something. We'll keep an eye out for Jerry."

"Good idea," my father said. Breakfast was included in the price of our rooms, and my father was eager to start getting his money's worth.

"Follow me," Granny said. "I want to show you two of the most legendary rooms in all of Stockholm."

We followed Granny around a corner and down a corridor. She stopped at a large door and opened it. "Good, it's open."

We entered one of the most beautiful banquet rooms that I had ever seen; the whole room sparkled.

"This is called *The Hall of Mirrors*," Granny said. "It was modeled after the *Galerie des Glaces* at Versailles. The Nobel banquets were held in this room until 1929, after which they were moved to City Hall."

"It's beautiful," Margaret said. "I've never seen so much crystal in all my life. And the frames on those mirrors!"

It was indescribable. "Granny, it reminds me of your dining room," I said.

"Thank you, dear, but my home is nowhere near as grand."

Granny was wrong, for the second time in her life.

"Can you imagine having a wedding here?" Margaret asked. "It's so idyllic."

"It is," Granny said. "Let's run along. I want to show you the *Wintergarden*."

We followed Granny again, and were soon on the threshold of the *Wintergarden*. The doors were open.

"This room is my favorite, of course," Granny said.

The *Wintergarden* was a conservatory brimming with lush green. It reminded me of two things at home: Granny's house and the conservatory at *Longwood Gardens*.

"Perhaps tomorrow we can relax in here before we're off to Arland again," Granny suggested.

"There you are!" Jerry said. "Breakfast is waiting; Dad's already on his third helping of cherry blintzes!"

"You look surprisingly rested," I said to Jerry.

"I think I'm just floating in a dream. I'll probably collapse from exhaustion as I'm descending the grand staircase tonight."

"The grand staircase?" I asked.

"Yes. Tonight the King and Queen lead a procession of the Laureates in City Hall. We descend a balcony from a large stairway to the banquet floor."

"Oh Jerry," I said, "don't even joke about something like that."

We laughed as we walked back to the restaurant and found our table. Dad was tending to a cherry stain on the front of his shirt; Mom was reading brochures. We took our seats and ordered a pot of coffee.

"Well, I know where I'm off to today," Mom said. "To the *Junibaken*."

"What's that, Mom?" Margaret asked.

"It's a magical fairy tale world based on the children's books by Astrid Lindgren. You know, the *Pippi Longstocking* series. Do you want to go?"

"No, Mom. I'm going shopping. But thanks."

"If you're going there, then we're splitting up," Dad said. "I want to see the *Globe Arena* and *The Milles Museum*. We'll have to meet back at the hotel later."

The *Milles Museum* was the former home of Carl Milles, the famed Swedish Sculptor.

"What's on your agenda today?" I asked Jerry.

"A luncheon at the American Embassy, and then back to the hotel to get into my tails and practice my speech one more time."

Dad became alert to our conversation when hearing the word *tails*. He still believed that Jerry would respect his wishes and get a haircut before the prize ceremony.

I put my hand on Jerry's shoulder. "You'll do just fine."

We ate our Scandinavian breakfast and split into factions for our varied excursions.

Granny and I got out of the taxi in front of The *Tekniska Museet*, the Museum of Science and Technology. I looked at Granny, noticing she looked a little jilted.

"Everything O.K., Gran?" I asked.

"Yes. It's just that this town brings back such memories. The last time I was here, your grandfather was on my arm. Sometimes I miss Stanley desperately; I long so to be with him again."

I put my arm around Granny. "One day you will be with him again," I said. "Who knows why God ended his life so tragically? Life and death are hard to fathom sometimes."

"I know," Granny said, brushing away a tear. "He was so young, with so much promise ahead of him. But look how fate has unfolded: Jerry has lived his grandfather's dream. Still, why he had to go the way he did is a mystery. I don't know how the good Lord is going to bring me home, but I hope I go in style and with a bang. Now enough of this sentimentality. Let's enjoy the day." Granny adjusted her wig and we entered the museum.

We browsed for several hours, fascinated by the Swedish marvels of technology. We approached the last exhibit, which would later become part of a permanent Nobel Museum. The Nobel Prize would celebrate its Centennial in 2001, and a permanent monument was underway.

"I didn't know that Alfred Nobel invented dynamite," I said to Granny. She didn't hear me; she was reading a document that had been mounted to a brass plaque. I walked toward her. "What are you reading?" I asked.

"It's William Faulkner's acceptance speech, which he read when he won the Nobel Prize in Literature in 1950," Granny said. "Read it, dear. It's a message to future writers."

I read Faulkner's speech, entitled "I Decline to Accept the End of Man." I was floored.

"Powerful, isn't it?" Granny asked.

I nodded.

"Just think," she said, "one day these archives will include the story of your brother. Stanley would be so proud, of all of you."

On that note we took a cab back to the hotel.

There was a knock at my hotel room door. It was the concierge, returning my tuxedo. The flight across the Atlantic had left it sorely in need of a pressing.

"Thank you," I said, taking my suit and handing the concierge a nice tip.

I quickly dressed and adjusted my bow-tie. There was another knock at my door.

"Granny!" I said, opening the door. "You look beautiful."

"Thank you, dear. I just wanted to let you know that I'm leaving for the Concert Hall now; I want to make a stop along the way. I'll meet you there," Granny said.

"Good enough," I said. "Be careful!"

"I will. See you there."

I looked at the mirror for a final inspection and walked toward the door to meet Margaret. Just as I opened the door, the telephone rang. I walked back toward the night stand.

"Hello?"

"Honey? It's me!" Maria said.

"Maria! Is everything all right?"

"Everything is coming up roses," she said, out of breath.

"Honey, what is it?"

"That couple that came to look at our apartment, they made an offer!"

"Yeah?"

"Yeah. Eight-forty!" Maria yelled.

"Life is good!" I yelled, loudly enough for my voice to cross the Atlantic.

"That's not all," Maria said. "Are you sitting down?"

I sat on the edge of the bed. "I am now."

"Dr. Hamberger called. My ear is fine; just a bad case of swimmer's ear. Nothing to worry about."

"Then why the dizziness?"

"I can't believe it, Tony," Maria yelled, "I'm pregnant!"

"What? When?"

"It looks as though our baby was conceived on Halloween; remember, when you came home early from Granny's?"

"Oh my God!" I yelled. "What kind of monster have we created?"

"Tony!"

"I'm just kidding. Oh, Maria. I can't believe it. I wish I was there with you right now. How do you feel? I'm going to see if I can get a flight out of here first thing in the morning. This is unbelievable—a baby!"

"I know," Maria said. "I didn't even realize I was late. There never seemed to be any reason to keep track."

"I love you, Maria. I can't believe this; a new house and a baby!"

"I love you too," Maria said. "But you'd better get going. Call me when you get in tonight."

"I will," I said. "Maria, I've never been happier."

"Me too, sweetie. Now you had better run."

"Maria, one more thing. Go into my sock drawer; in the back of it you'll find a pair of blue argyles. There's a present for you hiding in those socks."

"Really? Thank you. I'll talk to you tonight. Give my best to Jerry."

"Goodbye, love. And make sure to get some rest!"

"I will. Goodbye, Tony."

"Goodbye, my love."

There was a third knock at my door. It was Margaret.

"Margaret, I've never seen you look more beautiful," I said, still excited over Maria's news. Margaret wore a long gown of the most beautiful shade of purple. Purple must be our family color, I thought.

Margaret looked at me. "You don't look too bad yourself, Tony. In fact, you're glowing."

"Thank you," I said. "Shall we go?" I extended my arm, and Margaret and I walked proudly down the corridor. I was dying to tell her my news, but I would wait until after the ceremony. Tonight was Jerry's night.

Our parents were waiting at the elevator.

"It's about time," our father snapped. "The limo is probably ready to pull away without us."

"Mom," Margaret said, "you didn't tell me that your gown was purple too."

Mom's gown was several shades lighter than Margaret's, a pale lavender. My olfactory memory conjured the fragrance that had never failed to soothe me; I walked calmly into the elevator.

The limo was waiting downstairs for us, and we got in for the short ride to *Stockholms Konserthus*. "Your grandmother had better not be late," my father grumbled.

Within minutes we arrived at Hötorget Square. The four of us got out of the limo and walked triumphantly toward the steps of the Concert Hall.

Approaching the steps, Margaret cried out: "Look! There's a ponytail in the gutter!"

Sure enough, a ponytail lay sadly amidst the street debris.

"Who would just cut off his ponytail and throw it into the gutter that way?" Margaret asked.

"Who do you think?" Dad said. "Your brother finally came to his senses. I knew he would. I knew he wouldn't make a mockery of his whole family in front of the King and Queen of Sweden."

Margaret picked up the ponytail and put it into her evening bag. "I'll save it for Jerry," she said, "as memorabilia."

We climbed the steps and were ushered inside by the Royal Guards who stood greeting guests at the door. "Quickly, please," one of the guards said. "The ceremony is about to begin."

Another guard led us in procession to our seats, front and center, where Granny was waiting. Just as we reached our aisle, the lights dimmed and the violins sounded.

As the curtain rose on stage, my eyes were drawn to the huge Nobel banner that hung behind the Laureates, the Swedish officials, and members of the Royal Family. Huge drapes of periwinkle blue and yellow supported a bronze medallion which pictured Alfred Nobel. On either side of the medallion were bronze numerals announcing the year. The ceremony began.

Be it my lack of sleep or the news of my future child, or maybe the surrealism of the pomp and circumstance before me, I began to feel as if I was dreaming.

In my dream the King of Sweden announced my brother's feat, and Jerry walked proudly to retrieve his medal and diploma. As King Carl XVI Gustaf handed Jerry his blue leather document, everyone in our family wept tears of joy. Everyone except my father: he was wrenching his neck to make sure it had indeed been Jerry's ponytail in the gutter.

Jerry walked calmly to the microphone, and began his acceptance speech. My dear little brother, I thought, as Jerry spoke.

"And so," Jerry said, "Time has no meaning at the level of

order in which God exists. It is time to bring honor to the power that accompanies our new technologies. We shall go forth in uncharted waters with maps of honor; may God help us to respect our power. Thank you very much."

Jerry walked back to his seat, ponytail swinging.

"Jeez-Zus!" my father exclaimed, as the entire audience rose in a standing ovation.

The rest of the ceremony was a blur. Before I knew it, we were being whisked off to City Hall for the celebration banquet. My parents got back into the limo; Granny, Margaret and I opted for some fresh air. City Hall was just a stone's throw from the Concert Hall.

"Unbelievable," Granny said. "My life is complete."

"Gran, what did you do, cut your wig?" Margaret asked.

"Yes," Granny said. "I decided to wear it in a ponytail in honor of Jerry. On the way here I caught a glimpse of myself in a shop window, and realized how ridiculous I looked. Luckily I had your grandfather's Swiss Army Knife in my pocket, so I just clipped it off and tossed it into the gutter."

I looked at Granny's wig: sure enough, it looked as though it had recently spawned a ponytail. So the mystery of the ponytail in the gutter had been solved: it was a synthetic, and it belonged to my grandmother.

"So this is your ponytail?" Margaret asked, opening her purse.

"Yes, and I'm glad you retrieved it. I felt badly afterward, about having littered."

"Dad thought it was Jerry's ponytail," Margaret said. "Did you see the way he fumed when Jerry turned around to walk back to his seat?"

"I caught it," Granny said. "You'd think of all nights, that tonight he would behave. Nevertheless, nothing could spoil the magic of this evening. Let's go; the King and Queen are waiting for us."

We laughed as we entered City Hall. Our laughter ended when we noticed Mom and Dad just ahead of us in the receiving line.

"Oh my God," Margaret said, "Dad's stepping on the train of the Queen's gown! Is he totally oblivious?"

We had our audience with the King and Queen and were led to

the Blue Hall by the student volunteers from Stockholm University.

The Blue Hall was magnificent: archways supported by Corinthian columns spanned the entire perimeter of the hall. The tables were dressed regally in ivory and gold, with no shortage of flowers. We were led to our table and took a seat, waiting anxiously for the Royal Procession to descend the balcony. The grand staircase ended at the head table, which was covered with long-stemmed roses.

Once the Blue Hall had filled, the lights dimmed and trumpets announced the beginning of the procession. The King and Queen descended first, followed by the Laureates and other dignitaries. With the help of Granny's opera glasses, I was able to see the footprint of my father's rented shoe on the ivory train that followed the Queen. I then saw my brother, illuminated by the surrealistic blue light which dramatized the staircase and procession. It appeared to be the stairway to heaven; we looked on proudly. The celebration began.

There were speeches, tears, dancing in the Golden Hall, and a meal fit for a king. We celebrated madly in our dream, creating memories that I would one day recount to my own son or daughter.

As I led my mother to the Golden Hall for one last dance, I overheard part of a conversation between my father and last year's Laureate in Physics.

"You know," my father said, leaning closer to the unwitting gentleman, "I know exactly how the Nobel heirs felt. I too was gypped out of a fortune; my inheritance went to the butler and silver maid."

At that moment, something clicked for me. As I led my mother from the madness, God spoke to me: accept the things you cannot change. As we danced in the Golden Hall, I realized that my happiness would never again depend on something external, on someone else's behavior. My happiness would come from within. I was powerless to change anyone but myself.

At ten minutes to midnight we left City Hall for the short drive back to the hotel. As we left the building, my father began his commentary.

"I can't believe he didn't cut the ponytail. Did you see the way everyone was staring at him?"

"They were staring at him because he won the Nobel Prize, you stupid fool," my mother said.

"I'm a stupid fool?" Dad snarled. "I'd say that your Einstein in there is the one who looked the fool."

We stopped and looked at my father.

"Why are you looking at me? I'm the only one in this family with his head on straight. You people live with your head in the clouds. Look at what a mess you've made of your lives!"

"I beg your pardon?" Mom asked. "I'll have you know that I've just signed a contract with a major toy manufacturer. They're licensing products based on my children's book, which will be released in February, by the way."

"Mom," I said, "that's great. Why didn't you tell us?"

"I wanted to wait until after the prize ceremony," Mom said. "Jerry deserved his own limelight."

"Now that we're spilling all," Margaret said, "I have some news too. Les has asked me to marry him."

"That's wonderful," I said, congratulating my sister.

"We're all very happy for you," Granny said.

"I guess it's my turn," I said. "Maria and I are having a baby!"

"A grandchild?" my mother said. "I will never forget this night as long as I live. Anthony, did you hear what Tony said? They're having a baby!"

"Yeah, I heard," my father grunted. "Give my congratulations to Maria." He then began walking toward the street.

"Oh well," Granny said, "You can't win them all. Anyhow, we have a great deal to celebrate. Now tell me, Margaret, have you and Les set a date?" Granny and Margaret walked arm in arm, discussing the upcoming nuptials.

I took my mother's arm and we followed. "Don't be disappointed," she said. "Your father just doesn't see life as we do. All is not lost; God is giving you the opportunity for another chance, with your own child."

"Thank you, Mom," I said. "You know, all of a sudden my life has become crystal clear: I can be happy despite what anyone else says or thinks about me."

"Always remember one thing," Mom said, as we stood under the starry midnight sky on that fateful night. "Like Einstein said, there are only two kinds of people in the world: those who believe that everything is a miracle, and those who believe that nothing is."

On that note we approached the street, arm in arm, absorbing the starlight that reflected back to us our earlier hopes and dreams.

Granny and I got out of the taxi and approached the terminal at Arland Airport. I had secured an earlier flight to New York; Granny was off to Munich to visit Walter Water and from there would go on to Paris to spend the New Year with friends.

"It's a shame that Walkon couldn't make it to Stockholm," Granny said, "but his health is frail."

"You mean Walter," I corrected.

"Yes. What did I say?"

"You said Walkon."

"Oh," Granny laughed. "Walkon was an old nickname. We used to call Walter that because everyone looked at him as the god of the Physics Department in Munich. You know, Walkon Water."

I laughed, as Granny's flight to Munich was called for boarding. We hugged for several precious moments.

As we parted at the gate, Granny's last words to me were: "Never forget how much I love you. You are going to be a wonderful father."

Those words carried me to my departing gate and through the eight-hour flight back to New York.

As I walked through the gate at Kennedy, the first thing I saw was a purple light, radiating from Maria's heart. My glowing wife was adorned by the purple ruby from Madagascar, which dangled as a testament to the miracle of our lives together.

I held Maria in a long embrace. "It's a miracle," I whispered.

"There is no other way to explain it," she said.

We walked arm in arm toward the parking lot, reveling in the wondrous thing called life.

Thirteen

The rest of the world managed to transit the millennium without serious Y2K glitches, but my family was not so fortunate. Tragedy shattered our lives.

Our beloved Granny died on New Year's Day in one of Paris' most elegant hotels. This of course fulfilled her earlier wish: that she leave the world in style and with a bang.

Since Granny had gone on to Munich and Paris for a few weeks, she suggested that Maria and I house-sit and ring in the new millennium in Philadelphia. We jumped at the opportunity, eager for the enchantment and to escape Manhattan's Y2K crowds.

As I lay on the sofa in Granny's office, I noticed that the silver notes of Bach were beginning to lose their luster. I thought about doing a little touch-up for Granny while I was there; it would be a nice surprise for her when she returned. My thoughts were interrupted by Margaret's call: Granny would not be coming home. She had died earlier that morning in Paris.

I later discovered that Granny's exact time of death was 6 a.m. Paris time. As Maria and I welcomed the new millennium under the majestic Philadelphia skyline, my dear, sweet Granny was leaving our world forever, with a very big bang.

Although heartbroken, my pain was softened by the knowledge that Granny was once again with her beloved husband.

The new millennium brought other changes to our family as well. Jerry and his colleagues were busy at Princeton developing technology that was made possible, in part, by the generosity of Alfred Nobel.

My Uncle Harry was invited to the White House to accept an award from the EPA. He and Aunt Vicky finally resolved their marital difficulties, with a little off-hours' help from Maria.

My cousin Tommy finally came out of the closet, and Uncle

Harry and Aunt Vicky finally came out of denial. This created the opportunity for Margaret's friend Ivan to marry into our family after all: he and Tommy really hit it off.

Margaret's business got a big boost when our Nobel Laureate brother finally decided to get a haircut. Jerry had no idea that Margaret had issued a press release announcing the clipping of the royal ponytail. As usual, Jerry was a good sport.

Off hours, Margaret and Les were busy planning their wedding. We would be off to Stockholm again in the spring of 2001; they booked their wedding at the legendary Hall of Mirrors. The wedding would coincide nicely with Stockholm's centennial celebration of the Nobel Prize.

My mother, also known as children's author LeOna VitEllo, was busy working on her next book, based on one of the characters in my grandmother's letters. The last time I'd heard, Leona and big Anthony were still at odds, in a house on the main line funded by my mother's royalties from her toy line.

Maria started a new practice when we moved to Philadelphia in February of 2000.

I traded my office at SuperSoft for one with a bust of Mark Twain. Granny had willed her house to Maria and me, and we moved in almost immediately after the reading of the will. I then spent my days writing about ponytails. I hung a copy of William Faulkner's Nobel Prize acceptance speech on the wall of the office that I shared with my grandfather's spirit. When I needed inspiration, I read Faulkner's words, which Granny and I had discovered in the *Tekniska Museet*:

> I believe that man will not merely endure: he will prevail. He is immortal, not because he alone among creatures has an inexhaustible voice, but because he has a soul, a spirit capable of compassion and sacrifice and endurance. The poet's, the writer's, duty is to write about these things. It is his privilege to help man endure by lifting his heart…The poet's voice need not merely be the record of man, it can be one of the props, the pillars to help him endure and prevail.

It became my new career goal to lift the heart of man, just as mine had been lifted during that last year of the millennium.

The greatest lifting of my heart occurred on July 13, 2000, at exactly midnight, when my son Stanley was born. As my father held his grandson for the first time, I saw something that I had never before witnessed in my father's eyes: the birth of hope. Who knows what is possible in the new millennium, I thought.

The room adjacent to my office (the bedroom where my mother had once slept) became Stanley's nursery.

I leaned over and scooped my precious son from his cradle. As he lay sleeping in my arms, a tear of joy swelled from my left eye and fell onto Stanley's little hand. As I wiped it dry, I discovered something new about my son: he had a birthmark. However faint, it distinctly resembled a ponytail!? I returned Stanley to his soft world and went downstairs.

Life never ceased to amaze me. Why had something as arcane as a ponytail existed as such a powerful symbol in our family? I was content in realizing I would never know the answer. All I needed to know was that our ponytail incidents had been miracles.

Regarding the miracle of God's thirty-year sneeze, my mid-life crisis had finally ended, at an age when my fellow yuppies were just beginning theirs. My life hadn't been that bad, I reasoned, if I was one step ahead of the game.

I looked around in gratitude at the home Granny had bequeathed to me. As rainbows bounced in my own private hall of mirrors, I had but one thought: look what you have taught me, my dear, sweet Granny. You have spun a web of love so great, it will forever connect the fathers and sons and daughters who come after you.

At that moment, I realized that Granny was only physically gone: the beauty of her love was crystallized in my heart forever.

My new job was not only to lift the hearts of men; my most precious responsibility was to continue the legacy which had blossomed in that one perfect rose: my grandmother.